The Unnatural Woman

Dave Astho

Dedication

For all those who have gone before, those who are here now, and hopefully, those still to come. With special thanks to Jackie Collins, whose advice I followed to do a page a day and to Julian Wright for showing me it was possible.

Acknowledgements and Preface

I approached many literary agents and publishers with the manuscript for this book. The result was either an email rejection or no response at all - with the exception of one publisher in 2018. That publisher said: "We were intrigued by the plot, and the setting – following in the time-honoured science fiction tradition of turning a situation on its head in a future scenario as an allegory for the injustice or inequity in our own current society." They identified a number of weaknesses in my writing and declined to publish the book because of these, but at the end of their email said, "Whatever you do, don't give up, the story is good and deserves to be told really well."

I have endeavoured to amend the book in light of the weaknesses identified by them, and by others who have read *The Unnatural Woman*. I am sure it is still not perfect, but I feel the time has now come to stop adjusting, to stop approaching agents and to simply self-publish. In addition to my own satisfaction in completing the book there will, at last, be something to show to all those who have supported me in this project. I give a big, *Thank You,* to all of those people. I hope the end result is deserving of the effort you have made and patience you have shown.

Dave Asthouart, July 2022

Contents

Part 1: Inconsequential Injustice

Chapter 1: Meeting the Red Dress   9
Chapter 2: The Police Meet the Red Dress for the First Time   19
Chapter 3: May Asks a Question or Two   25
Chapter 4: And so to the White Court of the Magistrates   33
Chapter 5: Flop-flop   45
Chapter 6: Last Time White Court. Last Time No Red Dress   56
Chapter 7: The Orange Court. May Spots the Revolving Door   65
Chapter 8: Steph Shown the Revolving Door   73
Chapter 9: Tim the Thief, May the Mum and John the Lost   84
Chapter 10: John's Car, Tim's Reform, May's Cuts. The Door Turns 101

Part 2: But Everything has a Context

Chapter 11: The Bomb…and Humming in the Orange Court   111
Chapter 12: Charlie's Chicken Man and might Marginals Hum?   121
Chapter 13: The Causeway Café   131
Chapter 14: John in Hospital and the Green Court of Appeal   148
Chapter 15: The Red Dress Bombings and John Arrested   163

Part 3: Whose Justice and What Consequences for Whom?

Chapter 16: The Court of Truth and the Night of Smashing   175
Chapter 17: Morning of Rescue. Moment of Truth. House of Hope   208
Chapter 18: Meeting Marginals   247
Chapter 19: The Room of Eternal Reflection and a Martyr on TV   270
Chapter 20: And the Chamber was Empty   291

Epilogue

Epilogue   295

Part 1: Inconsequential Injustice

Chapter 1: Meeting the Red Dress

The red dress changed everything for Steph Hugo. It seems absurd to think that something as apparently inconsequential as a piece of clothing could do that– but it did.

On the night before everything changed she was at home looking out of the bedroom window after a long, but good day at work, in her job at the council offices - a job she had enjoyed for the past six years – and she felt she deserved the glass of wine that was in her hand. Her husband, John was away on business, and would not be back until the following evening. She was looking forward to having the big bed to herself that night. Her children – Tim aged ten and May aged twelve - were asleep in their rooms just down the corridor. She felt very lucky. She had a lovely family and here she was in a lovely house looking out at a beautiful June evening.

*

She felt very content. She had worked hard as a Citizen of Trueway and Trueway had rewarded her with all this – but Steph had secrets and secrets can be dangerous.

*

She watched the swirled clouds of white and grey slowly turn pink and the cool blue sky flame with orange and red before night extinguished the fire with her dark mantle and brought peace. Stars appeared and Steph briefly mused on how strange it was that darkness revealed those little pinpoints of light billions of miles away while hiding even the colour of the building across the street.

The fragrance of some evening scented flowers crept in through the open window, timidly bringing a little of the outside world into the room. She had read somewhere that these flowers gave off their scent at night to attract moths.

She drew the curtain closed but left the window open to allow in the sweet smell of the flowers – and hoped that no moths would follow it. Soft lighting came on automatically in the room illuminating pale pink walls embellished with beautiful paintings. Steph changed these pictures regularly, as was the custom in Trueway. The few essential furnishings were functional, tasteful, and like most of the house, made of sustainable or recycled material. A small table and a full length mirror were of considerable age – antique in fact.

She took a deep breath. The scent of the flowers was sweet. There had been no moth invasion. She drained her glass and put it on the table. She slid into bed – no duvet just cool, smooth sheets. With John not there, she lay in the middle of the bed rather than on 'her side'. She spread her arms and legs wide with self-indulgent, childish delight.

"House!" she said with authority, "Lights out," and the room darkened as the house computer obeyed.

"MyBook!" she said with equal authority and an ethereal blue light lit the room.

"Yes, Steph?" queried the gentle, friendly voice of the computer.

"Diary, MyBook – simply add … 'Good Day'."

"Job done, Steph."

"My Book! Sleep." The blue light faded.

Steph lay in her warm, soft cocoon. There was a fluttering in her stomach and she thought of the wings of the moths somewhere outside her window seeking out the flowers – but she knew that the fluttering inside her had nothing to do with the moths and the dying day, but was in anticipation of what she would do on the coming day when the children had gone to school and before John had returned. She had taken tomorrow and the following day as leave from work, and tomorrow she would climb the steps of the ladder into the attic for a secret rendezvous. This was not the first time she had ascended the ladder for this meeting. What Steph did not know, was that her climb into the attic tomorrow would be different, and that the evening now ending was the last evening of life as she knew it.

*

In the morning she went through the usual routine of ablutions, breakfasts and getting the children off to school. With the breakfast things cleared away she went upstairs, then through a small door on the landing and then up the ladder into the loft.

The attic was a bit like a spare bedroom. There was a single bed, some drawers, a full length mirror, a table and chair, and a small sofa. In front of the sofa was what looked like a coffee table draped in a white cloth with a few books on top. This 'coffee table' was in fact a large travelling trunk. It had been used as such, and whenever anyone removed the white cover the faded and torn remnants of stickers from destinations visited by someone long ago could still be seen to adorn it. The trunk was always locked. The children rarely came into the attic and although they had asked what was in the trunk, Steph had always told them that it was empty and that the key had been lost long ago. She had always felt guilty about this lie - for it was a lie - but it was easier, and safer, than trying to explain the trunk's content. It was that content that had compelled Steph to make her solitary visits to the attic.

When she went up the ladder on this fateful day the sun was well risen and it was warm – maybe warmer than the previous beautiful day. Even with the eco-shield and a high degree of regional climate control everyone lived at a place on the planet and the planet still rotated and made its orbit round the sun. Beyond the eco-shield therefore the background of daily and annual change continued and some days could be a little warmer or cooler than others, some longer or shorter and some wetter or dryer.

Once in the attic she stood a moment looking at the trunk in anticipation before removing the books and the cloth. She undid the purse on her belt and took out a small key. She unlocked the trunk and returned the key to her purse before taking off the belt that held it. She lifted the lid of the trunk and there it was - the red dress. She felt the same tingle every time that she saw it, and despite the warm day, convulsed momentarily with a shiver of excitement. She took it out carefully and walked with it to a shaft of sunlight that came through a window in the ceiling. The dress glowed - blood satin in the light. She gathered it and slipped it over her head. It felt cool against her as it slid down. She put her arms through the straps and adjusted them on her shoulders. She went to the mirror. She smoothed the dress with her hands. It clung to her. She turned sideways. She loved how it followed the line of her back and the way the short skirt curved over her bottom before making neat vertical ripples to the hem. She twirled and the skirt span out almost horizontal. She pulled her hair up, holding it in place with both hands like a bun as she twirled again. She was absorbed. She was aware of nothing but herself and the dress until the word: "Mum?"

At the hatch into the attic only the head and shoulders of Tim could be seen. She had not heard his feet on the ladder. Open mouthed, he looked at his mother through bewildered brown eyes. She returned his gaze and the silence between them was as cold and as hard as ice.

*

Is it possible for a person to reach forty years of age and to genuinely feel that they are content but in fact be lying to themselves – or at the very least be fooling themselves? And is it possible for that person's whole belief system to be shattered by a single act in the same way that a house of cards might be brought down by a single, slight nudge? That day, for the first time in her life – or for the first time she had admitted it to herself in a long while – she questioned who she was. She faced her family. There were questions and silences. There were explanations and silences. Her son, her daughter, her husband all trying to understand. Her emotions would swing from spirited defence to feelings of utter humiliation. No matter what she thought of the dress or her secret meetings with it she could not dispel the shame of the deceit. She had lied to her family. Repeatedly on that day and in the days that followed she had wanted to destroy the dress - purge herself of it, cleanse herself. But she hadn't. Maybe it was because she liked it too much, or maybe because she knew that nothing she did to the dress would remove the guilt and shame of her lie. It would be a futile act. Maybe it was all of these things or maybe something else that she couldn't or didn't want to admit to. Whatever it was she did nothing and the dress remained in the trunk in the attic.

Possibly it was only her imagination but she felt as if her whole family was aware of it lying there like a great weight above their heads - something not to be discussed further but something constantly present. Eventually, after about a week, John asked what she was going to do with it. With false casualness Steph shrugged and said she didn't know. She continued slicing carrots for dinner.

"I would have thought that the best thing would be to shred it," he suggested, "...cut it up with scissors - and then feed it through the recycling in bits. We wouldn't *have* to cut it of course, it could go as it is - but it would probably avoid any possibility of questions if we cut it first."

"Yes, you're probably right."

There was a silence. She pushed the discs of carrot off the board into the steamer with the knife blade.

"Probably best sooner than later." His words met no response. "I don't mind doing it."

"No, it's all right - just leave it." The irritation in her voice was clear and he felt the "it" was more a reference to the conversation than the dress. With equal ambiguity he left the kitchen saying, "Ok, I'll leave you to sort it," and there the discussion ended. John did not look back. He did not see the white of his wife's knuckles gripping the knife. He did not see her lift it and press the cold blade hard against her lips but he did hear her slam it down flat onto the chopping board. Was she angry at John and his pestering about the dress or was she angry with herself …or with a deep longing inside her and shame at that longing? Had the uncovering of her secret rendezvous forced her to question whether she should have taken a different path a long time ago? Had she been living a lie?

She knew that John would raise the topic again if she didn't do something, and worse still, might even break into the trunk and remove the dress himself if she didn't act. Tomorrow therefore she would do what was necessary before setting off for the office.

*

The following day after John had gone to work and the children had gone to school Steph went to the attic with a pair of scissors and a carrier bag. Again she positioned herself in front of the mirror. The dress was in the trunk behind her and she stood naked looking at her reflection.

A face with small nose, pointed chin and melancholy hazel eyes looked back at her with resignation from beneath a bob of auburn hair. She didn't think of herself as especially pretty. She was however pleased – and proud – of her trim, healthy body. She saw it as fitting testament to her lifestyle. These days, she rarely took advantage of the Trueway custom of adorning hair – but she had taken full advantage of the right to have body decoration and the tattoos of biography that swirled in a myriad of colours across the pale skin of her chest and around her arms had always given her – still gave her - deep satisfaction. They testified to her achievements as a Citizen, as a person. Many proclaimed the contributions that she had made to the protection of the planet and to the future wellbeing of Trueway – the new, oxygen giving trees she had funded and her certified use of renewable energy to reduce pollution. She even had a tattoo for the electricity she had generated through pedalling an exercise bike at the gym. A proportion of her salary, and therefore of the lifestyle she could afford, was consequent upon these and similar civic contributions.

Her efforts had also earned her privileges. These too were recorded in her tattoos and of these the one that mattered above all others was the large, floral 'EM2' that identified her as a woman permitted 'Enhanced Marriage with Two Children'. Population control in Trueway was very important and anyone wanting children had to meet strict criteria. The requirements to be met for permission to have one child were high but for two children they were *extremely* high. And not only did Steph have to meet the stipulated criteria. Trueway demanded that *both* parents qualify.

John, like her proudly displayed an 'EM2' tattoo amidst all his other tattoos of achievement. John was a good man. He was a good looking man too - tall and slim with brown eyes that smiled out from a kindly face beneath short cropped blonde hair. She would jokingly call him her 'blonde god'. Like her he had worked hard to better himself, to gain a good education, to obtain a good job and to meet the criteria for having a family with two children. Steph saw herself and John as good Citizens yet both harboured a suppressed resentment that Trueway did not always apply its criteria equitably across all strata of society.

Trueway strived to be egalitarian but it was not. There were no lords, ladies, kings or queens but there was wealth and there was privilege. For some people having a beautiful home and two children, seemed more easily won. These people were the elite of Trueway, known colloquially as 'leets'.

Steph had not been born into a leet family. She had been born poor. She had no significant social connections. It was the same for all the other children in the neighbourhood where she had grown up. Trueway ensured they had all received adequate education, healthcare and where necessary, social support, but Steph knew of only one former school friend who had achieved the right to have a child. Steph was aware of none that had achieved the right to have two. From her neighbourhood, she alone had been prepared to spend the years of effort necessary to meet the criteria of social achievements. Only she had been prepared to defer marriage until she had been able to prove her worthiness through a demanding period of living within the confines of a convent of The Good Sisters.

What was it that had made Steph different to everyone else? Fundamentally, it was that she was bright and had been encouraged.

Steph had shown herself to be a very able pupil at school and her mother had encouraged her to be the best Citizen possible. She had encouraged her to 'get on' and to 'move up in the world'. Stephanie, her little girl, was as good as any 'leet' and just as worthy of having two children. Steph believed her. Steph applied herself. Steph was pleased by her achievements. She was pleased by the smile of pride on her mother's face when the teachers said how well she did. She was pleased when the priests said what a worthy child she must be in the sight of The Great Spirit.

So it was that she worked on with diligence and determination from an early age. Then the unthinkable happened. At only forty years of age, Steph's mother became ill and died. Steph was devastated, as any child would be. She was bewildered too. Her mother was good. Why would The Great Spirit allow her mother to die? People were kind to Steph. People were comforting, but none could explain it. Some children, some people, faced with an event so huge, devastating and incomprehensible might have lost all faith, all trust. They may have taken, consciously or unconsciously, the attitude of, 'what's the point?' - but not Steph. After the kindness and the comfort, which ultimately resolved nothing, Steph found her own way. She worked harder and more fervently than ever. She worked for her mother. It was her duty.

Now, here she was standing looking at herself in the mirror, the same age at which her mother had passed away and had her future taken from her. Steph looked at her tattoos, she looked at her surroundings, she thought of her two children and she thought of John. All this she had achieved against the odds. All this had come from her years of dogged endeavour, of determination. No hint of discontent. No hint of being unhappy. This was what she had worked for.

"I did it, mum. I did it," she sighed with tears in her eyes. She turned to the trunk and took out the dress. She laid it on the floor. She thought it looked sad, as if it knew it was about to die. She took the scissors and lifted the hem of the dress.

"Goodbye - and thank you," she whispered ... but then, as she went to make the first cut, morning sunlight broke through the roof window startling the colour to life. The red filled her eyes, filled the room and her being. Her breathing became shallow. It was as if she was being engulfed, suffocated, consumed and the dress was screaming ... "I am blood!"

She could hardly breathe. She could hardly see, and as the redness subsided, she wasn't sure whether she had momentarily lost

15

consciousness. But, as her breathing became regular again, and the fuzziness behind her eyes cleared, she looked at the glowing garment and understood. She lay the scissors down. She lifted the dress to her face. She buried her face in it, breathed in through the musty material, filling herself with its essence. She kissed it, pressing her lips hard against the fabric in her hands.

"No, there is nothing wrong with you. There is nothing wrong with me. We are good." She knew at that moment that the shame and stain of her secret ... her lie … stemmed from not believing in, or even being aware of, that goodness. Her simple goodness was what mattered ... and now she knew her way forward.

*

The sun was still shining when Steph opened the front door to set off for work. The carrier bag that she had taken into the attic now contained her sandwiches. She would walk her usual route and see many of the people who routinely crossed her path on this daily journey ... all doing what they always did as part of their daily routine. So much routine. She had often thought to herself how easy it was to predict what a person would be doing at a certain time and on a certain day. Looking back at her own life she recognised that there were change moments, but after that - routine. June 14th last year at 08:10 - set off to work along the same path she was about to walk now. June 14th two, three, four or five years before that at 08:10 - set off along the same path that she was about to walk now. She knew nothing could be predicted 100% ... but felt sure it was at least 90%!

The first person she would meet would probably be, Charlie. He lived a couple of doors down in the cul-de-sac that contained her own property. He was an elderly blind man, and on a sunny morning was inclined to sit in a deckchair on his front path warming himself and listening to the radio. She hoped he would be there, and that today would not be one of those 10% days that ran counter to what she felt she could predict. She drew a deep breath, stepped out, closed the door behind her and set off.

He was there. She could see him almost as soon as she was out of her drive and onto the footpath. As usual there was no-one else about. Charlie's hearing was very acute and selective. With his left ear he would be listening to the radio but his right would be listening for her footfall. It wasn't long 'til she was within earshot.

"Morning Steph!" came his confident call.

"Morning Charlie - lovely morning again."

"What you got in your sandwiches today?"

"Cheese and pickle. Enjoy the sunshine."

"Will do my best..."

She watched him as she passed. Did she see a quizzical turn of his head? Did she detect an involuntary movement of his hand towards the radio as if to quieten it because he had picked up some unfamiliar sound? She half expected him to call after her, but he didn't. She was shaking a little but it was good that Charlie had been there and that their exchange had been so much as she had predicted, so much the usual routine.

She crossed the little road at the end of the cul-de-sac and almost immediately entered a small, municipal park. It was lovely, the trees heavy with leaves, the borders full of colourful flowers and the air carrying their scent – daytime scent. Her sandals scrunched on the gravel path as it wound between purple rhododendrons. Unless there was someone unexpected about then her next encounter would either be, 'the dog lady' or the 'bicycle man'. The latter would be riding his bicycle along the gravel path towards her and the former would be exercising her dog on the lawn. The dog lady always gave a polite "good morning" and the bicycle man always rang his bell and gave a cheery "helloo" as he peddled past. Today, as Steph approached a bend in the path, she could hear his tyres on the gravel before he emerged from behind the rhododendrons.

"Ding" went the bell but the confusion on the man's face after that automatic reaction explained the stifling of his normal verbal greeting. "Nice morning," called Steph in her usual way as he passed her. There was no answer. She walked on, not looking round to see whether he was looking back. The path emerged from the bushes and she could see the dog lady on the grass. She was a little way off. There was no doubt that she saw Steph, and even with the distance, would have recognised her, but there was no wave or call. The dog suddenly became of much greater concern than was generally the case, necessitating the woman's full attention, and compelling her gaze downwards.

The council offices were across a street on the far side of the park and Steph encountered one or two other people before entering the building. Some, like the bicycle man and dog lady, were people that she regularly saw while others were people that she did not recognise. Some looked away quickly, others stared, none spoke.

"Morning Jill," said Steph to the girl on reception as she entered the building.

"Hi ... Steph..." came the faltering response.

She met no-one in the corridor but the buzz of conversation in the open plan office stopped when she entered.

"Morning all," she called in the way she always did and went to her desk. She put her bag of sandwiches in the drawer. Her back was to the room. She sat down and switched on her computer. She was aware of a very, very quiet exchange behind her (more movements and signals than words) before Terry came over to her.

"Hi Steph, is everything OK?"

"Fine, it's a nice morning isn't it?"

"Yes, sure. Been a good June so far. "

She looked up at Terry. He smiled awkwardly.

"Everything's fine, Terry – really." She turned in her seat to her work colleagues. "Really, I'm fine."

Encouraged by Steph's calm manner and reassurance, Asha voiced their collective thoughts,

"...But Steph, you're wearing a dress!"

Chapter 2: The Police Meet the Red Dress for the First Time

It wasn't long before Steph was called to the manager's office just down the corridor.

"Hi Steph, take a seat," invited Fiona motioning towards one of the two easy chairs, both of which already had fresh, disposable sitting towels on them. Fiona was a large, smiley lady, who filled her office. There was always a bowl of boiled sweets on the table.

"Coffee?" she asked as she poured herself a cup from a thermos flask.

"No I'm fine."

"Well, I'll come to the point," said Fiona putting her coffee cup on the table and sitting down. "You have caused a bit of a stir. Why are you wearing a dress?"

"Why shouldn't I? What's wrong with it? Women used to wear dresses all the time. I'm not harming anyone am I? Its clean - if that's your worry."

"Oh Steph…please! I don't doubt for one second that it's clean. Come on, you know why I'm asking. It's extremely unusual." Fiona took a sip of coffee before adding, "Some would even say 'odd'." She paused and looked quizzically at Steph – but not long enough to invite a response. "Anyway, it's not what people expect. I bet work has come to a standstill out there!" She chuckled and leaned back in her chair. The chuckle had not been forced. Fiona was a good manager. She and Steph had always got on well and Steph felt a little abashed, wondering whether her tone may have been unnecessarily defensive – confrontational even. She wanted to speak but didn't know quite what to say. Fiona appeared to recognise Steph's difficulty.

"I dare say whatever has led to this may not be that easy to explain. I'll tell you what. Take the rest of the day off and we can talk about it again tomorrow. "

"Am I being suspended?"

"No, no - I just think it would be best if you took a little time - had a think. You could come in tomorrow - preferably without the dress - and you could explain a bit more. If it would be easier I could come to you, at home if you would prefer."

They sat silently. Steph didn't want to get into an argument, but equally didn't particularly want to go home. She wanted to get on with her work.

"If I take the dress off can I go and get on with my work?"

"Well yes, I don't see why not. I imagine there will still be questions from everyone and some tongues wagging but ..." She gave a shrug.

"Can I not work with the dress on?"

"I don't really think so Steph."

"Why not?"

"Oh come on Steph. I've already explained that the office has probably come to a standstill - and these are your friends and colleagues. Sooner or later someone will complain. I don't want it to come to that. If you take the dress off and start work then we will, I am sure, muddle on through. Failing that, I think that my suggestion of taking the rest of the day off and talking again tomorrow is best."

Steph was reluctant to take the dress off. Maybe Fiona was right, maybe she needed time to think.

"OK, I'll go and turn off my machine and get my sandwiches."

"Don't worry about that Steph. I'll go and get your stuff and turn off your machine. You're going to take the rest of the day off then?"

Steph nodded and gave a little, "Mmm" in response.

"OK then. I'll tell the others and send you a text this evening to see whether you want to come in tomorrow or would like me to come round. I've got the usual section managers' meeting first thing but should be OK about lunch time. Did you have anything specific that needed doing today - any meetings? I can give your apologies or arrange cover."

They looked briefly at the on-screen diary together. It all seemed so normal, so much the usual - two colleagues planning the response to an unexpected event. It therefore seemed so much stranger when Steph found herself alone in the corridor clutching her bag of sandwiches knowing that the office work was going on behind her - and that she was the unexpected event.

She wasn't sure what to do and sought refuge, and time for procrastination, in the lavatory. She entered a cubicle, put the lid down on the toilet seat and sat there. It was cool and quiet in the toilet. Her heart was racing but she soon became calm in the stillness and solitude. She sat, not really thinking of anything until she decided that she couldn't sit any longer. She stood up, undid her belt and laid it on the seat. She took off the dress. She carefully folded it and put it in the carrier bag with her sandwiches. She put her belt back on and left the building.

*

Steph did not want to go home. The day was getting warmer and she felt very free ... almost like a child skipping school. Without the dress she was inconspicuous - exactly like everyone else. No-one stared in surprise or avoided looking at her in embarrassment. She wandered along with no real goal. She glanced in shop windows as she wound her way through narrow pedestrian streets until she came to one of her favourite cafés. She selected a table outside in the dappled shade beneath a small lime tree, took her sitting towel from her bag and sat down. The day was warm with only a hint of a breeze. When the waiter came she ordered a coffee and a slice of lemon cake.

She sat sipping her coffee and enjoying the moist, crumbly delight. She wasn't thinking of anything in particular. She watched the people around her, and that occupied her thoughts. Work, home, the red dress, what to do? These issues were there. The reality would have to be faced. She would have to go home, talk to John, make decisions ... but right now, she would just sip coffee, eat cake and watch people.

Eventually, her cup empty, and the last delicious crumbs lifted to her lips with the end of a sticky finger, she went inside to pay. She decided that she would go to the toilet before setting off home. When she came out of the cubicle she was wearing the red dress.

*

Her walk to the cafe had been unremarkable. Her walk away from it was not. She was no longer another, invisible person.

"Oh Great Spirit!" was the first thing she heard from a young woman sitting with her friend at one of the tables. The other girl turned to look and her mouth fell open before she stifled a giggle. The two girls stared in disbelief. Steph smiled at them and walked past.

The majority of people ignored her or stared from a distance. Occasionally there was a jovial comment or question like where was the historical drama being filmed? At the road there were a few honks from the horns of passing glide-cars.

"Why is that lady red mummy?" asked a toddler pulling at his mother who was standing talking to other ladies with prams and push chairs. She and the others had not seen Steph approaching.

21

"What lady...?" said the mother turning then, " ...Never mind, come away. Come here." She pulled the child behind her looking venomously at Steph. "What do you think you're doing?"

Steph glanced across at the little huddle of women all of whom now followed the lead of their companion and made protective movements towards their offspring. "Leets," thought Steph judging by the lack of tattoos, and the fancy hair decoration. She ignored them and kept walking but the woman called after her, "You should be ashamed. Do what you like in your own home but doing stuff like that in public ... and in front of children! You're disgusting... pervert! Skin shamer! People like you shouldn't be allowed out – and certainly not near children!"

Steph wanted to confront her – show her the 'EM2'. Steph would lay odds that not one of those women was an 'EM2' but she didn't even call back, "It's a dress for pity's sake - people wore them all the time in the past!" She felt to do either would be pointless, and so kept walking in silence. Not rising to the challenge made her feel even a little superior in fact – and even more certain that the woman and all her leet cronies were probably only 'EM1s'.

She would return home via the park. The bicycle man and dog lady would not be there at this time of day. She wondered who would be. She became aware of the siren when she was about 100 metres from the park gate. It grew louder. She stopped to cross the road and could see the police car approaching with its blue light flashing. She stood at the kerb. The car pulled up. Two policemen got out and came over to her.

"Hello madam. I'm Police Officer Johns and this is my colleague Officer Williams." The officer waved his ID badge in front of Steph's face. "There has been a complaint and I am afraid I must ask you to accompany us to the police station. Will you get in the car please?"

"A complaint? A complaint about me?" asked Steph with a degree of incredulity. "What sort of complaint?"

"If you could just get in the car please madam. We will explain at the station."

"But what is the problem?"

"Please Madam, if you could just get in the car," said Officer Johns as Officer Williams held open the back door of the vehicle.

Steph sighed and got in.

At the station she was taken by a female officer to a small, well lit room with shiny cream walls. It reminded Steph of an old fashioned butcher's shop. In the centre of the room there was a table with an empty chair on one side and two chairs on the other, one of which was already occupied by a male officer. The policewoman went to sit next to her colleague and invited Steph to take up the seat facing them. The chair had a clean sitting towel on it.

"The towel is clean," said the female officer, "…if you would like to take off the dress."

"The dress is clean too," said Steph, taking the towel and putting it on the table before sitting down.

"I'm Officer Miller," said the man, "and this is my colleague Constable Thomas. Could you give me your name please madam?"

"Have I been arrested? Why do you want my name? And anyway haven't you got my name from the scanner?"

"No, madam, our bio-scanner does not tell us names … and no, technically you have not been arrested. I can make it a formal arrest and caution if you wish," said officer Miller, before adding quite kindly "… but I would prefer not to." Officer Miller then explained that there had been a complaint about a woman walking through the town wearing a red dress. The person lodging the complaint had said that she and others had been quite distressed as a consequence of being confronted by the person in the dress. There had been children present as well.

"So, who was this person making the complaint?" asked Steph though she had little doubt it was the opinionated leets.

"That is of no consequence," said Officer Miller. "The fact is that the complaint was made and so we, the police, are obliged to investigate."

"So, I don't get told who has complained. Do I get told what the complaint was? What is it I am supposed to have done to 'distress' this person?"

"Madam," interjected Constable Thomas. "We often get complaints of one sort or another that we have to look into. If you will just listen to my colleague and co-operate then I am sure we can sort this out."

Steph looked at them, finding it hard to conceal the contempt building inside her.

"So," said Officer Miller recommencing, "can you tell me your name please?"

Steph co-operated with the questioning despite her irritation. After basic details, she was asked about where she had been and what she had done that day. As Officer Miller asked questions Constable Thomas took notes on a digipad. The questioning took her to the point where she had entered the room in which she was now being interviewed.

"Thank you, Mrs Hugo. That brings us up to date, so-to-speak," said Officer Miller. "My colleague will print off the notes for you to read and sign." Constable Thomas stood up and went to the corner of the room where a printer had started to buzz away.

"Is that it?" asked Steph. "What happens then ... when I have read the notes?"

"Well, unless you think there is something wrong, my colleague and I will countersign and file them."

At that point Constable Thomas returned and placed the notes in front of Steph before leaving the room.

"So, have a read and make sure it is all correct," said Officer Miller. "Take your time. There is no rush."

Steph felt like simply signing to get the whole thing over with ... but decided it was best to read through to make sure that there was nothing that she disagreed with. While she was reading, Constable Thomas returned and whispered something to her colleague before leaving again.

After what seemed an age of silent reading Steph looked up. "OK can I have a pen please?" She signed and Officer Miller countersigned.

"My female colleague will sign it when she comes back."

"So what happens now?"

"We will just wait for your husband to arrive."

"What!"

"We have contacted your husband and asked that he come and collect you," said Officer Miller.

"Why? ... You have no right ... how dare you!" Steph was on her feet now. "How dare you!" she blurted. "What gives you the right ...," but before she could finish her sentence the door opened and there was John accompanied by Constable Thomas.

Chapter 3: May Asks a Question or Two

The journey home in the car was pretty much in silence.

"I need a cup of tea," said Steph when they got in. She headed off to the kitchen, the kitchen where the day had started so normally only a few hours before. "They didn't even offer me a drink at that damned station. Do you want one?"

"No, I'm fine," said John following her in and sitting down at the table.

"I'm sorry they called you. It wasn't my idea. I didn't know until you were standing there. I'm really sorry. Were you at work?"

"Yes, of course I was." Steph detected the irritation in John's voice even though he tried to hide it.

"Sorry." She sat down with her tea.

John sat silently looking at the table and fiddling with the keys to his glide-car.

"Say something," said Steph. "I am sorry. I really didn't know they were going to drag you out of work."

"It's not about being called from work, is it Steph? How can you sit there in that," he looked pointedly at the dress, "... and think I am worried about missing a few hours work? You have been arrested and taken to the police station. You have been parading yourself in the town." His voice was growing louder. "Hell knows what happened at your office, 'coz you certainly aren't there now and weren't there earlier!" He was almost shouting now. "Do you really think I am worried about a few hours work?"

They sat in silence once more. Steph took sips of her tea, the word "parading" repeating itself in her head.

"Are you going to say anything? Give me any explanation? Tell me what all this is about?" asked John more calmly.

Steph sipped her tea and just looked silently at the table. The silence continued until John spoke again.

"Well, the children will be home soon. You had better take that off. Probably best to put it back in the box for now. They won't expect us to be here. I don't know what you want me to tell them. I guess it will have to be *me* since you don't seem to want to speak. Anyway, go and take that off and we can work something out."

"I don't know what to say," said Steph as John stood up to leave. "I'm not trying to be difficult. I don't really understand myself ... it was just something I did. It felt right. It felt honest."

John leaned against the door frame looking at her a moment. "I'm going out to the car. I left my case and everything in there." He turned to go.

"I'm not taking it off," was all Steph quietly said, as he went.

*

"The other day, your dad and I had a talk and I decided that I would cut this dress up and put it through the recycling." Steph looked down at the dress and then at the silent faces of her family sat round the kitchen table. "I went to do it this morning after you had all gone and before I went to work." She paused. "I just couldn't do it. I couldn't cut it up. I realised that there was nothing wrong with the dress and that there was nothing wrong with me wearing it - that there was nothing wrong with me." She paused again. "Anyway, instead of cutting it up I put it on and went to work."

"What?" exclaimed May, her blue eyes wide in astonishment. "You went out like that ... like you are now?"

"Yes."

"But ... weren't you embarrassed? Didn't people stare?"

"Can I go and do my homework?" piped in Tim.

"In a minute Tim, let your mother finish what she has to say first," said John calmly.

"Yes, I went to work, but they asked me to go home. I went into town instead and then was arrested by the police after someone complained. Your father came to collect me from the police station. That's it really. That's why your dad and me are here now and not at work."

"So what's going to happen now?" May directed the question to her father.

"Well, that rather depends on your mother doesn't it?" John looked at Steph.

"Well, I'm not going to simply stop wearing it. Why shouldn't I wear it? I realised I was embarrassed before because I was ashamed of it ... but people used to wear clothes before ... people sometimes wear clothes now so I ..."

"Can I do my homework now please?" said Tim looking at his father.

"Yes, go on Tim."

Tim disappeared to his room with his school bag. John looked at Steph. She couldn't read his face.

"I've got some papers to get ready for tomorrow," he announced standing up "and then I will get on with cooking some dinner – veggie sausage and chip night!" he said with a smile at May, knowing it was one of her favourites. "Great," she said, trying to sound cheery as he left the room.

Steph looked at her daughter. She fully recognised the distress she was causing to her and the rest of the family. She regretted this immensely but could not escape the conviction that what she was doing was *right* and that she was somehow compelled to continue. She did not fully understand the root of this epiphany and was still working out for herself what she was trying to achieve and why. Her thinking however, had not prepared her for the question May asked when her father had gone.

"You're not going to be a terrorist ... or a prostitute, are you mum?"

For a second the question seemed so outlandish that Steph said nothing, but she quickly guessed the origin of May's enquiry.

"No, I'm not becoming a terrorist or a prostitute," she said with a kindly smile. "I guess you have been doing stuff at school about clothing in history. Sorry if I have brought the classroom home."

"It's just that at school they said that people like terrorists used to wear clothes for bad reasons like hiding bombs under them. That's why the *Clothing and Makeup Act* was necessary."

"I'm sure ... well I *hope* ... that your history teacher gave more reasons than that for why people wore clothes in the past!" smiled Steph.

"Yes, of course mum - they didn't have climate control and stuff, but the teacher said that clothes are really only worn today by people that *need* to wear them - like firemen for protection, or doctors in the operating theatre to stop germs. The teacher says that these are called the 'stipulated exceptions'. Anyone else is just ashamed of their skin or their body and that's wrong. The Great Spirit created people to wear skin and not clothes. Wearing clothes puts human creation above that of The Great Spirit and so is an insult to The Great Spirit."

Steph was astonished at the ease with which her daughter gave this explanation. Maybe she should not have been. She herself had been brought up and educated in Trueway. She knew the thoroughness of

27

teaching about The Great Spirit and the Book of Truth. She recognised the catechism from which May's words had sprung. Her surprise emphasised just how much she had come to question.

"And prostitutes?" queried Steph.

"Well … prostitutes just do," ventured May with less certainty, before suddenly adding, "– and maybe to cover up tattoos."

"Well, take heart my little May," reassured Steph as she reached across the table and took her daughter's hands, "I am not becoming a mad bomber or a prostitute. I wouldn't fit many bombs under this little thing for a start would I?" At that, May smiled. Steph smiled too and sat back in her chair as the tension subsided.

"Where did it come from - the dress … and don't be funny and say the attic!" May rolled her eyes, anticipating the kind of bad joke response her mother was fond of making.

Steph had anticipated this question and had prepared her answer – though, in her mind's eye, the question had been posed by John.

"You know, May, you are the first person to have asked me that. It was your Great-great-grandmother's. I wish I had a picture of her wearing it, but I don't. Things were different then - all a bit topsy-turvy from our point of view."

At that moment Steph's phone jingled indicating a text had come through. She looked. "Damn, I had forgotten about that. It's Fiona from work. Well, I can get back to her in a bit. Right now I need to wash this." She stood up and pulled the dress off over her head, relieved at the opportunity for a comfortable termination to the conversation. "Next time you do anything about the *Clothing and Makeup Act* at school, and they ask for reasons why we stopped wearing clothes, forget about terrorists - tell them it was to avoid the hours spent washing them!"

*

Fiona came round to Steph's house at 1pm the following day. The red dress was nowhere to be seen. Steph had taken it back into the attic to dry, suspended by the shoulder straps from a makeshift hanger made from a cardboard tube with a piece of string through it. Fiona looked relieved to see that Steph wasn't wearing the dress.

Steph made tea for them both and they chatted about work things while she did so.

"I see you are not wearing the dress," ventured Fiona with a pause as Steph handed her the tea and sat down.

"No, I washed it. It's upstairs drying. Living now has its advantages - imagine the amount of clothes' washing for a family in the past!"

"Yes indeed ... so are you saying that the dress is staying at home from now on - if only to avoid washing?" ventured Fiona hopefully.

"No, not really. I'm not saying that I want to come into work every day wearing that dress or any other. If I had come into work this morning then I probably ... no certainly ... would not have been wearing it. It's just the principle. I can't see any reason why I can't wear a dress if I want to. Can you?"

"Well, if we are talking 'in principle' and 'theoretically' then no, I can't see why you - or anyone else for that matter – shouldn't wear a dress if they want to. In *practice* however I think it's different. Like I said yesterday, it disrupted the office."

"Well, if there is nothing wrong with it - and you have just said that you don't think there is - then people in the office can adjust, and get on with their work as normal. They've known me a long time, most of them, and we get on OK ... so I don't see that it's a problem."

"It's not just what *I* think Steph. In fact my personal opinion doesn't matter at all ... it's what is right for the office. After you had gone yesterday I spoke to the Deputy Director and she took advice from our legal department. They say that wearing a dress is not illegal *in itself* but that if someone complained about you then it could lay you open to a charge of having caused distress. The DD felt that would compromise the department. She was therefore very clear, that if you were to come back, it would have to be on the understanding that you would not be wearing a dress."

Fiona sipped her tea. At first Steph said nothing. She hadn't been exactly sure what Fiona was going to say to her on this visit, but this ultimatum did not come as a surprise.

"So, if I refuse to give an unequivocal guarantee that I will not come into work wearing a dress, what happens then?"

"I think that it would lead to disciplinary procedures." There was a tone of kindly resignation in Fiona's voice. She was simply stating the inevitable.

"And if I agree *not* to wear a dress to work?"

"Well, I am not certain but I think that you would come back under some kind of probationary arrangement. I think that you might also be asked to agree not to wear it in public at all, since that might bring the department into disrepute. But, I'm not absolutely sure of that. I expect the legal department would be consulted again. You put us all a bit on the spot yesterday, and working out what to do was a bit rushed."

Steph remained silent so Fiona continued, "The DD realised that you may want time to think, so said that she was quite happy for you to take the rest of the week off ... more if need be. She also suggested that you may want to discuss things with Occupational Health." Fiona delved into her bag and produced some leaflets. "These give all the contact details for them," she said, laying the leaflets on the table as she stood up. "I want you back Steph. I want you in the office as you have been all these years. I don't really understand what is going on so I think you really should take up the suggestion to arrange a meeting with Occupational Health."

"I'll think about it," said Steph as she accompanied Fiona to the door and saw her out.

Steph felt 'empty' as she poured the undrunk, half cold cups of tea down the sink. Although she didn't fully admit it to herself, she knew then that she would never be going back to work.

*

She explained the situation to John that evening; particularly that she would not be going to the office for the next few days while she tried to decide what to do. He did not understand why wearing the dress - or as Steph insisted, the *freedom* to wear the dress - was so important to her, but he felt it best not to press her with questions.

In the days that followed the dress remained in the attic, and apart from the fact that Steph was not going to work, the Hugo household seemed to return to normal and life became more relaxed. In the evening, after the children had gone to bed, Steph and John would have a glass of wine. They would often sit curled up on the plump, cosy settee and maybe watch TV or listen to music or just chat. It must have been five or six days after Fiona's visit that John stood up to take the wine glasses to the kitchen before they went to bed when Steph blurted,

"I'm going to hand in my resignation tomorrow."

John froze by the living room door, a glass in each hand and looked at her in disbelief.

"I'm sorry. I've been trying to find a way to tell you and just been putting it off and putting it off … but I've got to tell Fiona something so …" She left the sentence unfinished and just looked at her husband. John stood a moment unsure of what to say – unsure of what he felt. Things had seemed so normal he hadn't really expected this.

"Right, I guess I'm surprised. You haven't worn the dress for days and things seemed to be getting back to how they were. Why can't you just carry on as you are now, as you have been for the past few days; in the way you had always done before all this started?"

Steph looked at him. He looked genuinely lost – because he was. She shrugged and looked away. Her voice sounded inadequate, even to herself, when she heard the matter of fact words from her mouth:

"There is nothing wrong with the dress. There is nothing wrong with me or with me wearing the dress." She looked at him. "So to agree to their terms is tantamount to accepting that there *is* something wrong with the dress … and therefore something wrong with *me*. I won't do it, so it's better that I resign than drag it out through a disciplinary." That factual explanation was the concluding distillation of what had been going on in her head since Fiona's visit. After a moment John spoke.

"Will you try and get another job? We can probably get by on my salary - but we may need to make some adjustments."

She looked back at him. *Good old John - always practical, always steady*, she thought with a smile to herself. She knew John didn't understand why she was doing what she was doing (after all, she was still formulating her reasons herself … feeling her way as issues confronted her). She knew she was lucky though. John's anger had already subsided and despite his lack of comprehension he appeared ready to support her.

"I can try for other jobs," she said. "I guess it will all depend on what's out there and what response I get. Whoever I approach will contact the council and ask for references so they are bound to discover what's happened before they offer me anything. Maybe I'll become self-employed … if I can think of some service to offer."

John nodded. "I'll take these to the kitchen. Then I'm off to bed." He smiled.

"OK, I'll sit a little longer. I won't be long."

After he had gone she could still see him in her mind's eye, standing there with the glasses and being so accepting. He was a good man. He was everything she thought she had wanted – a tall, caring handsome god with an EM2 tattoo. She also knew that he wasn't perfect. Because of the strict sex and reproduction laws in Trueway, Citizens took medication called, Desire and Aggression Modification Pills (DAMP). This helped reduce ardour, and for men especially, unwanted arousal in public. Couples were however allowed periods without DAMP, called DAMP Holidays. Steph knew that John had recently taken such a holiday. They, as a couple, had not been scheduled one, but she had found condoms in his drawer. With much embarrassment he had explained their use for masturbation during a government sanctioned element of male entertainment associated with the currently occurring World Games. She believed him. She had heard of these events and John was much more likely to engage in something sanctioned by Trueway than risk a secret affair. Nevertheless, what he had been doing had been a secret – something he had kept from her, just as she had kept the dress from him.

Chapter 4: And so to the White Court of the Magistrates

Steph submitted her letter of resignation. Fiona e-mailed to say how sorry she was to receive it. After that Steph felt as though she was on a strange mini holiday. The days were sunny, she had no work to go to and once John and the kids were gone each morning she could do as she pleased. She took to having a glass or two of wine in the afternoon and going for a walk. For about a week she enjoyed this new found freedom. She didn't wear the dress and oddly she forgot all about it - but the dress was not to be forgotten.

"Isn't that the body shaming woman - the one that was parading herself in front of the children the other week?"

The words came from someone in a small group of women with pushchairs. Steph had just come out of the supermarket. At first she only registered the words as an accidentally heard snatch of conversation. She was taken aback when she realised the comment was aimed at her. She glanced across at the group. They were all looking at her. She turned and continued walking.

"That's it - clear off! We don't want your kind round here. Your sort should be locked up – promoting your 'body shame' rubbish! My child is brought up proud of his body! You're a pervert, that's what you are – like all those other textilist weirdoes! Anti-Trueway, that's what I call it!"

Steph's blood started to boil. She felt her cheeks flush. She wanted to confront this woman - confront her self-righteousness. Couldn't she see the tattoos that made everything she was saying so obviously wrong? Steph wanted to confront her hypocrisy - the hypocrisy of criticising her while yelling angry abuse in front of her child – especially when Steph wasn't even wearing her dress and the child wouldn't know why his mother was yelling. She wanted to confront all this – but she didn't. She clenched her teeth and kept walking in silence and the woman and her little group made no move to follow.

Steph walked with no particular goal. She just needed to get away from the angry words but the words repeated in her head and her own anger simply increased. She found herself walking faster. She shot fierce, challenging glances at passersby. Her pace quickened further - almost marching. Her mind had shut off now but her feet were taking her home.

She was breathing hard with the exertion and her cheeks burned as she crossed the park. She was almost running when she burst through her front door and pounded up the stairs, then up into the attic. The dress was still hanging from its makeshift hanger. She stood looking at it a moment, panting and shaking. Her trembling fingers fumbled with the string and cardboard as she tried to get the dress off. She pulled hard at the string which cut into her hands before it snapped. She clutched the dress to her chest. A deep, animal growl escaped her clenched teeth before she dropped heavily to the floor in tears. She lay there, curled up clutching the dress until she had cried herself out.

*

When John got home from work May and Tim were watching TV. They had done their homework. Steph was not at home. May and Tim said that they had not seen their mother since breakfast. John had a cursory look round for a note. He couldn't find one but wasn't too concerned. It was Steph's night for doing the evening meal so he expected her home soon. She may even have popped out for some missing ingredient. He sent her a text.

As time passed with no word from her he began to feel uneasy. After an hour, with Tim and May asking about something to eat and Steph's phone just going to answer phone, John was beginning to think he should be checking the local hospital. It was very unlike Steph not to have made contact. Before he could do that however his phone rang. It was not Steph, or the hospital. It was the police. He was informed that Steph was well but that she had been arrested and could he come to the station.

John had no concerns about leaving May and Tim alone. They were sensible kids and once he had given them something to eat he knew they would just carry on watching TV. At the police station John was met by Officer Miller - the same officer who had interviewed Steph on the previous occasion. Officer Miller took John to an interview room.

"Thank you for coming in."

"Where is my wife? What's happened?"

"Your wife is fine, Mr Hugo. She is in one of the police cells."

John fell silent. Steph was in a prison cell. His wife, Steph in a cell.

"I'm afraid," said Officer Miller, "that there have been further complaints about Mrs Hugo being seen in town wearing a dress. Since this is the second time there has been a complaint, we have had to conduct matters more formally than on the previous occasion. Mrs Hugo was therefore interviewed under caution and offered the opportunity to have a solicitor present. Mrs Hugo declined the offer. The interview was completed about an hour ago."

John hung his head. He felt stunned.

"I'm afraid there is more," continued Officer Miller apologetically. "I think you should know that the complaint was made when Mrs Hugo was walking down Finch Street. When our officers arrived she was not only wearing the dress, but was dancing in front of the convent of The Good Sisters situated at the end of that street. The dancing doesn't make the charge any worse – but I just thought it was something that you should be aware of."

"Right," was all a very shaken John, could quietly say. Officer Miller didn't speak. He knew he had to give John time to take in what he had just heard.

"So," queried John after a few bewildered seconds "are you going to release her now that I'm here so I can take her home?"

"I'm afraid it isn't quite that simple this time. We have had to charge her with behaving in a manner likely to cause offence."

John's heart sank. "You're not going to keep her in prison, surely?"

"Well, that depends ... and is very much why we have asked to speak to you. We do not regard Mrs Hugo as a danger to the public and we would therefore like to release her on police bail until her case comes to court. However, we are concerned that Mrs Hugo may repeat her behaviour. We therefore feel it necessary to make her bail conditional upon her surrendering her dress until her case has been heard in the Magistrate's Court. Failing her agreement to that we would only be willing to release her on bail with surety of 500 standard units."

"Right, I see," said John as his mind began to focus on practicalities that helped blot out the image of his wife dancing in a dress in front of a convent. "Have you asked her whether she will surrender the dress?"

"Not yet Mr Hugo. We wanted to explain the situation to you first. If Mrs Hugo refuses to surrender the dress are you willing, or do you know of anyone else who may be willing, to provide surety of 500 standard units?"

"Oh, I will provide surety if it comes to that."

"Thank you, Mr Hugo. I'll ask for your wife to be brought up." He went to the door and asked a constable who had been waiting outside to fetch Mrs Hugo. He then returned and sat in silence with John until a knock was heard on the door. Officer Miller moved to stand up but paused. He leaned towards John and quietly said, "Just so you know, our officers got to Mrs Hugo before the TV people arrived – but only just."

*

Although Steph agreed to take the dress off prior to leaving the police station she was not willing to surrender it to the police. John therefore had to agree to the 500 standard units bail condition. Once home she explained to the children what had happened. Tim remained quiet. Steph felt unable to read his thoughts. May was generally supportive of her mother's stance - especially not giving up what she now regarded to be a family heirloom - but both she and Tim were obviously upset and concerned when their mother explained that she was going to have to go to court.

Steph had to admit that she was uncertain about the powers of the court and what the possible outcomes might be. She thought she may have to pay a fine. Her uncertainty however, and therefore her inability to reassure her children, made her wish she had accepted the offer of a solicitor at the police station. She promised that she would consult one the following day. With that knowledge Steph hoped that the children went to bed that night feeling less anxious – and to some extent they did, though intuitively they knew that their peace was in the hands of their mother and not someone called a solicitor.

Steph and John did not talk a great deal more about the day's events after the children had gone to bed. John appeared to accept the situation and to accept Steph's explanation that her behaviour had been a reaction to the taunting and that what the police called, 'dancing' had just been a few steps in response to a busker playing a jig on a fiddle.

The two of them now focused on what questions to ask a solicitor - and just as importantly, which solicitor. Although they had had some dealings with a firm in town this had been for the more usual family things – wills and house purchase. They had never had to consult anyone on criminal issues. They identified a couple of likely options through the internet, settled on a, 'Mr Shaw' and worked out the key questions they felt needed to be addressed. Despite the unusualness and potential stressfulness of the situation, they thought they had done as much as they could and felt surprisingly relaxed by the time they turned in for the night.

"I guess I have become more important in the eyes of the police now," said Steph as they went to bed.

"Why?" John looked puzzled.

"They gave me a cup of tea this time."

*

The following day Steph contacted Mr Shaw and explained her situation. He agreed to obtain further details from the authorities and they met to discuss her case a few days later.

"Come in, come in … do sit down," said a jovial Mr Shaw as he ushered Steph into his office and indicated a leather chair with a monogrammed, paper sitting towel ready in place. The office was small but airy and bright with a large window beyond which Steph could see the boughs of a beech tree dappled in sunlight. Steph estimated Mr Shaw to be in his late fifties, a small round man with an equally round and smiling face.

"Tea? Coffee? Water?" he queried.

"No, I'm fine - but, thank you."

"Right, then straight to business." Mr Shaw sat down behind his desk. He put on some spectacles and opened a file. "Well, Mrs Hugo, it seems you have been charged under Section 5 of The Public Order Act. I won't go into all the details of the legislation, but essentially this means that the police are of the view that you have behaved in a way that has caused harassment, alarm or distress to someone." Mr Shaw looked over his glasses at Steph. "Make sense so far?"

Steph nodded.

"Good, good," said Mr Shaw, "So, from the charge sheet, and from what you have told me yourself, the behaviour of concern is wearing a dress in public." Again he glanced over his glasses before continuing. "The police don't seem to be saying that you caused a kerfuffle, or anything like that, so I don't think there is any suggestion that you may have caused alarm in that way. Were you aware of anyone being upset – anyone who appeared distressed?"

"No, not this time. I did go out in the dress once before. A woman with a pushchair was pretty unpleasant to me on that occasion. I think it was the same woman who saw me earlier on the day we're talking about.

She was pretty abusive to me then as well … but I wasn't wearing the dress at that time."

"Mmm – right. Could this person have seen you again when you came out wearing your dress later that day do you think?"

"Well, it's possible – but I didn't see her."

"Right. Good. So, you were not aware of any problem until the police arrived to arrest you? Did anyone speak to you at all while you were out in your dress?"

"Well," said Steph, "some people did stare and there were some remarks … friendly I would say. One lady, I recall, said, 'Nice bit of retro'."

"Right, that all sounds very positive," said Mr Shaw sitting back and smiling.

"So, I am not being prosecuted for skin shaming or body shaming?" queried Steph.

"Oh goodness me, no! For a charge under that legislation you would need to be suggesting there was a need to cover up for moral purposes, or maybe because you think one body shape is better than another." He paused, a momentary look of alarm on his face. "You weren't carrying any placards or anything … were you?" Steph shook her head and Mr Shaw looked relieved. "No, of course not – and you have already told me that you didn't speak to anyone. On top of that you have a very impressive array of civic tattoos, which I can't imagine you are ashamed of, so no, this is just as the charge says - a simple case of, 'causing harassment, alarm or distress'. Right, now that we are all clear - let the game begin! What do you want to plead – 'guilty' or 'not guilty'?"

Steph was taken aback. What did he mean – "let the game begin"?

"I'm sorry Mr Shaw. I'm not sure I understand. I'm not aware of having alarmed, or distressed anyone, and I haven't tried to harass anyone so I'm not guilty of anything. I therefore plead 'not guilty' don't I?"

Mr Shaw leaned forward across his desk. "That sounds eminently sensible, Mrs Hugo – axiomatic even – but this is the law, and the law's the game! The question to ask is, 'Do I think I will win the game?'." Again he leaned back smiling before continuing.

"Say you plead 'guilty'. The police will be happy, the magistrates will be happy, you will get a small fine and everyone will go home. Everything will be over and done with - except, of course," and here he leaned forward again, "for the fact that you will have a criminal record."

"Well, having a criminal record seems a pretty big issue to me," responded Steph "and a damned good reason for pleading 'not guilty'."

"Indeed, indeed, Mrs Hugo, absolutely but remember the all important question – do you think you will win the game? Let's assume that you plead, 'not guilty'." He leaned forward. "If you do that then the first thing that will happen is that we will have to wait for another hearing! The magistrates will not deal with your case on the same day as your plea. The second hearing date could be anything from four to twelve weeks later. When that second hearing comes you might win. If you *do* win then you will not get a fine and you will not get a criminal record – the *best* outcome. But … and this brings us back to the game and the question … if you lose then you will not only get a criminal record but the fine will be bigger!" Once again Mr Shaw leaned back in his chair and smiled. "It's a game Mrs Hugo."

Steph looked at this smiling, Humpty Dumpty figure and wondered whether she and John had chosen the right person – a solicitor who called the law, 'a game'. Having always been on the 'right side' of the law everything she was now experiencing was new to her. Maybe the things that Mr Shaw was saying were 'normal' in these circumstances. These internal musings aside however she understood the point he was making.

"So, what fine am I likely to get if I am found 'guilty'?" she asked.

"Mmm – a minor offence coming before the court for the first time?" mused Mr Shaw aloud. He leaned forward again. "Maybe forty standard units if you plead 'guilty' and maybe 160 standard units if you plead 'not guilty' – and then maybe forty or fifty units 'costs'. It could be a bit more or a bit less. All depends who is in the chair."

"So, the court is trying to tempt me to plead 'guilty' … even if I'm not … just so I get off more lightly?" said Steph with indignation.

"One way to look at it," said Mr Shaw. "Like I said – it's a game."

There was a brief pause before Steph asked the question that Mr Shaw had been expecting.

"So, how likely am I to win if I plead 'not guilty'?"

Mr Shaw leaned back in his chair and made an open handed gesture.

"That, Mrs Hugo, is a question on which I cannot put a percentage figure of probability." Again he leaned forward across his desk. "The best

I can do is to identify some salient facts - facts that I have no doubt the police will refer to in their case. First, you have been seen wearing a dress on at least two occasions in town. On the first occasion someone was abusive to you because of it. We might therefore conclude that they were upset or alarmed. After you went out the second time someone made a complaint – the complaint that has led to the present charge. If the person that made the complaint was the person that saw you on the first occasion the police might argue, that as well as causing alarm, you were deliberately harassing that person. In defence we can say that you were not aware of anyone being upset, that you were simply going about your business, and that you did nothing to shock or alarm anyone. You had certainly not targeted anyone for harassment." Once again Mr Shaw leaned back and gave his open handed gesture. "There you have it Mrs Hugo, in a nutshell. If you were the magistrate what conclusion would you come to – 'guilty' or 'not guilty'?"

Steph felt cornered and angry. "But I've done nothing wrong! I haven't harassed anyone. If people are alarmed or distressed then that's their own stupid fault! I was just walking along – oh and at one point there was a busker playing and I did a little dance for a laugh. I wasn't being provocative, I wasn't pretending that I had bombs strapped under my dress, I wasn't shouting or waving a placard ... I just wasn't doing anything wrong! I *am* right aren't I? There is nothing illegal about wearing a dress?" Steph heard her voice gradually getting louder with frustration. "I'm sorry, I didn't mean to shout. It's just that it seems so absurd. I am being asked to plead guilty when I have done nothing wrong."

Mr Shaw waved her apology aside with a smile, "You are quite right Mrs Hugo, wearing a dress is not illegal in itself, or even doing a little jig in one and *I* am not asking you to plead guilty - for that matter neither is the court. All I am saying is that the police *could* put forward an argument that you caused distress and it is difficult for us to refute that by saying that a person was not distressed ... or that they *shouldn't* have been distressed."

Mr Shaw looked kindly at Steph. "The law can be a bit hard to fathom at times, but I hope that I have explained things sufficiently for you to be able to make an informed decision." He paused. Steph nodded silently in affirmation.

"Well, that's about it then. Would you like me to represent you at the hearing?"

Again Steph nodded her affirmation before adding – almost as an afterthought, "And how long will all this take?"

"The Magistrate's Court – we sometimes just call it The White Court - will probably hear your case in about a week's time I would think. I'm surprised that you haven't had a letter already. I can chase that up. If you plead 'guilty' at that hearing, as we have discussed, then they are likely to deal with it on the day. If you plead 'not guilty' then a date for a second hearing will be set - probably in a month to twelve weeks time."

Steph looked at Mr Shaw. She felt a mixture of resignation, disappointment and deflation. "Can I have a think about the 'guilty/not-guilty' issue and get back to you?" she asked.

"Of course, Mrs Hugo."

Mr Shaw stood up, came round the desk and extended his hand. Steph stood and shook his hand with a polite, "Thank you."

Mr Shaw opened the office door and with a smile, "Remember Mrs Hugo, it's a game."

*

John looked at Steph across the kitchen table after she had finished explaining all that had happened in her meeting with Mr Shaw. He knew that it would go against the grain for Steph to plead 'guilty'.

"Did you pick up, even if he wasn't going to say it explicitly, whether he thought that you would win if you pleaded 'not guilty'?"

"Not really. He just talked about what he thought the police would highlight in their case."

"So, do you think that the police have charged you because they think they have a strong case - strong enough to get a conviction?"

"Oh, I don't know!" Steph was irritated - not with John but with being in the position she was in. She kept going round the same circle of thoughts. She had done nothing illegal in wearing the dress so how could she be guilty of anything? Surely the law should be defending her right to behave as she wished if what she was doing was lawful?

"What do you think?" The words escaped Steph's mouth before she knew she was saying them. She didn't really want John to give his 'position' on the matter. She guessed that he would want everything over as quickly as possible and so would favour pleading 'guilty'. He would see the plea simply as a strategy to that end.

"Well, if you are likely to lose then I don't see the point in contesting it. It's a pity our Mr Shaw could not have been a bit clearer. He must have experience of the police and the cases that they choose to bring ... their success rate and the like. I wonder if there is anything on the internet. If we knew that the police win 90% of their cases then it would be a 'no brainer' I would have thought. On the other hand, if the odds are 50:50 or better, then ..." John shrugged his shoulders as much as to say, "up to you".

"But what about the principle? Do you really think that little me walking around in a dress could genuinely cause distress or alarm to anyone?"

John paused, "I think Tim was pretty startled when he saw you that first time in the attic."

Steph had not expected that. "Yes, but that's different. I mean in the street. It may be unusual ... but it couldn't really be alarming."

John shrugged. "I don't know. Maybe we should talk about it again tomorrow. Maybe I should see if I can get some facts about the police success rate," and with that he stood up.

Steph guessed that John probably wanted to say, "Never mind about all that. I really don't care," or "Shouldn't we think about us and about the kids in all this?" He was leaving now to terminate his involvement in a decision that he knew Steph would make for herself.

"Thanks. I know it's not easy, the fuss I'm causing..." she said as he went to the door, "...and I think about Tim and May. But, I also think that I have to do what I believe in and set an example to them, an example that says that you follow what you believe to be right, even if that creates hardship. I think that's a better example than just doing what we are told because someone more powerful tells us to do it - especially when we think that powerful person is wrong. Don't you?"

John stood in the doorway. He didn't speak, though Steph thought she saw a nod of agreement. Then, after a second gazing down at nothing in particular he looked at her and said, "Sounds like you have made your mind up on how you will plead then, doesn't it?"

Steph nodded.

*

From the time when she and John had left the police station to the time of the Magistrates' hearing Steph had not worn the dress. She was therefore naked when she appeared before the magistrates. Looking round the small room she now realised why Mr Shaw had said it was called The White Court. The entire room – walls, ceiling and sparse furnishings – were all white though the high backed seats of the three magistrates had different coloured headrests corresponding to the traditional colours of the branches of Trueway government - Civil (blue), Religious (yellow) and Martial (red). She had spoken with Mr Shaw beforehand. It therefore came as no shock to him when she pleaded "not guilty". As he had predicted, this led to a date being set for a second hearing a few weeks hence.

There was relatively little to do in preparation for the second hearing. Mr Shaw put together the relevant legal points and a statement from Steph emphasising the uneventful nature of her perambulation on the day she was arrested. With this he intended to argue that her behaviour should not have caused alarm to anyone. For their case the prosecution submitted the transcript of the police interview with Steph and two signed statements by witnesses. Steph was not surprised to read that both witnesses made reference to the children that had been with them and to the distress and confusion that *they* had felt. Steph was willing to bet that these witnesses were the same women that had been so abusive to her in the street.

On the day of the trial Steph's suspicions were proved correct when the prosecution called their witnesses. She recognised both women from the group with push chairs. Steph listened to what they said about being upset and about their children being upset. They referred to the first time they had seen Steph and said that they had been afraid that Steph may have been trying to hide a criminal tattoo. Steph did not think that their argument was very strong. She was therefore not overly concerned that Mr Shaw did not cross question them particularly strongly but instead called Steph herself to testify that she was unaware of anyone being disturbed or concerned until the police arrived to arrest her. The prosecution did not have any questions for Steph and so Mr Shaw gave a closing statement and the three magistrates adjourned to consider their verdict. Mr Shaw and Steph remained seated within the white bubble and made small talk until the three magistrates returned.

The chairperson gave the verdict.

"We find the defendant guilty as charged. It is evident from the witness statements and their testimony here today, that they were caused alarm and distress by the defendant's presence in town wearing a red dress.

This was something for which they were not prepared and which they could do nothing to avoid seeing. In terms of sentence we will impose a fine of 150 standard units and an additional fifty units prosecution costs."

Chapter 5: Flop-flop

Steph naturally felt guilty about the 200 units that her decision to plead "not guilty" had cost the family, made worse by John's uncomplaining acceptance of it all. In a perverse way she would have felt better if he had got angry, and told her that she should have been more pragmatic in her approach to the court. As it was, family life seemed to go on pretty much as normal, until a couple of days after the hearing when the children returned from school. Steph was reading in the living room. She heard them come in and heard their angry voices.

As brother and sister, Tim and May got along really well, so to hear any upset was unusual. Steph immediately put down her book, and was getting up to see what the problem was, when Tim burst into the room.

"I hate you! I hate you! ... you stupid, stupid!"

Steph was completely taken aback. "Tim ..."

Before she could say any more Tim had advanced a few steps towards her, his fists clenched, his face red with rage. She thought he was going to hit her. His fist went back, but then he burst into tears, turned and fled upstairs to his room slamming the bedroom door behind him.

Steph stood trembling a second then started to go after him. May was standing at the living room door.

"What's happened ... what on earth has happened ... May?"

"I tried to stop him - but he was ... well, like you saw him."

"But what is it? What has happened?"

"It's kids at school." May seemed quite calm. Steph looked towards the stairs. She couldn't hear anything ... maybe a faint sobbing. She turned to May.

"What about kids at school - what's happened?"

May explained that a small group of children had been goading Tim, saying his mother was a 'body shamer', that she had been to court and was a slut, a prostitute. There had been some fights - minor scuffles really - but teachers had had to intervene. The taunting didn't stop though, especially after school.

"How long has this been happening?"

"Since the day after the hearing. One of the kids brought the local paper into school. You were in it."

*

Tim eventually calmed. When John was home the family talked. It was explained to Tim that the court appearance had nothing to do with his mother being a prostitute or a 'body shamer'. Tim was an intelligent boy and, although this was quite an adult topic, was capable of understanding that his mother had been to court only because people had complained about her wearing a dress. Neither Tim nor May however said much to their parents. John said that he would talk to the head teacher the following day to see if he could ensure that the taunting stopped. The rest of the evening passed in the usual way, though the atmosphere was subdued.

"Hopefully, things will blow over once I have spoken to the head teacher," said John after the children had both gone to bed.

"I'm not going to stop." The words fell, unrequested from Steph's lips. It was as if someone else spoke them. It could only have been a second, two at the most, before John's incredulous, "What?" and yet the words, 'I'm not going to stop' seemed to hang in the air between them forever, an almost tangible thing, heavier than the air but floating in it.

"I'm not going to stop." She looked at him. "Now, more than ever it's important that I carry on. I have to show Tim and May that it's important to follow your conscience and not just conform because conforming is easier."

John was dumbstruck. He had assumed, taken for granted, that Steph, seeing Tim's upset, would have been 'brought to her senses', would have realised that what she was doing was hurting her children, her family and that there was then no question but that she would put the dress away forever.

"You can't be serious."

"We've explained. He can understand. Would you prefer that I set an example of giving in when things get tough?"

"No … no! I thought the example to set would have been, 'my children come first'!" John wasn't shouting - but the exasperated, incomprehension in his voice told Steph that this interchange was pivotal.

"You don't have to wear a dress," continued John. "Your wearing or not wearing a dress is not going to change the world. No-one will care if you stop wearing it. You haven't worn it these past few weeks so what difference does it make now?"

"*I* will care – and *that's* the difference it will make. I have to do what is 'right' - *that's* the difference it will make. I have to set an example - *that's* the difference it will make. I want Tim and May to look back and see that I stuck to my principles - *that's* the difference it will make. I have to show that I am not doing anything wrong. Those kids at Tim's school, those stupid, complaining women all go on about prostitutes and the like. Even May asked me if I was a prostitute or a terrorist - but I am neither of those things. If I stop now then it's as good as me saying that I am ashamed, that I was wearing it to be lewd or because I have body shame - not because that's what I have been charged with but because that's the way those stupid women with their push chairs see it."

"It sounds more like being pig headed to me. So what if a few women have the wrong end of the stick. We need to put an end to this now. We need to draw a line under the whole episode and get back to normality - or as close to normality as we can. I worry even now whether Tim, and possibly May, are already being labelled as, 'that daft woman's kids' ... maybe worse."

"Exactly, and for those very reasons I have to show that I am not something 'worse'."

John felt exasperated by this last, as he saw it, self-contradictory argument. "This is stupid, we are going in circles and getting nowhere," he said. "All I can see is that our children are upset *now* and that arguments and upset are likely to continue for as long as you persist in wearing a dress when you don't need to. Maybe, at some point in the future if you keep on with it they may - only *may* - think, 'good old mum - she stuck to her principles' - but right now, and possibly even in the future, it is causing them problems."

"Or causing *you* problems?" Steph regretted the words instantly, and in response to his silence, added somewhat lamely, "May hasn't said that she is having any difficulty anyway."

She wanted then to say, "Sorry" but the contempt in her husband's eyes told her it was too late. John calmly terminated the exchange."We're not getting anywhere. Let's just leave it. I will talk to the head teacher tomorrow, like I said."

*

John rang Tim's school first thing the following day, and was given a meeting with the head teacher prior to the start of lessons. Tim and May went to school as usual, Tim somewhat reassured by the knowledge that his father would already have spoken to the head teacher by the time he was in class.

The house seemed very big and empty to Steph when they had all gone. The events of the preceding day had upset everyone. The rest of the family were all busy now doing things, but Steph was here in this big, empty place. She had to get out of the house - but how? She paraphrased Shakespeare in her head - 'To dress or not to dress?'

She went to the attic, slipped on the red dress and looked at herself in the mirror. Why was she doing this? She went downstairs, grabbed her bag and headed for the front door. She stood there behind the door - a turn of the latch and it would open onto the world - her world, everyone else's world - her street, Charlie's street. She hesitated. She walked back into the living room and sat down. Maybe she should watch TV, make a cup of coffee. There was a noise at the front door and some mail tumbled through the letter box. She fetched it, saw there was nothing that looked interesting and put it in a neat pile on the corner of the kitchen table. She looked back at the front door. She didn't want to stay in, but she didn't know how to get out. She smoothed the dress. Again she walked up to the door. Again she stopped – undecided, but then pulled the dress off over her head and threw it on the floor before opening the door and stepping out. She stood there, letting the sun warm her. She turned. She could see the dress in a pile. She marched back in leaving the door open. She took a carrier bag from the kitchen, gathered the dress up, put it in the bag and left the house.

*

Steph had nowhere specific to go and nothing specific to do. She went to the glide-bus station and boarded the first bus that presented itself. She didn't require money or a travel pass of any kind. Like all Citizens, Steph had information coded into her bones - osteodata (or biodata as it was more commonly called). There were different 'levels' of activation that Citizens could opt for. Steph had opted for 'Functional Level 2'. This allowed such things as automatic scanning for travel and automatic payment in shops.

Within minutes she was trundling along, out of the town and into the countryside. It was a long time since she had been on a bus. It felt good - sitting doing nothing, yet doing something; sitting still in one place, yet moving to somewhere else. Here in the bus, she and all the other passengers were in one place, one time - but out there, just the other side of the window was constant change, an ever moving 'somewhere else'.

The bus was not full. Steph guessed, that at this time of the day, not many people travelled, and of those that did, the majority were probably coming into town rather than going out from it. She looked about her. Quite a few of her fellow travellers seemed to be elderly, probably retired people who were not constrained by work. There were a couple of Good Sisters – easily identified by their wimples – and one mother and her child.

Steph put her hand into the bag and felt the dress. Steph had grown up in a naked world. Growing up she had never questioned it. No-one questioned it. What was there to question? In history lessons at school she had learned about the transition from a clothed to an unclothed society. She knew that the transition had been controversial, that there had been much debate before the *Clothing and Makeup Act* was finally passed. Steph had learned (and now it seemed that May was learning) that the driving force to an unclothed society had been terrorism. A naked society prevented the concealment of explosives by suicide bombers.

Steph knew all this but what did that history matter now? Those terrorist events had occurred generations ago. Terrorist activity was very much a thing of the past. Yes, there might still be the occasional news item about a terrorist raid but Trueway citizens no longer died in bombings. As May had said, nakedness was part of Trueway doctrine. It was the cultural norm. That said, there were people who met in private to wear clothes. They were referred to as 'textilists'. Steph looked at her fellow passengers and wondered whether any of them dressed in secret.

She had been secretive about wearing the dress but now that had changed. Now she saw no reason why she should not wear it publicly. Mr Shaw had confirmed that it was not illegal *per se*. Every year people would march and dance through the streets wearing clothes made of paper as part of an event called, 'BodPride'. Yes, at the end of the parade the participants cast aside their paper clothes in a grand gesture of pride in their nakedness, but while the procession took place, no onlookers complained about the clothes. Nobody claimed they were alarmed or distressed and none of the participants were arrested.

Steph idly mused on clothes, no clothes and society's ways as she watched the countryside slide by outside. Occasionally the bus would stop to let passengers on and off. It pulled up in a small village. It was a place Steph had passed through but never visited. She noticed a tea room as the bus came to a halt, and so decided to get out and have a morning coffee.

*

The teashop had tables outside, and Steph sat enjoying the warm sun on her skin as she sipped her drink. The young waiter who served her wore a small apron in the pocket of which he carried a digipad. This acted as a notepad for taking orders and as a scanner to allowed customers to pay via their biodata. Waiters and waitresses generally wore these small aprons. It was recognised as necessary apparel, and so was a 'stipulated exception' to full nudity. She had never thought about it before, but with her current experience, she found herself asking whether it really was necessary – or whether it was just a tradition that nobody questioned. Maybe she was being churlish to regard it as hypocrisy.

Steph watched the young waiter. She thought he was quite attractive. She wondered whether she would find him *as* attractive without the apron. Did being covered enhance his attractiveness? In turn, would she be more attractive to him – or anyone else for that matter - if she were covered to some degree – leaving something mysterious to be discovered? As it was, even with his apron, she knew a great deal about him from his visible tattoos.

Biographic tattoos were not compulsory unless ordered by a court – usually to identify someone who had committed a criminal offence. Many Citizens however chose to have tattoos. The Book of Truth taught that The Great Spirit approved of such body markings as, 'an outward sign of inward grace'. Similarly, The Great Spirit had stipulated in The Book of Truth, that 'the grievous wrongdoer should be branded with a *Cain mark* so that all may know and be wary'. Only prescribed designs were permitted and strict criteria governed whether an individual qualified for any particular tattoo. Only when all the official documentation was in place, would a designated Civic Tattooist be able to apply the specified image.

From the 'NON' tattoo on the waiter, Steph knew that he was a 'Non Reproductive Citizen'. This meant that he would not, indeed could not, have children. Clearly, to have chosen to have this tattoo, he was as proud of his non-reproductive status as she was of her ability to have two children. She could not see a tattoo to proclaim that he was homosexual, but with her 'EM2' tattoo and the age difference, she concluded that he was probably not having the same internal musings as herself. She turned her attention to the village in front of her.

There were not many people about. It appeared to be quite a sleepy place. She noticed a restaurant a little further along the street on the opposite side. It looked nice. There was also the tower of a pre-Trueway church peeping over the rooftops opposite. She liked churches, especially those that retained aspects of the pre-Trueway reforms. A village church like this one might have many original features. She finished her coffee and went to look at the menu in the restaurant window. There was a nice selection at a reasonable price. She made a mental note to tell John. It would be a new place for them to try. He would like the church too if it had original features. She found a narrow passage that wound up to some steps into the church yard.

She was disappointed to find the church locked. There was a sign however saying that the key could be obtained from the cafe across the street - the same cafe at which she had had coffee. *Pity I didn't know that when I was there*, thought Steph. It wasn't far though so she went back down. The attractive waiter fetched the key for her with a smile, and she returned. The church was cool inside and there was a musty smell. She made a slow circuit, reading the occasional memorial plaque, and running her fingers over recumbent effigies of notables long dead. Her feet made the only sound.

She edged into a pew and sat looking at the windows, and the coloured light that fell from them to give transient staining to the stone flags. For centuries this church had stood here, maybe replacing some even more ancient place of worship or tradition. What languages and what liturgies had these stones and their predecessors rung to before the modified liturgy of Trueway?

She pondered. Beliefs change. Behaviours change. It happens all the time - both religious and secular. She found herself musing on how some changes would be vehemently resisted and others readily accepted and how that resistance or acceptance seemed independent of 'good' or 'bad' since what was seen as good at one time, would be seen as bad at another time. She looked around her. She wondered whether any poor soul, clinging to an 'old' belief or promoting a 'new' belief, had been dragged from this church to be burned alive as a heretic in former times.

She shivered. Was it her thoughts? Was it the damp atmosphere of the church? She took the dress out of the bag and wrapped it round her shoulders like a shawl. She sat a little longer. She thought of John, of Tim and May. She thought of her own childhood and her mother. She thought about the passage of time, the things an individual achieves while here on Earth and the things an individual leaves for those that come after. She shivered again. Why was she thinking these things? She guessed it must be something about churches and 'holy' buildings. What was she - Steph Hugo - going to achieve or leave behind? Had she achieved all she was going to? Were her children her shared contribution and legacy to the world? She gently stroked the dress. "What did *you* leave to the world Great-great grandmother of May?"

It was time to go. When Steph left the church the dress was no longer around her shoulders. She was wearing it.

*

Steph locked the church door and went across the street to the cafe. At first the waiter seemed not to recognise her. He stood looking at her, transfixed. It wasn't until she held the key out to him that he muttered a surprised sounding, "Oh".

"Thank you for the key," said Steph as she left. There was no answer.

She crossed to the bus stop on the opposite side of the road to where she had got off. The little timetable in the bus shelter indicated that buses ran frequently and it was only a few minutes before one arrived and stopped.

A few people got off and Steph moved forward to board.

"Sorry miss I can't take you like that."

"Pardon?" said Steph, knowing full well what the driver meant.

"I can't have you on the bus like that madam ... that dress. I'm sorry."

"Why not? What is the matter with it?"

"Madam, please. I don't wish to have an argument. I can't take you like that."

"Is there a rule book or something from your company that ..." but again Steph was not allowed to finish.

"Can you please get off the bus madam? I have a schedule."

Steph stood looking at him.

"Please madam. I can't let you on." There was a tone of apology in his voice - a plea to let him be on his way.

"Get off the damned bus, you trollop!" came a call from one of the passengers. Then, emboldened by the first, a second voice piped up, "Yeah, you're a trouble maker you are. Seen all about you in the paper. Get off!"

Steph looked down the bus at the passengers waiting to continue their journey. Despite her indignation Steph did not see any point in 'making a point' with this bus driver and his passengers.

"OK - I'll take your number if that's how you wish to behave," and Steph exaggeratedly looked at the man's ID plate as if memorising his number before stepping back onto the pavement.

The bus pulled away and she watched it go; watched the faces of passengers – a few haughty glances but most avoiding looking at her. She had seen a few tattoos when she looked down the bus, but doubted whether any of the arrogant shouters had an 'EM2' … or any number of the other tattoos that her own skin boasted, and which reflected the dedication and service that she had given to the community. She had noticed the bus driver had a tattoo for funding 100 trees whereas she had one for 5000. Maybe, as she stood there watching the bus shrink with distance, her own perspective finally changed. Nobody on the bus had sprung to her defence. Nobody had spoken to support her. Nobody had said, "Look at the tattoos on her arms showing the service she has given to all of us." If any of them had had such thoughts, those thoughts were not strong enough to make them voice their opinion.

Had everything for which she had striven been a pot of gold at the end of the rainbow? Had she found the pot of gold, only to discover that others did not give it the value that she did? Maybe that was why so many 'leets' did not have tattoos. The pot of gold came easily to them, and so was taken for granted.

As the bus disappeared Steph turned to go but spotted something blue in the gutter. She bent down and picked up a fluffy child's toy – a little rabbit. She looked up the road. One of the people who had got off the bus had been a woman with a push chair. Steph just caught a glimpse of her disappearing round a corner a little way off. She ran to catch up.

"Excuse me! Excuse me!" called Steph, as she continued her pursuit of the woman with the pushchair. The woman turned. She was elderly. Probably the child's grandmother, thought Steph. "Did you drop this?" Steph, proffered the little blue rabbit.

"Oh! My goodness, yes. Oh thank you. Stephen look, it's Flop-flop. You must have dropped him." A little boy of about three years of age rubbed his eyes and yawned, then looking up and seeing his toy, reached out with both hands. Steph crouched and handed it to him.

"Oh thank you so much," said the lady smiling at Steph. "What would we have done if we'd lost Flop-flop?" she continued looking down at the child, "My goodness we're lucky this lady spotted him, aren't we? Say 'thank you' to the lady Stephen."

"Thank yooouu," singsonged the boy.

"That's quite all right, Stephen. Bye-bye." Steph gave a little wave.

"Thank you again. Where was it?"

"By the bus stop. It must have fallen as you got off."

"And you look as though you ran to catch us. Oh you are so kind. It's my grandson's favourite. He takes it everywhere."

Steph stifled a chuckle at the woman's exuberant expressions of gratitude, "That's quite all right, really it is. I'm glad Flop-flop and Stephen are reunited. Right, I must get on, bye. And bye-bye to you and Flop-flop," said Steph smiling down at Stephen with his rabbit as she turned and walked back. When she got to the corner she stopped. There, down the street was the bus stop where people had jeered at her. She glanced back at Stephen and his grandmother. It was only then that it struck her that neither Stephen nor his grandmother had given any indication of having seen the red dress. All they seemed to see was a kind gesture. The tears welled in Steph's eyes. They hadn't seen the dress. They had seen her – her kindness, her goodness. They had just seen *her*.

*

Steph decided that she would not attempt to board another bus and so, with no alternative, began walking back to town. A few vehicles passed her as she walked. There was no indication from the majority that they saw her - though they must have. A couple tooted their horns and there was the occasional shout of, "Nice one" ... or something similar.

After about an hour she came to the outer buildings of another village. This was a larger settlement than the one she had just left. Pedestrians began to appear. As with the motorists, most did not interact with her to any significant degree. Some stared. Some ignored. A few smiled. She passed a school. Children were in the playground. Most continued their games, their chatting. There was a whistle or two which Steph thought were directed at her and she turned and smiled at a girl who called out, "My mum has a dress like that".

Steph continued her journey through the centre of the village. A man crossed the road and walked along beside her. "Y'all right?" he enquired.

"Fine, thanks. You?"

"Yeah - fine. This for charity or something?"

"No - just like wearing it."

"Right, nothing wrong with that. Good luck to you, that's what I say."

The man continued walking next to Steph.

"Personally, I think there's a lot to be said for clothes ... not that I would want to be wearing them myself ... just that I think they gave variety. Anyway - good luck to you."

"Thanks," said Steph as the man crossed back over the road and turned up a side street.

Before Steph left the village she heard the sound of the police car siren. The car passed her, pulled up at the kerb and two police officers got out and came over to her. Villagers watched as she was escorted to the car and driven away. As Steph looked out of the car window she thought she saw the man that had spoken to her in the watching crowd. In the weeks and months to come Steph would wonder whether it was this man that organised a group of the villagers to stage a protest that was featured in the local press where several of them dressed in clothes - mainly red - and carried banners saying things like, "Be free to be free" and "Dare to wear."

Chapter 6: Last Time White Court. Last Time No Red Dress

"There was a restaurant in the village," said Steph to John as they sat at the kitchen table. She said it to break the silence. He had again collected her from the police station, and after sitting down with the obligatory cup of tea he had said nothing.

John wasn't interested. He was exasperated.

"We can't carry on like this." He looked up at Steph. "*You* can't carry on like this."

"I don't want to cause a problem. People were really nice to me most of the time. Why should I stop doing something that isn't wrong and isn't illegal just because someone ... someone in a minority it would seem ... decides to complain?"

"Why? Well how about '1' - it's cost you your job; '2' it's reduced our income; '3' it's upsetting me; '4' it's upsetting the kids; '5' it's making you a laughing stock and gossip point? Do you want me to go on? Do I need 6, or 7 or 8 reasons? What is the critical number? ... Well?" John was shaking. Steph had never seen him like this.

"I'm sorry. I ... I don't know what to say."

"How about, 'I will stop'? That would be something good to say."

"I can't. It would be like saying I want to stop freedom."

"Freedom? Whose freedom? I want to be free of this nonsense. I want to be free to go to work without wondering if I will get a call to fetch you from the police station. I want to be free of not worrying whether Tim or May will come home crying because someone has taunted them about the latest headline in the local paper about their mad mother!"

"I'm sorry."

"Don't be 'sorry' - just stop doing it!" John stared intently at Steph for the briefest moment before adding. "I won't collect you again if it happens."

Steph knew this wasn't an idle threat. It wasn't even a threat. It was simply a statement of fact. John would not come and collect her or, she assumed, stand surety for her bail. She looked at him with a sadness she could not explain. All she could quietly say, as much to herself as to him, was:

"Why do they see my dress and not my tattoos?"

"Could it be because you *cover* them with it?" came the answer with angry sarcasm. Steph made no rejoinder. She knew that a great many of her tattoos were visible when she had the dress on. But she had not been picturing herself at the bus stop or anywhere else where she had been wearing it. No, in her mind's eye, she was seeing herself standing naked in the court room.

*

Following her arrest in the village Steph had been taken to the police station. She had been asked if she wanted legal representation. Steph remembered her regret at having not said "yes" to this question before, and so had asked for Mr Shaw. To her surprise he was available and attended the interview. Although Steph and John had not been overly impressed with Mr Shaw's performance in Steph's first trial, she had asked for *him* because he knew her case. Having sought his involvement this second time at the police station, Steph and John agreed that they would continue with Mr Shaw for the forthcoming trial. For a second time therefore Steph entered the office with the tree outside the window to discuss her case.

Mr Shaw put on his glasses and looked at the papers in front of him. "The charge is very much the same as before, so I don't propose to go over things with which you are familiar, Mrs Hugo. I must however draw your attention to this paragraph here." Although Steph had her own copy of the papers Mr Shaw handed her his copy in which a paragraph had been highlighted. Steph had seen it when the papers had come through to her. It said that the prosecution was intending to apply for a *Behaviour Restriction Order (BRO)*.

"Yes, I noted that when I read through," said Steph.

"Do you know what a *Behaviour Restriction Order* is?" asked Mr Shaw over his spectacles.

"Well, I am as familiar as most lay people I guess - it's an order that bans someone from doing something."

"That's it precisely. The prosecution - effectively the police - have given notice of their intention to apply for what is called, 'a *BRO* on conviction'. This means, that if you are found guilty of the offence, they will ask the court to impose a *BRO*. The *BRO* will almost certainly ban you from appearing in public in your dress ... or any dress for that matter."

"Right, and if I ignore the *BRO*?" asked Steph.

"Back to court," said Mr Shaw.

"Well, that happens now ... so it seems a waste of time," said Steph dismissively.

"Ah, maybe, to an extent." There was something ominous in his tone and in the deliberate way he removed his glasses before continuing. "But there are *significant* differences." He looked unwaveringly at Steph as he spoke. "The first is that nobody has to make a complaint. If you disobey the order, and the police see you, then they can arrest you. The second difference is that breach of a *BRO* can (and most probably would) result in a custodial sentence rather than a fine. The court could also require you to be given a criminal tattoo."

Steph began to understand the gravity of Mr Shaw's demeanour.

"So, you are saying that I could go to prison or be literally branded a criminal?"

"I doubt that you would be given a 'Cain mark' tattoo the first time you breach a *BRO* but I think it almost certain that you would be given a prison sentence. Of course, the court cannot proceed with a *BRO* if you are acquitted, so we will do the best we can to defend you against the current charge. I have to say however, that the paperwork is so very similar to the first time we went to court, that I fear you will be found guilty should you decide to contest the case."

In contrast to Mr Shaw's ponderous gravity, Steph's response was swift.

"So, again I have to decide whether to plead, 'not guilty' and fight ... or just roll over and plead 'guilty' ... and you think either way the outcome will be the same?"

Mr Shaw maintained his gravity and nodded.

Steph sat without speaking. The thought of prison frightened her. She looked down at her tattoos and the thought of being forced to have a criminal tattoo terrified her ... and angered her in equal measure. She looked at the tree out of the window; the dappled sunlight. She looked down at the highlighted text on the papers Mr Shaw had given her. She closed her eyes. She inhaled deeply, held her breath a moment in silence and then, as she released it, got to her feet.

"Thank you Mr Shaw," she said in an even tone as she handed back his papers. "Send me your bill as soon as you are ready."

"P-pardon ...I-I- I'm sorry ...?" stammered Mr Shaw in surprise.

"You can send me your bill. No offense to you Mr Shaw, but if you think it likely that I will be convicted, and it makes no difference how I plead then ... well," Steph shrugged, "... there is no real point in me having a solicitor is there? Maybe you were right last time. Maybe it is, 'just a game'." With that she left Mr Shaw's office.

*

Having been through the process once Steph was not surprised, when having pleaded 'not guilty' her case was not dealt with at the initial hearing but she again had to wait for a second hearing to be scheduled. When the day of the second hearing arrived Steph sat with nobody beside her on the white seats facing the three magistrates in their high backed chairs. When asked to confirm her plea she reaffirmed 'not guilty' to the charge of having caused alarm and distress. Without Mr Shaw she felt nervous, but she had specifically asked John not to take the day off work to be there. She felt she would be better in front of the court without him watching her.

There was only one witness called by the prosecution. This was the Head Teacher from the school in the village where Steph had been arrested. He testified that several children had been upset by seeing Steph, and that he had been asked if she was going to attack them or their parents or anyone else in the village. He had assured them that they were safe. Steph cross-questioned him.

"How many children were upset?"

"Several."

"Can you be more precise ... two? ...twenty?"

"Well, I spoke to at least three or four who were asking me about the 'lady in red'."

"When you say they were 'asking' about the lady, that doesn't sound as if they were necessarily upset. What makes you say they were upset?"

"Well, one little girl was in tears ... and a couple more were close to it."

"And that was because they had seen a lady wearing a red dress? Might it have been due to anything else?"

"All I can tell you is that the duty teacher brought them to me, and there was a lot of commotion amongst the children because of a woman who had walked past the school wearing a red dress, and this girl and one or two of her friends were upset and were asking if you - sorry the lady in the dress - was a terrorist."

"Did your duty teacher, or any of the children, say that the lady in the red dress had approached them or spoken to them or done anything alarming - anything other than walk down the road?"

"No."

"Apart from the three or four that you mentioned who were upset about something, did any of the other children comment to you about the lady in the red dress?"

"No."

"Did you ask any of the other children about what they had seen?"

"No, I was only concerned about calming the situation down and getting back to normal."

"So you personally were not worried or afraid or alarmed? You didn't think something terrible was about to happen?"

"No."

Steph finished her questioning at that point. She hadn't called any witnesses and regretted that she had not obtained the name of the man who had walked beside her for a short distance.

The prosecution summed up their case - essentially that a very reliable witness - the Head Teacher of the school - had contacted the police about a person, who by walking down the road wearing a red dress, had caused alarm and distress among his pupils which he then had to spend time addressing. Steph, in making her final submission emphasised that she had not behaved in any way that was threatening. No-one had spoken unpleasantly to her or given any sign of being distressed. In fact there had been one man who had spoken to her very positively and there had even been one child from the school who had called across to her to say that her mother had a dress like the one Steph was wearing.

The magistrates retired to consider the case. When they returned the Chair explained that although Steph may not have done anything threatening she knew that there was a likelihood that her behaviour would cause alarm. The testimony of a reliable witness confirmed that alarm had been caused. The court had no choice therefore but to find Steph "guilty". As on the first occasion a fine was imposed and costs awarded. Then however the Chair explained that the police had applied for a *Behaviour Restriction Order*. In light of the fact that this was the third time that Steph had been arrested, and the second time in a relatively short period that

Steph had been brought before the court, the court would agree to the imposition of the order. The Chair read the order:

Stephanie Hugo will not, without reasonable excuse, appear in a public place wearing a dress or any other garment other than in circumstances recognised specifically to require such dress, for example as protection against hazardous substances. This order will come into force immediately and will continue until deemed no longer necessary by a court.

Steph was told that she would receive all the details of the BRO in writing including details of the appeal procedure if she considered the order inappropriate. The court adjourned.

*

Steph had been naked for her court appearance but when she returned home she immediately put on the dress for a while. She took it off before the children and John returned. She told them what had happened in court and then the evening went on as usual. Steph did not say what she was going to do now and her family did not ask. Steph wondered whether the lack of enquiry was because they *assumed* that she would obey the court order or because they *feared* that she would not.

The outcome of the court hearing was again reported in the local newspaper. Both Tim and May said that it was being talked about at school, though there had been no more fights.

Steph remained at home for the next few days. She felt she needed time to think. There had been a few e-mail messages, mainly from people at work who had seen the newspaper articles. Some of her social media accounts had attracted some unpleasant comments from people that she was unable to identify, but generally people that she knew were either supportive or were refraining from comment. No-one had come to visit.

As advised, the written notification of the BRO arrived by post. She read it and the process for appeal. She felt that she ought to appeal but wasn't sure what to say in relation to the grounds for appeal beyond, "I think you are wrong" and a reiteration of what she had said in court about having done nothing to upset anyone. She wondered whether it was worth the effort of appealing anyway. The outcomes from her appearances in court so far flew in the face of reason as far as she was concerned, so why should judges listening to an appeal suddenly start accepting her view? Reluctantly she felt that she needed to take legal advice.

Although her head told her that she should find an alternative lawyer to Mr Shaw she felt so despondent that she could not bring herself to start explaining things to someone new. She therefore rang his office and arranged a meeting. Even as she did so, she knew that she was creating a problem for herself - whether to wear her dress or go naked to Mr Shaw's office.

If she understood the *BRO* correctly then to step outside her front door wearing the red dress would mean that she was breaking the law. She didn't want to break the law, but the more that she thought about this restriction, the more absurd and unfair it seemed to her. As far as she knew there was no law for anyone else saying that they could not wear a dress in public. Celebrities who dressed up to make money for charity were lauded in the media for their efforts ... yet here she was, a criminal if she did the same. The more she pondered the more she was convinced that her treatment was *fundamentally* wrong and that she had to fight this injustice. In order to do that she would have to lodge her appeal. To lodge her appeal she needed the advice of Mr Shaw – and that brought her back to the problem of whether to go to Mr Shaw naked or wearing the dress.

From the day that she first went out in the red dress she had been 'flexible' in when she wore it. Although she was convinced in herself that she was doing nothing wrong in wearing it in public she had, nevertheless shown deference to convention, and gone naked for her meetings with Mr Shaw and her appearances in court. Now, as she pondered events, she began to feel uneasy about her 'flexible' approach. She began to feel that she was not being true to herself. If she believed there was nothing wrong in what she was doing then she should not 'cow tow' to convention. The fact that she now had a law saying that she could not wear the dress made no difference. She recalled, from her history lessons when she was a child, that some great freedom fighter had said something about people having, "*a moral responsibility to disobey unjust laws*". She should be free to wear the dress if she wished. The law was therefore 'unjust' so therefore she had a 'responsibility' to oppose it. She would go out wearing the dress when she went to her appointment with Mr Shaw.

*

Steph did not manage to reach Mr Shaw's office. John received a message from the police to say that his wife had been arrested. She was currently in custody at the police station. The police anticipated that she would shortly be moved to the local prison and remain there pending trial for breach of the *BRO*. He was welcome to visit her before the transfer took place if he wished.

John was escorted to the police cell where Steph was being held and an officer remained with him while he was there. Steph was seated on the edge of a bed. She was still wearing the dress. The conversation was awkward. John wanted to be supportive but was finding it impossible to understand why his wife was behaving as she was. She knew that in going out in the dress she risked arrest and yet, so soon after her court hearing and the imposition of the *BRO*, that was exactly what she had done. Steph in her turn felt that there was little more she could say to try and explain why she was doing what she was doing and so they focused on practical things - what she needed if she was going to remain in custody, how long she was going to remain in the police cell before being moved to prison, when she would see a lawyer - and so on. The officer who had accompanied John thought that Steph was likely to remain in police custody for one or two days before being transferred - but she couldn't be sure. She felt that Steph would have everything she required for at least her first night in the police cell.

John agreed to go home and bring back toiletries, books, and the like the following day. As he stood waiting for the officer to unlock the door to let him out Steph said,

"Give my love to May and Tim."

John turned and almost gave a casual, "of course" (though this would have been to prevent his lips saying, "if you hadn't been so stupid you could tell them yourself") but, when he looked down at her she seemed so small and the place where she was so alien that a shiver shot through his shoulders.

"Yes, I will ... of course I will."

John made his way home with his wife's voice in his ears, "Give my love to May and Tim" and the image of her in his mind's eye. It was as if she was saying goodbye.

At home he did as Steph had asked and passed on her love to Tim and May after which the family went through the motions of an ordinary evening. The children went to bed and when John checked on them a little while later they were both sleeping soundly. He eventually went to bed himself. He felt weary, but before getting into bed he looked at himself in the full length mirror - in very much the way that Steph had done - and unbeknown to him, some of what he thought was similar. He ate sensibly and exercised regularly and felt that he was in reasonable shape for a man his age. He had worked hard as a Citizen and his civic tattoos testified to that. He was proud of them. He would never want to have them covered up. When he was away on business, with people who did not know him, he would see the glances at the 'EM2' tattoo and at the names 'May' and 'Tim' beneath it. He assumed that the majority of people recognised this for the significant achievement that it was. He felt certain that many would be envious. It did not occur to him, that anything more than a handful, would pay it as little attention as he paid to the 'NON' tattoos that he came across. Maybe it is impossible for an individual to step fully into another person's shoes – no matter how sensitive or empathetic that individual might be. Maybe it is impossible to fully shed that egocentric standpoint.

He was proud of his tattoos and he had felt sure that Steph was proud of hers. Why would she want to have any of them concealed by a dress? Did she have a psychiatric problem? Should she see a doctor? Was it some form of involuntary skin shame or body shame? Mr Shaw and the courts had made clear that the issue bringing her into conflict with the law was neither of these things … but there may be something fundamental in her personality; something beyond her control that was compelling her to wear the dress. Maybe he would talk to her about seeing a doctor when she was released from custody.

There was no point in thinking about that now. He needed to get some sleep and so went to bed.

*

When John arrived at the police station the following morning he was informed that Steph had already been transferred to the local prison. He remonstrated a little but was told that there was nothing that could be done and that he now needed to contact the prison. The staff there would be able to explain their visiting arrangements and advise him about the things he had brought for Steph.

Chapter 7: The Orange Court. May Spots the Revolving Door

Mr Shaw visited Steph in prison. She felt a little embarrassed, remembering her parting words the last time she had seen him, but he seemed unperturbed. His tone however was serious when he spoke. He explained that when her case came to trial it would now be before a jury. Steph agreed to have him represent her.

Mr Shaw had been granted access to Steph in her prison cell. He however, as her lawyer, was privileged. Since her arrest, in fact since leaving her house to visit Mr Shaw, Steph had refused to take off the dress. To Steph's astonishment this refusal resulted in her being kept away from other prisoners. She did not share a cell with anyone and she was not allowed to go to any communal areas. This meant that she did not exercise or eat with other inmates. It also meant that she was not allowed in the communal visiting area. This in turn meant, that with the exception of her legal adviser and prison staff, she was not able to have any visitors. She was not allowed to see John, Tim or May ... and they were not allowed to see her. She was in solitary confinement for wearing a dress and refusing to take it off.

Steph *was* allowed books and a radio. She was also able to write and receive letters. So it was that the isolated and letter based phase of Steph Hugo's existence began.

*

Hi John. Thanks for your letter which I see you sent on Tuesday but which I didn't get until today (Saturday). It is now 9pm. Today has been much as usual. Breakfast was brought to me at 8am. I didn't see the warder who brought it and she (or he) did not say anything - it just came through the hatch. Your letter was pushed under my door around mid-day ... no idea why food comes through the hatch but letters under the door!!! I hope that you and the kids are well and I am sorry for being such a pain. I haven't been taken out for exercise today. Last exercise was three days ago I think. Still, I can walk briskly up and down in the cell to keep the leg muscles and the lungs/heart working! I haven't had any feedback from Mr Shaw recently so don't know any more about when my trial will take place. Thanks for the copy of the drawing that Tim did at school. It looks really great. Tell him how lovely I think it is. Well, I can hear the sound of a trolley coming down the corridor. That will be the last drink of the day. Bye for now...

Once Steph had finished her letter she put it in an envelope. She addressed the envelope but she didn't seal it. She had been told that any letters would need to be read by the prison authorities before being sent.

*

A week later Steph wrote a second letter.

Hi John, Mr Shaw visited this morning. A date still hasn't been set for the trial. I will let you know that as soon as I find out. We went through the arguments that we can make in defence and the likely angle that the prosecution will take (though we haven't had any paperwork through yet). He thinks that there is a possibility that the judge will ask for psychiatric reports ... I guess because what I am doing is seen as unusual. Mr Shaw says that I don't have to agree to any assessments if I don't want to. As with the 'guilty/not guilty' thing he wouldn't advise me one way or the other ... simply told me the potential pros and cons. You didn't say much in your last letter about the kids and what they have been up to. Food in here isn't too bad. I was taken out for exercise yesterday and I am hoping that I will get the chance to exercise today as well. Bye for now...

Steph put the letter in an envelope and left it unsealed as before to be collected by a warder later that day. The envelopes were provided by the prison. The writing paper was not. Steph wrote her letters on pages ripped from a little note book that she always carried in her bag and which she had been allowed to take with her to her cell. In the outside world she had mainly used this notebook for jotting down odd things she needed to remember or for shopping lists. She had written, 'Stuff' on the front cover. She had not expected that she would be tearing pages from it to write letters from prison.

Having written the address on the envelope Steph again picked up her little notebook of 'Stuff' but this time did not tear out a page. Instead she found the next clean sheet and wrote:

Dear diary ... really? Am I really starting this with, 'dear diary'? It sounds like something from a novel of long ago. Maybe, 'Dear Red Dress' or

'Dear family or dear world … or 'Me?' Yes, 'ME' - that's what it is really, isn't it Steph Hugo? You're talking to yourself – just like all those other 'diarists' – talking to themselves but pretending. Pretending they are talking to someone else, to the universe, to posterity – to anyone, everyone – but really? Just to themselves. Just to myself.

Why am I here in this prison?

Why am I doing this?

Steph looked round her; looked at her cell. She looked down at her legs, at the red dress under the pad on which she was writing. Again she asked herself, "Why am I here?" She did not have the energy to answer or to try and think of an answer. She put the pen and pad down on the bed.

Steph didn't write anything more in her diary on the days that followed. She continued to see Mr Shaw periodically, and to write letters to John and the children. Letters from John continued to be pushed under her cell door by an anonymous hand, and her food continued to be put anonymously through the hatch. The occasions on which she was allowed out for exercise continued in their erratic and infrequent way, and she continued to pace her cell to compensate. She continued to wear the red dress and she continued to be kept away from other prisoners. Other than Mr Shaw, and the occasional warder taking her for exercise, Steph saw nobody until one day she was startled to have her cell door opened and to find herself confronted by a rotund young woman with ruddy cheeks that shone almost as much as the teeth in her broad, white smile.

"Hello Mrs Hugo, I'm Reverend Somes, Prison Chaplain," beamed the apparition, proffering her hand.

"Hello," said Steph, as her arm was jolted up and down by this round, rosy girl.

"I hope that you don't mind me visiting," said The Reverend pulling over the chair to which Steph had silently directed her while she herself sat down on the bed, "– and my apology for taking so long to get to see you." The Reverend gave no further explanation of what had delayed – or indeed prompted – her visit but instead, immediately set about a nervously delivered ten minutes of chatter. There was discussion of what Steph was doing and why she was wearing the dress. There was talk of religion and of how Steph could always ask to speak with her, the Prison Chaplain, any time she wanted to. There was also quite bit of informal chat about their respective lives – Steph's family and the Reverend's personal life, especially her recently acquired kitten.

Despite the frenetic onslaught – or maybe because of it – Steph found herself suppressing a smile and decided that she quite liked this jolly priest and was a little sad when she stood up to leave. The Reverend Somes was about to knock on the door to attract the warder when she suddenly said,

"Oh, Steph you haven't got a 'never-flower'," and immediately plucked a yellow, paper bloom from her own hair and held it out to Steph. Steph's hand moved to take it but her inner smile faded and she let her hand drop. Steph had forgotten that it was November and close to the, *Never-we-Forget* celebration when Trueway remembered its military heroes.

"No, it's all right Reverend. It is kind of you to offer ... but I don't..."

"Oh, I'm sorry." The Reverend Somes looked confused – but then assumed Steph's refusal was due to her inability to make the customary donation. "Don't worry about paying. I am more than happy to make a donation on your behalf ... or you could arrange one with the warder if you didn't like that."

"No, Reverend. I simply don't buy one or wear one. I used to but what is the point in remembering if we keep on making the same mistakes? What is the point in sentimentally remembering once a year the heroes of generations past when we don't apply the lessons to the people of the present?"

"But we have learned the lessons. We have had peace all these generations because of their sacrifice and the lessons we learned from those times," said the Reverend in genuine bewilderment. Even with all the time in the world, let alone this departing moment, Steph felt that she would not be able to explain – or even want to explain – why she didn't wear a 'never-flower'. She had not felt able to explain this, even to John, so she was not going to try to tell this happy blancmange her reasons. She simply smiled and said,

"It's alright Reverend. It is a nice gesture. Thank you ... but no," and with that a puzzled Reverend Somes knocked the door and was let out while a thoughtful Steph Hugo sat back down on her bed. She ran her fingers through her hair, knowing that on the scalp beneath was concealed a small tattoo, of which even John was not aware, and she reflected on just how many secrets she had kept alongside that of the red dress.

*

It was about a month after the Reverend's visit that the day of Steph's trial arrived. Steph saw very little of proceedings because of her refusal to remove her dress. Not being allowed to attend her own trial infuriated her … but although this occupied her thoughts when she was back in her cell, the image that she could not dispel was of the courtroom itself. As with The Magistrates' Court everything – walls and furnishings – was the same colour, but unlike the calm white of The Magistrates' Court, this place was a garish orange. Mr Shaw had spoken of it as The Orange Court, but nevertheless, it had been an assault on the eyes that refused to disappear from her brain! And maybe that was what the Trueway justice system intended – a visual shout of, "Watch your step!" to the defendant.

*

John sat down alone and read the newspaper article about the trial.

Stephanie Hugo, unemployed mother of two was sentenced to three months in prison today by Judge Pollock after being found guilty of breaching a Behaviour Restriction Order (BRO). The BRO bars Hugo from appearing in public wearing clothes. The prosecution alleged, that in defiance of that order, Hugo was arrested by the police after a member of the public notified them of a woman in a red dress in the High Street.

Prior to the hearing Hugo had appeared in the dock wearing a dress.

The Judge said: "It is not appropriate to the setting in which you find yourself this morning – a court of law – and there are certain standards. Appearing dressed does not meet these.

It may be, that coming in as you have, could be a contempt of court. I ask you, Stephanie Hugo, are you prepared to undress and appear appropriately?" Hugo replied: "I think I am dressed appropriately."

The judge told Hugo, that since she had refused to undress, she would be found in contempt of court. This meant that she may face even more time in jail regardless of the outcome of her trial. The judge then ordered Hugo to be returned to the cells, and the trial continued in her absence. She was represented by her solicitor, Philip Shaw.

It was claimed by the prosecution that Hugo appeared wearing a red dress in a public place in breach of a Behaviour Restriction Order. The arresting officer gave testimony.

During the hearing Hugo's solicitor said that his client was determined to continue wearing clothes.

"She engages in this behaviour because she believes that human beings have a right to freedom as long as they are not harming others. She wishes to celebrate herself and her heritage as a human being, whether clothed like her forbears or naked," he told the court. "She has no perception of any wrongdoing. She accepts that she is subject to a BRO but does not regard this as legitimate."

The jury returned a verdict of 'guilty'. Judge Pollock said he had no choice but to impose a custodial sentence. The sentence was backdated to when Hugo had been taken into custody. Hugo was therefore released shortly after the ruling because of the time she had already spent on remand. Upon her release however Hugo continued to refuse to remove the dress and so was immediately re-arrested and returned to prison.

John put the newspaper down. He hadn't really wanted to read it but felt that he had to know what was said. He expected that there may be questions or silent looks at work, or what he would find even more awkward, words of sympathy and understanding. He also feared the children coming home upset from school because of things that may have been said to them by pupils who had read the account of their mother's trial. As it was, the article had been quite factual. Having been in court himself he knew there were a few minor errors but nothing sensational had been written. The report was accompanied by a photograph that the newspaper photographer had snapped through some railings behind the court. It showed Steph being led inside from the police van. Her hands were cuffed. She was looking away from the camera and her face wasn't visible. John was grateful for that, but she was clearly wearing the dress.

John didn't want to face the children when they came home. He felt what was happening wasn't fair to them. He didn't understand their mother's behaviour so how could he explain it to them? He felt cold but he also felt a growing resentment as he stared at the paper on the table before him. All that kept going round in his head was, *Why does the paper call her 'Hugo' and not 'Mrs Hugo'?*

*

To John's relief neither Tim nor May reported any significant unpleasantness from pupils at school. May read the report in her father's newspaper but Tim just got on with his usual, after school routines.

"How long will mum be in prison now?" asked May.

"I don't know. I guess it will be like before. She will be held on remand until a trial date is set and then the trial will decide if she is innocent or guilty and then ... well if she is innocent she will be released but if she's found guilty then ... well I guess it's up to the judge."

May thought for a moment.

"But mum was released this time ... and she's still in prison. If she keeps wearing the dress she'll be in prison for ever ...." May looked at her father.

John wanted to say that she was a silly girl and hadn't understood. May wanted her father to say the same, but he couldn't. It seemed an absurd possibility, but May had voiced what had been at the back of his own mind. If Steph continued to wear the dress she would continue to be in prison. May understood her father's silence and her eyes filled with tears. John put his arms round his little girl and held her close. He was as bewildered and as helpless as she was, and found comfort himself, in her embrace and tears. He could understand those. He could continue to strive to be a father to his children but was he still a husband, or had his wife left him in favour of a red dress?

*

The period that Steph was held on remand pending her next trial was similar to before, about three months. Since her arrest on the way to see Mr Shaw she had been in prison for a total of six months with only a few minutes freedom after the last trial. John had not been there when she was released and re-arrested, and so had only seen his wife inside the court room. They had exchanged letters, but that was all.

From the most recent of these letters, John had learned of Steph's intention to represent herself at her forthcoming hearing. She wrote:

I don't see the point in using Mr Shaw. He hasn't been successful so far, and as long as he is there, they can do what they did last time, and keep me out of the court room with the argument that I am being represented so it doesn't matter. If he's not there then I will be able to address the jury myself and I think that is the only way I can get an acquittal ... to address them myself wearing the dress! The last thing Mr Shaw said was that he thinks my only line of defence is that the BRO is unlawful. I don't agree. I haven't told him that, but I'm going on what I know about myself and the ordinary Citizens who will be among the twelve jurors. All I can do is explain what my 'reasonable excuse' is for breaching the BRO, and that is: ... I did what I thought was right. What I am hoping is, they won't convict me if they think it's absurd. And it is absurd, once a person stands back and objectively and impartially examines the evidence. A dress is not indecent.

I know the prosecution will go on about how I have walked past a school, how in other instances people have been out with their children, how I am acting outside social norms, and I presume they'll try and put forward the argument that I am not denying breaking the court order of being prohibited from wearing the dress in public - all true of course but ....

John didn't continue reading. He closed his eyes. He understood what his wife was saying and he agreed that Mr Shaw had not been effective ... but he felt that getting another lawyer would be a better strategy than trying to 'go it alone'. John didn't think that the prosecution would say anything about Steph having walked past a school. He wasn't a lawyer, but he could see that the only question the jury would be asked was whether Steph had breached the BRO. If the answer was "yes" and she had no reasonable excuse for having done so, then she was guilty. John had written to his wife to tell her all this but doubted that she would change her mind and get a fresh lawyer. When the day of the trial came therefore he was not surprised to find that she remained unrepresented.

Chapter 8: Steph Shown the Revolving Door

John arrived early at the court and positioned himself at the front of the public gallery. It was a different court room to the one he had been to before – but like all the courts of this type it was decked out in garish orange. He was the only person there. He felt glad about that, and hoped that no-one else would show interest. The less interest there was, then the less publicity there would be, and so the less likelihood of any difficulty for the children at school.

To get to the public gallery in this court room he had had to climb two flights of stairs. From where he now sat he had an almost bird-like view of the court. The raised dais where the judge would sit was opposite with an imposing orange leather chair. The headrest did not display the blue, yellow and red of Trueway government. This was to emphasise the separation and independence of the judiciary at this level. The court was *of* Trueway but not subject *to* Trueway. In front of the dais were the tables and benches for the lawyers and their teams. John wondered what the court would do, given that his wife had elected not to have a defence lawyer.

Already there were some people, two women with orange hats, in the courtroom below busying themselves around these tables. John thought they may be clerks or ushers but wasn't sure. To the right of the tables and benches there was a bank of seats facing across the court. John counted twelve seats and assumed that these must be for the jurors. To the left of the tables and benches were more seats facing across the court. *Were these for witnesses?* John wondered. There was also a raised, box-like structure. *Was this the dock where Steph would stand?* It was all so unfamiliar. John didn't know.

The figures in orange hats glanced up at John but paid him no further attention after that. They bustled about moving papers and arranging glasses of water and the like. They exchanged the occasional word. John was surprised at how clear their words were but paid little attention until he heard,

"If she comes up undressed then we'll admit her and if not then we won't."

John was startled. They were clearly talking about Steph. Who was this person - a clerk or the judge herself? Whoever it was it sounded as though a decision of some sort had already been made. Had he understood correctly? Were they saying that Steph would be allowed in court only if she was naked? As if to answer this unspoken question a man wearing a white wig (subsequently identified by John as the prosecuting barrister) then joined the two ladies in the well of the court and was given fuller information by the same speaker.

"Mrs Hugo has been given a message that if she comes naked to the court then the trial can proceed. If she refuses to take off the dress then she is to come up and be addressed by Judge Willis."

Shortly after this more people entered the court and took up seats. Then,

"All rise" - it was the other orange hatted lady who gave this instruction so confirming to John that she was the usher. A door in the wall behind the judge's chair opened and a man with a red ceremonial wig entered and sat himself in the large leather seat. John assumed this to be Judge Willis. The court sat down.

*

"What can you tell me, Mr Phillips?" asked the judge looking at the white wigged barrister.

"Mrs Hugo has no legal representation your honour. She has elected to represent herself. A printed copy of the BRO has been given to her and the BRO is the only written material that I propose to give to the jury on behalf of the prosecution. Mrs Hugo has also been given a copy of the prosecution case and evidence - the police statement. I have no idea what Mrs Hugo's argument is. This is not about Mrs Hugo wearing a dress but about her disregard for a court order - the BRO."

John was astonished ... was all this happening in the absence of his wife when there was no defence solicitor? Where was Steph?

"Thank you," said the judge, "and the case is not about 'bad character' - and neither is the BRO itself ... though the background to it *could* be. Do you have anything you wish to say at this point Mrs Hugo?"

"No, Your Honour," came Steph's voice from beneath John. The dock was under the public gallery! John peered over the rail but could not see the dock at all. When had she arrived in the dock? He didn't know. Had she heard all that had been said since the judge entered? Had she been there before then?

"Thank you. I see that you are wearing a red dress. That is not appropriate for a court of law. Are you prepared to remove it?" asked Judge Willis.

"No, Your Honour," came Steph's voice again - a little shaky John thought.

"Mr Phillips?" The judge looked towards the prosecuting barrister.

"I completely oppose Mrs Hugo being in court wearing a dress," responded Mr Phillips. "It is not appropriate to the setting ... the dignity of the court. Furthermore, it is contrary to the terms of her *Behaviour Restriction Order* ... this being a public place and the jurors being members of the public. If Mrs Hugo insists on wearing the dress in that knowledge then she is choosing not to participate in the trial."

"Mrs Hugo?" The judge looked towards a place beneath John.

"I don't see why, in the interest of a fair trial, I should not represent myself wearing the dress that is the thing at issue. The jury would see there is nothing wrong with it. It is part of the evidence," came Steph's disembodied voice.

"I do not wish to see your dress in my court Mrs Hugo. Have you seen the police evidence?"

"Yes," came the voice.

"Do you have any issues that you wish to raise with me about that evidence?"

"No." John noticed the absence of "Your Honour" in Steph's responses.

"I will ask you for a final time Mrs Hugo whether you will remove the dress that you are wearing. If you do not, then I agree with Mr Phillips, that you are choosing to absent yourself from the court. Do you understand?"

"Yes, but I ..."

"I do not wish to discuss it further Mrs Hugo. If you understand then I will simply ask you - will you remove your dress?"

"No."

"In that case you will return to the cells. You will be called back as and when you need to be spoken to ... officer, please? ... thank you." Judge Willis waited a few moments - presumably while Steph left the dock. He then turned to Mr Phillips.

"Mr Phillips, we will have to proceed with caution in these circumstances. I would want to, 'get it right' - so if you feel that there are any issues, procedural or otherwise, please stop me. Right, we will take a short break before calling the jury to be sworn in."

*

John sat in disbelief at all that he had just witnessed. How could this be happening? How could a trial take place without the defendant and without any defence? How could the prosecution barrister be called upon to guide the judge? It was like the referee asking the captain of one team in a football match to advise him. All this because his wife had some cloth on her body ... a different part of her body to the members of the court for whom it appeared to be satisfactory ... mandatory even ... to have something on their heads! Worst of all, his wife being told - "... *you* are choosing to absent yourself from the court" ... when it was the judge making the decision!

*

The jury consisted of eight men and four women of varying ages. Once sworn in the judge addressed them. He explained that Mrs Hugo was not present because she wished to appear in court wearing a red dress. John noted that he didn't say why Steph's determination to wear the dress prevented her from being in court.

The judge explained that there were two parts to a hearing - the first part in which the prosecution presents the case against the defendant and the second part in which the accused person (or their representative) presents the defence against the charge. He explained, that on this occasion, the court was going to hear the prosecution case against Mrs Hugo in her absence. When the court was ready to move on to the second part of the hearing - the case for the defence - Mrs Hugo would be invited to remove the dress and give her side. The judge emphasised (to his credit, John thought) that the fact that Mrs Hugo was absent from the courtroom was not to be read as an indicator of guilt. The jury must listen to the evidence and come to their decision on the basis of that.

With these preliminaries complete Mr Phillips was invited to make the case for the prosecution. He provided the jury with a printed copy of the *BRO* and the charge that Mrs Hugo had breached it. He then called, as witness, the police officer who had arrested Mrs Hugo - PC Draper.

"Constable Draper, can you please tell the court the circumstances of your involvement on the day of Mrs Hugo's arrest?"

"Yes. Mrs Hugo had been released following her last trial. Prior to her release it was anticipated that she might continue to wear her dress. If she did so, this would be in contravention of the *Behaviour Restriction Order* that had been imposed. Myself, and another officer, Constable Ferdinand, were therefore despatched to meet Mrs Hugo on her release."

"Thank you, officer. Can you now please tell the court what happened when Mrs Hugo *was* released?"

"Yes. My colleague and I met Mrs Hugo. As expected, she was wearing a red dress. I invited Mrs Hugo to remove the dress. She refused. I asked Mrs Hugo if she understood that she was subject to a *Behaviour Restriction Order* that banned her from wearing clothes in public. She said that she knew that she was, but that she would still not take off the dress. We therefore arrested Mrs Hugo and took her to the police station. She declined the offer of a solicitor and so we interviewed her without one."

"Thank you officer, that was very clear. Was the interview recorded?"

"Yes, the interview was recorded and then transcribed."

"Thank you. Now, can you confirm that this is the transcript of that interview?" Mr Phillips handed PC Draper a document of a few pages. The constable briefly looked at it before saying

"Yes, that's it."

"Thank you, officer. Please remain where you are for the moment."

Copies of the interview were distributed to the twelve jurors before Mr Phillips addressed them.

"As you can see, the document runs to some five pages. You may read the full document at your leisure in due course, but I would like to draw your attention to some key exchanges between Mrs Hugo and the interviewing officer. In order to do this I will ask PC Draper to read Mrs Hugo's words and I will read the words of the interviewing officer. Could you all please turn to the second page and the penultimate paragraph? The interviewing officer - Constable Ferdinand - starts by saying: 'Why is it ...' ... have you all found that?" There was some turning of pages and confirmatory nods from the jury.

"So, I will continue as Constable Ferdinand:

'Why is it Mrs Hugo that you don't wish to take off the dress?' " Mr Phillips looked towards PC Draper.

" 'I don't want to. I don't think there is anything shameful about it'," read PC Draper from the transcript.

" 'But you do understand and accept that the court has issued a *BRO* in relation to your dress wearing activity that states that you must not appear in public wearing a dress?' " quoted Mr Phillips.

" 'Yes, I understand all that ... but the order also says that I shouldn't do it unless I have a 'reasonable excuse' doesn't it?' " quoted PC Draper.

" 'So, are you saying that you have a reasonable excuse?' "

" 'Yes, my reasonable excuse is, ... well, it's like a big person ... stronger than you ... saying, 'do this!' ... when it doesn't make sense ... so I don't do it just because a bully says, 'do it' ... I can't, it's going against my truth'."

Mr Phillips raised his hand to indicate to PC Draper that he wanted him to stop. He turned to the judge.

"That is all the questioning that I have for my witness."

PC Draper left the witness stand and Mr Phillips turned to the jury.

"There you have it ladies and gentlemen of the jury ... I will quote again from the transcript ... 'so I don't do it just because a bully says, 'do it' ... I can't, it's going against my truth'. Mrs Hugo sees the court as a bully. The court is not a bully. The court has considered Mrs Hugo's behaviour and issued an order. The fact that Mrs Hugo does not like that order, and regards the court as a bully for issuing it, cannot constitute an excuse for not doing as the court has ordered. I doubt that most criminals like the orders made against them. If we accept what Mrs Hugo says as a, 'reasonable excuse' then we would have to agree to every criminal in the land being acquitted if they said that they did not like their *BRO*. Obviously we cannot do that. I therefore put it to you, that there is incontrovertible evidence from the police, that Mrs Hugo contravened the *Behaviour Restriction Order* against her, and did so without any reasonable excuse whatsoever. I therefore urge you to return a verdict of 'guilty' as the only reasonable conclusion that you can come to."

Mr Phillips sat down.

"Thank you Mr Phillips." The judge turned to the jury. "We will take a short break now and reconvene after lunch - say 2:15. While you are at lunch please refrain from talking to anyone about the case and do not do any research in relation to the defendant."

The usher called for the court to rise. The judge left and the court emptied.

*

John made sure that he was back in the public gallery in good time for the 2:15 start. He was surprised to see someone else there, seated in the back row. He didn't recognise the man and the latter did not make any eye contact, so John simply returned to where he had been sitting before.

When the court reconvened, the jury was not summoned immediately.

"Mrs Hugo," the judge looked towards the area beneath where John was sitting as he had done before. "I will ask you again whether you are prepared to remove the dress so that you can present your case and any evidence to this court."

"I want to give evidence but I want to do that without prejudice. I want to speak to the jury as I am so that they can see me and the dress ... it is all part of the evidence."

"Do you understand Mrs Hugo, that I will not have you in that dress in my court, and that if you do not remove it then you will be absenting yourself from this court and not have the opportunity to address the jury?" The irritation in the judge's voice was unmistakable. *He isn't used to anyone defying him,* thought John.

"The fact that you don't like the dress is subjective, and that is not what a court should be. You are prejudiced and the ..."

"Mrs Hugo," the judge interrupted, "there are a number of people in this court who do not need to see you in the dock, and see your dress in defiance of the court and in defiance of the order against you. There is no reason for you to wear it."

"That is just prejudice, you are prejudiced and you are making the court prejudiced. My intention is to argue that me and this dress are not indecent and I will be contradicting myself if I agree to take it off ... that would be the same as agreeing that there is something shameful in wearing it ... everything I stand for is based on that point ... that me, the dress and my heritage are not indecent." Steph was almost shouting and her voice was shaking.

"Well, you have been given the choice to address the jury but have absented yourself. I will continue without you. Take the prisoner back to the cells."

All was silent below John. He felt for his wife. During the lunch break she had clearly become angry at what she saw happening, and realising that she was not going to be allowed to speak to the jury while wearing her dress, had decided to at least speak her mind to the judge. John wanted to go to her. He wanted to put his arms round her and hold her in the same way that he had held May. She would be in the cell - probably still shaking with rage ... but she was a prisoner and he wasn't allowed.

The jurors were summoned and filed in. The judge addressed them.

"Ladies and gentlemen of the jury, as you can see Mrs Hugo, the defendant, is not in the dock for the second part of this hearing. I have asked her to remove the dress that she is wearing in order to give her defence, but she is not prepared to do so. I have made clear to her that I am not prepared to have her wearing the dress in front of you. She may have wished to say to you that the dress she is wearing and she herself are not indecent. That is not the point. The issue before you is whether or not Mrs Hugo breached the terms of her *Behaviour Restriction Order* - her *BRO* - and, if she did breach that order, whether she had a reasonable excuse for so doing. Simply not liking the order of the court is not a reason, and if that were accepted as a defence, could lead to anarchy.

Do not hold against Mrs Hugo the fact that she has not given evidence. That is not an indicator of guilt. It is for the prosecution to make the case against Mrs Hugo that she is guilty. Mrs Hugo has to prove nothing.

In order to find Mrs Hugo guilty you must be sure that she *knew* of the *BRO*, that she *understood* the restriction it placed upon her and that, despite this, she breached that order without a reasonable excuse. In the absence of Mrs Hugo, or of council for the defence, I direct you to the five page transcript of Mrs Hugo's interview to aid in your deliberations. In relation to wearing the dress Mrs Hugo says, 'I don't think there is anything shameful about it' and then later, in refusing to comply with the *BRO*, 'it's like a big person ... stronger than you ... saying, 'do this!' ... when it doesn't make sense'. I am now going to ask that you retire to consider your verdict. Please choose one among you to act as your spokesperson. It is important that you *all* agree on the verdict."

With that the jury, escorted by the usher, left the court room. The judge also left. John remained where he was in the public gallery and the various other members of the court below him relaxed and chatted. After about ten minutes the usher returned and advised the clerk that the jury had reached a decision. The clerk telephoned the judge to tell him and to ask whether he wanted Mrs Hugo back in court before the jury was recalled. Evidently he did, since the clerk then asked that Mrs Hugo be brought to the dock.

A few minutes later and the judge entered. He looked again to the location below John.

"I am advised that the jury has reached a verdict. Are you prepared to remove the dress so that you can be present to hear its verdict?"

"No."

"Then you will return to the cells ... please officer ... thank you."

There was a pause while Steph left the dock.

The jury was called and all filed in. The judge addressed its members.

"Mrs Hugo has declined again to remove her dress and so will not be present. Have you come to a verdict?" A man at the front of the jurors stood and said, "We have."

"And is that a verdict on which you are *all* agreed?" enquired the judge.

"It is, Your Honour."

"And how do you find the defendant, Mrs Hugo, guilty or not guilty?"

"Guilty, Your Honour."

"Thank you. You may sit down. Thank you all for your deliberations in what has been an unconventional hearing. Your work is done, though we will continue now with the question of sentencing. Thank you all once again, the usher will see you out."

Once the jury had gone Steph was again summoned to the dock. John wished that he could see her ... and more importantly that she could see him, know that he was there for her, supporting her.

"Mrs Hugo," began the judge, "the jury has considered the evidence and has found you guilty of breaching the terms of your *Behaviour Restriction Order*. It now falls to me to consider what sentence I should impose. Would you wish to be represented for sentencing?"

"Pardon?" Steph's voice from beneath John was now almost inaudible.

"You may want someone with you to suggest what the sentence should be."

"Oh ... no, no I don't."

"In that case, Mr Phillips can you tell me about any previous offences committed by Mrs Hugo that I should take into consideration?"

Mr Phillips gave a factual summary but finished by advising the judge that the maximum sentence open to him for breach of a court order was a five year prison term.

"There you have it Mrs Hugo. Do you have any comment on what Mr Phillips has told me?"

There was silence from below John.

"Very well then," continued the judge, "you have been found guilty and this is not your first offence. From your perspective ... and correct me if I am wrong ... you see nothing indecent in what you do. That however is not the issue here today. What we are considering is whether or not you have disregarded a court order. The jury has concluded that you have. Is there anything you wish to say before I pass sentence? It will be a custodial sentence so if you wish to draw my attention to anything, any mitigating circumstance, this is your opportunity."

The judge paused but no sound came from the dock. John didn't know whether Steph was shaking her head, sitting impassively or what.

"Very well," resumed the judge, "although I accept that you genuinely do not believe that what you are doing is offensive, you have nevertheless, disregarded a court order, and have shown repeatedly now that you are likely to do this again. I would urge you to think carefully about your action since if you persist you will find yourself in a revolving door of imprisonment and release. In light of your history of offending, I sentence you to sixteen months imprisonment. Any time already spent on remand, will of course, be deducted."

The court adjourned. John remained where he was until the court room was entirely empty and silent. He was alone. His children were alone. His wife was alone. What was she doing now? Where was she exactly? In a cell, here in the court building? In a van, heading towards the prison? Was she already there? It wasn't that far. His wife was going to prison for more than a year. He couldn't believe it. How had all this come about? Maybe it wouldn't be the thirteen months that he calculated. Maybe she would get time off, 'for good behaviour'. He had heard that phrase in the press and in casual conversation ... usually in a derogatory tone when someone wished to emphasise how "soft" the courts were: "Oh yeah, sure he got five years behind bars but with time off 'for good behaviour' he will be out in two ... even though the old lady had a stroke just after he robbed her. Call that justice?" John wondered whether people would call what he had just witnessed in the court below him 'justice'. He wondered whether anyone would even know what had gone on. There were other people in the court that he hadn't identified ... maybe one of them was a reporter.

Maybe the man at the back of the public gallery was a reporter. John looked back. The man had gone. With his head full of thoughts and muddle, John left the public gallery.

Chapter 9: Tim the Thief, May the Mum and John the Lost

John made his way downstairs to the main lobby of the court building. No-one paid him any attention. No-one knew or cared who he was or that his wife had just been given a sixteen month prison sentence. As John left the building however he was brought to a halt by the sight before him. There, at the foot of the imposing steps leading up to the entrance of the courthouse, stood three men holding placards. Two bore the words, 'Free To Be Ourselves' and the other 'Free Mrs Hugo'. The men stood impassively. One wore a red hat, one a red silk sash and the other a 'grass skirt' made from fronds of red, crepe paper. A few people stood at a distance watching them. Some giggled. Some took photographs. Other people walked past without a second glance. John could see two policemen standing a little way off, observing the scene.

John continued on down the steps and past the three protesters. He didn't recognise any of them and none of them looked at him as he went by. They maintained their static positions, simply looking ahead with an air of silent defiance. John made his way home. He wondered how long the three would stand there. He wondered whether the police would take any action - ask them to move on? Ask them to take the 'clothing' off? Arrest them? Had he not been so absorbed in his own thoughts he may have waited to see, or spoken to the three protesters to find out who they were. As it was he wanted to get home to be with Tim and May. He wanted to be sure that when they came in from school, he was there, and able to explain that their mother would not be home for some time.

*

May and Tim listened impassively as John explained that their mother had been found guilty of breaching her BRO (a term with which both children were now fully familiar). He told them of the sixteen month prison sentence, but that Steph would not be in jail that long because of the time she had already spent 'on remand' (another term they now knew well). John didn't say anything about the three protesters, and after he had imparted the outcome of the trial, the evening took on its usual activities.

With the absence of Steph from the family home for so many months slightly new routines had developed. John generally cooked - though May increasingly took on those duties of her own volition. Visits and calls to take away food services filled in the gaps occasionally and sometimes they went out to eat. Overall, the household had adapted.

May in particular appeared to adjust well to her mother's absence, and to having a mother who was in the news for criminal activity. John did his best to emphasise to both children, that even if they couldn't fully understand what their mother was doing, she was not behaving in a way that was intended to hurt others, so in his eyes, it was *technically* criminal ... but not *really* criminal.

John was pleased to see no discernible difference in the way Tim and May were treated by their friends. As far as he could tell, none of the parents had advised their children to stay away from the Hugo's. Certainly the parents *he* met behaved positively towards him and showed no reticence in letting their offspring spend time with Tim and May. It was therefore no surprise to find a little gathering of May's friends in the house when he came home from work only a week after the trial. They were busily engaged in one of their favourite pastimes – body painting.

"Hello, MaysDad" chorused three girls as he entered. He was always referred to as, "MaysDad" by her friends. He wondered whether the girls referred to the other parents in that way ... "AmysDad", "VickysMum". He never asked. He was happy being, "MaysDad". It was a nice balance between the uncomfortably familiar "John" and the unnecessarily formal "Mr Hugo".

"Alright you lot. I'm making tea - anybody want anything?"

The girls were engrossed, and there were just mumbles that amounted to, "No, we're OK". John headed for the kitchen. He was followed by one of them - Amy. She was the young sister of Anita. The latter was busy with May painting decorations on Mina's stomach. Amy, being that little bit younger, was sometimes left out - especially when her older sister and friends were engaged in something as delicate as body painting, where a wrong brush stroke would result in irritated admonishment – especially if they were using henna.

"Y'alright Amy?" enquired John.

"Yep," came the cheery response as Amy proceeded to pull herself up to sit on the work surface by the sink. This was common practice for Amy, who for some reason, preferred to sit elf-like on the work surface rather than on a chair. Seeing what was about to happen John began what had almost become a ritual between them.

"Towe..."

"I know, I know .... towel!" piped Amy grinning, though she didn't rush off to the living room to get her sitting towel since she knew that John would now tear off some kitchen roll for her. This done she placed it on the work surface and clambered up. She sat with her arms wrapped round her shins so that she could rest her chin on her knees and watch him.

John smiled at the little pixie.

"How's MaysMum?" asked Amy.

"As far as I know she's OK ... but obviously being in prison isn't nice."

"I'm glad I'm not in prison ... and I'm glad my mum isn't either. MaysMum's in prison 'cos she wears a dress ... that's why she's in prison isn't it?"

"That's about it."

"That's stupid. If I had a dress on now I wouldn't need this bit of paper," said Amy indicating the kitchen roll beneath her.

Out of the mouths of babes, thought John, and smiled. Although he knew that this was not the rationale for Steph wearing the dress, it pleased him that this little girl was siding with his wife on the basis of a sensible reason for clothing. He looked at her, perched on the work surface. There was an absurdity to the towel. There were probably more germs on her fingers and grubby little feet than her bottom and although children were taught to wash their hands they weren't required to wear protective gloves or socks. Then again, thought John philosophically, most kids don't sit on the kitchen work surface with their feet up!

"You may have a point there young Amy ... maybe you should be a lawyer when you grow up. Right now little pixie would you do me a favour? Hop down from your toadstool and go see if Tim wants a drink or anything."

When a little clutch of girls accompanied May home Tim would generally disappear to his room so Amy knew where she had to go. She soon reappeared.

"Not there."

John looked perplexed. "Where's Tim?" He called through to May as he poured his tea. (John always made tea the traditional way, in a pot).

"He dropped his school stuff off and went out ... 'business' he said," came the reply.

John, with Amy behind, went through and joined the girls.

"What do you mean 'business'? He's ten years old!"

"Dunno," May did not look up from her detailed patterning around Mina's navel.

"Hey, hey ... stop please, look at me." The decorating stopped. Both May and Anita looked up. Mina, already lying still seemed even stiller. Amy, realising that the older girls might be in a bit of trouble, adopted her pixie pose on the carpet in the hope of a little entertainment at their expense.

"I don't know dad. He often goes out after we get in from school. He's usually back before you get in though."

"How long has he been doing that?"

"Oh I don't know ... maybe ..." Before May could finish there was the sound of a key in the front door. Tim had come back. He headed straight for his room.

"Hold on mate, can you come here please?" called John. "I thought you were in your room when I got in. Where've you been?"

"Logan's." Logan was Tim's best friend, so it was plausible, but John thought the answer came just a little too hesitantly.

"May said you've been going out quite often after school. Is it always to Logan's?"

Tim flashed a glance at May. "It's not that often."

"Well, however often doesn't matter. The point is, I assumed you were at home, and when I asked May where you were she didn't know. What if something happened? If you were going to Logan's why didn't you simply say?"

Tim shrugged, not looking at his father. "Sorry, can I go now?"

John could see no point in pursuing the questioning further right then - and didn't wish to humiliate his son in front of his sister and her friends. "OK, apology accepted. But think in future. Say where you're going."

As Tim headed sulkily towards the stairs up to his room John heard a muttered, "I do have a mobile phone, you know." John ignored the comment, but the atmosphere in the room was no longer comfortable and the body decorating project was rapidly brought to a close. The girls left, and May tidied away the paraphernalia, before beginning to prepare dinner. The Hugo household was subdued for the remainder of the evening.

It was a few days later that John was asked to come urgently to Tim's school for a meeting with the head teacher. John had been worried, that as a result of the publicity about Steph, his children might suffer some bullying. It was therefore a shock to him to learn from the head teacher that bullying had been taking place ... but that the perpetrator was Tim. It seemed that Tim had been threatening some of the children; forcing them to give him money, sweets, toys, small electrical goods and the like. These would be hidden in his school bag and then deposited in a 'stash' behind a shed in a friend's garden. John was not surprised to learn that the friend was Logan. The latter, it seemed, had not been particularly active in extorting money and goods from the children, but had acted as a 'fence' for selling items to some older children. The enterprise had come to light when Logan's mother accidently discovered the stash while looking for some garden shears. Logan confessed immediately, and told his mother what had been happening. Tim had maintained a sullen silence when questioned, but several children testified to what had been taking place, and their stories tallied - one with the other and matched the items found in the stash. John was told that Tim was suspended for a fortnight, and that he must keep him at home until the school's disciplinary committee had met to decide what action to take.

John did not question Tim immediately on getting home. He wasn't angry, just shocked and puzzled. Why was Tim doing this? Before he spoke to him he wanted to consider possible reasons. He felt he needed to be prepared. The one reason that John kept coming back to was drugs. Although Tim was only ten years old there had been stories in the press - exaggerated, scare stories John had always thought - about increasing numbers of pre-teen children experimenting with chemicals. Now, with his own son stealing money, he feared they may not just be scare stories. Why else would he be obtaining money by this method? Steph and John had never been unwilling to give their children money if they wanted something ... and the children in their turn had not been greedy and demanding. If Tim felt he needed to steal to get money then it *had* to be for something that would not meet with his parents' approval.

When John sat down with Tim to discuss what had been taking place he wasn't sure which of them was most fearful of what might emerge. Despite having convinced himself that Tim was going to say that he needed money for drugs, John didn't leap straight in with any accusations, but simply told Tim what the head teacher had said. John asked whether it was true. His son confirmed that it was. John took a deep breath.

"Why, Tim? Why?"

The boy looked down at the table. There was an almost imperceptible shrug of his shoulders. John thought that maybe the 'why' question was too big a leap – and maybe it was, but a significant part of Tim's reluctance to say anything, was because the extortion racket involved others besides Logan and himself. The head of the operation was a girl called Claudia, and Tim was really just doing what Claudia wanted. Tim liked Claudia - but also feared her. He wanted to impress her, but he was also afraid of what she might do to him … or get a huge bully called Vaz to do to him … if he didn't obtain the things she wanted. He didn't want to tell all this to his father – partly because of embarrassment, but also because it would get Claudia and the others into trouble – though Tim did not know whether that was mainly motivated by loyalty or fear … two forces that had a fluid relationship within him. He was glad when his father broke the silence with another question.

"How long has it been going on?"

"A few weeks."

This was better.

"So, what have you taken, and who from?"

"Some money from Hardeep. An old phone from Karen. A bike lamp off ... "and so the list went on. Tim had no difficulty in recalling the items and the victims. Sometimes he would identify something with which to try and justify his actions, such as Hardeep having lots of money and being a show off about it.

Now that Tim was talking John thought he would try again. "But why do this in the first place? It doesn't matter if Hardeep is rich ... it doesn't give you the right ... or the need ... to rob him ... So why, Tim? Why are you doing all this?"

Tim shrugged again. John remained silent. Tim looked at the table then briefly at John before muttering, "dunno". John continued to say nothing. After what seemed an age Tim looked up again.

"I don't know ... why not?"

"Because it's wrong. Come on Tim ... you know that. We've always taught you and May to be kind to other people ... and you always *have* been. You know right from wrong and stealing is wrong ... isn't it?"

"So will I get punished?"

John hadn't thought about this - well, not beyond the exclusion aspect of it, but realised that there would almost certainly be further consequences.

"I expect there will be some punishment ... and you will certainly have to give things back, or compensate the children in some way, if you no longer have what you took from them."

"Will I go to jail?"

John suppressed a smile. "I don't think that is likely - but what you have done is serious and if you were older then possibly ..." John was intending saying, "possibly you might" but left the sentence hanging as a thought dawned. "Tim, you're not doing this because you want to go to jail to be with mum are you?"

This idea of being reunited with his mother through crime had not occurred to Tim, but he realised that if he agreed that this *was* the reason, then the interview would probably stop. His father would have the answer to his 'why' question. Tim nodded. John took this as confirmation that Tim had been stealing in a childish attempt to get sent to jail to be with his mother. All thought of drugs evaporated in John's mind.

"Oh my word." John went round the table to his son and cuddled him. Tim broke into tears -tears that came unexpectedly ... as did the tears in John's eyes. They stayed like that, holding each other a while, 'til John reached for some kitchen towel.

"She'll get out mate," said John as he wiped Tim's face with the paper. "I'll write to mum and tell her what has happened. We better get cleaned up ... May will be home soon - and I need to do something about food." John smiled at his son. "You OK?" Tim nodded. The interview about the stealing was over.

Tim knew that he would have to go into school with his father and 'face the music' as he had heard adults say. *Adults say some stupid things*, he thought. His father would tell the head teacher that his son had been stealing in an attempt to get sent to jail to be with his mother. Would they believe that? His father did, even though it wasn't the truth. Tim didn't feel he had lied ... just allowed his father to believe what he wanted to believe.

The truth behind Tim's stealing was more complex – and it wasn't just the other children like Claudia that were involved. Tim didn't fully understand himself why he was doing it. Yes, there was Claudia and the others but there were also thoughts, ideas and emotions all jumbled inside him - a jumble in which someone 'good', his mother, was in jail - a place for people who are 'bad'. So what was good and what was bad? And had all the things he'd been taught been true or false? Before going down the wrong track, John had come close to the edge of that jumble when he had waited, and in the stillness, Tim had asked, "Why not?"

*

John was shocked by the choice offered to him, when at the head teacher's request, he returned to the school with Tim. The head teacher, Mrs Smollette, invited John and Tim into her office. They were introduced to a gentleman who was already there - Reverend Fellows, Chair of the school's Disciplinary Committee. Mrs Smollette explained that the committee had met and discussed Tim's behaviour. She looked at Tim.

"Reverend Fellows, myself and the other committee members - senior teachers and governors," she said, glancing at John, "were very, very concerned about what you have been doing, Tim. We recognise that you have always been a good boy, but that does not mean that we can ignore what you have done and the harm that you have caused to others." She looked again at John. "The committee concluded that Tim's behaviour comes into the category of, 'very serious misdemeanour'. His activities had an impact on several other pupils - his victims - and that demands both restitution and punishment. Those victims, and their families, require recompense and justice - a justice that is both done and *seen* to be done. In terms of recompense, Tim must return every item he has taken to its rightful owner, and where that is not possible, pay for a replacement. In terms of punishment ..." she looked at Tim and then back to John, "...the offence of, 'very serious misdemeanour' would normally result in automatic removal from the school. In light of Tim's former good conduct however the committee felt that you, as his parent, should be given an alternative and so the committee is offering corporal punishment as a means to avoid his permanent removal from the school."

John sat in silence, not believing what he was hearing, all thought of explaining Tim's reasons temporarily swept from his consciousness.

"Obviously, that is a stark choice, and from your silence, I can only assume was not expected," said Reverend Fellows. "And we would not expect that you make a decision here and now. You obviously need to go away and discuss it with ..." the Reverend Fellows faltered "... family or friends."

The Reverend's hesitation refocused John. "But that's just it," he said looking first at the Reverend and then the head teacher, "Tim's mother isn't there to have that discussion ... and that's what this is all about, that's why he's been doing it. I talked to him and he explained. He's been doing all these things because he thought he might get sent to prison, and so be with his mum. He misses his mother. We all do," John looked at his son. "We all do, and Tim was just trying to do something about it and get to be with her." He looked back to Mrs Smollette. "Tim doesn't deserve punishment like this."

"It is not for me to judge Tim's motives, Mr Hugo," said Mrs Smollette

"But surely his motives are important."

"That is as maybe, but the Committee has charged me with advising you of their decision, and seeking ... in a reasonable time as suggested by Reverend Fellows ... *your* decision regarding the choice it has offered you."

"But surely they needed to know why Tim was doing what he was doing before ..."

"Mr Hugo," interrupted Reverend Fellows, "I understand what you are saying, as I am sure Mrs Smollette does, but at this juncture we must take one step at a time. Now, further to this meeting, Mrs Smollette will write to you summarising the Disciplinary Committee's decision. The letter will formally seek your response, and will also explain how you can appeal the decision if you feel that it is incorrect."

"So, when you say corporal punishment, what does that mean?" asked John, realising that neither Mrs Smollette or Reverend Fellows were in a position to do anything other than advise him of the Committee's decision.

"All that will be covered in the letter, Mr Hugo," advised Mrs Smollette. "The letter should arrive in the next couple of days. For the time being you must keep Tim at home."

"Do you ... or indeed Tim ...," queried Reverend Fellows looking at Tim, "have any further questions?" Neither John nor Tim spoke, and in that brief silence Mrs Smollette rose to her feet.

"I know that there has been a lot of 'grown up' talk," she said looking at Tim, "and if you didn't follow everything, then I am sure that your father will explain further at home. For now, I'm afraid that you can't come back to school ... but I'm sure your father will explain." She held out her hand to John to signal the end of the meeting.

*

The letter arrived as predicted.

"...either, be removed from the school or be returned for corporal punishment. The latter to take the form of twelve cane strokes to the buttocks".

John read and re-read those words. Twelve strokes. His son, a ten year old boy - twelve strokes of a cane. It was barbaric. John rarely became angry but this made him physically shake with rage - a rage that seemed to emanate from the pit of his stomach and fill his whole body. A ten year old boy, given no understanding, given no real opportunity to explain himself and these sanctimonious people feeling that they were being generous by offering this appalling choice ... in light of his 'former good conduct'! Obscene! Obscene!

At the end of the letter there was a tear off slip to be returned with John's decision and signature:

"(1) I do not accept the decision of the Disciplinary Committee and wish to lodge an appeal

OR

(2a) I accept the decision of the Disciplinary Committee and agree to remove my son from the school

OR

(2b) I accept the decision of the Disciplinary Committee and agree to my son receiving corporal punishment

Please delete as appropriate and return".

John looked briefly at some enclosed papers headed, "How to Appeal" but felt too angry to do anything other than put everything back in the envelope. He would do nothing until he was calmer.

*

From the moment he had read the letter, John had been determined that his son would not undergo such barbaric punishment. Now, as he sat reading through the paperwork more calmly, his head was telling him that he needed to lodge an appeal. However, he imagined an appeal to be a quasi-legal procedure, and what he had recently witnessed in his wife's trials made him fearful of that. He felt sure, that if the Disciplinary Committee could be made aware of the full facts, then they would see the injustice of their decision. Then, surely, they would withdraw their ultimatum and so obviate the need for a formal appeal hearing. He required help to pursue this approach however, and where better to turn for such help than the bedrock of everything good - Trueway itself.

He and the children were regular worshipers. Steph had been less devout, but Tim and May had been brought up in general acceptance of the teachings of Trueway, and as a family, they attended major celebrations. He and Steph were on speaking terms with the local priest - Reverend Shakhan. John would go to him. John wanted to believe that the right way forward could be arrived at through reason rather than a battle. He knew that Trueway made much of being good and doing what was right, but it also made much of forgiveness. If John explained everything to the Reverend Shakhan, then the priest would see that Tim was deserving of forgiveness, and then intercede on his behalf with Reverend Fellows. John was sure there were passages in the core religious text of Trueway ... The Book of Truth ... that would support his position and so, before contacting the Reverend, he took The Book of Truth from the shelf in search of the relevant verses.

*

The Reverend Shakhan welcomed John with a warm handshake and the offer of a cup of tea - with biscuits, of course.

How very 'Reverend', smiled John to himself.

"I am sorry about your wife John," began Reverend Shakhan as they sat down in the cosy living room. John sank back into the deep easy chair and then felt he looked too casual and sat forward, elbows on knees.

"Thank you. It's a very difficult situation ... for her and for us, especially the children ... and that's really why I asked to see you ...."

The Reverend's housemaid then rattled in with a trolley carrying a large teapot covered in a cosy, two china tea cups with roses on, matching saucers, milk jug and sugar bowl, a tea strainer and biscuits on a green plate. John smiled at the site of the tea strainer, pleased to see that he wasn't the only person still making tea in a pot with loose tea.

"Thank you, Mrs Finch."

"Reverend, Mr Hugo," she said, nodding by way of greeting and goodbye all in one.

"Do help yourself John, though I should give it a minute to brew ... oh and *do* use the strainer ... Mrs Finch makes tea the traditional way."

"Thank you," said John, starting to lean back and then awkwardly sitting forward again.

"I'm sorry, I interrupted. I think you were just starting to tell me about you and your family at this difficult time."

"Well, about Tim specifically, Reverend. You see he's been in some trouble at school ... I'm not sure if you are aware or how much you know..."John hesitated, but as Reverend Shakhan only leaned forward to pour milk into a cup, continued, " ...but in short he's been stealing and everything he's done has had to be considered by the Disciplinary Committee."

"Yes," nodded the Reverend pausing in his task and looking at John with an expression that somehow conveyed both concern and an invitation to continue.

"Well, the Committee has concluded that I must either allow Tim to be caned or I must withdraw him from the school ... and well ... well, I think that is a totally unfair and unjustified ultimatum."

"I see. That *is* a very difficult position for you ... and the boy. Do you take milk?"

"Yes ... please."

"The Disciplinary Committee can appear quite firm at times - some might say 'harsh' - but they do have to be fair to all sides in an issue and see things from the different perspectives of those involved." The Reverend handed John a cup of tea. "Please help yourself to sugar."

John was beginning to feel that the Reverend probably *did* know about Tim and had already determined which side he was on. He began to feel his visit was wasted but then the Reverend asked a question.

"What is it that makes you feel that the decision of the Committee was unfair and unjustified John? Do you feel that the Committee has missed something? Is there something they should have taken into consideration, but did not?"

"Well, I think the first thing is that they didn't seem to consider *why* Tim was stealing." Again the Reverend gave a look as if to invite John to continue, though John thought he detected a little anxiety in his eyes. "Well, I talked to Tim all about it and ... well, silly as it may seem ... but he is only ten ... well, like I said, silly as it may seem he was doing it because he thought that stealing would get him sent to prison and then he could be with his mum."

"Well John, I don't think that is 'silly' at all. I think that it is a testament to the love your boy has for his mother - and to the strong family that you are. The Committee did not know about this?"

"No, Tim only told me this after his initial exclusion and before we went back to see Mrs Smollette and the Reverend Fellows."

"Well, it seems to me that the Committee should have known about that. As I said, they have to consider everything that is relevant - and that seems relevant to me. I am not part of the Committee of course, and although I know Reverend Fellows, I cannot say what the Committee would make of the information you have just given me. What I can say is that I think they should have known about it."

This was better. John felt that he may have judged the Reverend Shakhan's position too quickly.

"Thank you Reverend, it is good to hear you say that. I haven't really discussed this with anyone and ... well, you know ... when you go over things in your head you keep telling yourself you're right ... but then you have a doubt ... so, well, it is good to hear someone else say that the Committee might have got it wrong."

"We are all fallible John, including committees," smiled the Reverend.

"Yes, that's exactly it!" blurted John putting his cup down. "That's exactly why I came to see you Reverend. We are all fallible and the Book of Truth talks about forgiveness and who could be more deserving of forgiveness than a child? I know you know the book back to front, I am sure, but I wrote down the quotes." John took a piece of paper from his hip bag and unfolded it. He hurriedly read several passages aloud one after the other:

'Judge not, and you will not be judged; condemn not, and you will not be condemned; forgive, and you will be forgiven' ...

'Pay attention to yourselves! If your brother sins, rebuke him, and if he repents, forgive him'...

'Hold to forgiveness, command what is right, and turn away from the ignorant'...

'To understand everything is to forgive everything'

"Righteousness is the one highest good; and forgiveness is the one supreme peace; knowledge is one supreme contentment; and benevolence, one sole happiness'"

John stopped and looked up.

"Well John, I can have no argument with any of that can I? And neither, I am sure, would the Committee," smiled the Reverend Shakhan.

"Well, there are probably other quotes (and maybe I've collected too many anyway) ... but my point is that The Book of Truth repeatedly talks about, and praises, forgiveness, so I was hoping that you, as a priest, could go to the Committee - maybe through Reverend Fellows - explain about Tim's reasons for what he did and ask them to reconsider their decision ... ask them to be forgiving."

The Reverend put down his tea. He was silent for a moment. He put his hands together. Was he praying? John wondered.

"I would like to help you in this way John ... and your boy, of course ... but it is not the appropriate course to take. There is an appeal procedure for situations such as yours. That is the correct route for you at this point. It is not that I don't want to help you ... and indeed, if you felt that as a priest there was something I could do to assist you in compiling your appeal, then you have only to ask. It would not be appropriate for me however to go to the Committee - or to Reverend Fellows - while the appeal option is there for you to take. I dare say that isn't what you wanted to hear me say ... but it makes sense doesn't it? Use the appeal. That's what it is there for."

John reluctantly had to agree. He had hoped that he could avoid the formal procedure ... but had to accept the Reverend Shakhan's reasoning. In fact, he felt guilty that he had put the Reverend in the position of having to say what he had just said. It seemed obvious to John now that he should not have asked him, as it were, to circumvent the formal procedure.

John left with the Reverend giving him as amicable a handshake as when he had arrived. John knew that what the Reverend had said was right and he felt stupid for having gone to bother him - but for some reason the one thought that kept popping into his mind was that he should have taken one of the biscuits ... but hadn't!

*

"What's up John? ... You seem glum."

John had been going over stuff as he meandered home, and the questioner was right - he was glum. The words brought John to the here-and-now and he looked up to see Charlie sitting in his deckchair enjoying the glorious July weather.

"Oh, hi Charlie ... yep guess I am a bit glum." John was not surprised that a blind man - well Charlie at any rate - had perceived his state of mind. Over the years John had come to realise that once within earshot, Charlie could *hear* almost as much as someone else could see.

"Fancy a beer?" offered the inquisitor.

"Yeah, sounds like a good idea," responded John automatically – though the punch from a shot of whisky appealed more, despite the heat of the day! "... in the fridge?"

"Where else?"

John went through to Charlie's kitchen, took two cans from the fridge and brought them out. He handed one to Charlie and then sat himself on the ground. "Cheers," he said cracking it open.

"Your good health, John. How's Steph? How much longer has she got to go now?"

"Hell ... I should know that to the day shouldn't I? ... Thing is my head has been full of dealing with Tim. He's been in some trouble."

"Oh, I'm sorry to hear that, John."

"No, it's OK Charlie … I should still know about Steph's sentence. Mmm … it's about a year still to do ... but I don't know what happens about 'time off for good behaviour'."

"Right - that should bring it down ... though I'm not sure by how much ... maybe six months do you think?"

"Yes, maybe. That would be good. I don't know whether she gets told that sort of thing or if I have to go to a lawyer or something. I'll write to her. She'll be wondering why I haven't written already, especially since it's our wedding anniversary. I'll have to tell her about Tim. She doesn't know anything."

"So, what is it that's happened with Tim? ... if you don't mind me asking. I don't want to pry – and congratulations."

98

"Thanks. No, you're not prying Charlie." John explained about Tim's stealing and the ultimatum from the Disciplinary Committee. "I went to the Reverend Shakhan to see if he could intervene and tell the Committee Tim's reasons - but he said he couldn't."

"He told you to use the appeals procedure I guess," volunteered Charlie.

"Yes, that was it exactly."

"Well, he's probably right. Makes you wonder though doesn't it?"

"Sorry Charlie, I'm not with you ... 'wonder' what?"

"Well, what they are for ... priests and the like. You go to him for help ... and he's a nice man from what I can tell ... and he says, 'use the appeal'. You go away and use the appeal. Say you win. You then go back to Reverend Shakhan and he says, 'There you go John, I said the appeal was the right course to take'. Or maybe you lose the appeal and go back to Reverend Shakhan. What's he going to say then? Will he say, 'Right John, you have followed procedures ... but they have got it wrong. I will fight your corner – let's go see them now' ... or will he say, 'The appeal panel had all the information John, and so they must have come to this decision on the evidence before them. It's not for me to question that'? What do you think John? Fighting talk from him or acceptance? I know what I think ... and like I said, I don't think he's a bad bloke ... just part of the system."

"Well, maybe you're right. I don't know." John felt totally despondent. "Guess I'll have to sort out the appeal stuff."

"There's no harm in giving it a try."

"The way you say that sounds like you don't think I will win, Charlie."

"Not for me to say John - just that I don't trust 'the system' ... cynical old fool that I am ... and it's probably worse than that. I don't think I trust *systems* not just *the* system!!" - Charlie gave a wry smile. "Systems serve themselves. They decide what's right, what's wrong, what's good, what's bad - and those things change with the system. Take your wife. She's in trouble for wearing that dress. Is that dress hurting anyone? Is Steph hurting anyone? Of course not ... but the system says she's doing something wrong. If the system was one in which everyone wore clothes then to go around without clothes would be 'wrong'. See what I mean, it's all arbitrary ... right and wrong, good and bad ... all system dependent! It just comes down to power and the status quo."

John was silent. Charlie was bleak sometimes.

"Sorry John, I have been going on a bit haven't I?" John didn't answer since Charlie looked thoughtful. "I'm sorry, John. You don't need to listen to an old man ranting. Your wife is in jail and your son is in trouble and all I do is rant. You probably don't know this John, but when I was young I was a lawyer. I no longer have a practice certificate of course, and I haven't put a case together for years, but if you need help drafting your appeal then don't be afraid to ask me. I know the sort of stuff that has to go into these things. Despite my ranting and scepticism you've got to try for the lad's sake – and I would love my ranting cynicism to be proved wrong."

Chapter 10: John's Car, Tim's Reform, May's Cuts. The Door Turns

With Charlie's help John put his appeal together. Even with that help however, his appeal was unsuccessful. From the time John first learned of the choice facing him - caning for his son or removal from the school - there had been no doubt in his mind that it would be the latter. Now, he was even more certain. The Appeal Committee had been told Tim's explanation for doing what he did, and still they insisted on this harsh punishment or his removal. If they, as a school purporting to promote Trueway values, were so hypocritical in their lack of forgiveness ... then John felt that Tim was better off in another school anyway. Not only that, but he would not allow May to stay at such a school either. The problem was finding a new one.

Although all the schools were happy to take May, it took John several weeks to identify a school that would accept Tim. He started by approaching nearby schools with good reputations but found himself moving further away and becoming less 'picky' with each rejection. When eventually he found a school that would take Tim, and that also had a space for May, it was a considerable distance from where they lived. The children were capable of using public transport but going to and from the new school would make their day very long. Additionally, the area where the school was situated was one which did not have a good reputation, and John was anxious about them travelling alone. He began to wonder whether the whole family should move, but they all liked their current house and the area where they lived, so he didn't want to do this. May was upset at the thought of leaving her present school and all her friends – especially when she had done nothing wrong - and was doing well in her lessons. John empathised but said he could not tolerate her being at such a hypocritical school and that she would adjust and make new friends. It would also be a help for Tim to have his sister there in a place where he would otherwise be with nobody he knew.

John explained the situation to his employer and asked if he could have some sort of flexible start and finish times to enable him to accompany his children to and from school ... at least to begin with. To John's relief - and surprise - it was agreed. Sitting at home by himself that evening after the children had gone to bed he thought about why he had been surprised at the firm's agreement - why he had *expected* refusal. At first he explained it to himself 'logically'. They were a small firm, and Tim was no concern of theirs, so it was natural to expect that they would say that John's family problems were things for him to resolve outside of work. This had not been the basis of his expectation however. He had not thought it through in that way. His expectation had been emotional. He had been to the head teacher seeking understanding, and been rejected. He had been to the priest seeking understanding, and been rejected. He had been to the Appeal Committee seeking understanding, and been rejected. He realised that he had come to expect rejection and lack of support. So, when he went to his firm he expected the same - yet his firm, who had no responsibility towards Tim, said "we'll help". A tear rolled down John's face. This was not how the world was supposed to be. The others should have helped. They should have helped because he and his family were *good* people, and good people should be supported when they have a difficulty.

But maybe the world was no longer seeing John and his family as good people. He had a wife in prison and a son who had been excluded from school for theft. How was the world seeing him and his family now? How was he seeing the world now? John thought of Charlie and his comments about right and wrong, good and bad. John did not go back to the Reverend Shakhan.

*

In his next letter to Steph John explained what had been happening with Tim. He explained about the new school for both children. He also explained about the flexible working arrangement that he had negotiated. He hoped, that in response, she would say that she would accompany the children to school as soon as she was released. This, of course, would mean abiding by the BRO and not wearing the red dress. Despite being sympathetic to her family's predicament however Steph did not make such a commitment when she wrote back. Nevertheless, John hoped that once released she would 'see sense'.

Life in the Hugo household settled into the adjusted routine. An earlier breakfast was followed by John accompanying the children to school before going to work. In the evening John usually brought the children home and then went back to the office. Sometimes he remained at home and worked in his study. Increasingly May helped out with preparing the evening meal. To John's relief both she and Tim appeared to settle quickly into this new school. They didn't mention any particular friends ... or enemies for that matter ... and there were no adverse reports from the staff. In fact both children were praised for their work and effort. Tim in particular took to his new school with enthusiasm, and John was pleased that he didn't seem to miss friends from his old school.

Claudia and the gang had watched proceedings with apprehension and Tim had received messages making clear how he would suffer if Claudia or any of the others were implicated in his thefts. He received no thanks from Claudia for his loyalty.

Shortly after starting his new school however Tim had encountered Vaz in the park. Tim had tried to turn and walk away, but the bully had called to him and Tim had been too afraid to run. The lad had approached until he was just inches away, towering over Tim. Despite believing that he had done all required of him by the gang, Tim had still not dared to look up and meet the gaze of this colossus. Instead he had just stared at his huge chest. Then, in a hushed voice, Vaz had simply said:

"You didn't blab, Hugo. All what they done, and you didn't blab. Thank you." He then turned and Tim watched him lope away. Tim didn't know that Vaz had been thrown out of two schools already, and that to have been implicated in the extortion racket would have had dire consequences for him. A 'thank you' from Claudia was what Tim really wanted – craved even – but this quiet 'thank you' from the giant Vaz made an impression. That said, he didn't want a further encounter with him and he didn't want to get sucked back into that group. From then on he steered clear of the park and other haunts where he knew they might go. He even stopped visiting Logan.

Despite all the issues around her brother, the move of school forced upon her, and the additional support she was voluntarily providing at home, May too appeared happy – though May was one of those children that people often referred to as 'deep' and it wasn't always clear what was happening below the surface. Outside school her old circle of friends remained loyal and still continued to visit – something that helped maintain the illusion, if not the reality, of all the other changes in her life having minimal impact.

The 'new' family situation imperceptibly became 'normal' and routine. John and the children were not allowed to visit Steph because she refused to remove the dress so 'mum' was included in family routine only via letters. At first they were quite frequent in both directions, but then became more intermittent. In January John and the children had sent Steph a birthday card, and then in April photographs of Tim on his 11th birthday and a month later photographs of May as she became a teenager. For her part Steph sent letters of congratulations. The months came and went, almost imperceptibly, in their eco-shielded way. On a day-to-day basis this life without Steph seemed increasingly less of a strain – certainly to John. He ceased to think of his life as something he had to endure until Steph came home. Although John would not have admitted it, even to himself, he was thinking less and less about his wife. He was therefore startled when he received a letter from Steph containing her release date. He had known that her sentence was likely to be commuted – but it still came as a shock.

John immediately told Tim and May, and the calendar was consulted. It would be a Friday in three weeks time. Unfortunately, Steph had not provided her exact time of release. Neither had she said whether she would like John to be there to give her a lift in the car or whether it was her intention to come out still wearing the dress. John felt he needed to know all this.

The turnaround time for letters to and from the prison was quite long - about a week. All letters (in and out) were opened and checked by the prison authority, but John could never understand why this seemed to add so much time to delivering or sending. John was not allowed to telephone Steph and although Steph was able to telephone out she could never predict when she would be allowed to make a call. As a result calls could easily be missed and on more than one occasion John had returned home to find an answer phone message from her or been in a position where he was not able to take her call on his mobile. Steph therefore rarely telephoned. John was able to e-mail the prison for a printed message to be passed on to Steph. She was not allowed to email back but John thought that if he emailed immediately then there would be sufficient time for her to write a letter in response. He emailed his questions. A week later he received Steph's letter in response.

Hi John. Your e-mail was passed on to me yesterday evening. I don't know exactly what time I will be released, I'm afraid. From talking to my warders it seems likely that it will be mid to late morning. If you want to be there to meet me then I guess you would have to hang around. I would love a lift if you are able to be there but obviously if you have to be at work I understand. I have worn the dress all the time I have been here and I am determined that I will leave the prison still wearing it. Sorry I can't be more precise about the time. Give my love to May and Tim.

So, thought John, *she will come out wearing the dress. Hopefully, if I am there she can get in the car and I can bring her home without any fuss and we can talk everything through.*

*

The prison was on a main road about half a mile from the centre of town. John made enquiries with the prison to see if he could obtain a more accurate release time for Steph, but all he was told was that it would be between 10:00am and mid-day - pretty much what Steph had said. John asked whether there was somewhere that he could park his car and wait for his wife. He was informed that there was nowhere within the prison grounds for visitors, friends or relatives to park. He would have to park on the street or in a public car park.

Prior to the day of Steph's release John investigated his options. There were parking bays for five cars on the street opposite the prison - but waiting was limited to twenty-five minutes. The rest of the road was marked as "no parking". There was a public car park only a short distance away but it was behind high buildings. John could probably find space there but would not be able to see when Steph came out so would have to leave his car and stand on the pavement until she emerged. It wasn't ideal but it was the best he could do.

On the day of her release John arrived at the car park at 9:30am. He paid for three hours parking and walked to the main road to wait outside the prison. There appeared to be only one entrance to the prison grounds used by both vehicles and pedestrians so John assumed that Steph would emerge, onto the road at this point. For some reason he felt he shouldn't wait immediately by the entrance and so stationed himself on the opposite side of the road.

There was only an intermittent stream of traffic to and from the town and John was confident he would be able to get across to his wife as soon as he saw her. He paced up and down. The occasional vehicle went in and the occasional vehicle came out of the prison - a red and white barrier rising and falling each time to allow their passage. There were very few pedestrians around, and only one or two entered or left the prison. As

105

time passed, John began to wonder whether his assumption was correct - was this the only way in and out? Was he waiting in the wrong place? There appeared to be no one else waiting for a prisoner to emerge. Maybe Steph was the only prisoner being released that day.

By 10.30 John was becoming increasingly anxious. He knew that Steph had a phone with her ... but wasn't sure that it would be charged and therefore whether she would be able to call him if she came out of another entrance. John felt that he was going to have to go and ask someone. There was what looked like a porter's lodge next to the red and white barrier so John crossed the road and went to see if there was anyone on duty. He looked through the window. There was a chair and table but no signs of an occupant. John began to wonder whether he should venture further. He could see that there were security cameras so presumably someone inside the building was watching what he was doing.

As he was considering what to do a police car pulled up. Two police officers, one male and one female got out and another officer then parked the car in one of the twenty-five minute parking bays. The driving officer remained with the vehicle and the other two stood chatting on the pavement a few yards from John. They didn't approach him or ask what he was doing but their presence made him feel awkward and he found himself walking back over the road to escape them while he thought about what to do.

As he arrived on the far pavement and turned to look back there was a flash of red as Steph emerged from behind the porter's lodge. Immediately John started back towards her but, before he reached the pavement the two police officers had begun speaking to her.

"... refuse then you will leave me with no choice," John heard the male officer saying as he approached.

"There is nothing wrong with it and I am hurting no-one," he heard Steph say.

"Steph!" said John as he came up between the two police officers and hugged his wife.

"John! Oh John!" beamed Steph as she squeezed him.

"I'm her husband Officer ... my car's just over there in the car park. I can take her home now."

"I'm sorry sir," said the male officer, "but this lady is committing an offence."

"But my car is just over there. I'm here to pick her up and go home."

"I'm sorry sir, but unless Mrs Hugo removes this dress she is committing an offence and I am obliged to arrest her," said the male officer.

"We have already asked your wife to remove the dress and she has refused," said the female officer.

"Mrs Hugo, for a second time, will you please remove the dress ... and then if you wish, take the lift being offered by your husband," said the male officer.

"Come on Steph, the car's just over there...," imploredJohn, but his wife ignored him.

"I'm sorry Officer," said Steph calmly, "but there is nothing wrong with my dress. Am I hurting you or anyone else?"

"I am not intending having a debate Mrs Hugo. For the final time are you prepared to take off the dress and go home with your husband?"

"There is nothing wrong..." began Steph but her words were drowned out by the male officer.

"Mrs Hugo I am arresting you for being in breach of the ..."

"But this is ridiculous...," began John as the officer continued and the female officer began to lead Steph towards the waiting police car.

John remonstrated and tried to convince the officers of the pointlessness of what they were doing when his car was 'just over there', but it was to no avail. Steph calmly complied with the police and got into the back of the police car. The door was shut and the female police officer got in beside her through the door on the other side. The male officer, having finished his standard speech took up the front passenger seat and then they were gone.

John stood there on the pavement, a lost and lonely man. His wife had been there and now she was gone. It was almost as if she hadn't been there at all ... almost as if he was still waiting for her to appear. John stood there for several minutes before walking slowly back to his car where he sat for even longer just staring at the car park, not really thinking anything. Eventually he drove home.

*

After her re-arrest Steph was taken to the police station. Sitting in the police cell by herself she took out her pad of 'Stuff'.

John, John, John. It was so, so good to see you. I'm so sorry. Why didn't I just run or take it off and come with you? Oh John I wanted to. Or am I just writing and feeling that now? Out there what was I feeling? Defiance? Resolve? Hell, hell, hell, what am I trying to do? Hell, my head's a mess at times.

Thank you for coming John. I'm sorry.

*

May and Tim were very upset to find that their mother had not come home. John feared that this might trigger another episode of difficulty with Tim but in the days and weeks that followed there was no sign of this. May too appeared to adjust, though she showed more anger than Tim initially. It was mainly directed at the police. Several times she went through variants of the same theme - the injustice of targeting her mother and of wasting police time on something trivial.

"They were waiting for her!! They were waiting for mum --- three of them and a car! They called her 'Mrs Hugo' so they knew it was her ... and must have come just for her ... all that just to arrest mum because of her stupid dress!"

At no point did May ask why her mother or her father hadn't put up a greater struggle or why wearing the dress was more important to Steph than getting home to be with her family, but John sensed that these questions were latent and that some of the anger was directed at him and Steph even though May did not explicitly say so. To an extent John was right but May would not have been able to put into words the emotion she felt towards her parents in the way that she could towards the police. Similarly she would not have been able to put into words the way she felt about her brother – or even herself. In her mind what the police had done was simple – they had lain in wait – an ambush for her mother. It was a simple situation of bully and victim; of good and bad. Her mother and her father however she regarded as good people, yet they were causing her pain.

Maybe, if they were good people, it was somehow her fault? Was her mother intentionally getting taken to prison in order to get away from her? Was she herself – May – the fundamental problem? She worked hard at school. She worked hard at home and yet still her mother did not return – she had not been there for her 13th birthday. When her brother was in trouble it wasn't just him that changed school, but she had been forced to move as well, even though she had done nothing wrong. It was as if he mattered but she didn't. It all pointed to *her* as the problem. If she was good then she wouldn't be treated in this way. But she felt that she *was* good and was doing good things – doing her very best.

Her friends liked her so maybe she should be angry at her parents for not seeing what her friends could see. Or maybe if she was bad then she should behave even more badly – a bit like Tim did – since it wasn't worth constantly trying to be good if she didn't get it right and if her family did not recognise it. None of this, of course, was in any way explicit in her mind. She could not have articulated any of this – but the ferment was there fizzing and bubbling down deep - while the surface waters were calm. Nobody noticed the little cuts she made on her arm, disguised among the lines and dots of henna design.

*

John went over and over the events outside the prison and pondered his own reaction to them. His daughter was right; the police had definitely come to meet Steph and to arrest her if she did not comply with the request to remove the dress. He felt there was little more he could have done. Steph showed no sign of resistance to the police. Why was she doing this? Why was she so ready to go back to jail rather than take off the red dress? Why was it more important to her to do that than to be with him and the children? What was she trying to achieve? When would it all end?

John put these things in his next letter to Steph. She responded.

It was lovely to see you - even if it was brief - and I can understand your puzzlement. After the arrest I was sitting by myself in the police cell. I had a piece of paper. I took a pen and wrote, 'what am I trying to do?' This self-questioning is a constant habit of mine, as I often forget why I am doing what I am doing. That may sound bizarre, but it really is only an indication of the constant back and forth my mind goes through at times. Anyway, the answer came quickly: I'm not trying to do anything. I've succeeded already by following my truth. That's all anyone can do. No one can do better, and it leads us to wherever it leads.

By imposing the BRO on me the court - society if you like - is saying in effect that I should act according to the expectations of others and not according to what I think is true. I think that is an unworkable guide to live by. I don't mean by that, it can't be done, but that it doesn't work. It is the opposite of freedom.

I hope one day that Tim and May will understand that I have to live according to what I think is right. What sort of an example would I be giving to them if I just did what I was told or what was easy and ignored my conscience? I'm sure in the end they will understand and I hope they will be proud of me.

In the end, thought John, *in the end. What about now Steph? What about them missing you now? What about me missing you now? What about now?* John wanted to support his wife but increasingly he was seeing what she was doing as selfish. Yes, he understood what she was saying about behaving according to her conscience ... but she was talking about wearing a dress! He agreed that she should not be in prison for such a trivial offence ... but in his mind it was just that – 'trivial'. No matter who it had belonged to, no matter what principle of personal freedom was at stake, wearing a dress was trivial, and in John's mind, there was a higher principle ... being there for your children!

Part 2: But Everything has a Context

Chapter 11: The Bomb…and Humming in the Orange Court

The bomb was unexpected. John first heard about it from a colleague at work. Steph first heard about it through whispers and snatches of overheard conversation. The children first heard about it from their head teacher at school and came home anxious and bewildered.

All that was known initially was that there had been an explosion in one of the outer districts of the town. Information of what had happened passed by word of mouth to begin with and there were various stories - a gas leak, a bomb, a crashed helicopter. At first the Trueway media simply said, "an incident" but within hours was reporting it as having been *likely* to have been a bomb and then, later in the day, that it *definitely* had been a bomb. The speculation after that was all about who had planted the bomb and why.

This speculation continued since no person or organisation came forward to claim responsibility. The bomb had exploded inside a Trueway temple and about half the building had been destroyed. There was some damage to nearby property but nobody had been killed or injured in any way. The absence of casualties was attributed to the time that the bomb exploded – 3:30am - when there were very few people about. Had the bomb been targeted at Trueway? Had the bomb been targeted at this particular building or area? Was the timing of the blast due to the opportunity that the bomber had to plant the device … or was there an intention to damage property but avoid hurting people? Speculation, speculation, speculation.

As with all news however the speculation and concern began to fade - for most people at any rate - as time passed and nothing further untoward occurred. It was only a few weeks before the event disappeared from the headlines, and went from being the most important, all consuming issue of concern, to a tedious, "oh that again" whenever it was mentioned.

The children soon forgot about it - well, in their day-to-day activities and conversations at least. Steph and John put it to one side in their minds and got on with the everyday. Charlie did not forget it.

*

The bomb blast played on Charlie's mind. It wouldn't leave him alone. As time passed it seemed to concern him more. The fact that it disappeared from the news concerned him. The fact that other people seemed to forget about it concerned him. Charlie lay in bed in his dark world and he pondered the bomb. What he came back to again and again was distance. It was distance that he pondered most - distance in time, distance in space. Distance, he concluded was making people ignore and forget about the bomb.

Charlie was an elderly man, and yet he could not recall ever having heard of a bomb blast in the heart of Trueway during his lifetime. This was the only confirmed occurrence of which he was aware. At first he couldn't understand why he kept thinking about it while other people seemed to forget about it. The first bomb blast in the heart of Trueway in living memory ... yet within a few weeks it was history ... and that was it. That was what Charlie concluded. The bomb blast had become *history,* and like all the other history that was taught in school or that people learned about through books, visits to historic houses, the internet, museums, videos and films it had become somewhat unreal. As time passed the bomb blast became more distant in time and with that distance, less real. People knew it *was* real ... just as they knew that the medieval armour in the museum had genuinely been worn by a knight, but just as the reality of that armour blurred with the fiction of stories like King Arthur, so the bomb blast faded into being, "just another story". What surprised Charlie was the *speed* with which that happened. The distance in time from the present to medieval knights was centuries, but the distance in time from the bomb blast was weeks and days.

Then there was distance in space. The blast had occurred over the other side of town. Apart from people who lived there and saw the damage daily it was, 'the other side of town' ... or 'district' ...or 'territory' ... or even, 'continent'. As soon as the media stopped coverage, then there were no reminders.

Charlie stopped talking to people about the bomb blast - even though it occupied his thoughts a good deal of the time. He wondered whether there were other people like himself, who were still concerned, but who simply stopped talking about it. People who became embarrassed by the response they elicited of, "oh not that again". He assumed that there probably were such people - people for whom the "distance" rule did not work, people who, like himself had something in their personality or something in their past or something in their upbringing or something in the wiring of their brains, that meant that they could not ignore the bomb blast, that they could not push it into history; into a fiction.

*

Charlie's underlying preoccupation with the bomb did not diminish his concern about Steph. He was fond of her and had been upset when John had explained the circumstances of her release and immediate re-arrest. That had been some months ago, and since then, Steph had again been held in prison on remand awaiting yet another trial.

"How's Steph?" enquired Charlie one evening when John was passing. "Has she said anything more about what she is going to say in her defence ... or about her defence strategy?"

"Hi Charlie ... no, she hasn't said anything more than what I told you last time."

"Well, like I've said before John, I think she should get some good legal representation, and stop trying to go it alone."

"Yes, I've tried telling her that, but she won't listen. She says that she wants to address the jury and feels that if she has a representative then it gives the court the perfect excuse to exclude her from the trial."

"Well, the judge did that before anyway ... so ..."

"Yes, I know Charlie, I know."

"You sound weary, John." John didn't answer. He was weary. In the absence of a response Charlie continued. "The hearing's next week isn't it?"

"Yes, Monday 11:00am."

"Will you go?"

"Yes, of course!" said John with indignation. Charlie was surprised by his tone. He hadn't intended to imply that he thought John might not.

"Sorry, John, I put that badly. I just meant that if you are going I wondered whether you would like me to come too. In fact I'd like to come if you are happy with that."

"Yes, of course Charlie. It's a public hearing. You don't need my permission." John paused, hearing the continuing harshness in his response. "Sorry, now I'm sounding irritable. Yes, Charlie, yes, I'd like you to come. It will be good to have someone to talk to about it - whatever happens - someone who was there besides me."

*

John assumed that they would travel by glide-car - but Charlie suggested walking.

"I like stretching my legs," he said. When walking by himself he used a long cane for checking the pavement in front. He had it with him when they set off but linked arms with John and trusted his companion.

"What are you anticipating, John?" he asked.

"Well, I'm not sure. I was shocked by what happened last time - Steph not being allowed to speak and everything. I got hold of the court listing and it's a different judge this time - a woman, Judge Mills. Maybe she will be more tolerant."

"Well, we can hope, can't we?" said Charlie, with what John perceived as a lack of conviction.

"You think it will be the same as last time then?"

"Well, you know me John -- ever the cynic! ... But I would like to think that it will be different. Let's hope the old judiciary proves me wrong ... and I would like them to ... for Steph's sake." He squeezed John's arm. "I like Steph and she deserves to be treated fairly."

John appreciated Charlie's expression of affection for Steph. He knew it was sincere. They walked in silence for a bit.

"I wonder if the press will be there," mused Charlie aloud. "There's usually someone from the local rag."

"Yes, probably. The basics of what goes on gets reported somewhere by someone," said John. "There were a few people in the court room last time - ushers and the like - and I worked out the roles of most of them. There was one who I thought might be a reporter." They again fell silent for a while.

"How's Tim doing at school now?" ventured Charlie, and the topic of conversation moved to the children and from there meandered through various subjects interspersed with silences as they walked. They were discussing the quality of different beers as they approached the steps of the court building.

They were in good time, but to John's surprise there were already a couple of people in the public gallery. He and Charlie had to sit in the second rather than the front row. The hearing was in a different court room to the previous time and instead of being above the court they were on a level with it - separated only by a glass screen. John told Charlie of his surprise at finding other members of the public present. Charlie simply shrugged and said, "Well" in a tone that John could not interpret. They waited in silence until the words, "All rise" heralded the entrance of Judge Mills and the start of proceedings.

*

The tone of the hearing was set from the beginning. Almost the first thing that Judge Mills said was that she intended to deal with Mrs Hugo, "in the same way as Judge Willis. If Mrs Hugo appears naked then we will have her in court. If not then she will have forfeited her right to participate."

The defendant was summoned to the court, and to John's delight, Steph suddenly appeared in the dock only a few feet from him. She smiled at him through the glass and gave a little wave in response to his.

"She's in the dock, Charlie ... I can she her. She waved to us," whispered John.

"Which way?"

"Over to our left"

Charlie gave a tentative wave and smile, and despite the fact he could not see her Steph smiled and waved back.

"She saw, Charlie. She smiled and waved."

John was then silent as the judge addressed Steph.

"You are wearing a dress Mrs Hugo. I think you know from the hearing with Judge Willis that this is not considered appropriate in a court of law, and furthermore, places you in breach of your *Behaviour Restriction Order*. I am therefore going to ask you to remove it. If you agree then you will be allowed to remain in court and participate - presenting your case to the jury by way of your defence. If you do not, then I will have no choice but to return you to the cells. Will you agree to remove the dress?"

"With respect, Your Honour, the dress, and me wearing it, is part of the evidence that I wish to present to the jury. There is nothing wrong with it, and for me to remove it, just because there is an order that does not make sense, would go against my conscience. And anyway, I am

115

standing here now, in full view of the court and a public gallery with people in it - so how is that any different to me being here for the rest of the trial and addressing the jury?"

"I am not here to have a debate Mrs Hugo. Will you remove the dress?"

"I have already said that I will not. I will not do something that doesn't make sense just because someone bigger says I must for no good reason."

"In that case I will ask you to return to the cells. Have you been provided with the case documents of the prosecution?" Steph nodded. "Is there anything in those documents that you wish to challenge?" Steph shook her head. "Are there any points that you would wish me to put to the jury in your absence?" Again Steph shook her head. "In that case, I will ask that you are now taken back to the cells, until I call for you again. If there is anything that you think of, that you do wish to challenge in the prosecution case, or if there are any points that you wish me to present to the jury on your behalf, then please have them ready for when I call you back."

At a nod from the judge the officer escorting Steph then turned her round and she left the dock. As she did so one of the people in the public gallery also got up and left.

The trial then proceeded. It was almost a carbon copy of the one that John had attended earlier in the year. The jury was sworn in. The absence of Steph was explained to them. The prosecution presented its case, describing Steph's release and rearrest outside the prison very much as John recalled it. The jury was then asked to leave, and return ready for the remainder of the trial, in an hour and a half. After they had gone Steph was returned to the dock. She was asked by the judge whether she had anything to say against the prosecution case or anything to say to the judge for passing on to the jury. There was nothing that Steph wanted to say on either count. She was returned to the cells and the hearing was adjourned for an hour and a half. Charlie and John found a cafeteria in the court building and had coffee and cake.

When they returned to the public gallery it was empty and they took up seats on the front row. The hearing was soon reconvened and the jury brought back. The judge explained that Mrs Hugo had forfeited her right to present her defence in person by refusing to take off the dress. Judge Mills explained that Mrs Hugo had been offered the opportunity to make any points to the jury through the judge but had declined to do so. In the absence of any such defence the judge said that she would not call upon the prosecution to give a summary. She then summed up the case herself and directed the jury on the points of law that they had to consider ... essentially whether Mrs Hugo had breached the *BRO*, and if she had, whether there was any sound, reasonable excuse for her having done so. If there was not then they were to find her guilty.

The jury retired to consider their verdict.

"What do you think, Charlie?" whispered John.

"Who's here?" came the unexpected response.

"John looked round. To his astonishment the public gallery was full – every seat in every row was occupied. He had been vaguely aware of movement behind him, but had been so absorbed in the court room events, that he had not been aware of how many people had entered. Clearly Charlie, with his acute and selective hearing, had been.

"People," whispered John, "...lots of them. The place is full!" Charlie said nothing but he linked arms with John.

It wasn't long - five minutes at the most - before the jury filed back into the court room. Their verdict was unanimous: "Guilty". The judge thanked them and dismissed them. She asked that Steph be returned to the dock.

"Mrs Hugo, the jury has found you guilty. It is therefore my job now to pass sentence. Before doing so I will ask the prosecutor to provide me with a summary of any previous convictions."

Steph stood impassively in the dock while the prosecutor went through her case history, finishing with a reference to the sentencing guidelines which, given Steph's blatant disregard for a court order, he felt should be implemented to the maximum custodial sentence. The judge thanked him before turning to Steph.

"Do you have anything you wish to say Mrs Hugo - anything you believe I should take into account before sentencing - anything mitigating in your favour?"

"As I have said before, I have done nothing wrong, and I have to follow my conscience."

"In that case, having considered the evidence and your previous history of offending, I sentence you to two years in prison. Take Mrs Hugo back to the cells please."

John, who had been looking at his wife all the time, waved but Steph did not seem to notice as she turned and went.

At exactly the same moment that she disappeared from sight a low hum began. It was almost inaudible at first, but as the judge started to speak again it gradually became louder. John realised that it was coming from the other people in the public gallery. He looked around him as it grew louder and louder. The people – men, women, all very ordinary looking - were sitting motionless staring straight ahead. They made no movement but each, with lips just slightly parted, was exhaling a long, low, monotonous, "nnnnnnnn" sound. The judge, as she became aware, stopped speaking. She and the prosecutor exchanged glances. She stood up - apparently about to address the public gallery - but instantly, as if signalled by the conductor of an orchestra, the sound stopped. All was still. All was silent. No-one moved. John was suddenly aware of how tight Charlie's grip had become on his arm.

John looked over his shoulder. Before the judge could say anything the person at the end of the row behind John stood up and proceeded to walk out. The rest of the row followed suit and then the next row and so on until only Charlie and John remained. Judge Mills gathered her papers, the usher called, "All rise" and the proceedings came to an official end.

John helped Charlie to his feet and was beginning to edge along the seats to the door when he noticed that every one of the seats in the public gallery had a piece of red paper on it cut in the shape of a dress. He took one.

*

The walk home had an urgency. Charlie seemed quite agitated. He said very little as they walked, but what little he did say indicated that his agitation was due more to the strange humming than the events or outcome of Steph's trial. He seemed to calm a little once he was back home.

"I'm sorry, John," he said as the latter opened a can of beer for each of them.

"It's OK ... I don't like to see you upset ... but that noise business was spooky. It gave me the shivers too."

"I know ... but I am being selfish. You have just seen your wife sentenced to two years in prison ... and all I'm doing is rushing you home because of me."

"Leave it Charlie. Like I said, I can understand. It was spooky."

"What did you pick up, John? As we were leaving, you paused and picked something up off one of the chairs."

"You don't miss a thing do you Charlie? Well, that was spooky too. All of the chairs had one of these on them." He took the dress-shaped piece of paper from his pocket and handed it to Charlie. "It's coloured red - like Steph's dress."

"And it's been written on in ball point pen too," commented Charlie, running his fingers over the surface.

"Really? I hadn't noticed that." Charlie handed the piece of paper back to John who read aloud, "'You can jail the revolutionary but you can't jail the revolution'. What's that supposed to mean ... well apart from the literal obvious?"

Charlie didn't respond immediately. He raised his beer can to his lips and paused before quietly saying, "Unhappiness, John. It means unhappiness. It's just a question of how much and for whom." Charlie took a sip of beer and then simply said, "Poor Steph."

John wasn't sure whether this reference to Steph was directly linked to the message on the paper dress, or was Charlie now thinking of the trial and Steph's two year sentence. John went with the latter.

"Yes, I waved as they led her away ... but she didn't seem to see me. I suppose you go a bit blank when you have been told something like that. It's only just starting to sink in for me. Even if she doesn't serve all of it, Tim could be a teenager by the time she is released. And it was all so unfair Charlie. I'm glad you were there. You heard what happened. She wasn't allowed to speak to the jury - convicted without being allowed to defend herself ... and all that crap about not being allowed to face the jury because the BRO prevented it ... she was there in court in full view of everyone! No offence to you intended Charlie. You know what I'm saying."

"No offence taken, John. Actions speak louder than words and a lot of political correctness is just words. We can cover things up, tell lies and hide the truth with words ... or with the absence of words. It is more difficult to do that with actions. Have you always known that Steph had a red dress? You don't have to answer that if you don't want to. I don't want to pry into your personal life. Regard it as rhetorical if you want."

"No, that's OK Charlie. Like you I don't take offence or think you are prying. The truth is I had no idea about the dress until Tim discovered his mum wearing it when he came home unexpectedly from school. It was a bit of a shock to all of us."

"So, Steph had a secret that she had kept from you and the kids. Are secrets a kind of lie John?

"Not really, Charlie. I don't think so anyway."

"Do you have secrets from Steph? Again you can regard that as rhetorical."

John thought a moment. Charlie had the ability … and maybe the bravery … to touch things that other people didn't. Knowing that John had just seen a huge injustice perpetrated against his wife, and that he had been thrown into confusion by the humming noise and the paper dresses, most people would have simply shown sympathy, empathy, understanding – but instead, Charlie was mercilessly peeling back the skin on this raw wound to get to even deeper pain nerves.

"Yes, Charlie. I have secrets. We all have secrets, don't we? I didn't know about Steph's dress … and there are things – mainly small – about me and my life that I have never told to her. Maybe I shouldn't even admit that to you. I didn't know about the dress but I knew there were things that I held back and so I guessed there were things that she held back too. I think that we had a tacit agreement not to pry; a silent, mutual agreement that there were things that just shouldn't and wouldn't be talked about or asked about. We had a good life, two wonderful kids and good jobs. We were respected and successful Citizens – a respected and successful family. We were stable. I guess we didn't want to risk upsetting all that by questioning and thinking about things from the past."

"And then the dress went and spoke for itself," added Charlie.

They finished their beers in silence and John said he had to go and collect the kids from school. By the time John left, Charlie seemed less agitated … but both he and John were trying to understand and integrate everything that had been heard, seen and said over the past few hours.

Chapter 12: Charlie's Chicken Man and might Marginals Hum?

John didn't see Charlie for a couple of days. He hadn't been sitting outside like usual and so John went round one evening- taking half a dozen cans of beer. He felt guilty about constantly drinking Charlie's and it provided a 'comfortable excuse', in John's mind, to go and make sure that Charlie was OK. He also needed someone to talk to. He had been reading about the trial in the media and he felt upset and angry. He took the local newspaper with him and some notes of what he had read on line as well.

A bit subdued, thought John as Charlie invited him in.

"Everything OK Charlie? Haven't seen you out for a couple of days – oh and I've brought a few beers. I'll stick them in the fridge."

"Yep, I'm fine – and thanks for the beers. Use mine for now though, since they're chilled."

"Will do." John returned with two cold cans. He cracked them open and handed one to Charlie.

"To be honest John I've been feeling a bit odd. It was the trial. It sort of rattled me. I keep thinking and my head gets sort of 'spinny' and overloaded."

"Right. I've been going over and over it myself," said John as he sat down. He'd not seen Charlie like this before, so felt the best approach was simply to behave as he usually would. "There have been some reports in the media. Have you heard any of it?"

"I caught some on the radio - but they didn't say much."

"Well, there's been stuff on-line and in the newspapers. A brief bit on TV local news as well. What was it that 'rattled' you Charlie - was it that humming noise or the way the trial went?"

"All of it really, John. All of it," came the slow, despondent answer. But then, as if a switch had been flicked, a more alert Charlie asked, "What sort of things have they been saying in the papers?"

"Well, it was all pretty factual. I've got the paper with me so I could read the whole article if you want," ventured John with a little more confidence. "... though it was mainly just a report of what happened - and you were there so you know all that. There were no massive errors in what was said, but I was frustrated by what they didn't say. They mentioned the fact that Steph wasn't allowed to stay in court because she refused to take off the dress ... but they made no comment on the unfairness of a trial where the accused has no opportunity to offer a defence to the jury."

"It sounds pretty much like what I heard on the radio, John. If the newspaper, TV and online media reports were anything like what I was listening to, then nearly all the focus was on the rights and wrongs of wearing clothes – mostly the 'wrongs'.

"Absolutely, Charlie. There was some really bigoted stuff – especially in the on-line comments from the public. It was mainly about body shaming and calling Steph a pervert. It was upsetting – and it made me angry too since these people were all hiding behind fictitious, on-line names. Can I read you some stuff? I just want to get it off my chest."

"Of course, John. I can probably guess the kind of thing – but I would like to hear, especially if sharing it helps you."

"Thanks, Charlie. These are all comments that followed the online version of the local newspaper. I'll start on a positive note. This was probably the best thing I read.

'I was shocked that Mrs Hugo was not allowed to address the jury because she refused to remove the dress she was wearing. The jury therefore convicted her without hearing her case in defence of her actions. Before that point I would not have believed such a thing possible in a Trueway court."

"That *is* good to hear," said Charlie. "I wonder if that person was in the public gallery."

"No indication, Charlie. There was just an on-line name – 'defender' … nothing more. Whoever he or she was, their comment pushed a button and some of the responses were dire. Someone calling themselves, 'blanco' said this,

She should have got the dress off then. She was warned, repeatedly yet decided to go ahead with keeping it on. Until clothes are accepted as the norm in the public space then she should get naked when required. Such as in court.

Then someone calling themselves 'Tinka' said,

Exactly. It's like she thinks access to justice is a basic human right that should be available to everyone. Utterly ridiculous. If you can't obey the rules, you shouldn't expect to have human rights.

I couldn't believe that Tinka person!" John looking up from the piece of paper. "Does he or she really think human rights should NOT be available to everyone? It beggars belief ... or are these comments the sort of stuff an old cynic like you would have expected Charlie?"

"Yes, I suppose this 'old cynic' did expect something like that. And was I right about the focus on the rights and wrongs of wearing clothes?"

"Yes, pretty much. Some people saying that it was disgusting - that clothes were there to emphasise a person's sexuality – an argument I don't get at all - some going on about the dangers of terrorism and loads and loads about Steph being a body shamer and a skin shamer. I think it was that stuff – the body shaming stuff – that I found most upsetting. Steph once asked me why people saw the dress and not her tattoos. I was angry with her at the time ... but I think I understand a bit more now how she felt."

Charlie stayed quiet a while before asking, "Did the media say anything about the noise from the public gallery or the cut-out paper dresses?"

"Yes ... yes, they did," responded a thoughtful John. "I'll read what it said in the local paper: 'Towards the end of the trial, after Hugo had been sentenced, there was some noise from the public gallery and the majority of people watching the trial left. Some paper leaflets in the shape of a red dress were left behind with a slogan written on them - *You can jail the revolutionary but you can't jail the revolution.* Police are investigating this'. That was all any of the reports said about it. Don't know if I expected anything more. How about you?"

Charlie didn't answer. He rubbed his leathery face and sighed. He remained quiet for quite a few seconds as if going off into a reverie. He then started a strange monologue. To John, it seemed to, 'come from nowhere'. It appeared unrelated to Steph, the trial or anything of what John had read to him – but John was transfixed by Charlie's sombre intensity.

"Survival John, *that's* what I think - survival. I think it's all pretty much as Darwin said - what survives, survives; what works, works- the tautology of life. People usually say that Darwin went on about, 'survival of the fittest' ... but I think that that's misleading, because I think people interpret 'fittest' as meaning 'strongest' or 'healthiest' when actually it just means best suited to the environment - the circumstance. Some female spiders, as soon as they have become pregnant, eat their male partners whereas some seagulls travel thousands of miles to meet the same partner in the same place year after year to breed. You don't get much more diverse than that ... but it *works* in both cases.

Well, I say 'it works' ... but even that has to be qualified. It works in the sense that it enables the parents to successfully create offspring and maintain the species. Humans can be a bit different - humans have *religion*. For humans is 'survival of the species' always the goal? Maybe some humans see survival of the physical state as irrelevant, since survival of the soul is the key thing. If you think like that then sacrificing yourself makes sense ... its martyrdom. The martyr is born to die ... death being the route to survival of the soul ... the 'fittest' soul and the survival of the correct 'soul species' in that 'other place' ... heaven, if you like. In the words of the song, 'Are we any more than we achieve or what we leave?'."

Charlie 'looked' at John. "What sort of survival are you interested in John ... and what would you *do* in order to survive?"

John liked Charlie and he enjoyed the sometimes slightly quirky discussions he had had with him over the years, but he felt slightly irritated by this monologue and question that seemed to ignore the events of Steph's trial.

"I don't know Charlie ... not something I've thought a lot about."

"Maybe it's something that needs to be thought about." Charlie's words sounded like an admonishment. "A lot of people can die - maybe all people - when survival of the soul is more important than survival of the body."

John didn't want to pursue this line of conversation. He was thinking about what had happened at his wife's trial. He wanted to get some things off his chest and maybe talk about what might be done next. What Charlie had started talking about he saw as abstract and irrelevant.

"Maybe you're right Charlie. I'm not sure – but I thought the Terror Wars had dealt with all that religious stuff generations ago. Anyway, you didn't seem surprised by the on-line public comments." John hoped that this would draw Charlie back to the trial and bring a close to the Darwin discussion. Charlie appeared to recognise this.

"Yes, the Terror Wars ... you're right ... and the comments were pretty much what I expected. I'm sorry, John. I guess I went off on a bit of a tangent. It's just that Steph has started to bring up things that I had buried.

I remember the first time she went out in the dress. She had taken cheese and pickle sandwiches to work. She told me that as she passed me out the front ... but I heard something, something nervous in her voice ... and something else, something very faint and out of place. I thought I must have been mistaken, but I hadn't been. I had picked up the feint swish of her carrier bag against the dress.

As the weeks passed it became evident that Steph's outing in the dress wasn't a one off adventure. I didn't realise initially she was going to continue wearing it so doggedly, but when I did, it dredged up memories of everything that had led to my disenchantment with the law. It was then that I started to get worried for Steph. She had led me back to, *The Chicken Man*."

*

"I doubt that you will have heard of *The Chicken Man*, John. It was one of the first cases that I took on as a young barrister. I had good eyes in those days ... and I would like to think that my legal mind was just as sharp and clear as my vision. Anyway, this man believed he was the embodiment of a chicken. It probably sounds comical. He would prance around silently in the street being a chicken. Most people paid him no attention. One day, however someone complained and *The Chicken Man* was prosecuted on the basis of an archaic law dating from the earliest days of Trueway. The law had been designed to protect the rights of a religious group of chicken worshippers from ridicule. The last member of the sect had died years before so this piece of law had no real purpose. It was an anachronism - but the legislation had never been repealed.

At the point when I took on the case my client had been ordered by the White Court to stop imitating a chicken, but he claimed it was his right. In fact he *was* a chicken so the court could not tell him to stop. As a result he breached the court order and things escalated – just as they are escalating with your Steph. I defended him in the Orange Court. I put together a sound argument. I was optimistic that we would win and that *The Chicken Man* would be acquitted. I was therefore shocked to hear what I considered to be a very biased summary by the judge. I felt sure his words influenced the jury who then found *The Chicken Man* guilty.

I was still quite junior in the law firm for which I worked so I discussed the case with the head of the firm. I thought that maybe I had argued badly or misinterpreted the salient points. She, however, thought that I had argued well and that the judge was wrong in his summing up. She felt that we should take the case to the Appeal Court. We did that, but the appeal was dismissed. I read the ruling and was incensed. I could see, what appeared to me, to be a completely obvious error of reasoning. In fact, the decision appeared to be bizarre and irrational – a blatant miscarriage of justice.

Again I raised all my concerns with the head of my law firm. Again, I fully expected her to point out to me where my thinking was at fault, where my naivety and emotion had blinded my legal mind … but she didn't. Again, she said she agreed. The appeal court decision was wrong. She felt that we should seek leave to appeal to The Supreme Court. We did so, but leave to appeal was denied.

I went to her yet again to ask what we should do now – and the answer that she gave is what has made me so anxious for your Steph. The head of my law firm simply said that we should do 'nothing' - because there was nothing more we *could* do. Having been denied leave to appeal to The Supreme Court the process, and with it *justice*, was at an end. She left it at that."

Once more, Charlie paused and sipped his beer. For a moment he turned his sightless eyes to the floor. If it had not been for the twitch in Charlie's jaw, as he nervously and repeatedly clenched his teeth, John might have thought that Charlie's pause was for dramatic effect. Impatient though he was to see where Charlie was leading with his recollections, John remained silent. Charlie turned to John.

"All courts have rules. The Supreme Court is no different. The Supreme Court would only become involved if the case had major issues regarding a point of law. Although the court of appeal may have erred the Supreme Court could not see that it had a role. In effect, the Court of Appeal was the end of the line. It was, in terms of the issues of this case, the highest court. It had the last word." Charlie hung his head with the finality of defeat.

"Well, I suppose there has to be someone or some 'body' that has the last word." John thought this sounded hollow in the face of the dejected figure that Charlie now presented, but to fill the silence if nothing else, added, "I guess, in this case, the last word was with the Court of Appeal. In another case it may have been the Supreme Court… and whichever court it is, there's no guarantee they'll 'get it right'."

"Absolutely true, John," came the surprisingly alert response, as Charlie suddenly sat erect and took a swig of beer, "but the error, to me seemed so obvious that I couldn't get it out of my head. I couldn't, still can't, square a senior judge ... three judges in fact, since there are two others on the appeal panel as well as the lead judge ... making that sort of mistake. Then I started to wonder. What if it wasn't a mistake?

I started to wonder, what if it was calculated? What if that Appeal Court judge knew that he would have the last word and that, as long as his reasoning met the requirements of *law*, he would not be challenged? What if, for his own reasons, he wanted to support the decision of the judge from the lower court - maybe even support that judge as a person? The more I thought about it the more I began to understand. At the end of the day, the law only provided a framework, and within that framework, it was human beings that made decisions, and human beings had their own agendas.

I started to consider the other humans involved in the case - not just the judges and lawyers - but family, friends, journalists, supporters, detractors, critics. I realised they were all coming to the case from their personal perspectives, and with their own agendas. If that agenda coincided with my client's agenda then all well and good ... but if not, then his agenda didn't matter. In fact that was it ... that was what troubled me. My client's agenda was irrelevant. The reason he was doing what he was doing, was irrelevant. All that mattered was how other people saw it, and chose to use it or ignore it, as fitted *their* needs and purposes. The courts didn't care about his reasons for breaching court orders ... only that he had breached them, and both supporters and opponents alike only cared about *what* he was doing, not his *reasons* for doing it." Charlie's hand was tight around the half empty beer can and it made a crack as it buckled slightly in his grip. The sound seemed to still his agitation and he continued more calmly.

"And that's why I am so uneasy, John. You don't fully understand why Steph is doing what she is doing ... but does it matter what *her reasons* are? When it comes to the courts it will be her actions, not her reasons that are on trial. When it comes to the media, it will be whatever slant they want to put on it that will be the focus. Then there are these people that were in court - the ones who left the paper dresses. Do they care about Steph's reasons? What is their agenda? Do you see why I am anxious John? I don't know where this could lead for Steph ... but I fear that wherever it leads may have little to do with whatever reasons she has for doing what she is doing." He took a sip from his dented can before asking,

"What level of biodata ID do you have John?"

*

This last question ... tagged on the end of what Charlie was saying ... appeared to have nothing to do with anything that went before - but John was resigned to the apparent random nature of Charlie's thought processes. He just hoped that he wasn't inviting another, unfathomable monologue like that on Darwin, when he answered, "Functional Level 2".

"Right," nodded Charlie, "- like most people – 'shop & ship'. Why did you opt for that?"

"Well, it seemed the most convenient. If I go shopping or travel I don't have to queue to pay or get tickets since my biodata will be scanned as I leave the shop or get on the glide and my account deducted accordingly. I couldn't see any reason why not to opt for it. What about you?"

"Just Level 1 - I don't have much use for anything else and so I opted for the minimum. What level do you think those people who left the paper dresses had, John?"

"I don't know, Charlie. Can't say that I had given it any thought. Probably different levels, depending on their points of view ... just like you and me."

Charlie nodded. He sat still with his eyes closed as if deliberating before quietly saying, "Or maybe they didn't have any level."

John was silent. He didn't quite know what to make of this. Everyone had some level of biodata encoded just after birth. Even if a Citizen chose not to opt for one of the higher, 'functional' levels their bones already contained the minimum ID data.

"Well, they must have had some level ... everybody has some level."

Again there was a brief hush before Charlie spoke.

"Not if they are 'Marginals' John."

Now John really had no idea what to think, or how to respond.

"Have I embarrassed you, John? I don't generally talk about my views on Marginals. Some people don't think they exist at all. What about you, John? Do you think that they are real? Do you think I'm mad?"

"No Charlie, no, I don't think you are mad. I don't see why anyone would say that Marginals *don't* exist."

"Really, John? Going back a few years, I seem to remember there being questions about whether they had all died out."

"Maybe – but I think that idea was pretty quickly debunked. So no, I don't think you are mad Charlie … but I don't see why you would think that the people who were in the courthouse were Marginals."

"No, I am probably reading too much into it. I guess I am just too suspicious, too cynical. It's just that so little was said in the media about what happened or about who the people were. It just left me wondering whether the absence of comment was due to an absence of interest or an absence of information on who these people were … and the only way there would be absence of information would be if there was no biodata."

"Well, maybe Charlie. Who knows … hey?" John wanted to go, but didn't want to do so immediately since he didn't want to give Charlie the impression that he was leaving because of the direction the conversation had taken. Charlie, maybe sensing all this, voluntarily changed the line of discussion to beer, and they happily supped and chatted a while longer on that, and other non-contentious bits and bobs, until John said he needed to be going.

"Sorry if I went on a bit," said Charlie as he held the door open.

"No, Charlie - lots of interesting - and helpful - stuff. I'm grateful."

"I hope Steph is OK. Pass on my best wishes when you're next in touch with her."

"No problem Charlie."

"And John," Charlie paused, "try and persuade her to get out of there. I know it's not up to her … but you know what I mean - co-operate more. I've probably left you thinking I'm a bit mad … but I am worried for her."

"Nothing me and the kids would like more, than to have her out of there and back home Charlie," said John over his shoulder as he walked down the path, then added with a contrived chuckle, "but she's stubborn!"

*

John passed on Charlie's best wishes to Steph in his next letter. He also told her about the humming noise in the public gallery, and asked if she had heard it. He told her about the cut-out paper dresses left on the seats and what had been written on them. He told her about his discussion with Charlie. He told Steph about Charlie being concerned for her, about his exhortation to her to co-operate in order to get out of prison, because he thought she could be in danger. He told her all these things, but the letter he received back a week or so later reiterated Steph's resolve to continue wearing the dress in defiance of laws and rulings that she saw as wrong.

For several weeks after that John did not mention anything further in his letters about Charlie's misgivings. Neither did he make any suggestion that Steph should stop what she was doing. Then the note came through his door.

Chapter 13: The Causeway Café

The note was in an envelope with John's name and address on it but there was no postage stamp.

Dear Mr Hugo

I hope that you do not mind me writing to you unannounced in this way. I have exchanged several letters with your wife while she has been in prison. I think that what she is doing is wonderful and very courageous. So many of us admire her for standing up for the right to be clothed, for having no shame in what is shameless. We recognise that the authorities are likely to maintain their prejudiced stand and so, in my most recent letter to her I have offered the opportunity, when she is next released, to spend time with myself and other like minded people if she wishes. I have a house and land where she would be able to wear clothes freely in a safe and secluded area. There would be no risk of arrest. Obviously I am aware that she is married, and has a family, so felt I should write to you directly to invite you to meet me, and possibly some others from our group, to talk about the offer that I have made. I usually call in at the Causeway Cafe for a drink on a Saturday morning and thought that may provide a suitable place for an initial meeting and chat. I will be there around 11:00am and hope that you will accept the offer ... the coffee is on me!

Best wishes

Robert.

Of all the thoughts that started to buzz in John's head on reading this, the one that was uppermost, was the startling realisation that he was not the only person corresponding with Steph. It had never occurred to him that anyone else would be writing to her. There was no reason why other people shouldn't ... but he had simply made the assumption that no-one did! The wording of the note from Robert also suggested that Steph had been writing back to him. She had said nothing about this in her letters. John wasn't sure what feeling this was creating ... mistrust? Jealousy? Confusion? Irritation?

All these emotions seemed to be in there, vying for dominance ... and they didn't dissipate when he told himself that this, 'Robert' might be making it all up! In fact they were added to, since he now felt disappointment in himself that his first reaction had been to believe the note. At that point 'irritation' won and John decided there were more pressing things that he needed to be getting on with. He pushed the note back into its envelope, dropped it on the kitchen table and went out into the sunshine.

*

John looked at the note again in the evening, once the children had gone to bed. As well as there being no stamp or post mark, Robert had not included his address or surname. This made John very suspicious. He knew, from his own correspondence with Steph, that if this person was writing to his wife, then it will have been necessary for him to disclose exactly who he was and where he lived. Without this information the prison authorities would not have passed any letters on to her. For what reason would this person therefore not disclose the same to John? It didn't make sense.

He was rapidly concluding that the note must be some sort of hoax -- but if it was a hoax, then to what end? Could it be someone from the media wanting to get to talk to him? John decided that was unlikely since he could see no reason why anyone from the media would try to conceal his or her identity. He thought of Charlie and what he had said about the Marginals. Could this, Robert be one of the people who had been in the court and left the paper dresses? The note spoke about a group of, 'like minded people' ... and that seemed to be in the context of clothing. John wasn't ready to accept Charlie's thoughts about Marginals ... but some sort of group could be involved.

John remembered the little huddle of people holding banners when he came out of the court several months earlier. Maybe Robert was one of them? That seemed more plausible ... but then, that would suggest that the note was unlikely to be a hoax ... but if it wasn't a hoax why hadn't the person put their full name and address? John felt he was going in circles. Against his better judgement he found himself thinking that the only way to get answers was to go to the Causeway Cafe.

*

The Reverend Somes entered Steph's cell - her face beaming. As Prison Chaplain she visited all the prisoners - unless they specifically said that they did not want to be visited. Owing to the number of prisoners however, and her other duties, the Reverend's visits were infrequent and this was only her second visit to Steph.

"Hello Steph - it's been a while. I really wish I could get to see people more often. Have you heard from John recently? How are the kids?"

132

Steph smiled. She realised that the Reverend was a professional, and had probably looked at some notes to remind her of Steph's details ... but it was good that she had taken the trouble to do so, and asked about John by name.

"Yes, judging by his last letter they are all fine, thanks. And I think that you had just got a kitten last time we spoke ...?" Steph didn't need notes. She didn't get visitors so remembering her previous conversation with the Reverend was simple.

"Haha --- bigger every day. I hated leaving her in the morning ... but she's lovely to cuddle up with in the evening ... when she's of a mind that is! She's like you Steph ... very independent. You're still wearing the dress I see."

That was good, thought Steph, *from kitten to my dress in a single breath*. "Yes, indeed. Maybe I am a reincarnated cat."

"Tell me again why you won't take it off Steph," continued the Reverend Somes with a slight smile (the only acknowledgement of Steph's quip).

"There is nothing wrong with it. It harms no-one. It is my choice and nobody should interfere with it. Surely the question is, why *should* I take it off ... just because the 'big bully' says that if I don't he will keep me locked up? Is that the way we should behave Reverend? Do what we are told because it will hurt us if we don't? Abandon conscience and truth for expediency and comfort?"

"Not at all Steph. I respect you greatly for following your conscience ... but you must think of others ... be considerate to their wishes. What you do upsets people. I'm sure that you don't want to do that."

"If they are upset at something that isn't intrinsically upsetting, then that is a problem for them to address. It is not for me to go against my conscience - my truth - in order to resolve a problem that they create for themselves. You don't look particularly upset by being in here with me, so why should anyone else be upset?"

"There are differences aren't there Steph? Differences between me as Prison Chaplain coming to a cell where I know I will find, 'The Lady in the Red Dress' and someone coming across you unexpectedly in the street - maybe with children."

At the mention of children Steph could feel her hackles rise. Why did people always seem to take it as unquestionable that children would be upset ... even damaged in some way ... by seeing her in a dress? She would not rise to the bait.

"Differences?" queried Steph, deciding that her best tactic was to let the good Reverend keep talking. It would be interesting to see how she dealt with the dilemma of accepting the goodness of an individual remaining true to their conscience while promoting the 'party line' of conformity - an irrational conformity in Steph's view.

"Well, as I said, Steph - expectation. We all know, from history, that the abandonment of clothes was a rational development. The primary reason for wearing clothes was to hide things ... this was most evident in the period of Terrorism when clothes concealed weapons and bombs ... especially bombs for suicide attacks. If you have nothing to hide, then you have no need for clothes. When people see you in your dress their reaction is one of anxiety ... 'what is she hiding?' ... they think."

"Oh, come on!" said Steph standing up and twirling round, "there's nothing to it. It doesn't even have sleeves. What can I hide under this?"

"Well, that's what you say Steph ... but I don't think people react or think rationally when they are shocked or surprised. Then there are also the moral arguments."

Here we go, thought Steph.

"Clothes weren't just used to hide bombs. The essence of clothes is concealment of reality - deception - and through that deception an immoral manipulation of power. Clothes could be used to assert authority - even by their design. Those in power would have suits with big shoulder pads to make them look physically strong, even if the body underneath was weak. Clothes could be used to maintain dominance - while nudity increased vulnerability. Clothes could be used to allure and tempt, to emphasise sexuality - concealment to entice and excite with the anticipation of hidden pleasures ... pleasures to be desired ... but withheld beneath the clothes until the wearer chose to reveal. Withholding that which is desired gives the withholder power. So, power and concealment go hand-in-hand Steph, whether it be sexual power or social power. Surely you can see that? Through the abandonment of clothes – and makeup don't forget - through that abandonment and through the honest and open portrayal of ourselves for what we are, we have removed all that ... and here, in many people's eyes, are you trying to bring back that wickedness of concealment and deception. The reason we have BodPride, and legislation that safeguards against body shame, all stems from this."

Steph pictured the pushchair group of name-calling women and found it difficult to imagine them having a train of reasoning like the good Reverend - not that she thought the Reverend was making much sense.

"Don't get me wrong Steph," continued Reverend Somes. "I am not suggesting that you have deep desires for concealment and manipulation of power ... but all I'm saying is - think of how others see it, and show a bit of consideration."

"You're right, Reverend. I don't have desires for concealment or manipulation of power ... and I don't think that my little dress could achieve that. I just like wearing my dress ... and since I don't have any ulterior motive, and am not directly harming anyone ... I don't see why I can't be left alone."

The Reverend looked at Steph as if deciding where to take her argument next ... or even whether to continue it at all.

"The thing is Steph, people, even the most tolerant, can't understand why you are doing what you are doing. There seems no need for it and so they see it as perverse ... perverted even. Everyone knows that there are people who enjoy dressing ... and they *do* dress - sometimes alone and sometimes as members of a group. They do this in private however. You, on the other hand, seem to want to parade yourself in public ... and that upsets people, and they don't like it."

"But if I do it just in private ... as I used to by the way ... then it means that I am ashamed of it ... and there is nothing to be ashamed of, so that is why I do it in public."

"Yes, but..."

"..and I don't 'parade'," interjected Steph, "I simply go about my business like anyone else."

"Yes, maybe that was the wrong word," conceded the Reverend apologetically, "but it is the way that people see it, I think ... simply because they can't see a rational explanation for what you are doing. In the past people needed clothes ... especially in this region ... to keep warm and there are occupations today and places today where clothes are worn because they are essential - but seeing you in the middle of the street wearing a dress, when there is no obvious need for it, makes people suspicious and uncomfortable. 'What is this woman about? What are her motives?' ... they ask themselves ... and conclude the worst."

Steph was both amused and irritated by the way that the Reverend considered that she could see inside other people's heads and know their thoughts. Was it divine revelation?

"Maybe you should advise the courts to sentence me to hard labour in the unprotected Arctic regions beyond the margin," suggested Steph with a smile to lighten the mood. "That would be ironic wouldn't it? ... wearing the dress ... but under *more* clothes!"

"I doubt I will be able to influence the court ... and I certainly wouldn't be suggesting that if I could!" chuckled the Reverend as she stood up. "Well, I better be off. Have a think about what I said Steph." With that and a smile, she left.

*

The Causeway Cafe was a busy and very public place, so John did not feel that he would be in any immediate danger by going there to meet this person, Robert. Nevertheless, he felt uneasy given the unanswered questions in his head. He felt his best guess, regarding Robert and his, 'group of like minded people', was that they were simply a club that met privately to wear clothes. John had never given much thought to these groups, not even when Steph started to wear the dress. He didn't know what sort of people attended them and it was only on Saturday morning, minutes before he set off for his rendezvous, that it occurred to him that he should find something out about such people. He hadn't left himself much time, but he did an internet search on clothes wearing groups and found that the generic term for them was 'textilists'. He skimmed the key points in the *Truepedia* entry. These read as follows:

Textilists:

This is a generic term for a diverse group of people who have a preference for wearing clothes.

Textilism is a cultural and political movement practicing, advocating and defending the social wearing of clothes, most but not all of which takes place on private property.

People interested in the social wearing of clothes can attend designated clothe-wearing areas and other types of ad-hoc clothed events. At these venues, participants generally need not belong to a textilist club.

The section on 'textilist ideals' caught John's eye.

It is generally agreed by textilist organisations that eroticism and blatant sexuality have no place in textilism. Fundamental principles cited by textilists for wearing clothes include:

Spirituality — man is more than an animal and clothes emphasise this fact

Equality — nudity builds social barriers. Social wearing of clothes leads to acceptance in spite of differences in age, body shape, fitness, and health.

Liberty — no one has the right to tell others or their children that they must be naked.

Truepedia also identified the following arguments against wearing clothes:

- there is no justification other than body protection - such as in cold situations;

- covering bodies encourages the idea of shame: - some bodies should not be seen because they are ugly; some body parts should not be seen because they are private

- wearing clothes is unnatural - it is against the laws of nature,

- wearing clothes is a 'throw back' to less educated, less enlightened times

- wearing clothes is dishonest and deceptive because it hides or encourages hiding of the true self

- the wearing of clothes encourages deviant sexuality by making bodies secrets to be hidden or withheld on the one hand and sought out unnaturally on the other.

John felt more comfortable with these final points. They made sense to him. Being naked *was* normal, and these reasons for remaining naked corresponded with his thinking on the subject. He checked the time … probably just long enough to look at something on the Marginals before he left. Although he wasn't convinced by what Charlie had said he thought he would look at the *Truepedia* entry - if only to convince himself that 'Robert' was not one! John quickly scanned the *Truepedia* summary so allowing himself sufficient time to get to the cafe. It read:

The Marginals:

This term refers to a group of people who continued to exist outside the revised political and religious unification that took place following The Terror Wars. It is generally accepted that they were members of breakaway terrorist groups who fled the unified forces, and who went into hiding in the inhabitable fringe beyond the borders of the Unified Territories. This fringe area or 'margin' consists of a belt of as little as five miles in some places and probably a maximum of about 100 in others. There are also some inhabitable 'patches' that do not directly abut the unified territories of Trueway but exist as 'islands' in the broader area outside Trueway sometimes referred to as The Outlands. In the immediate post-War period there were occasional skirmishes in the margins as Unity forces flushed out and neutralised any remaining terrorist pockets. It is thought that the term 'Marginals' first came into play at this time as a single designation for these, often geographically and frequently politically and religiously, diverse terrorist elements.

Feeling that he had now done all he could to prepare himself for his encounter, John set off.

*

The Causeway Cafe was buzzing ... as it usually was. It was named after its location on a stretch of pavement called *The Causeway* which, in years gone by, had been a walkway affording safe passage through the marshy ground adjacent to the river that ran through the town. Now it was a pedestrian area with bric-a-brac shops, art galleries and bars. John did not feel comfortable here ... but neither did he feel threatened. It was a 'Bohemian' area ... possibly considered 'avant-garde' ... but not 'dangerous'. There were lots of young people around ... chatting, vaping, laughing -- making a controlled noise -- which again made John feel a little out of place. It reminded him of his student days. He felt that he had moved on a long way in life, since then.... and he didn't really belong here anymore. For some reason it seemed to him that Robert wouldn't belong here either. John had expected that he would need to leave it to the mysterious note writer to identify himself but it wasn't necessary. No sooner had John entered the cafe than he saw a middle aged man wearing a hat and a silk scarf round his neck. *What clearer sign could someone give that they were a textilist?* thought John, as he walked across the cafe.

Before John reached the man however, he was intercepted.

"John," said a young man hurrying towards him and extending his hand in greeting, "I'm so glad you came. I was afraid that you wouldn't. I'm over here in the corner," and he pointed towards a table where a young woman sat sipping a coffee from a tall glass. She stood as they approached. "This is Lisa," said the young man, motioning John to take a seat. "Can I get you a coffee or something?"

"Yes, thanks ... black, please ... thanks." John took a disposable towel from the dispenser, sat down and smiled somewhat nervously at Lisa.

"Have you heard anything recently from Steph?" asked the girl.

"No, not for a while," answered John, feeling a little irritated that this girl, who he didn't know, was asking him about correspondence with his wife as if they were all old friends.

"How do you know Steph?" asked John.

"Oh, only through Rob," smiled Lisa. "He writes to her, and tells me what she writes back."

"I was surprised to get his note, and to learn that he and my wife had been corresponding. She hadn't said anything."

"Well, your wife is becoming quite well known. I suppose a few people have written to her. She seems very courageous - very principled - and I think people ... well, some people ... admire that."

"Yes, Robert talked about, 'like minded people'. I guess you're one of the people he was talking about?"

"Well, I suppose," smiled the girl, "but you had better ask him." On that cue the young man reappeared at John's side with a cup of black coffee. John thought he looked to be in his twenties, with skin colour and facial features that suggested maybe Arabic or Jewish heritage – though the man's blue eyes hinted at a more complex ancestry. Lisa smiled up at Robert. "John was just asking about the 'like minded people' that you mentioned in your note to him. He wondered whether I was one of them ... I advised him to ask you."

"Haha - yes, like minded, I have no doubt," he smiled back. "So, anything recently from your wife, John?"

"No, I was just saying to your friend here ... to Lisa ... that I hadn't had anything from her for a little while. How long have *you* been writing to her ... and what was the last thing you received? Has she said anything in response to the offer that you mentioned in your note ... to come and stay with you when she's released?"

"I've written to her three or four times and had a couple of letters back - but not one since I wrote and offered her a place to stay. I hope that she will accept. Of course, the point of inviting you here today was to get your thoughts on *that* but obviously, you would be very, very welcome to come over as well, if it was something you would like to do."

"Well, with due respect," said John holding up his hand as if to stop traffic, "can we slow things down a bit please? Who exactly are you? I don't know the first thing about you and yet you are inviting my wife and myself to your house to stay. You also say she will be with 'like minded people' - whatever that means, so ... who exactly are you, Robert and who are the people you are talking about?"

"Of course John, of course. I have been going way too fast, and haven't been at all considerate. I apologise. My name is Robert Cray. I work for a firm of engineers - Colman's - if you have heard of them? And I have a property the other side of Fordington. Day to day I am as you see me now, but at home I wear clothes and frequently have friends round ... maybe for a meal ... and we enjoy dressing for dinner and relaxing together in that way. We sometimes have themed evenings and dress to a particular period ... but usually it is just casual clothes. Some may be genuine, old items - possibly passed down through a person's family, while others are modern copies."

"A couple of people in particular are good at the latter," interjected Lisa, "they have sewing machines and have scoured antique shops and places for patterns. Some of the stuff they make is really nice."

"So, would you describe yourselves as 'textilists'?" ventured John.

The couple looked at each other, with what John interpreted as a conceited smile that said, "Oh these conventional people, always wanting to put us in a box." He was therefore taken aback when Lisa gave a very forthright answer.

"In a word, 'yes'. The thing is that when you give a group a name, people somehow forget the variation that can occur within that grouping. We know that there is a group of animals called 'dogs'. The range of shapes, sizes and colours of the animals we call 'dogs' does not surprise us because we are familiar with them. We know them well. For things with which we are less familiar we somehow forget that variation can occur and assume homogeneity. Did you notice that man with the hat and scarf when you came in? You seemed to be heading in his direction."

"Yes," John nodded, "I thought ..."

"You thought, 'he's wearing something'," continued Lisa, "so he must be the person I have come to meet ... he must be a 'textilist'. Yes?" Lisa smiled. "But here are the three of us sitting chatting, and to an outside observer we are indistinguishable. There is no indication which of us is, or is not a 'textilist'. For all I know, John - you may be one." Lisa smiled broadly.

"I'm glad that Lisa mentioned the man that you spotted when you first came in. I could see that you were heading in his direction and I wanted to intercept you before you got there ... not just to avoid the mistake, but because that man is a good illustration of the variation that can occur within a single label. I've explained how Lisa, myself and our friends enjoy meeting and dressing. It's very much a social thing ... almost a hobby. In fact, for some, it probably could be described as a hobby ... Janet and Tom who do the sewing?" He directed his question at Lisa who nodded her confirmation. "But that man, the one you were approaching, sees it much more as a political thing - human rights and that kind of stuff. He wears small things in public, like the hat, to make a statement. He sticks to places like this though, where he knows that he won't ruffle too many feathers ... if any. Do you regard Steph as a 'textilist' John?"

John had not been ready for the question and realised, to his surprise, that he had not thought about it. Steph was Steph - his wife - she wasn't someone he needed to categorise. "Well, I guess it's like you say, people are different. I could ask you the same question, whether you regard her as such. I don't think she is like the man in the scarf and hat ... but I am not sure that she is like you and your friends ... well, as far as you have described them and yourselves." John realised he still had only the most general idea of how Robert, Lisa and their friends spent their time ... whether dressed or normal. "I think the red dress, and her insistence on wearing it, is very personal to Steph. I don't think she has a political agenda ... but neither do I think she is interested in wearing clothes for social evenings as you have described."

John felt a certain dislike in discussing his wife with these two strangers, and in trying to 'explain' her to them ... particularly since he didn't fully understand what she was doing himself. Maybe he felt a little anxiety verging on jealousy too ... a sense that they, as clothes wearers, had a link to Steph that he did not ... even if he was convinced that they did not understand her, and what was driving her, any more clearly than he did. "When you have written to my wife have you described the sort of clothes wearing that you do - talked about having friends round - eating and such?"

"Oh yes, I've mentioned it and described the place and the space that we have ... basically told her that she would be free to dress, undress and go about her business as she wished. There would be no compulsion to join in with any 'social' type events if she didn't want to."

"Well," interjected John, "I'm not convinced that it will appeal to her at all ... but I guess we will have to wait and see what she says when she gets back to you." John had nearly finished his coffee and was feeling that he would like to terminate the meeting pretty soon.

"So, would you like to come out and see the place, John?" ventured Lisa. "Just to see what it's like?" John thought Lisa sounded like a kindly matron trying to encourage someone to visit a care home for an elderly parent.

"Maybe - but let's see what Steph says first," suggested John. He pushed his coffee cup forward on the table and moved his chair back. "Thank you for the coffee," he said looking at Robert and preparing to stand but the latter looked back at him and made as if to speak, but paused. John looked at him quizzically.

"We said that there are different people under the term 'Textilists'," said Lisa, as if to help the situation. "I think Rob has some concerns for your wife."

"Concerns?" queried John looking at Robert, "concerns about what?"

"Well, as Lisa says, there are different groups of people who you might put under the label 'textilists'."

"Yes, we've established that," interjected John. "We have spent most of our time sitting here talking about it." John did not try to hide his irritation. "If your main reason for inviting me here was to talk about some concerns that you have for my wife then I would like you to get to the point." He looked intently at Robert.

"OK," came the resolute response. "You were in court for your wife's last trial, weren't you? John gave a small nod of acknowledgement. "Something unusual happened in the public gallery didn't it, John?"

"You mean the noise?"

"Yes, that and the leaflets in the shape of a dress ... and the fact that there were so many people there at all. Didn't you find all that strange, John?" There was no pause for an answer. "The people that came and left those leaflets and that made that strange noise were, for want of a better word, 'textilists' ... but they were not 'textilists' in the sense that Lisa and I are 'textilists' ... or indeed in the sense that the man in the hat and scarf is a 'textilist'. These people use the freedom within the current laws to meet and dress and behave in similar ways to people like Lisa and myself but they have a more fundamental political agenda, and probably more dangerously, a religious agenda. The 'textilist' label is a convenient one for them. It is a worrying use of the label for people like Lisa and me. The authorities have no concern really about a group of people sitting round sewing clothes and playing, 'let's dress for dinner'. They do have concerns about a group that might cause unrest. The people that were in the public gallery at your wife's trial are such a group. The authorities try to watch them - when they can identify them ... but how do you tell one of them from someone like me or Lisa? We are all this homogeneous group known as 'textilists' and, as such, we are all as dangerous and all in need of surveillance and distrust."

"And Steph...?" queried John. "Are you saying that Steph - locked in prison as she is - is in danger from this group in some way?"

"Not directly from the group - no, but if the authorities think that she is associated with the group then yes, I think that she may be."

John was silent. He looked at his coffee cup rather than either of his coffee companions. John's natural trust in law, justice and authority had been seriously damaged by what he had witnessed in his wife's treatment by the courts, and even by his son's treatment by the school, but what was being suggested to him now was that the authorities may, in some way, penalise his wife because of a suspected association with a group she knew nothing about. This seemed too incredulous. John looked at Robert and Lisa and wondered exactly who they were. He still felt he did not really know. He didn't trust them, even though they seemed to be wanting to help his wife. John wondered exactly what sort of danger these two people thought Steph might face, but instead of asking that question, the words that almost involuntarily came from his lips were:

"Why can't the authorities tell one lot of people from another? Surely they will know who was in the public gallery and whether one of you was in that public gallery or not. I assume they scan biodata when people come in and go out. In fact, you seem to know a lot about what happened so maybe I should ask you whether you were there. Were you?"

"We weren't there John, though we had direct feedback from someone who was," said Lisa, "And don't assume that biodata will always give accurate information on who is who, where they go and what they d..."

"What Lisa is saying John is that this group is devious," cut in Robert with what John fleetingly thought was a nervous glance at Lisa. "Anyway John, the key point we are trying to make is that we *do* think that your wife may be in some danger, and maybe that if you came out to our place, you could get to know us better and we could explain more fully." He took a piece of paper from his pouch. "Here, this is my phone number. Give me a ring and we can find a time when you could come over ... and maybe then you could talk to your wife about things. I just feel that if she were a little more co-operative with the authorities she could have the opportunity to come and join us for a while the next time she is released. I think it would be of benefit to her - help her see the bigger picture."

"Well, at the moment she has quite a long prison term," said John, "so it will be a while."

"But you could come, John," encouraged Lisa.

"And your wife may even lodge a successful appeal against her current sentence," added Robert. John had thought about the possibility of an appeal and determined to mention it in his next letter to Steph. For now, he felt he had heard enough from his coffee companions.

"Well, I would certainly like to see my wife out of prison ... so I will write to her about an appeal. Regarding your offer ... I will think about it ... and like I say, write to her and get her thoughts." With that, John stood, shook hands, thanked them again for the coffee and left.

*

"Do you think he will ring?" asked Lisa once John had gone.

"I don't know. I am not good at falsehoods am I, Lisa? It's difficult, pretending to know about a group of people who are putting Steph in danger, when I don't know who they are myself. I don't think I was very convincing."

*

Charlie listened as John read him the note from Robert and gave an account of the meeting that had taken place at the Causeway Cafe.

"What do you make of it, Charlie?"

"Don't suppose you have had chance yet to ask Steph if she knows this Robert, and the girl, Lisa?"

"I've written to her, sent her a copy of the note and explained what happened at the cafe. There hasn't been time for me to get anything back from her yet. I felt a bit stupid, because the one thing I didn't ask the two of them, was exactly what danger they thought Steph was in ... the obvious question really ... but, well I was busy puzzling about stuff. I have obviously asked Steph to confirm that she has been corresponding with this man, and if she has, whether he has said anything to her about her being in danger. I've asked her what she thinks of this offer of his ... to go and stay at his place."

"Well, I've been feeling uneasy about Steph - and this whole business of the note and the cafe meeting doesn't make me feel any better, John."

"What's your gut feeling, Charlie? Do you think I should trust them?"

"I don't know if you should trust them, John ... but I don't think you should ignore them. I think you were right to go to the café. I'm not sure about a visit to the house though. Maybe wait 'til you get something back from Steph. I don't know that there is much point in doing anything 'til you know where she stands on all this."

John was rather relieved by Charlie's counsel. He had felt reluctant to make further contact with Robert, and had been thinking that he would wait and see what Steph said. It was therefore good to hear that Charlie was of the same opinion.

*

It was two weeks before John received a letter from Steph.

Yes, I have had a few letters from a man called Robert Cray. It was interesting to read your description of him. I had pictured him as older than you describe. The copy of the note was interesting too. It's the first time I've seen his handwriting. Everything he writes to me is word processed and he just initials it 'RC'. He has said that he has a house and that I would be welcome to stay there for as long or as short a period as I wanted and that he has several friends that dress in private ... seems they have quite a wardrobe between them. It was a nice offer and I have been polite in my letters back to him but not committed one way or another. He hasn't been pushy in any way and certainly hasn't said anything to suggest that he thinks I am in any imminent danger. I didn't mention anything to you in earlier letters because I wasn't really intending taking up his offer - certainly not until after I had come home. I suppose then it might make an interesting visit, but I hadn't contemplated staying there. I don't see the point really. I don't really have any interest in dressing for social reasons. I have explained in my letter to him ... or at least tried to explain ... that wearing the dress is about freedom and not about a need to enjoy clothes or socialise in them. I wasn't sure that he would understand what I was on about, and the fact that he has written that note to you just confirms that he hasn't grasped what I am saying. If you are curious and wanted to go and see the place then obviously you can do ... but not really with a view to me going there to stay.

Did he say anything to you about what danger he thought I was in? Like I said, he hasn't said anything in his letters to me - but that might just be him being circumspect because he knows that all correspondence (in and out) gets opened and read by the prison authorities.

The rest of Steph's letter contained the usual talk and questions about the things of life. How were the children? What else had John been doing? Was John well? She had had a bit of a cold. The food she had been eating. What she had been reading, and so on. She said nothing about her plans for when she was released. The date was almost certainly still some way off but John assumed that she would be determined to leave prison wearing her dress, as she had done before. If she did that, then he feared the obvious consequence would be immediate re-arrest. Even if there was no immediate danger to Steph in the short term, there was clearly a long term danger ... life imprisonment! Then, at the end of the letter - almost as an afterthought it seemed, she added:

Oh I should also say - while we are on the subject of people writing to me (which we were earlier in this letter) - that a barrister called Mark Welsh wrote to me offering to draft papers seeking leave to appeal against the last conviction on the grounds that it is unsafe because I was not allowed to represent myself. He said he is so incensed by what is happening that he is willing to do it for free. Imagine that!! A barrister offering to work for free!! I wrote back to him and said 'go ahead'!!! I'm now waiting to hear from him again. I expect he will come to see me - hopefully with a draft of what he has written. I'll keep you up to speed with how things go on that front.

She then signed off. John immediately checked on-line for information about 'Mark Welsh'. There was indeed a barrister by that name. What John read impressed him. Mark Welsh had a practice based in the capital, he had a good reputation and had been involved in a number of high profile cases. He wrote about law issues in a respected newspaper. But what stood out to John were the references suggesting that Mark Welsh had a strong sense of justice and was recognised for defending people who were not wealthy if he felt their cause was just. Assuming that it was the same Mark Welsh, then Steph seemed to have obtained support from a very useful ally. *At last*, thought John, *we might be able to find a way out of this nightmare.*

*

In the days that followed this letter from Steph, John relaxed more than he had in quite some time. He told Charlie about Mark Welsh.

Charlie knew the man by reputation and Charlie, like John, seemed to relax more, now that he knew Steph was not fighting her battle alone. Given all that Steph had said in her letter, John decided not to make any further contact with Robert.

Life in the Hugo household went on as usual. John had not told Tim and May about the meeting with Robert and Lisa. He hadn't said anything about Charlie's concerns either. He told them about Mark Welsh and the possibility of an appeal against their mother's conviction. Naturally, this pleased them as much as it had pleased him. Both children continued to do well at school. Tim had made a few friends and both he and May now travelled to and from school by themselves. With the children now quite independent, John no longer required any special arrangements from his employer and he was able to concentrate fully on his work. Barring Steph's continued imprisonment, things again felt reasonably 'normal' to John and in April and May first Tim and then his sister enjoyed their birthday celebrations. This general good mood was boosted further when John received a letter from Steph saying that Mark Welsh had been granted leave to appeal. This meant that a senior judge considered that there was sufficient concern about Steph's conviction to warrant a full hearing at the Court of Appeal.

Charlie counselled John not to get too excited. The fact that an appeal was going to be heard did not mean that it would be won ... though even sceptical Charlie admitted that it was very positive news. He also told John it was likely to be at least six months before the appeal was heard. John was disappointed, but not surprised by this news. He was also annoyed. If his wife's conviction was quashed and she was released, then who was going to give her back those six months? John fleetingly wondered about the possibility of compensation for wrong conviction, but the thought of more legal battling made him shudder. He just wanted the whole business of the dress and prison to come to an end. The first point where that could possibly happen was the appeal hearing, so John accepted that he just had to settle down and wait six months. What John did not know was that events were going to take place in those six months that would have far reaching implications for everyone, and profound consequences for Steph.

Chapter 14: John in Hospital and the Green Court of Appeal

World peace was a great achievement - possibly the greatest achievement - of the Terror Wars. For the first time in the history of humans there was no international conflict. There was no 'international'. There were no nations. Under Trueway, there was but one humanity. Under Trueway everyone was a Citizen and every Citizen had equal opportunity and equal access to health care, social care and education. Some may be more able, some may be more wealthy, some may be more powerful – but that was the perpetual way of nature. It was the way of The Great Spirit.

If pressed, politicians would accept that, beyond the border of Trueway, there were The Outlands, and within them, a scattering of non-Citizens known as Marginals. If pressed, politicians would say that these Marginals were nothing more than the inconsequential remnants of terrorists defeated in The Terror Wars. If pressed, politicians would admit that there was occasional unrest here or there.

Everyday Citizens were familiar with the periodic news report of some conflict - some 'troubles' - but it was nothing major and was soon quelled. Such troubles might be attributed to an incursion by Marginals or some disgruntled, misguided or deviant faction of Citizens. Nature inevitably produced such variants of humanity - and they undoubtedly had their place in the plan of The Great Spirit. The regular police in the location of any such trouble was generally more than adequate to address the situation but there was also a small military presence across the globe that could be called upon if necessary.

The Trueway Armed Forces spent the majority of their time doing exercises so that they would be ready for any conflict should it arise. There were, however, regular debates about the appropriate size of the military and periodic debates about the necessity of maintaining a military at all.

Military and police personnel were naked like other Citizens, unless in a situation that necessitated clothing, such as for protection or carrying equipment. Crime and conflict, although probably more frequent than reported in the media, were nevertheless not a major threat to most Trueway Citizens. There was certainly no need for the police or military to be dressed and armed in readiness at all times. The police in particular acted more as *Citizen Helpers* than enforcers of law, and identified themselves simply through a hat, arm band or bag with insignia. In the event of an emergency requiring clothing and equipment, officers on the beat were able to obtain these quickly from 'pods' that were located on just about every street corner in large towns and cities.

The pods were regularly checked and maintained, but were rarely used for their intended purpose – that is, until the major troubles started.

The attacks generally took the form of explosions, often targeting Trueway government buildings or temples. At first their linked and co-ordinated nature was unclear - a temple attacked in a northern town one day then a government building in an eastern town a week later. Only when the frequency increased did the World Government accept that there was a concerted offensive by some group, or linked groups, against Trueway or some aspect of it.

John, very much like most other people, took little notice at first. He remembered the bomb at the temple earlier that year and how that incident had quickly disappeared from the media. Many people played down the new "wave" of bombings as an exaggeration, created by a news-starved media inflating the usual minor troubles that occurred everywhere. Unlike the earlier bomb, none of the recent explosions had occurred anywhere near where John lived. This contributed to the ease with which he was able to ignore them. The fact that nobody was able to identify who was behind the bombings and what purpose they had, contributed to the speculation that they were contrived by the press.

"Have you noticed the number of police wearing clothes?" asked one of John's colleagues at work with indignation. "Any excuse. It's not as if there were any bombs going off round here ... assuming they really are bombs anyway."

"Well, I feel sorry for them," said John, "that gear looks very hot and uncomfortable. Anyway, I guess it will all die down soon." He was wrong.

*

John found himself counting the lights on the ceiling as he was hurried along the hospital corridor on his back with a drip attached to his arm. The blast had flung him to the ground and he had been showered with debris. He didn't remember that however. It was only later that it was explained to him that a bomb had exploded across the street from where he had been walking.

"Eighteen, nineteen...," John didn't know why he was counting the lights. He was still dazed and wasn't even fully sure of where he was. He was turned into a room, and the bed that he was on, came to a halt. People in white aprons were around him. Nurses and doctors he guessed. He was told he was in hospital. He was told that he had been in an accident. He was asked whether he remembered. He was asked if he had any pain. He was asked to move arms, legs. He was asked if he knew his name, his date of birth. Suddenly, with urgency the fog cleared ... "Tim, May ... where are they?" He began to get up only to be gently prevented with calming words. Tim and May had been at school. They had been contacted to say their father had been in an accident but was thought to be OK. They were here, in the hospital, and he would be able to see them shortly.

The doctors were satisfied that John had no immediate life threatening injuries. He was advised that he was to remain in hospital overnight, and that they would carry out some scans and further tests, before deciding whether he was fit to return home. He was left with a nurse who began to clean the superficial wounds he had sustained from flying debris. While she did this she told John more about the incident. There had been an explosion at the Trueway temple close to John's office. There had been very few people about and only John and one other had been injured. There was no confirmation yet of what had caused the explosion but speculation was that it was a bomb, similar to those that had been used to target Trueway establishments across the globe.

John listened. "And Tim and May ... my children ... they're here? They weren't with me when it exploded?"

"No, they were at school. They are with one of our social work team at the moment. As soon as I have finished cleaning you up we will bring them in." She applied a dressing to a wound on John's chest and cleaned a few more on his right side. Can you roll onto your left side?" requested the nurse indicating which way she wanted John to turn. She dabbed at a few places but then had him return to his supine position. "You seem to have taken most of the blast on your right side. This cut on your chest appears the deepest." She indicated the one onto which she had put the dressing. "The bandage on that will need changing every twenty-four hours, for a couple of days. I've cleaned the rest. As long as they are kept clean, then I don't think there is a need for any dressing."

The nurse went and stood about half way down the bed so that John could see her clearly rather than sideways on. "How do you feel in yourself?" she asked as she took off her paper apron and scrunched it up to put in the bin.

"A bit bewildered I think ... but OK. I don't remember it. I feel a bit sore."

"Any headache?"

"No. A bit muzzy, maybe ... but that's all."

"Do you want any pain killers?"

"No, it's just a stinging feeling where you have been dabbing and dressing the cuts. I'm OK. I would just like to see Tim and May now though. What's going to happen if I have to stay in here?"

"You can discuss all that with the social worker. He will help sort those things out. You won't have anything to worry about." She gave John a reassuring smile. "John ...?" she said, with a slightly puzzled frown.

"Yes?"

"Hold your hands out in front of you."

John had thought all the immediate tests had been done, but did as requested.

"You've been like that since you were admitted - since you were caught in the blast possibly."

John looked at his hands. His left hand was open but his right hand was a fist - clenched shut.

"Nobody noticed at first," continued the nurse, "All the tests seemed OK so the doctors advised to ignore it until you were fully conscious, and then see whether you were able to open your hand voluntarily."

John looked at his right hand. He gradually uncurled his fingers. There was no pain or difficulty. In the palm of his had lay a piece of crumpled red paper.

"May I?" asked the nurse, looking at the shapeless mass in John's hand.

"Of course," said John, as much mystified as the nurse. She took the piece of paper and carefully flattened it out as best she could. The paper was in the shape of a small, red dress - exactly like the ones that had been left on the seats in the public gallery of the court room.

*

After seeing their father, May and Tim were allowed to return home. John gave his consent for the social worker to remain with the children at the family house overnight, rather than have them looked after in temporary foster care. John was discharged the following day and there was no need for further social services involvement. Apart from anything else the incident brought home to John how insular he was in many ways. The only neighbour he talked to (beyond 'good morning' and such like) was Charlie, and he had no close relatives nearby with whom May and Tim could have stayed had it been necessary.

When John got home the children had already gone to school so he went round to Charlie's place. He was greeted by the welcoming smell of coffee, and there were two mugs on the kitchen work surface as if Charlie was expecting him.

"You must have a sixth sense Charlie ... or are you going to tell me you were just making coffee for yourself anyway?"

Charlie smiled. "You're quite right John ... all us blind people have a sixth sense. It's called *awareness.*" He chuckled. "So, how're you feeling? I heard about the blast, but it wasn't 'til the social worker came back with May and Tim, that I learned that you were one of the people directly caught up in it."

"I have a few cuts and bruises - but nothing serious," said John as he sat down with the coffee that Charlie had poured. "There's a cut on my chest from flying debris. The dressing on that will need changing each day for a while – but May will be able to help with that. Otherwise just minor scratches, so I guess I got off lightly. I don't actually remember the blast but at some point I ended up with a piece of paper clutched in my hand. I didn't let go of it 'til I was with the nurse dressing my wounds." He placed the cut out paper dress into Charlie's hand. "As you can feel Charlie, it's exactly the same as the ones left in the public gallery at the court. It's red as well."

"No words?" queried Charlie. "I can't feel anything ... but it is pretty crumpled."

"No, no words on it that I could see. I don't know exactly where it came from. I don't remember picking it up. I was pretty dazed."

"Sounds like you haven't heard, or watched the news either John." It was true, despite having been involved in an incident that would have attracted media attention, John realised that he had not looked at a news paper, listened to a radio, watched television or streamed any news whatsoever since being admitted to hospital. "Several red paper dresses - I guess like this one - were found in the vicinity of the blast," explained Charlie. "What's more, it's emerging that similar cut-outs have been found in association with other blasts, in other parts of the world."

"Really? I don't recall reading or hearing anything about that before."

"No, neither do I," mused Charlie. "The reports of the earlier blasts were not very detailed - maybe that's the reason. Maybe the media thought these were the usual isolated incidents, and just gave them the standard coverage. I don't know the reason, but things are changing. People are asking questions. It doesn't seem to be going away like usual and I think people are getting worried."

"Why a red dress Charlie? Is it just coincidence that it's like the ones left at the court? These bombings can have nothing to do with Steph."

"I don't think that they have anything to do with her - but something is going on. I don't know whether the media aren't reporting stuff, or the authorities aren't releasing information, or the people behind these incidents are simply not identifying who they are, and what they are about. Maybe it's simply that - a group that wants to be disruptive and mysterious. Maybe they don't have a purpose. Maybe the red dress is just a good symbol. I can't imagine that many people, beyond those living locally, will have any awareness of Steph or any interest in what she's been doing."

*

"Ooowwww"

"Oh really dad ... it was just a few hairs. It's not my fault if the nurse stuck the plaster over the hairs on your chest ... and you're the one that asked me to help change the dressing." May smiled a wicked daughter's smile. She peeled away the dressing. The wound was quite deep and her amusement subsided with the realisation that things could have been so much worse for her father.

"Does mum know what's happened?" she enquired.

"I intend writing this evening. I don't think anyone from the hospital passed on the information to her, about what happened. I suppose I should have asked. It doesn't really matter. There is nothing she can do ... and I'm basically all right so ..."

"There's stuff in the news about little bits of red paper cut in the shape of a dress," said May. "A friend of Tim's at school even brought one in that he said had come from near where the bomb went off ... said his dad got it. Did you see anything like that?"

"Yes, when I was at the hospital. I had one in my hand. I guess I must have picked it up. Maybe before the bomb went off ... maybe after. I don't remember the blast or what I was doing immediately before. I know I had come out of work for some reason."

"They say these paper dresses have been found at other places where bombs have gone off. It made me think of mum and her red dress."

"Yes, I was discussing that with Charlie earlier today. It's odd ... but purely a coincidence."

"There," said May snipping through a piece of tape and patting it gently down on her father's chest, "and I haven't taped down any hairs."

"That's 'coz you ripped them all off with the last plaster," smiled John with fake indignation. "Thank you 'nurse' ... looks like a good job. Well, you better get ready for bed. I'm going to write to your mother like I said. You can leave the scissors and stuff. I'll deal with that."

May kissed her father's forehead as she got up, "Too kind Papa --- too kind." She looked back at him and smiled as she headed off to the bathroom. She was glad he was all right.

Tim was already in bed and fast asleep, and once John had looked in on May and wished her 'good night', he settled down to write to Steph. He had barely started when there was a loud and insistent knocking on the front door. It was late and John was not expecting anyone. The knocking came again ... demanding in its rapid, loud repetition. He went to the door and looked at the security viewer to see who was outside. There were three people - one woman, naked and two men, both dressed and with police hats and insignia visible.

John had no intercom on the door or security chain so opened it a crack.

"Yes?" he enquired.

"Mr Hugo?" came the response.

"Yes," confirmed John.

An ID card was thrust towards his face.

"I'm Detective Inspector of Police Collins and this is my colleague Sergeant of Police Walton. The lady with us is Mrs Hammond, Senior

Officer in Social Services. May we come in?" John felt pressure on the door pushing it open. "We have a search warrant." The sergeant waved some papers towards John and the door was pushed more firmly as the three stepped forward to enter. John resented the unnecessary forcefulness. He was not a criminal and would willingly let them in, yet now they were creating resentment, as they barged past him into the hallway.

"What's going on? Why are you here?" John's questions were ignored.

"I would be obliged if you would go and sit over there Mr Hugo." The Inspector pointed to an armchair. "Where are your children?"

"In bed ... what is this? Why...?"

"As I said Mr Hugo we have a search warrant. Mrs Hammond, will you go and get the children out of bed please?"

This was too much for John. He moved forward to get between Mrs Hammond and the stairs. The sergeant intercepted him and pushed John backwards, so forcefully that he fell into the armchair.

"Keep an eye on him, Sergeant," said the Inspector. "I wouldn't try anything like that again Mr Hugo. Neither you nor your children will be hurt, but I repeat, I have a warrant and I want all of you in one place. I would therefore be obliged if you would co-operate, and not cause me any more difficulty."

Mrs Hammond, a matronly lady, looked apologetically at John before disappearing upstairs to return moments later with two bewildered young people who immediately ran to their father.

"You're May aren't you?" said the Inspector. May just looked at him and then to her father, but before John could say anything, the Inspector continued. "Will you go and get your phone and any tablet, computer or similar device that you have. If you know where your brother keeps his bring me those as well please." He looked at Tim.

"It's on my bedside cabinet," said Tim.

May did not move but looked at her father.

"Mr Hugo? Please?" requested the Inspector.

"Since you haven't had the courtesy," said John pointedly staring at the officer and then addressing his daughter: "These people are the police and have a warrant to search our house for some reason. You had best go and get your phone and Tim's." May went back upstairs.

"What phones, tablets and computers do you and your wife have, Mr Hugo?" John was escorted to the various locations to retrieve these. All the devices were laid out, and John was given a receipt for each one as they were placed in a box by the Sergeant.

"Thank you, Mr Hugo," said the Inspector as he and his two colleagues prepared to leave. We will check the content of all of the devices. If there is nothing untoward then they will be returned."

"But I need that equipment for work, for emails and all sorts ... so do the kids ... what is all this?"

"I assure you, Mr Hugo that we will be as quick as possible in carrying out our checks."

"I want to know what is going on ... why do you have a warrant and what is all this about?"

"We just need to run checks, and hopefully eliminate you from our enquiries."

With that, all three left with the box of equipment. Tim, May and John stood in silence - a stunned disbelief. John's silence contained anger. May's silence, shock but Tim's silence contained bewilderment as to why the people who had imprisoned his mother for wearing a dress were now invading his house wearing clothes.

*

To John's surprise all the equipment was returned the following day. An unclothed, female officer delivered a box containing everything. She was cordial and unsmiling. She required him to give signed confirmation that everything was returned undamaged, and then she left. Before she did so, John again attempted to establish what had prompted the raid, and what it was they had been looking for, but the police officer said that she was unable to help. She had simply been asked to return the equipment. She suggested that John write to the Chief Constable or to the Head of Homeland Security, if he wanted to pursue matters further. At one time John would already have written, but once he had tested all the devices, and found that they worked, he felt disinclined to spend any more time on the matter. He did however discuss the whole incident with Charlie.

"Do you think they may have done something to the equipment ... you know, planted bugs or spyware in them?" queried John.

"What makes you think they would do that?"

"Well, I don't know. I guess because the stuff came back so quickly."

"Mmmm, possible," mused Charlie, "but it would only take a matter of minutes for them to transfer all the data from your devices onto their own system. They could then investigate at their leisure, and look at it again in the future, so there was no real need for them to keep the hardware a long time. If your anti-virus software has not detected anything, then I guess the only way you could check for some form of malware would be to take the equipment to an expert. Even then it may not be something that would be easily recognisable. I don't really know enough about these things." Charlie paused. "And they didn't give you any indication why they were doing this? What they were looking for?"

John shook his head. He had his suspicions, but didn't want to voice them.

"John?"

"Oh, sorry Charlie - no, no they didn't say anything."

"So, will you write and see if you can find out?" Knowing John, Charlie thought he may write to the Chief Constable, though he himself doubted that this would result in any kind of meaningful answer. Charlie was therefore surprised when John, after a pause said:

"No. I thought about it - but I suspect it would get me nowhere ... and anyway, although I haven't wanted to admit it to myself, I keep coming back to thinking that it is to do with Steph in some way. I think they see her with her red dress, and they see these paper dresses at the bombing scenes, and they think there must be a link. I know there isn't, but it's the only reason I can see why two clothed police officers would suddenly appear at my house to take communication equipment - and be so aggressive about it!"

"Maybe Steph will say something in her next letter," suggested Charlie. "If they suspect her of having anything to do with the bombings, then they will presumably question her."

"Yes, and I'll write and tell her what has happened here. I know they open all the letters, but I don't see any reason why they should sensor or object to us corresponding about it."

"No, they possibly pass on copies to the police anyway. I'm glad she has got the appeal under way, John. The sooner she is out of that place the better. Pity these things all take such a long time."

To John's amazement - and to Charlie's when John told him - the wait for the appeal was not going to be as long as was initially expected. In her next letter to John, Steph explained that her appeal date was being brought forward. Neither she nor her lawyer had been given a reason for this, but instead of a hearing in maybe September or October, it was now going to be in June.

*

John, with Charlie and a few others shuffled into the public gallery of the Appeal Court. This time the room and furnishings were entirely green. It gave John a sense of fresh new growth in Spring; a sense of hope and promise.

John wasn't sure, but he thought one of the people in the public gallery may have been the man with the hat and scarf that he had seen in the Causeway Cafe. If it was him he was fully naked now. There were some notices on the benches (including the ones where John and Charlie were sitting) advising that these particular seats were within view of video cameras. John wasn't sure what video cameras were being referred to, but did notice a large video screen that was visible to the whole court.

As with the other hearings he had attended, John could see an array of official people already busy in the court. He assumed that one of them was his wife's barrister - Mark Welsh. John was in the process of describing to Charlie what he could see, when the video screen lit up - and there was Steph's face. John told Charlie.

"They're not letting her into the court then," said Charlie. "It must be a video link from the prison." Before John could say anything further the usher called for the court to rise and three judges entered and took up their seats. A female judge sat in the centre, and was flanked on either side by male judges. The proceedings started with the briefest explanation of the purpose of the hearing. Steph was asked to confirm who she was, and if she could see and hear the court through the video link. This done, Mr Welsh was asked to present the case on behalf of the appellant.

John was pleased by what he heard. Although there were references to aspects of legislation and legal precedents that meant little to him, the core argument seemed compelling. Mark Welsh made very clear that, in the interest of fairness and justice, the judge in Steph's last trial should not have excluded her from the proceedings.

"The only justifiable reason for exclusion," argued Mark Welsh, when summing up "would have been disruptive behaviour on the part of my client since that would have prevented the court from functioning. Mrs

158

Hugo, however, was not being disruptive in any way, and so she should have been allowed to remain in court and to address the jury. Since the jury was deprived of Mrs Hugo's defence, the conviction is unsound."

In addition to this Mr Welsh argued that if the judge did not like Steph wearing a dress in court, then the judge should have arranged for Mrs Hugo to present her case by video link. Finally, Mark Welsh announced that he was also seeking leave to appeal against the sentence, which he considered to be excessive, for something that actually caused no harm.

When Mark Welsh sat down John felt very positive. Steph appeared to have been listening intently, but John couldn't gauge how she felt about her barrister's performance from her face on the screen. John gave a little wave in the direction of the screen but saw no reaction from Steph. He wasn't sure if she could see him or not.

The case in opposition to the appeal was given by a man who John thought said very little of any substance. He spoke about respect for the court and protection of the jury. He felt that exclusion from the court was necessary and proportionate. John was not impressed and hoped that the three judges would not be impressed either. When the court adjourned for them to make their decision he felt that things had gone well.

The appeal hearing resumed a mere twenty minutes later. The lead judge began by summarising the events of the court hearing in which Steph had been excluded. She then summarised Mr Welsh's arguments and then the arguments in support of Steph having been excluded. To John's dismay she then dismissed Mark Welsh's main argument by reference to the *Behaviour Restriction Order.*

In our judgment, were the Appellant to have appeared clothed in front of the jury it would have been a further breach of the Behaviour Restriction Order and that is the end of the argument. That a court should contemplate concurrence with the commission of a criminal offence during proceedings is a bizarre notion and, without more, fatal to the Appellant's submissions. The suggestion that the judge "ought to have been very slow, in the absence of any disruptive behaviour, to set any conditions about being naked" misses the point. The judge could not with propriety have put herself in the position of agreeing to the commission of a crime. The Behaviour Restriction Order was in place and it prohibited behaviour the applicant sought to legitimise.

John could not believe what he was hearing. He had seen his wife stand in the dock of that court in her red dress. She had been in full view of the court and the public gallery. She had spoken. The *BRO* had not stopped the judge from allowing Steph to do that, so how could it be argued that it had stopped the judge from allowing exactly the same when the jury was there?

John did not pay much attention to the rest of what the lead judge said though he noted the usual passing of blame to his wife - Steph knew that the consequence of refusing to undress would be exclusion from the hearing, so it was *she* who was absenting *herself*.

The appeal was dismissed. The application for review of the sentence was also rejected - Steph had repeatedly disobeyed the *BRO* and so should expect increasingly long sentences.

John's heart sank. What he regarded as the meaningful arguments of Mark Welsh, were being dismissed by illogical reasoning. He felt angry and frustrated. He wanted to stand up and shout ... but feared that would achieve nothing ... or possibly make matters worse. Having delivered her verdict on the appeal and the application for review of sentence, John assumed that the hearing would now be closed. Instead the lead judge looked towards the screen from which Steph's impassive face was observing and being observed.

"Mrs Hugo, you have heard the verdict of this court. Have you understood that your appeal has been dismissed?" enquired the lead judge. "If not, then I am sure Mr Welsh will be able to advise you further."

"I understand what has happened." Steph's voice was calm and controlled. "My appeal has been rejected." She paused, looking down - and then straight into the camera. "You feel that the judge at my last trial behaved correctly in refusing me the right to address the jury in defence of my actions. You say it would be 'bizarre' for her to have allowed me to wear my dress in court, because it would have meant the judge was supporting an illegal action - the breaching of my *BRO*." Again Steph looked down silently and then back at camera. "Yes, I understand all that ... and I understand that this is the law ... but I also now understand that the tail of the law is wagging the dog of justice ... and worse still, the tail is broken." Again she paused, looking straight ahead at the camera this time. "I know all this because I also know that your decision makes no sense. I stood in the dock of that court, wearing my dress. The judge saw me. The court saw me. The people in the public gallery saw me. It was only the jury that wasn't allowed to see me - or hear me. The people that could affect the outcome of my trial, were the only people denied the right to see me stand there. It wasn't the *BRO* that kept me away from the jury - it was the judge!"

John wanted to leap to his feet and punch the air screaming *Yes! Yes!* Steph had voiced his thoughts - summed it all up. He may still not fully agree with what his wife was doing ... but he was proud of her!

"Thank you for confirming that, Mrs Hugo. If you believe that this court has erred then I am sure that Mr Welsh will be able to advise you on any appropriate course of action. Do you have any further comment that you wish to make at this point?" John felt there was a smug satisfaction in the judge's tone. He thought of Charlie and the Chicken Man and wondered whether this judge knew that she had just had the last word, no matter what Mr Welsh might try.

"Nothing that I haven't said already, Your Honour. It is a matter of freedom ... the freedom to be oneself as long as it does not harm others - and I have hurt no-one."

With a nod from the judge to the usher the screen went blank. "All rise" was called and the hearing came to a close. John and Charlie left the court in silence. To John, the green of the court now seemed more the green of mould, decay and despair than the green of new life and hope.

While John and Charlie were making their way out of the courthouse, Steph was being taken back to her cell from the video room. A section of the route took her along a short corridor that was actually an enclosed bridge over a small footpath. There were windows along both sides and Steph could see that it was starting to get dark. How long had it been since she last saw an evening sky? It reminded her of a time, almost exactly two years earlier, when she had stood looking out of her bedroom window, smelling the fragrance of night scented flowers and musing on stars. There was no fragrance of night scented flowers coming through these sealed windows. There was just a mild smell of disinfectant from whatever was used to clean the floor. As she left the view behind she realised that she had forgotten to send birthday cards to Tim and May.

*

It was about a week later that John received a letter from his wife. He did not know that it would be the last. She asked him to give her love to the children, and apologised for having forgotten their birthdays. She asked that he pass on her belated birthday wishes. She had been unable to purchase cards. She talked in a matter of fact way about the appeal hearing. She said that Mark Welsh had prepared a further appeal, this time to the Supreme Court. She also mentioned that her case had been referred for further investigation by the police, 'in order to eliminate her' from 'recent incidents of unrest' where paper cut-outs of a red dress had been found. John wrote back. He didn't tell her about the police raid. He didn't want to worry her. He did say how angry he had been at what he had witnessed in the Appeal Court but how proud he was of what she had said. He was never to know whether she read his letter.

Chapter 15: The Red Dress Bombings and John Arrested

John peered at his door security viewer. He recognised the police officers and social worker from their previous visit. There was also another female officer. The two male officers, as on the previous occasion, were dressed. *Why do they always come at this time in the evening?* he wondered to himself with irritation. He opened the door with a vexed, "Yes?"

"I'm Detective Inspector of Police Collins and this is my colleague Sergeant of Police Walton. The lady with us …."

"Yes, I know who you are," interrupted John, "what do you want?"

"As I was saying, this is Mrs Hammond of Social Services and Police Constable Hargreaves. May we come in?" said the officer, finishing his set speech.

John gestured towards the living room and all four entered. As soon as they reached the living room and John had turned to face them the Inspector spoke again.

"John Hugo, I am arresting you on suspicion of involvement in recent incidents of unrest. You do not have to say anything. But it may harm your defence if you do not mention, when questioned, something which you rely on in court. Anything you do say can be given in evidence."

"What?" exclaimed John.

"I would be obliged if you would accompany my sergeant." He gestured to the sergeant who went to John's side and took hold of his arm.

"Hold on, I haven't done anything. What about…"

"Mrs Hammond and officer Hargreaves will wake your children and ensure that appropriate arrangements are made for their care, unless there is someone that you would like us to contact for that purpose," said the inspector anticipating John's question.

"There isn't anyone. This is absurd!" remonstrated John.

"I would be obliged, Mr Hugo if you would accompany my sergeant calmly, otherwise I will be forced to use handcuffs."

"Why? This is absurd," repeated John. "I have to explain to the children! They'll be confused and upset."

"What's going on?" It was May. Woken by the unusual voices, she had come out of her room and was now standing at the foot of the stairs.

"It's OK, May," said John. "There seems to be some sort of mistake, and the police think they have to arrest me for something. It will be just like the business with the computers. Anyway, I'm not going anywhere 'til I know what is going to be done about looking after you and Tim." John looked defiantly at the sergeant and then at the social worker, Mrs Hammond. The latter looked uncomfortable but her voice was steady when she spoke.

"With your permission Mr Hugo, I will remain here with the children, if the inspector has no objection to that." She looked at Detective Inspector Collins.

"That is a social care matter. I obviously leave the arrangements to you."

John looked at his daughter.

"It's OK, dad," said May in a very mature way. "I remember this lady from last time - and I also saw her when you were in hospital. Tim and me will be OK."

"I'll make sure everything is fine, Mr Hugo. You needn't worry about Tim and May," reassured Mrs Hammond. "I'll stay here tonight and then, if need be, I will arrange for one of my colleagues to come and take my place tomorrow. I know this is difficult. I *am* sorry."

John, despite his unease and growing anger, knew that there was little he could do other than to comply, and this Mrs Hammond at least, seemed to have a degree of genuine concern. More importantly, May appeared comfortable with her.

"Go and get Tim," said John to May, before turning to the inspector with a cynically cordial tone, "assuming I can tell my son what is happening?"

Detective Inspector Collins made no comment, but did not instruct his sergeant to take John out forcibly, probably sensing that John would not show resistance once he had spoken to his son. May returned with Tim.

"I have to go to the police station, Tim. Look after your sister while I'm away," said John with a joking smile. "This is Mrs Hammond. You remember her from before? And this lady is a police officer... sorry, I've forgotten your name ... will you be staying with Mrs Hammond?"

"I'm Police Constable Hargreaves. It probably won't be necessary for me to stay," she glanced questioningly between Mrs Hammond and the inspector. The latter looked at Mrs Hammond who shook her head.

"Right Tim," continued John, "Mrs Hammond will stay here with you and May tonight. Hopefully we can get all this sorted out quickly and I'll be back as soon as I can." John kissed his children, and with a reassuring, "They'll be fine," from Mrs Hammond following him up the hallway, he left the house with his police escort. There was a police car waiting outside, and to John's surprise, there was another parked just up the street. As he was driven away, John saw police going to Charlie's house. Through the entire journey John witnessed a level of police activity that he had never seen before. Police on foot, escorting people (occasionally in handcuffs) or knocking on doors, police cars and vans, with lights flashing (but no sirens sounding), either on the move or parked outside houses, sometimes with people being led out to them.

*

John had assumed that he was being taken to the police station, so was surprised when the car turned into the car park of a local school. There were other police cars, and what looked like military vehicles there. People were being escorted from them into the building. John's queries about why he - and other people - were being brought here was dismissed with a simple, "Instructions".

Once the car had stopped, John was taken into the building by Sergeant Walton. He was lead to the school hall where he was left, with what he estimated to be about another two hundred people. Some were standing chatting. Some were sitting or lounging on the floor. A few had secured folding seats from somewhere. Although Sergeant Walton had gone, John noted other police officers standing at intervals around the hall, and a couple stationed either side of the entrance. All were clothed and all carried batons.

John edged cautiously into the room, moving slowly between people, looking to see if there was anyone he recognised. He wondered where Charlie was. Had he been brought here? Were some people being taken to other places? After a few minutes wandering and seeing nobody that he knew, John approached one of the police officers.

"Excuse me, how long are we going to be kept here?"

"I'm sorry sir. All I know is that my shift ends in another hour," smiled the young officer.

"So, why are we here?"

"I'm sorry sir. I really can't help you. I just have my instructions."

"And what are they?"

"I'm sorry sir, I really can't help you." The young policeman looked about the room, and John realised that he was not going to obtain any answers from him - and doubted whether he had any to give.

As John walked away a middle aged man smiled at him. "You won't find anything out. I've tried ... and a few others too. I don't think the chaps with the batons know anything."

"How long have you been here?" enquired John.

"About an hour," smiled the man. He seemed very accepting of the situation.

"So, do you have any idea why we are all here?"

"Not the slightest," came the resigned response.

"I have to say, you seem very calm about it."

"Well, I expect they will let us all go pretty soon. I worked for the police for a while. For the day-to-day stuff they're fine ... but anything unusual and they haven't got a clue - the management especially. They'll let us go 'coz they won't know what else to do with us. It's probably just an overreaction to the bombings. I expect someone, somewhere has said that 'nothing is being done' and so they are doing 'something'. I wish they would hurry up though. I'm getting hungry." With a shrug that said, "There you go, I've said my piece," the man sauntered off into the throng.

Although John was amused by the man's nonchalant demeanour, he wasn't reassured by it. There may have been some truth in what he had said, but the man probably did not have two children at home to worry about. Suddenly there was a lot of shouting and John found himself being swept backwards as people surged towards him. John ran to one side where the surge was less concentrated. He continued in a rough arc until the cause of the commotion became visible. To John's horror a man was on the floor with three or four police officers hitting him with their batons. People in the crowd looked on. Some hid their faces to block out the site. Some screamed. No-one came forward to help. Pointlessly, more police entered the hall and formed a cordon between the incident and the crowd. A stretcher was brought in by people wearing paramedic armbands, and the limp body was loaded onto it then rushed away. Apart from some sobbing the hall fell into a shocked silence.

In that silence some step ladders were brought to the spot where the man had been beaten. A uniformed, middle aged woman entered the hall with a megaphone and mounted the steps. The incident had left the crowd in a horseshoe around her. She stood there like an actor in an ancient Greek theatre.

"Thank you all for your patience," she said, through the completely unnecessary megaphone. "We believe that we have identified and apprehended the person that we need. I would ask for your continued co-operation, and thank you in advance for this." As she spoke some trestle tables were brought in and lined up along the wall behind her. "You will shortly be invited to empty your shoulder bags for inspection. After that you will be allowed to leave."

The process of inspecting shoulder bags took a couple of hours. Due to where he was standing, and the way the queuing process was arranged, John was there for most of that time. As each person left, they passed through a scanner. John wondered whether this was reading bio-data or scanning for something such as metal. Possibly it was doing both. Possibly it was doing something else. John didn't know. He was confused by the whole process - but overriding (or possibly compounding) his confusion was anxiety. He had been made anxious by his arrest and separation from his children, but that anxiety had been intensified by the sight of the man being beaten. And it wasn't just the violence of the act. John recognised the man. It was the person he had seen in the public gallery at the Appeal Court, and John was now certain that this was the same man that he had seen wearing the scarf and hat at the Causeway Café.

*

When John eventually got home, in the early hours of the morning, he found Mrs Hammond asleep on the sofa. He didn't wake her. He looked in on May and Tim. All was quiet. John hadn't thought about where Mrs Hammond would sleep. He looked at the gently snoring figure and smiled. He quite liked Mrs Hammond - *even though you wouldn't make a good guard dog*, he thought. He sensed something genuinely caring about her. May seemed comfortable with her too - and he had come to regard his daughter as a good judge of character.

John didn't feel tired, but knew that he should try and get some sleep, so lay down on his bed and stared at the ceiling in the dim light. He had walked home, and the walk had calmed him a little, but left him with questions. What had it all been about? Why had all those people been collected and processed in the way that they had? Why had the 'hat and scarf man' been singled out, and beaten so savagely? Maybe there would be some answers in the news reports. He hoped that there would be. With that vague hope to counter the questions circling in his head, John drifted into a deeper sleep than he might have anticipated.

He was woken by May asking if he was intending to go to work. She and Mrs Hammond had been up a while and had made breakfast for everyone.

"I didn't realise that you had come back home, Mr Hugo," said Mrs Hammond as John, still unshaven, joined Tim sitting at the kitchen table. "May has shown me where everything is – but mainly out of courtesy, since she has been completely in charge. I have been but the kitchen porter to head chef May!"

"Thank you," said John, "this all looks great ... and I'm hungry."

"What happened, dad?" asked Tim, voicing the thoughts of everyone, as they started eating. "And when did you get back?" added May.

"Well, it was all a bit odd," began John, and recounted the events of the previous evening. When he had finished he looked at Mrs Hammond. "I don't know what it was all about. You were with the police Mrs Hammond, surely something was explained to you?"

Mrs Hammond shook her head. "I was only told that several people were to be brought in for questioning and that, in your case and one or two others, there were children in the house who would possibly have no adult to look after them as a consequence. I didn't realise it was as big an operation as you've described."

"And the 'questioning' didn't amount to much either," added John. "I asked more questions of them than they asked of me ... and didn't get any answers."

"A couple of people from school say that their parents were questioned ... or whatever it was," said May flicking through contacts on her phone.

Phones, tablets, TV and computers were generally not allowed at the table in the Hugo household ... but John considered the circumstances exceptional. "What about the news?" he asked.

"Says that there were police operations all over the place." May said no more before handing the phone to her father. She remained silent, but held his gaze a while before continuing with her breakfast. John couldn't interpret the enigmatic look in his daughter's eyes. He glanced at Mrs

Hammond and at Tim, both of whom appeared oblivious as they ate. He looked down at the screen and then understood. The news report about the night's events was titled, "The *Red Dress* Bombings".

*

When breakfast was finished Mrs Hammond tidied stuff away while John and the children prepared for work and school as usual. During the day John read several reports of the night's events and viewed news footage on TV and other media outlets. The term "Red Dress Bombings" seemed universal. Even his work colleagues had begun to use the phrase. All the reports were general and quite vague. Although they said that the police operation had been in connection with the bombings, and that arrests had been made, there was nothing to say why certain people had been rounded up by the police and not others. Sadly, despite having given the bombings a name, the authorities seemed no further forward in establishing the purpose of the attacks or who was behind them. Initially very few people had been injured, but inevitably, like John himself, some people had been caught in blasts. A few had now been reported killed.

All of the explosions had been close to Trueway religious or administration buildings. This led John to avoid them wherever possible. He would cross the street if he knew he was approaching a temple on the same side that he was walking. He told May and Tim to try and do the same. Paradoxically however, John noticed that temple congregations seemed to be increasing. Where once there had been a handful of people - often elderly - on the streets outside a temple following a service, there now seemed to be a crowd. The press picked up on this as well, explaining it as a proud reaction of ordinary Citizens, to show that they would not be cowed by cowardly acts of terror. As a complement to this courageous stance, the security in buildings - once a casual matter - became much stricter. If one worked in a Trueway building, then one knew that the body scanners would now definitely be well maintained, and used to scan every individual who entered.

Despite the 'defiant' increase in temple attendance - if indeed that was what it was - John sensed a growing unease and tension. Just because buildings symbolic of Trueway seemed to have been the targets up until now, that was no guarantee that this would continue to be the case. Where would the next bomb blast be? Will it be here in this street? Was that person over there a "Red Dress Bomber"? Anyone, seen carrying a larger than average bag, was eyed suspiciously. Despite the police sweep, and the arrest of some people, the blasts continued to occur. Conversations, and media coverage, started to focus on the lack of police progress in identifying perpetrators, and the inability of the authorities to stem the wave of attacks. A dangerous mix of resentment, fear, anger and suspicion was growing in the ordinary Citizens of Trueway.

Although temples, civic offices and courthouses had been targeted by the mysterious bombers, John was not aware of any explosions associated with prisons. In this he took some comfort. Steph's lack of freedom at least meant that she was not exposed to the terror threat now faced by himself and other Citizens.

*

Steph was aware of what had been occurring in the outside world. She had a radio, and even though she was not allowed to mix with other prisoners, she could overhear conversations. Some prisoners would even call out to her in person. The warders too spoke to her about what had been taking place. She therefore obtained quite a broad spectrum of opinion, even if she couldn't discuss things in quite the same way as people on the outside. She was keen for further insights from Mark Welsh, when he came to see her, in her cell. As had been the case with Mr Shaw, he was the one person from outside the prison who was granted this privilege - assuming one didn't count the priest, who Steph regarded more as a 'friendly warder'.

Mark was due that day to give feedback about his application for leave to appeal to the Supreme Court. She had been sent the paperwork that he had prepared in pursuance of this. She could see it was a well constructed, professional document, but she felt that it had missed some important points. Sadly, due to the statutory time frame, she had not been able to raise her concerns with him prior to it being submitted.

As soon as Mark Welsh arrived she could tell that the news was not good.

"We've been refused leave to appeal haven't we?" she said before he could speak.

"Yes, I'm afraid so," he sighed, seating himself on the simple wooden chair that formed part of Steph's limited furnishings. "The judge felt that there was no significant point of law being brought into question by the

Appeal Court decision. He therefore felt that it was not in the public interest for the Supreme Court to consider the decision further."

"But the Appeal Court decision was illogical!" blurted an incredulous Steph. "You can't say that I wasn't allowed to speak to the jury, because that would mean I was in breach of the *BRO*, and at the same time accept that I was in court, *in breach of the BRO*, ten minutes before they came in!"

"I understand your frustration, but the Supreme Court deals with points of law and ..."

"And denying a person a fair trial, and then justifying that on the basis of an illogical argument, isn't a 'point of law'? You didn't even mention that illogicality in your submission, so we will never know whether it would have been considered a 'point of law', will we?"

"I didn't mention it because the arguments have to be ..."

"On what *you* regard as 'points of law'," interrupted Steph again, her voice shaking with frustration. She had not anticipated that she would challenge Mark Welsh in this way, and her outburst was as much a surprise to herself as it was to him. She liked him, and thought that he had genuinely done his best for her, but once again she felt that lawyers ... the law itself ... was missing the point ... missing *her* point ... and, as she had said to the Appeal Court judge, the tail of law was wagging the dog of justice.

"I'm sorry." His apology was genuine. They fell silent for a moment. Steph, who had been standing all this time, sat down on the edge of the bed. They remained silent, both looking at the floor until he spoke again. "There's more I'm afraid." Steph looked up. At first he did not meet her gaze.

"Yes?" she enquired of his silence. He glanced at her, and then away again before continuing.

"I'm sure that you have heard about all that has been going on ... the bomb blasts, the police raids?"

"Yes, I have the radio, papers and so on." She didn't understand his hesitancy, his awkwardness.

"You know that they have been finding red dresses cut from paper at the scenes of the bombings?"

"Yes, of course I do. The police are even investigating me further, in order to 'eliminate me from their enquiries'. I was told that just after the appeal court decision." She was becoming impatient.

"They are calling the bombings, 'The Red Dress Bombings'."

"Yes, I know all that Mark ... come to the point." The slow progress of his faltering questions was starting to unnerve her as well as irritate her.

"Well, I have been informed that your case has now been referred to The Court of Truth."

*

"So what does that mean for me?" Steph's forthright question to Mark Welsh, spoken in her usual confident tone belied the anxiety she was feeling. She had heard of The Court of Truth, but knew very little about it. Her anxiety stemmed from that lack of knowledge and the vulnerability that accompanied it. She was moving into unknown territory. She felt she may be crossing a significant line.

"Well, if you mean 'ultimately', then obviously I don't know. The best I can do is explain about the Court, and try to answer any questions that you have about it. So, to begin with what, if anything, do you know about The Court of Truth?"

"I don't know much at all. I don't remember much of what I learned at school ... it all seemed so boring then ... and now it only seems to crop up once in a while in news broadcasts or dull sections of the media. The only impression I have is of a bunch of old men who pontificate on things, and like to think they are significant, when in fact they are largely symbolic ... a bit like an old fashioned monarchy in a parliamentary democracy. How am I doing?" The question, tagged on the end, was intended to sound a little flippant ... an attempt to continue giving the impression of confidence. She didn't know why.

"It's only my opinion," began Mark in answer, "but in many ways, I think you are right. I probably shouldn't say that, since the Court is a part of the World constitution, and its creation facilitated a great deal that otherwise would have been impossible. The birth of Trueway, at the end of The Terror Wars, was brought about largely by the leaders of world religions coming together in order to maintain their own existence in the face of challenges from fundamentalists.

Initially therefore Trueway was only a *part* of the new, post-Terror Wars political landscape, and on the surface at least, was primarily a spiritual entity. Being unified however gave it great potential for political power in the world. Civil groups and political leaders did not want secular decisions to become dominated by religion. In many ways the religious leadership of Trueway took a complementary stance. They wanted their role to be primarily spiritual. That said, however, they did not wish to be marginalised politically. The diplomatic solution was for Trueway to become a unified World order resting on the three pillars of Civil, Ecclesiastic and Martial that we know today. The Court of Truth was created as part of that process and its proceedings were always to be overseen by a cleric. It had no direct place in government, yet had influence. As its name implies it is a judicial - or quasi-judicial - body but in many ways it can be regarded as a kind of parliament ... or at least a chamber of a parliament." Mark Welsh took a breath and was about to continue but Steph interrupted.

"Mark - stop! You're going to have to go soon and the prison will be making demands of me - lunch or shower or exercise or something - they always do. I appreciate the history lesson but I need to know the implications for *me*. What's the difference in my case being considered by The Court of Truth rather than an ordinary court? Why am I being referred to them? Do the police think they have found something out about me that means they have to hand over the case to this court? For that matter who has made the decision that my case should be referred? What's going to happen, Mark? What do I need to do to start preparing? Do I need to prepare?"

"Yes, sorry Steph. I don't know what, if anything, the police have found. The referral of your case came through the *Combined Interests Council*. Under normal circumstances this tends to be a bureaucratic talking shop that reviews World events and provides advice to government. The major world event at the moment is the seemingly unstoppable wave of bombings.

The lack of progress in establishing the perpetrators of these attacks has left the Council unable to give government any meaningful advice. Since pieces of red paper in the shape of a dress have been found at all the bomb sites and since similar pieces of paper were found in the public gallery following one of your trials and since you wear a red dress and refuse to remove it the Council probably think there may be a link. Now, you may or may not have anything to do with the unrest, but from the point of view of the Combined Interests Council, the only way to find out is by referral to The Court of Truth."

"OK," said Steph nodding, "so now what happens? Will there be a hearing? What do we do in order to get ready for this?"

"Well," began Mark, again sounding hesitant, "I can't help you a great deal with this. Yes, there will be a hearing, but The Court of Truth is not an adversarial court. It is an inquisitorial court. There are no lawyers to prosecute or lawyers to defend ... and there is no jury. For a Court of Truth hearing there will be a bench of three people - a senior cleric, senior civil judge and senior military representative. They are charged with investigating the matter in question and establishing *the truth*. These courts occur very infrequently since it is rare for there to be cases or issues which cannot be addressed solely by the common courts."

"So, you won't be there? It will be just me and these three people?"

"There may be witnesses called and there is likely to be a group of observers as well as court officials for recording matters. I will not be there in my capacity as your lawyer. I am not certain at his stage whether I will be permitted to be there at all."

Steph looked aghast at this information. She had felt her treatment by the courts so far had been prejudiced ... but at least it had a degree of transparency. What she was hearing about The Court of Truth was leading her to feel increasingly isolated. This court was sounding almost secretive.

"And will I be accused of something specific ... or are they just conducting an inquiry ... fishing around for something?"

"It is possible that you will be charged with something from the start. The court will then be there to investigate the truth of that charge, or it may be that the hearing begins without a charge, and investigates whether one will or will not be made."

As Mark spoke there was a rattling at Steph's cell door and the cover of the observation window slid back. Mark's consultation time was over. He looked at her as he left - an enigmatic glance. He went to speak but the warder ushered him out. The door slammed. The key turned. The observation window cover slid shut ... and Steph knew that it was too late to ask the one question that was at the root of her anxiety.

Part 3: Whose Justice and What Consequences for Whom?

Chapter 16: The Court of Truth and the Night of Smashing

Steph was woken early next morning by a warder telling her that she was to be moved to a different prison. Sittings of The Court of Truth were in the Capital, and she needed to be close to the court room. It was still dark when she was escorted from the gate into the waiting prison transport van. It was now early July. The van drove her and her escorting warders for about an hour. When Steph was taken out the sky was beginning to lighten. She found that she was at an airfield. Steph didn't recognise it. She assumed it was probably a military or police facility. A helicopter was waiting. Air travel of any sort was rare in Trueway, being very expensive and dangerously polluting. Land based transport, such as cars, buses, trains and pods, all used clean, highly efficient glide technology. Aviation for regular transport was largely a thing of the past. Helicopters were used almost exclusively in cases of emergency, when a glide would not be practical for one reason or another. Steph had only flown once before in her life. Her stomach churned at the site of the machine, and the sound of its rotas already turning. She faltered but was urged forward by her guard. She sat with her head down staring at her feet. She didn't even want to look at her dress. She felt sick, and the flight seemed interminable, but eventually the helicopter touched down at another small airfield.

Her legs were shaking and she felt unsteady as she stepped out onto the tarmac, but she breathed the air – the fresh air – and it calmed her. Steph didn't know where she was or how near she was to the centre of the Capital. All she could see was the airbase and a few trees. She was escorted across the tarmac to one of the buildings, through a door and down some steps to where a private, underground autopod was waiting. Once inside, the warder keyed in the code and the driverless pod sped her and Steph away on the final leg of the journey. About forty-five minutes later the pod came to a halt at an underground platform, and from there Steph was taken through a door directly into the new prison.

As Steph's journey had been taking place, media sources around the world had been receiving details of the progress being made by the police and the authorities regarding the "Red Dress Bombings". Following the raids and arrests the group behind the bombings had now been identified. It was around mid-day when John heard the news that a group called the *Individual Freedom Alliance* (IFA) had been named as the organisation responsible. John, like everyone else, then started to devour the media reports to try and establish exactly who and what this group was.

As was often the case, the media reports all seemed to say much the same thing. Throughout the world the police raids had resulted in arrests of people implicated in the bombings. These people were very varied - different age groups, ethnicities and socio economic backgrounds. They all had one thing in common however. They all belonged to textilist groups of one sort or another. At last the media ... and the world ... could put a face to the 'enemy'. All of a sudden, people who had generally been regarded as harmless eccentrics, took on a new and more sinister persona. The textilist groups had been used as a cover for a subversive, anti-establishment, anti-Trueway revolutionary organisation – the IFA! Now, the red paper dresses left at the scene of the bombings made sense. The red dress was a symbol ... a 'flag'! The newspapers, and other media, were not slow to exploit this, and pictures of a red dress emblazoned with the letters 'IFA' in black, became a potent headlining image to articles.

Putting a 'face' to the enemy however did not stop the bombings. Why should it? Arresting a few people - people who may not even have been senior in the IFA - was not going to curtail the group's activities. Added to this, the relatively sparse military and police establishment, was woefully too small to carry out the massive investigations necessary. Everyone realised that there must be explosive stashes, that there must be people moving around planting the devices, yet not a single person had been caught in the act and not a single stash had been uncovered. These 'failings' were clear to all. The problem was emphasised in the news media and discussed in parliament in the days that followed the initial naming of the IFA. The solution was simple - a volunteer support service made up of good, Trueway Citizens was needed to supplement the regular members of the police and armed forces. Recruitment began.

*

Steph's new cell was not dissimilar, in its Spartan sparseness, to her former one - but was maybe a little larger. The walls were painted a deep maroon. The one warder that she saw during the remainder of her first day was a pleasant woman - civil and business like - who delivered Steph's food. The food itself was acceptable - possibly a little better than that in her previous prison - and she had had a choice of some quite varied options. Overall, Steph's first day in her new place of confinement, was unremarkable apart from the quiet. Steph could hear almost nothing coming from the other side of her cell door. There was no clanking of a tea trolley, no prisoner or warder voices and certainly no sounds filtering in from the 'free' world. She didn't even have a radio in this cell. Whether because of the silence or exhaustion from travel or a combination of the two, she had a good night's sleep.

The following day she woke and completed about twenty minutes of physical exercise (something that had become a daily routine with her) before washing. She then waited and before long breakfast was brought to her cell. After that she took paper from her bag to compose a letter to John explaining that she had been moved. It was not long after she had started however that her warder returned to collect the breakfast things.

"I wouldn't get too settled at your letter writing," she advised as she picked up the tray, "the court is already assembling, so it won't be long until you're called." Steph was so surprised at this that the warder was gone and the door closed before she could speak. Steph had not expected that anything would happen for a while. She had been here less than twenty-four hours and a court was assembling. She felt uneasy. She didn't know why exactly. Maybe it was because it seemed purposeful. Her arrests, imprisonment and trials to date had undoubtedly had a purpose, but they seemed to follow a well rehearsed and familiar script. Everyone played their part. The outcome may be 'this' or it may be 'that', but the process moved forward in its usual, predictable (and often ponderous) manner. The decision from a trial, at the end of the day, may result in celebration or disappointment for her - but then the next act in the play would start. What she was experiencing now felt different. It felt to her that this court actually wanted to find something out. It was not going to waste time. It was going to pursue its goal. She sensed the outcome was important.

Steph did not formulate all of these thoughts explicitly in her mind, certainly not in those first minutes after the warder's announcement. Had she been asked at that moment what made her uneasy she would probably have simply said, 'it's different'. It was not long before two warders came to escort her to the court room, where that difference would find visual form.

*

John sat chatting and supping beer with Charlie - unaware that his wife was now spending her first evening in a new prison. John always liked to get Charlie's 'take' on events so had come round to do just that. On the night that John had been arrested and taken to the school, Charlie had been visited by the police but not taken anywhere.

"I thought at first that they must have concluded that I wasn't involved in anything, but having listened to your description of the disorganisation in the school, I think they were just at a loss to know how on Earth they were going to cater for a blind man." Charlie took a sip of beer. "Have you been in touch with Steph?" he asked.

"I wrote to her just after the appeal, but not since the night I was arrested."

"Do you think she knows that they are now calling the bombings, 'Red Dress Bombings'? It worries me John. I've told you that before ... but now, with this name being given to all this, it worries me even more. I guess she is still wearing the dress?"

"Yes," confirmed John ... "well, as far as I know. I mean I don't know otherwise. I suppose, if she has heard about what is happening, she might have taken it off to distance herself from events and suspicion ... though being in jail she is clearly not involved ... but knowing Steph I imagine she is carrying on as normal ... and that means wearing the dress."

"No-one is ever beyond suspicion, John. When you write to her, you tell her that Charlie is worried. Tell her I miss her, and will she please take off the dress so she can get out, and then I can see her again. Write 'see' in capital letters ... she will find that amusing."

John chuckled. "Will do, Charlie ... but I don't even think *your* 'charmingness' will change her mind. What do you think of this latest little idea - volunteers to support the police and military?"

"Oh, the *Police and Military Volunteers*. I did think about going along to ask if I could be in charge of *surveillance*" scoffed Charlie "... but I was afraid that they wouldn't see the joke. They seem so disorganised that they might even have agreed, and signed me up for the job! What about you?"

"No," said John – in a more emphatic tone than he intended, and he quickly added, "I've got enough work to do as it is," though inside, he was thinking that there was a time when he would have been first in line. Then, as if to convince *himself* as much as Charlie, "Anyway, I doubt that this *PMV* will achieve much. If the 'regulars' can't organise themselves and get it sorted out then... well … no offence but ...."

"Absolutely, John - absolutely. Another beer?"

"Oh, absolutely."

*

Steph walked with the warders along the corridor from her cell. The floor of buff coloured stone was smooth and cool beneath her bare feet. The walls either side were of the same stone – smooth and unadorned. A diffuse light descended from panels in the ceiling. There were some other cell doors in the short corridor, but Steph could hear no sounds coming from the other side of these. In fact it was eerily quiet. The two warders had arm-band insignia, but otherwise were naked. Like Steph they had no footwear so the walk would have been almost completely silent if it were not for the faintest swish of the red dress. It made Steph think of Charlie, and that first morning when she thought that his ultra- sensitive hearing had picked up something different as she walked past him on her way to work. She fleetingly wondered whether Charlie thought of her. John wrote that he did.

At the end of the corridor the three of them mounted some stone steps and went through a door into a small room. There were three seats against one wall. The warders directed Steph to the central one before seating themselves either side.

"You'll be called in a minute," the first warder advised, and pointed to a door on the opposite wall to the one through which they had entered. The three sat in silence. A minute passed, then another. One part of Steph wanted the 'call' to come, but another preferred just sitting. The minutes ticked by.

"Is there a loo?" asked Steph, breaking the hush.

"They'll call you shortly ... not long."

"Yes, but if I need to..."

"No - you went before you left your cell and you haven't drunk much. It's just nerves. You'll be fine. This session won't be long."

Steph fell silent. She wasn't desperate for the toilet. The warder had said, 'this session' and Steph realised ... probably what she had known but not thought about ... that there may be more than one sitting. How many? What was going to happen at this one? The warder seemed familiar with proceedings, so Steph began a question,

"So what is going ...," but before she completed her sentence, the door that had been pointed out to her opened, and a young man leaned through,

"Mrs Stephanie Hugo?" he called in a querying tone, as if there was a room full of potential Mrs Hugos. Steph stood and went to him, followed by one of the warders.

"If you will just follow me, Mrs Hugo," requested the young man, "... and please use the hand rail to steady yourself." He turned, and began to ascend a flight of about ten steps. Steph did as she was asked and the warder followed her, closing the door behind. Steph watched the heels of the young man as he preceded her. She had a vague awareness of a room coming into view as she ascended the last few steps, but it wasn't until she was at the top and the young man stepped to one side, that she was able to truly see the court. She faltered and gripped the hand rail. She felt the hand of the warder gently steadying her from behind.

"It's OK Mrs Hugo," reassured the latter, "just go to your left and sit down."

Steph looked to her left and there were three seats. The young man now occupied the farthest one and was indicating to Steph to take the seat next to him. She did this and the warder came to sit on the remaining seat. Steph found herself in a glass fronted box. This was the dock. It was not dissimilar to the other docks in which she had stood when on trial, but the scene in front of her was unlike anything she had experienced before.

*

At the moment that Steph was taking up her seat in the dock, John was sitting down at his office desk. The children had gone off to school as usual. He had a couple of meetings scheduled for that morning and was about to go through some papers in preparation. His preparation, and all activity in the office however, was interrupted by an announcement from the general manager over the tannoy, informing staff that recruitment for the *Police and Military Volunteers,* was taking place in the staff canteen.

Recruitment officers would be there all day, and anyone wishing to become a volunteer could go at any convenient time to register.

The announcement was followed by a general buzz of chatter and discussion. One or two people had clearly made up their minds and were either definitely going to volunteer ... or decidedly not going to. More frequently however people seemed to be chattering in an attempt to make a decision. As the day wore on a steady stream of John's office colleagues went off to the canteen. They returned with leaflets and a few sported pale brown arm bands bearing the letters 'PMV' in red. John himself went down at lunch time - but only to get a sandwich. A few tables had people sitting round eating, but one corner of the room was sectioned off. A large banner made it clear that this was the *PMV* recruitment point. A young woman and a middle aged man were busy welcoming new recruits and earnestly explaining things to them with many reassuring nods and smiles. Although John had no intention of volunteering, he was curious to know what was said in the leaflets that were being handed out. He felt sure he could find the information on-line, and so resisted the temptation to go over and take one, or to ask any of his newly volunteered colleagues.

By the end of the day, John realised that the vast majority of the people around him had made the journey to the recruitment point, and there were many arm bands in evidence as he set off home. He saw more *PMV* armbands on his journey and realised that he was very much in the minority. At home that evening Tim and May reported that there had been announcements about the *PMV* at school. The children were not allowed to volunteer, but the role of the *PMV* had been explained to them. They thought that all of their teachers ... the majority anyway ... had become volunteers. When John went to bed that night his overwhelming feeling was one of astonishment at the speed with which this volunteer force was being assembled.

*

"Will the prisoner please stand up," came the request from the central figure of three seated on a dais opposite Steph. Steph did as she was requested. "Are you Stephanie Hugo?" For a second Steph did not answer, still somewhat awestruck by the scene in front of her. In the silence she was prompted by the questioner, "Just answer, 'yes' or 'no' please ... are you Stephanie Hugo?"

"Y- Yes," came Steph's faltering response.

"Thank you Mrs Hugo. Please step forward, closer to the front of the dock." Again Steph did as requested. The central figure, a portly, oriental man in maybe his fifties or sixties, then began to explain who he and his two colleagues were, but Steph was not really taking in what he was saying. She had known that there would be a panel - a bench - of three people. She also knew that there were likely to be some observers. All this had been explained to her - if somewhat hurriedly - by Mark Welsh. What he had failed to tell her was that the court itself would be more like a small amphitheatre of tiered seats, and that everything – walls, ceiling, floor and furnishings would be in the deepest shade of indigo, with only the three judges and the dock brightly illuminated from above. Neither had he explained that the 'observers' would be so numerous. They ascended – tier upon tier behind the three judges, a cliff of pink, brown and black flesh that retreated from the light until it became one with the shadow; with the building. Some heads were bald, some grey, some more youthful with hair decoration. She registered white wimples – Good Sisters – scattered throughout this wall of flesh. She registered a few swirls of tattoos. She could not see Mark Welsh.

How many people? She blocked a group of about ten, and then tried to estimate how many blocks – but they began to merge. She started to count the rows instead, but the rows might not be the same length –and then there were the ones in the darkness. Steph began to feel sick. The lead judge was still speaking, she could see his lips moving, but there was no sound. He was getting bigger… smaller… bigger… smaller… coming… going …

"Mrs Hugo ... Mrs Hugo ..." Steph opened her eyes. She was lying on the floor of the dock. The young man was kneeling beside her. She had fainted. "Can you sit up?" He had his arm under her neck and shoulder. The warder was squatting on the other side of her with a paper cup of water. Gradually Steph raised herself to a sitting position.

"Thank you," she said, taking the cup of water. It was cool.

"There's no rush," reassured the young man. "You fainted. Sit where you are until you feel OK - then we can get you a chair. Have you hurt yourself at all? I've called for a medic."

She didn't feel any obvious pain. "I don't think so." Steph sipped at the cool water. She took some deep breaths and looked about. She couldn't see the court - just the floor and walls of the dock. She glanced up to the upper part of the dock - the glass box part. She could picture the view from where she had been standing.

Steph sat still. There was a movement behind her.

"Hello," said a smiling young woman who now crouched down beside her. "I'm Dr Geelman. What happened?"

"She fainted," interrupted the young man before Steph could speak. "She began to sway, but I managed to catch her as she fell, so she didn't hit the floor or anything. I eased her down. She doesn't seem to have hurt herself."

"What's your name?" enquired the doctor of Steph, ignoring the young man.

"Steph Hugo."

"Did you faint Mrs Hugo?"

"I think I must have done," said Steph.

"Do you hurt anywhere?"

"No - I don't think so."

With the assistance of the young man Steph was helped to a chair and the doctor performed a few routine tests before concluding that Steph was fit to continue.

"I think you simply fainted Mrs Hugo – but do tell the warder if you feel nauseous or develop a headache or your vision goes funny. OK?"

"Yes, thank you," confirmed Steph with a nod, and the doctor left.

With the doctor no longer standing in front of her, Steph could again see the court room. It was empty now - just the dais backed by rows of unoccupied indigo seats.

"Do you feel able to carry on?" the young man asked.

Steph nodded. "Yes, I'm fine now. Thanks. Just the heat, I think." Steph smiled at the warder who took the water cup while the young man signalled to someone at the side of the court. A few moments later the chief judge and his two colleagues entered, and went to their positions on the dais.

"Hello Mrs Hugo," said the judge in a kindly manner, "how are you feeling?"

"I'm fine now, thank you."

"You started to sway a bit, but I think that the usher managed to catch you as you fell, so I do hope that you have not injured yourself."

"No, I feel fine now. Thank you."

"It can be a bit daunting I know. Procedures do require however, that the whole court is assembled for the hearing, and that includes, not only myself and my two colleagues here, but the body of learned colleagues as well. I had, more or less, completed the preliminaries before you fainted and while the full assembly of the court was present. I have therefore adjourned the hearing until tomorrow. Did you manage to hear what I said earlier?"

"I'm sorry," replied Steph apologetically, "I missed a lot of it."

"Well, no matter. It is quite a standard script for the commencement of such a hearing, so in the presence of my two colleagues, I will summarise."

"I am Judge Primate, Justice Couchan. As you may have deduced from the yellow wig that I wear, I am a Justice Ecclesiastic. These are my colleagues the Justice Civil," he indicated a slim black woman of about forty years sitting to his right wearing a blue wig, "and the Justice Martial," a white man of similar age and build to himself wearing a red wig. "Our colleagues, whom we have dismissed for the present but who will again join us tomorrow, are all senior members of The Court of Truth and are termed *The Assessors*. They will help us in our task, giving us counsel and comment as we need it." He paused and gave a fleeting smile. Steph felt that his eyes hardened before he continued.

"We have officially required that you appear before Us, Mrs Hugo, in order to obtain truthful answers to the questions that We will put to you and then, in our turn, act towards you in accordance with law and right.

We act in the name of truth and justice, and with the blessing of the deepest spirituality, will seek to fulfil the duties of Our office for the exaltation of The Great Spirit and preservation of Trueway. We therefore, and most charitably, warn and advise you Mrs Hugo to speak the whole truth upon all questions that We address to you, so as to bring about a more prompt resolution of the Action and the relief of your own conscience. We would exhort you to avoid all subterfuges and falsehoods of such a nature as might turn you aside from a sincere and true avowal." He paused and smiled. "Now, I think it is probably best if you go back to your cell and have a lie down. We will reconvene tomorrow. I look forward to seeing you then." With that, Justice Couchan and his two colleagues rose and left.

Steph was escorted down the steps, and then accompanied back to her cell by the two female warders, where she did indeed lie down. Everything she had seen and heard confirmed that this was unlike any previous courts or hearings that she had attended. She didn't remember everything that had been said by Justice Couchan. The thing that most struck her was the way he had switched between the use of "I" and "We", between being another human being concerned for her welfare and being an instrument of the court. She felt she should continue her letter to John ... and she had nothing else to do ... but she could not concentrate. Organising her thoughts seemed too difficult.

*

John went to work the next day and the children went off to school as usual. Again the arm bands were very much in evidence. John had forgotten to look at the recruitment pamphlet on-line. Given the number of people with armbands, he wondered whether the *PMV* documentation placed emphasis on wearing them. In a world where footwear and a bag were the only accessories generally in evidence, it was strange seeing this brown and red insignia adorning so many people. He noticed a few individuals like himself at work with two bare arms, but not many. Nobody openly commented on the fact that he had not volunteered or asked him why - but he nevertheless felt that he was seen as an outsider. He told himself that it was just his imagination, and indeed the day's activities progressed pretty much as they always did. He contributed to discussion in a meeting that morning in the way that he always would. He asked questions and gave answers. On the telephone, and in video chats, he was treated no differently to how he would have been on any other morning.

By lunch time John had pretty much forgotten about his feeling of being 'an outsider' and was becoming habituated to the arm bands. He went out into the sunshine to eat his sandwiches in a nearby park. He sat on a bench, enjoying the bird song. He wondered what Steph was doing. She seemed to be kept well informed of what was happening 'on the outside', so thought she was probably aware of the volunteer force. He idly wondered whether her warders were wearing *PMV* arm bands. He assumed not, given that they were in professional roles akin to the police anyway. Since his most recent chat with Charlie he still hadn't written to Steph, and resolved that he would do so when he got home that evening.

The afternoon passed quite uneventfully, except that the office was almost deserted for about an hour when all the *PMVs* were called to a meeting. John was left 'holding the fort' along with the handful of others who were not volunteers. John wondered how the office would manage if *everyone* was a volunteer, and whether these meetings were going to become a frequent occurrence.

*

Steph was unaware of the arm bands. She was unaware of John in the park thinking about her as she sat in her cell eating her lunch. She had been told that the court would see her later that day, and at about 3:00pm, her two warders arrived to collect her. Again they made the journey along the stone corridor to the little room, and again the young man called her and she ascended the stairs to the dock. This time, when asked to stand she did not feel faint. Now she felt nervous - but prepared - as she was confronted by the three justices backed by the tiers of Assessors within the indigo cave.

"Good afternoon Mrs Hugo," began Justice Couchan, "I hope that you are feeling fully recovered."

"Yes, I feel fine Your Honour - thank you."

"We are here with one purpose - the pursuit of 'truth' - and to that end I remind you of what I said yesterday, namely that my colleagues and I, with the blessing of the deepest spirituality, will seek to fulfil the duties of Our office for the exaltation and preservation of Trueway. Do you understand what I am saying Mrs Hugo?"

"Yes, that is plain enough," responded Steph.

"Good," smiled Justice Couchan. "Then may We also remind, and advise you Mrs Hugo, to speak the whole truth upon all questions that We address to you. As preliminary to this therefore We would ask that you swear an oath upon the Holy Book of Truth." On these words the usher stepped forward to Steph's side and handed Steph a copy of the book.

"Please take the book in your right hand," requested Justice Couchan. Steph did as she was asked. "Now, Mrs Hugo, do you swear, on this the Holy Book of Truth, to speak the truth on the questions that We address to you?"

Steph had no desire to tell lies but didn't like the open-ended nature of what she was being asked to agree to. What if they asked her personal things? "I don't know what it is you are going to question me about Your

Honour; perhaps you may ask me about things which I don't think I should tell you."

"In that case I will be more specific," said Justice Couchan, "and say that We would ask that you swear to speak the truth on the things that you will be asked about concerning the Faith, and of which you know of relevance to your case."

Steph thought that this sounded more acceptable - if a bit odd and archaic. She was generally familiar with the text in her hand, and she certainly had a clear idea of what had been happening to her regarding 'her case'.

"In relation to what you have said, Your Honour, I swear to tell the truth."

"Thank you Mrs Hugo," smiled Justice Couchan, "I will now hand you to my colleague, The Justice Martial." He indicated the gentleman to his left.

"Good afternoon Mrs Hugo," began The Justice Martial. "We understand that you have had correspondence with a Robert Cray. Is that correct?"

"Yes, someone called Robert Cray wrote to me in prison," answered Steph quite promptly.

"You say, 'someone', Mrs Hugo. Are you implying that you did not know this person until he wrote to you in prison?"

"That's correct, Your Honour ... but I don't see what this has to do with 'Faith' or my case ... which is what I thought Justice Couchan said I was going to be asked about."

"All things are to do with 'Faith' Mrs Hugo since all things are to do with 'truth' and the faith of Trueway *is* 'truth'. I thank you for your answer. In one of his letters to you did Mr Robert Cray not say, 'We think that you are wonderful ... The stand that you are taking. ...You can count on our support'?"

Steph was irritated by what she regarded as the man's pomposity but she honestly could not remember what Robert Cray had written to her, so was happy to say as much. "I don't know, Your Honour. A few people wrote to me in prison. I don't remember everything they said."

"Do you remember the answers that you gave them when you wrote back, Mrs Hugo? More particularly do you remember the answers that you gave to Mr Cray?"

"Again, Your Honour, I really couldn't say. Maybe if you were to read something back to me that I wrote at the time I might recall it ... I don't know."

"I will indeed Mrs Hugo. Will the usher in the dock pass Mrs Hugo, *Documents 1A* and *1B* please?" The young man stepped forward to Steph's side and handed her two pieces of paper - photocopied letters. Steph immediately recognised her own handwriting on one. The other was word processed but with the 'RC' of Robert Cray at the end. Both documents had sections highlighted in yellow. The Justice Martial spoke again.

"Do you recognise the document marked *1B* as being something that you wrote, Mrs Hugo?"

"It certainly looks like my handwriting ... I'm just reading ... yes, I remember this." Steph looked up.

"And do you recognise the document marked *1A* as being from Robert Cray?"

Steph looked at the document. "Yes, I do remember this letter."

"So, Mrs Hugo, for your benefit and the benefit of this court, I will read the highlighted area on document *1A* - the document that you agree is part of a letter from Mr Robert Cray to you,

'We think that you are wonderful, wearing your red dress no matter what the authorities say. The stand that you are taking for the simple principle to be yourself and wear clothes if you wish is an example to us all. It must be very hard on you. You can count on our support'.

...and now Mrs Hugo would you please read from your letter back to him what it was that you said ... just the highlighted section will do."

Steph skimmed through the letter, reminding herself of the context. She didn't want to read something that was misrepresenting her thoughts.

"When you are ready, Mrs Hugo," prompted The Justice Martial.

"Yes, I'm just reading the bit that comes before the highlighted section ... reminding myself of my thinking." It all seemed pretty innocuous to her so she read the section highlighted as requested.

"Right, just the highlighted section:

'Thank you for being supportive, Robert and for your words of encouragement. There are times when I wonder if it's all worth it. I know what I do may appear unreasonable to many. On the surface it appears trivial. But I am not coming from a position based on a surface desire to be free to wear what I want, where I want. Rather, it stems from a commitment to act in line with my truth. What's the difference? I suppose essentially it matters in the last case but doesn't so much in the first. Only *I* know what matters to me and only *others* will know what matters to them. Nothing can be classed as unimportant in respect of someone's behaviour / expression as we never know where they are coming from. Yesterday I actually wrote on a piece of paper, *Why bother? Really, why bother?* Then I wrote what came as a response, *To be free. To act in truth is to be free.* That's how obvious it is when your mind doesn't start fearing the consequence of your decision - the political and career-path implications etc ... of which, long term, you can't actually figure out, anyway, as there's so many unknown factors involved. What I am doing affects us all, whether we realise it or not. In fact, if what I am standing for is fundamentally freedom, then *nothing* is more important.

To go deeper, if we fundamentally are being true to ourselves, united, then we'll be at peace. What creates stress is where that unity is broken by thought. Therefore thought is the only cause of stress. Next time you are stressed out ask yourself, is it the circumstance that's causing it or my thinking? We like to blame the world *out there* but the reality is it's *in here* where we should look to find the answer to our problems. The only way I have become convinced of what I am saying is by putting it to the test. That's why I go on about writing my thoughts down on paper whenever I'm not feeling OK. It works.

Anyway, as you can see, there's a lot more behind what I am doing than meets the eye. What I am doing is challenging some really big fundamentals - in myself first off, and then consequently as I change it will change around me'.

That's it - the highlighted section," finished Steph looking up.

"Thank you, Mrs Hugo," smiled The Justice Martial, "And do you still agree with what you said to Mr Cray in your letter - what you have just read to the court?"

"Yes, though I can see my grammar was a bit off at times!" smiled Steph back.

"Thank you Mrs Hugo. I would just like to draw the court's attention to one or two key points.

---First, Mrs Hugo tells Mr Cray - and now this court - that even though wearing a dress may appear 'trivial' it is not since it stems from her desire to act in line with - and I quote - '*my* truth'. I emphasise '*my*' since I anticipate that the court will want to return to this later.

---Second, Mrs Hugo tells Mr Cray - and now this court - that she *acts* in accordance with this truth - *her* truth. And why? In order to be '*free*'. She is therefore telling Mr Cray, is she not, that freedom comes from following *one's own* truth? But then:

---Third, she seems to say that this way of seeing things goes hand-in-hand with - even stems from - not fearing the *political* and personal implications of following this personal truth. So she quite clearly sees a political dimension to what she is doing which is interesting when,

---Fourth, she says that, 'if we are being true to ourselves, *united*, then we'll be at peace'. Again I emphasise a word intentionally - '*united*' a curious word when juxtaposed with this idea of individual truth - yet not so strange when one recognises the political dimension to what she is doing. And that dimension becomes clear and succinct in the final point I bring to the court's attention when,

---Fifth, she admits, 'there's a lot more behind what I am doing than meets the eye. What I am doing is challenging some really big fundamentals - in myself first off, and then consequently as I change it will change around me'.

So it is clear that Mrs Hugo has an agenda of political change in what she is doing. There can be no doubt about this since you have heard it from her own lips, here today. Furthermore I believe that through her correspondence with Mr Cray - and there are more letters in a similar vein - that she has encouraged him to pursue such change by following her example of following whatever it is that he, and others like him, regard as their personal 'truth' ... and he, in his turn, has made clear to her that her words will not go unheeded - 'You can count on our support'. And again I will draw the court's attention to that word '*our*' since it indicates that Mr Cray is not simply speaking for himself. He is the spokesperson for a group. A group that we have only recently come to recognise for what it is, in light of the chaos and upheaval it is causing under the banner of the symbol you see before you in this very court - the red dress!" By this point The Justice Martial had risen to his feet and was pointing an accusative finger at Steph - a pose which he held a fraction longer than was necessary to emphasise his point.

Given the auditorium like setting, applause would not have seemed out of place at the end of this speech, yet as he resumed his seat, there was silence. Steph stood impassive. Justice Couchan's calm, deliberate voice broke the quietude.

"Our thanks to you, The Justice Martial. Mrs Hugo, do you wish to say anything in response to what you have just heard from my colleague?"

Steph felt a little shiver run through her body. She felt as though she had been watching something that had nothing to do with her - a play almost - and she wasn't ready for 'audience participation' - her participation.

"Say anything about *what* exactly, Your Honour?" she asked, hearing her own words coming as if from someone else, so separate did she feel from what was happening.

"Well," said Justice Couchan, "this reference to what you call 'my' truth. Tell us a little more about what it is that you mean. This is The Court of Truth so this point is fundamental to our purpose. Surely truth is truth - or are you saying that we can all make up our own truth?"

"Well, Your Honour, I think it's like conscience, our sense of right and wrong," Steph felt herself coming back into her own body as she spoke. "We all have it and it governs our thoughts and actions. It's pretty simple really, isn't it? We all know what it is, and how to access it. And it's *always* there when you need it, so I've found."

Justice Couchan nodded his head, but looked serious. There was no smile. "Conscience is indeed very important Mrs Hugo, but conscience does not prevent two people, both acting in accordance with their conscience, from coming into conflict if they start from two different points of belief or value. This is where there has to be an arbiter, a touchstone of absolute truth. This is Trueway. Trueway, as expressed in The Book of Truth and through the deliberations of the most senior clergy regularly assembled, cannot err, being ruled by the deepest spirituality of Trueway – The Great Spirit. Will you refer yourself to the guidance of this body of ultimate truth?"

Steph took very little time to formulate her answer. "I do what I do in accordance with my conscience, my truth. If we are talking in terms of spirituality and deep religious beliefs, then I can't see that my conscience comes anywhere but from that deepest spiritual guidance. I believe indeed in Trueway; but ultimately for my words and deeds I rely on my conscience. I believe that Trueway cannot err or fail; but as to my words and deeds, I have ultimately to submit to the voice of my conscience and to whatever deep spirituality underlies that and guides that. In short, I refer myself to that spirituality and to myself - my truth. As to whether I will submit to a 'truth' provided by Trueway I can say no more."

Justice Couchan, in the heavy silence of the court, pondered this response before asking:

"Do you mean by this to say that you have no judge on Earth other than yourself?"

"I have nothing further to say, Your Honour. If my conscience comes from the deepest spirituality – The Great Spirit - then it is to that spirituality that I look in everything I do, and to none other."

Again Justice Couchan pondered before asking:

"And how do you know that this voice of conscience that gives you your 'truth' is unerringly good? Might you, as a fallible human, be following a false truth - an evil truth even ... evil masquerading as 'conscience'?"

"If it was evil then it would be telling me to do things that hurt others - that's where true evil is, isn't it? In hurting others? My voice of conscience has never told me to do anything that harms anyone. In being true to myself I hurt nobody and so I cannot see that there is anything evil about it."

After this Justice Couchan did not hesitate in his next response which he delivered in a grave tone:

"If you will not believe in Trueway, if you will not believe in the unerring nature of The Book of Truth and of the most senior clergy then you are putting yourself above Trueway and above truth ... and I can assure you that you will be judged accordingly since no individual is above truth."

"I can say no more to you than I already have," said Steph after a pause.

Justice Couchan looked long and hard at Steph. She returned his gaze. His look, she felt, was one of bewilderment. Eventually, after a deep intake of breath, he spoke again.

"Let us move on. Do you accept the conclusions drawn by my colleague from your letter, that there is a political dimension to what you are doing in wearing this red dress and following your truth?"

"Only in as much as I believe in freedom and that people should be allowed to do as they wish - as long as they are not hurting other people."

"But you consider that that freedom should stem from the conscience of the individual and not from obedience to the laws of Trueway?"

"I don't see that there should be a problem. I want to wear my red dress. I don't hurt anyone in doing that so why should the law want to stop me?"

"But do you not see the selfishness in what you do, Mrs Hugo? You say that you do not hurt anyone but there are complaints about you. You offend people. Surely that is hurting others and for that reason alone you should desist from what you are doing?"

"But why, Your Honour, are these people offended? What is *offensive* about a piece of material? What is *harmful* about a piece of material? The complaints they make are irrational and based on prejudice. They see me in my red dress, and because that is unusual and different, they complain - even though I am not hurting them or even threatening to hurt them, but simply going about my business. Why does the law want to support that kind of irrational thinking? If I were to say that I was offended by a waiter wearing an apron would that be reasonable grounds for demanding that he remove it or that he should be put in prison?"

"That is a different matter Mrs Hugo, an entirely different matter. We all know why a waiter wears an apron. Trueway is never unreasonable. There is a reason for a waiter wearing an apron. Maybe you could tell us your reason for wearing a red dress?"

"It is a family heirloom. I like it and I want to wear it."

"You see it as simply that Mrs Hugo? Then why do you say in your letter, 'there's a lot more behind what I am doing than meets the eye'?"

"There is more to it than meets the eye because the law and Trueway make it so. If I was left in peace then there would be no more to it than me simply wearing an old dress because I like it."

"So, Mrs Hugo, that brings us back to the political dimension. You believe that the law - Trueway itself - is wrong, and you think that Trueway should change to see the world according to *your* truth. Is that correct?"

"I see what I am doing as harming nobody and so intend to continue what I am doing, and by example, support freedom - the freedom of the individual to behave in accordance with that individual's truth."

"And if I tell you Mrs Hugo, that beyond these walls, beyond this court and across the globe your example is being followed by individuals who are blowing up buildings and killing people what would you say then?"

Steph was silent. She had not expected this sudden assertion. From when she was first told that she was to be investigated further in order to 'eliminate her' from police enquiries she knew that that phrase was a euphemism. That had been proved by her referral to the court in which she now stood. Now, she felt a chill. In her answers to Justice Couchan, Steph felt that she had been honest. She was expressing her thinking - the philosophy that had propelled her in her wearing of the red dress. She had felt on firm ground, confident in her intellect and the soundness of her fundamental argument but now, with this question, she could see a direction being taken that was leading outside her rehearsed thinking.

"I am aware that there has been unrest - but it has nothing to do with me. I have set no example that suggests that anyone should bomb anyone else."

"But, Mrs Hugo, you have argued - here in this very court - that people should act in accordance with their own truth, with their conscience and that that is freedom. What if that conscience - that individual 'truth' - *does* encompass bombing? Paper cut-outs of a red dress have consistently been found at the site of bombings. Cut-outs of a red dress were found on seats in the public gallery following one of your trials. Are these things coincidence, Mrs Hugo? Some might see them as evidence of you being a ring leader, an instigator of this unrest. At the very least do you not think that you have become a symbol for defiance of Trueway and for the pursuit of change?"

"I have never advocated doing anything that harms anyone. I have not encouraged anyone in that respect. On the contrary I have said explicitly that all I want is to be free to do as I wish as long as what I do does *not* harm anyone. I am not responsible for people bombing and I am not responsible for people leaving cut-out paper dresses in places where they have bombed. I don't know why they are bombing or why they are leaving paper dresses ... and the last thing I heard, was that the authorities didn't even know who was doing the bombing or why."

Justice Couchan looked to his colleagues either side and there was a brief, whispered exchange.

"Forgive me Mrs Hugo, I was not aware, that since your prison move, you have not had access to a radio and information from the world at large. Progress has now been made on identifying those responsible for the world wide bombings. They are a group called the *Individual Freedom Alliance*. This group - the *IFA* - has been organising, preparing and implementing their plans under the guise of various textilist groups." Justice Couchan paused. "I take it, Mrs Hugo that you are familiar with the term 'textilist'?" Steph nodded. "Do you regard yourself as a textilist, Mrs Hugo?"

"No. – No, Your Honour."

"I think possibly others do, though that is not something that I intend to pursue at this time. Whether or not you regard yourself as a textilist ... and whether in fact textilism has any substantive connection with what is taking place as regards bombings or is nothing more than camouflage for the *IFA* remains to be seen. The key point however is that the *IFA* operated via textilist groups, and among those identified and arrested by the police, was Robert Cray - the same Robert Cray with whom you have had correspondence, the same Robert Cray to whom you said there was more to what you are doing than meets the eye ... and the same Robert Cray that said to you, Mrs Hugo, "You can count on our support". These are facts, Mrs Hugo, facts that I and my colleagues will need to consider further. I think they are facts that you too need to consider further. I will therefore adjourn this hearing at this point. We will reconvene tomorrow morning at 10:30am.

*

As Steph was being led back to her cell John was watching the *PMV* staff returning to the office following their meeting. The final part of the afternoon passed normally, and at the end of the day John returned home. May prepared a lovely salad for the three of them after which John intended to settle down and write the letter to Steph, as he had resolved that lunch time. His resolve was galvanised when, during the meal, May said that children at school had asked whether her mother had anything to do with the bombings. John was startled. Although he knew that everyone was affected by what was happening, he somehow thought that children would just be passive in this world of adult events.

"Why on earth have they asked you that?" he blurted out, not disguising his surprise.

"Daaad!" came the equally undisguised cry of incredulity from May, "Mum's in prison for wearing a red dress! The bombings are being called The Red Dress Bombings! How obvious does it have to be?"

"It's worse in my class," said Tim quietly. "They say she *is* the bomber. I've told them she's in jail so can't be and that they're stupid, but they still say it ... some of them anyway."

John was flabbergasted. He asked if they had reported these things to their teachers. May hadn't but Tim said that he had. It seemed that he had received a conciliatory and supportive hearing and that the children concerned were told that they were to say nothing further about Tim's mother - but there was no further action taken.

"I wish mum wasn't doing this," said Tim. "I wish she was home and that it was like it used to be when mum loved us."

"Mum does love us," came May's quick rejoinder.

"Of course she does," added John immediately - startled at Tim's words. Tim didn't argue. He sat silently and the tears began to roll down his face. John hurriedly knelt beside him and put his arms round his son. John didn't speak. He just held him. When, after a second or two he looked at May he found his daughter looking blankly back at him, silently weeping too.

Later that evening John wrote his letter to Steph. He and the children wanted her back - *needed* her back.

*

It was precisely 10:30 am when Steph stood in the dock for the third time.

"Good morning Mrs Hugo. I hope that you have had a good night's rest." Justice Couchan smiled briefly at Steph, but did not wait for a response. "We also hope that you have considered the facts that were put before the court yesterday, and have come here today prepared to assist Us further in Our pursuit of truth. To that end We would remind you of the oath that you took previously. We will not ask you to repeat it.

Yesterday We established that you had been in correspondence with one Robert Cray, a man known to have involvement in a group called the *Individual Freedom Alliance* - a terrorist organisation involved in bombings, the like of which have not been witnessed since the end of the Terror Wars. We also established that you personally promote the belief that individuals should be free to behave as they wish according to their own conscience ... their own 'truth' as you put it ... albeit, as you would insist, that those individuals do not harm others - though it seemed to us that you also regard yourself as the arbiter of what constitutes 'harm'. Finally We drew attention to the red dress, and the way it further links you to the unrest that is being experienced by our society at present - though whether that involvement is active or symbolic we reserve judgement. It is to this dress that We turn our attention today. Do you have anything you wish to say before We begin, Mrs Hugo?"

"Will I have the opportunity to have a visit from my husband and children? I haven't seen them for some time, and I am not even sure that they are aware that I have changed prison. Have they been told?"

Justice Couchan looked to his two colleagues. There was a little discussion before the Justice Civil - speaking to Steph for the first time, and sounding somewhat apologetic said, "That is something that we are not sure of ... whether they have been told of your move. We will look into it." Then, with a perceptible change in her tone, "As for *seeing* them, you are fully aware that the only thing that has prevented that in the past has been your refusal to remove the dress that you insist on wearing."

"Thank you." said Justice Couchan. "I am sorry, Mrs Hugo, that we cannot be clear at the moment regarding your family's knowledge of your prison move, but as my colleague says, we will look into that. However, her point about visits and your insistence on wearing the dress is well made and brings us to Our questioning today. We will begin with two things that you said yesterday regarding your behaviour. First you said, 'I do what I do in accordance with my conscience, my truth. If we are talking in terms of spirituality, and deep religious beliefs, then I can't see that my conscience comes anywhere but from that deepest spiritual guidance', and then second, when asked why you insist on wearing this red dress you said: 'It is a family heirloom. I like it and I want to wear it'. Do you remember saying those things Mrs Hugo?"

"Yes, I remember."

"So, Mrs Hugo, are you saying that you think your desire to wear this dress ultimately comes from that deepest spirituality? That that spirituality moved in you to prescribe the wearing of the dress?"

"I don't think the wearing of the dress - *per se* - is all that important. I didn't start wearing it because I was told to do so by anyone - but, as I have said, because I like it. If you wish to see that as stemming from a deep spirituality I will not contradict you. I don't really know where our deepest desires and motivations stem from."

"Did it appear to you that this desire - this motivation to wear a dress in public - was lawful?"

"Everything that I have done has been in accordance with my belief that I should be free to do as I wish as long as I do not harm anyone - that is acting in accordance with my conscience. It would have been the same if it was doing something other than wearing a dress. The key principle remains the same - to be true to my truth. "

"Mrs Hugo, We will ask you bluntly - did you start wearing this garment at the request of Robert Cray?"

"No."

"Looking back now, do you think you did well in deciding to wear - and in persisting to wear - this dress?"

"Yes. I have done nothing wrong or that is not in accordance with my principles."

"Principles are important, Mrs Hugo. Would you agree however that sometimes there can be conflicts of principles? For example, you have asked whether you will have the opportunity to have a visit from your family, since you have not seen them for some time. We have pointed out to you that your inability to have visits was a consequence of your refusal to undress for regular visiting sessions. You therefore barred yourself from having visits from your family. You put the principle of wearing your dress above the principle of being caring to your family, did you not?"

"I don't think so, Your Honour. I did not make the rule that said that my family could not visit me unless I removed my dress. That was the decision of the authorities."

"Yes, but you had the opportunity to make a decision to put a visit from your family before wearing your dress, yet you chose to keep wearing your dress. Let me put it to you again now. Will you consent to abandon the dress you wear in the event of your being permitted to have a visit from your family?"

"I would have to think about that, Your Honour."

"Obviously We would not wish to rush you in this. On the contrary We would encourage you to think about it carefully. We would go so far as to suggest that you pray for guidance in this matter since, if your motivation stems from a deep spirituality that guides your personal 'truth' as you seem to believe, then prayer may be the way to access that and gain guidance."

For the briefest moment Steph wondered whether she should pray - but it was the briefest of moments before she asked, "So, are you saying that I will not be allowed to see my family as long as I wear this dress? After all, I am here in court wearing it. I have not been permitted that before so I don't see why, if I am allowed to stand before all these people wearing my dress, that I shouldn't be allowed a visit from my family while I continue to wear it."

Then, to Steph's astonishment, as if triggered by her reference to them, the tiered bank of Assessors behind the three Justices came to life and began calling down to her - exhorting her, for so great a benefit, to consent to take off the dress. First they called individually but then in twos and threes until it became difficult to distinguish words in the great cacophony that developed. The chaotic sound enveloped the room - enveloped Steph - growing louder until it was almost unbearable. Then it stopped suddenly for one, maybe two seconds until, as one, the Assessors gave their demand, "Undress!"

In the silence that followed this command Steph stood shaking, but as the silence continued, an ice cold resolve of anger filled her. She would not be bullied. Any thought of prayer evaporated.

"No," she declared to the Assessors, "that is not in my power: if it were, it would soon be done! I'd rather die than be bullied into doing that just because *you* say so with no more reason than you feel you have power. That's just mindless bullying - the big over the small, the strong over the weak!"

"Do not be hasty, Mrs Hugo - reflect on it, pray," suggested Justice Couchan, "pray to know if it would be proper for you to remove this dress, in order that you may receive a visit from your family."

This exhortation only increased Steph's anger. As the clamour from the Assessors had risen she had expected Justice Couchan to subdue them, but he had not. It all seemed part of the proceedings. She would not be intimidated. She would not be bullied.

"I cannot remove my dress. I cannot therefore see my family. I beg of you, permit me to see my family as I am, in this dress; this dress does not break any civil law, and as far as I am aware, is not contrary to *any* laws of Trueway."

199

"Mrs Hugo," said Justice Couchan, "you say that you *cannot* remove your dress but it would be more truthful, would it not, to say *will* not? You say that the wearing of it breaches no law ... yet you have been found guilty by the civil courts of breaching laws, and have been imprisoned as a consequence of wearing the dress. Possibly your reasoning is too simplistic. Myself, my colleagues to left and right and all the Assessors here present are ecclesiastical, civil and martial persons of consummate knowledge, experts in law, both human and spiritually divine. It is our desire in these proceedings to pursue the truth, but to do that with both kindness and piety. We do not seek vengeance or punishment. On the contrary, Our desire is to assist you in gaining your return to the way of truth and spiritual salvation.

With this in mind, and because you are neither well enough taught nor instructed in these difficult matters, We offer you the opportunity to choose for counsel, such of the Assessors as you shall be pleased to point out. If you do not, of yourself know how to make this choice, We offer to do it for you, and to point out to you some who will counsel you on what you have to answer or do. Of course, that is always on the condition, that in matters of pure faith and truth you will answer yourself, and would, as previously reminded, do so on your oath to speak the truth on those things which are personal to yourself."

Despite the convoluted nature of this monologue, Steph did not have to think long before making her response.

"I do not wish to argue about 'cannot' or 'will not' in relation to removal of my dress. I thank you for your offer of counsel, but I have no intention of desisting from the counsel of my own conscience - my own truth. As to the oath, I am ready to speak the truth as I have said before."

"Thank you, Mrs Hugo. If you change your mind regarding counsel, the offer remains open. I will now adjourn this hearing 'til 10:30 tomorrow morning when I hope that we will be able to draw this to a conclusion." Justice Couchan looked briefly at Steph in silence and then asked that she be escorted back to her cell.

*

As Steph's third hearing had been taking place John had been busy in the office as usual. He had posted his letter to her on his way to work, unaware that she was no longer at the prison to which he had addressed it.

The children had gone to school as usual, but with strict instructions to contact him by phone if they suffered any further bullying.

John's morning passed without incident or anything remarkable. No meeting had been called for the *PMV* staff, and the office routine had followed its usual course. At lunch time he ate sandwiches in the park and his thoughts were very much with Tim, May and Steph. He was unaware that Steph's thoughts had been with him, May and Tim only a little while earlier as she requested the court's permission for a visit from them.

John returned to his desk and was settling into the afternoon's business when the news came through of the latest Red Dress Bombing. At first it seemed little different to previous incidents and so the office routine was only briefly interrupted by the announcement. It was also several hundred miles away which removed that immediate level of concern for personal safety. Then came the news that there had been some deaths associated with this bombing. One of those killed had been a very senior politician. This was the first death of its kind. John was not surprised when, late in the afternoon, *PMV* staff *were* called to a meeting. Again, he and a few others were left to get on with what they could until the meeting was finished, and the arm band wearing *PMV* staff returned. When they did come back, there was a tension that John could not fathom. Everyone went about their business. There was no further discussion of the bombing or of what had transpired in the *PMV* meeting, but something was different.

John sensed the same difference on his journey home. He tried to figure out what it was. Were people quieter than usual? Maybe. Were people avoiding looking at him? Maybe. Was it just his imagination? Was this feeling going to dissipate, just as his feeling of being an outsider had dissipated a few days previously?

At home Tim and May reported that there had been no further comments at school about their mother - despite the bombing and death of the politician. John was relieved and didn't think any more about his feelings of unease. After the children had gone to bed, he watched some news reports about the bombing. As well as the obvious physical damage, and human distress caused by the blast, there were angry scenes broadcast from the area near where the incident had occurred - crowds demanding that something be done. There was an interview with the family of the dead politician. John felt very sorry for them. Despite the police having identified the group behind the bombings, and despite people having been arrested, the politician's family and the public at large were understandably angry that the attacks had not been brought to a halt. John went to bed.

It was about 3:30 in the morning when he was woken by the telephone. John always kept his phone on the cabinet by his bed. He peered at the insistent display – *Charlie* - John was too sleepy to wonder why Charlie was ringing him at 3:30am. He just answered, "Hello Charlie."

"Get out John. Get the kids and get out of the house. They are coming. They're at my door!"

"What... Charlie ... what are...?"

"Just do it John. Get the kids out the back way ... Now John, now!" Charlie was screaming down the phone, then there was banging in the background and shouting, and John realised he was hearing some of it from the phone and some from outside.

"Charlie ... Charlie what's happening? Charlie...?" There was no answer. Charlie's phone was still on and John could hear voices and noise but Charlie wasn't answering. John went to the window without putting the light on. He peered through the blinds. There was noise - the sound of things being smashed - and lights in the direction of Charlie's house. The angle prevented John seeing clearly, but there seemed to be a lot of people judging by the long shadows being cast. He had no idea what was happening but action overtook thought, and John was soon in the dark of his back garden with two bewildered children.

Instinctively he had not turned on any lights, and the three of them had grabbed almost nothing but shoes in their rush to exit. They were soon out of the gate and in the alley that ran along the back of the properties in the close. There was still noise and light from the direction of Charlie's house so they went in the opposite direction. As they did so there was banging much closer to hand. John looked over his shoulder as he hurried the children along the alley. He saw lights coming on in their house and the muffled sound of voices shouting and things being broken, and then an almost explosive smash as one of the windows went - then another and another. John was dragging Tim by the hand and almost running while May, constantly glancing back over her shoulder, endeavoured to keep up. The shouting and the destruction taking place in their house was no longer muffled. Only as they put distance between themselves and the havoc did the sound become less.

There was enough ambient light to see where they were going ... but exactly where they were heading, John did not know.

*

Children can be very accepting and very resilient. Despite having been rushed from their beds into the night neither May or Tim complained. They could easily see that something extraordinary and terrible was taking place. They didn't know why but they didn't ask their father for explanations. They instinctively knew that now was simply the time to be alert and prepared. There was therefore no questioning or moving when John stopped suddenly and roughly pushed his children back against a wall.

After their initial headlong rush, they had felt safe enough to walk, and had been wandering silently for about fifteen minutes. John had steered the little group away from the main thoroughfares using side streets and alleys instead. Every so often the sound of voices and things breaking grew louder or lights went on in a house in an otherwise dark street. These signalled the need to change direction. It was this avoidance strategy that formed the only steerage to their otherwise aimless course. They were just about to exit an alleyway onto a small residential street when John had pushed his children against the wall. He pressed himself against the bricks alongside them, his arm instinctively across them holding them back. The children knew their father had glimpsed something as he was about to enter the street, but what, they did not know. They listened. There was a background noise of shouting and breaking ... but it was quite distant. They could hear nothing coming from the street a few feet away. A little bit of the street was visible to them just beyond the walls of the alley, but not much - especially when trying to see round their father.

The three stood pressed against the cold bricks in the dark. Then, only just perceptible, May thought she could hear a sniffing, whimpering sound. She moved her head and her father's hand pressed her just a little harder to the wall. The sound grew gradually louder. It was definitely coming from the street. Whoever, or whatever was making it, was getting closer to the end of the alley. It didn't seem like the sound of something threatening but all three of them became increasingly tense at its approach. A figure came into view - first to John and then the children. It was a woman. She was walking slowly, sobbing. The three stood still in the dark. At first she

203

did not look down the alley, but when she did she emitted a little cry of fear as she perceived the shadowy figures.

"It's all right," said John stepping forward towards the slightly greater light of the street. The woman was about to run, but stopped - possibly seeing the children who moved forward behind their father. "It's all right," said John again, softly and reassuringly. Then to his astonishment the woman asked,

"Mr Hugo, is that you?"

It was then that John recognised her. He didn't know her name, but she was a woman who worked in the bank where John had his accounts. She had served him many times over the years. He moved forward, and the woman all but fell into his arms with relief.

"I'm sorry," she said.

"There's nothing to say 'sorry' for," John assured her. "What has happened? What *is* happening? I guess you're caught up in all this like us?" The woman was shaking - shivering - the involuntary movement visible even in the poor light. "I'm sorry. I'm asking too many questions. Let's find somewhere to sit down." John knew where he was, and that there was a very secluded little park - more a garden - down a track between the houses just a short distance along the street. All appeared dark and quiet in that direction. He put his arm round the woman's shoulders. "Come on - there's a little garden up here. We should be safe there. Hardly anyone knows about it."

The little group silently made its way up the street. Despite being a small road, the houses were big detached buildings. They loomed over the little party. John turned into a dark gap between two of the houses. May and Tim recognised the street where they were, and had been this way many times, but had never noticed this track. It became darker as they moved away from the street and the two children kept close to the adults. When it began to seem that they would not be able to see the way forward John stopped. As May's eyes adjusted to the increased dark she could see a bench overhung by bushes. There was just room for the four of them. John sat at one end with the woman next to him and then May and then Tim. John took his arm from around the woman.

"How are you feeling?" he asked. She had stopped crying and appeared to have stopped shivering. The night was not cold so John assumed her shivering had been due to her state of shock.

"I'm OK now, Mr Hugo. Thank you. How are you ... and your children of course?" she asked turning to May and Tim.

"Well, physically we are all right, I think? ... Kids?" enquired John.

"Yes, were fine," they said in unison.

"I had a phone call from a friend ... oh hell ..."

"What is it?" said the woman, anxiety in her voice again.

John had thought of Charlie for the first time since fleeing the house with the children. What had happened to Charlie? There was nothing John could do now.

"Nothing, it's nothing," John reassured her. "I just thought of someone - the man that made the phone call warning me to leave the house. I don't know if he is all right." John leaned forwards - elbows on his knees, his head in his hands. "What's going on? What on earth is happening?" His questions were rhetorical. He didn't really expect an answer but the lady from the bank provided one.

"It's the *PMV*," she said simply. "I didn't sign up."

John, still leaning forward, looked at her as best he could in the dark. "What do you mean - the *PMV*?"

The woman seemed much calmer now. "All this smashing and stuff." (The sounds were still audible in the distance). "It's all being done by the *PMV* ... probably not officially ... but I have a good friend - Beth - at the bank. She signed up. She told me - warned me - that there may be trouble tonight, following the death of that minister in the Red Dress Bomb attack. You don't have an arm band Mr Hugo ... and you're here in the middle of the night in a park with your children, so I guess you didn't sign up either?"

John nodded and then said, "No, no I didn't join." The lady from the bank continued her explanation.

"According to Beth, the authorities are totally perplexed about what is going on with the bombings. They have made arrests and allegedly discovered this group - the *Individual Freedom Alliance* - that they say is behind it all, yet despite this and the arrests, the bombings continue and now a politician has died. So now it's a scatter gun approach ... assume that anyone who has not joined the *PMV* has something to hide so put fear into them."

"So, because you hadn't joined the *PMV* and your friend Beth had warned you, you have stayed away from your house?" asked John.

"I suppose that would have been the sensible thing ... but I didn't really believe it. I like Beth - but what she was saying seemed too fantastic, too extreme to be true. I stayed at home. It was about 1:30 this morning when the doorbell rang - persistently. I opened the door and about ten men pushed past me into my house, many of them wearing clothes. They rushed into the dining room and started smashing things - not wildly, but systematically and with precision. I tried to stop them but was dragged back. I ran out of the back door and headed for the police station. I intended to ask for police protection. When I got there I was greeted in the usual civil fashion at reception, but when the senior police officer came he just shouted at me: 'Non-*PMV* do not get protection from us! Vacate these premises!' He actually chased me back into the street and in the direction of my house. He kept behind me. I didn't know where to go so I kept on 'til I was back in my back garden. Once I was there he ordered me to remain and not leave under any circumstances.

Facing the back of my house, I was able to watch how everything was being systematically destroyed under the supervision of the men of law and order - the police. I could hear the crunching of glass and the hammering against wood as windows and doors were broken. Books, chairs, beds, tables, linen, chests, bits of my piano, my radio, my computer, everything ... all were thrown through the holes where the windows or doors had been.

In the meantime, a mob - probably more than forty or fifty people - had gathered and was standing around the building. Among these people I recognized some familiar faces, people I had served in the bank, trades people, who, only a day or a week earlier had been happy to deal with me. This time they were passive, watching the destruction of my home without much emotion. Eventually, and despite the warning, I could stand it no longer and simply ran. Nobody pursued me. I don't think anyone really noticed me, so intent were they all on the destruction - either doing it or watching it. I ran and ran. I could hear other incidents and so just tried to keep away from any noise or lights. Eventually I stopped running and just wandered aimlessly – 'til I met up with you."

*

The party of four continued sitting in the garden in the dark. John told the lady from the bank about the call from Charlie. That led on to talking about Charlie himself - what little John knew. There was some mention of

Steph ... but probably not as much as might be expected, given what had driven them to be huddled together in the night. There was some talk of respective work places. Some talk of school from Tim and May. Some talk of better times. The thing avoided was the thing that was at the back of all their minds - what now? What do we do next?

Gradually the sky lightened, and with the dissipation of the dark, the realisation that the noises of the night - the smashing and the shouting - had also given way to ordinary sounds - some birds, some distant traffic. The lady from the bank said that she would go home. There was nowhere else to go. John wanted to suggest an alternative ... but there was no alternative that he could offer. He didn't know himself what he was going to do. It was agreed that the four of them would, with caution, endeavour to make their way to her house.

Chapter 17: Morning of Rescue. Moment of Truth. House of Hope

As John, the children and the lady from the bank began their journey Steph was waking up in her cell. She went through her usual morning routine - go to the toilet, then a bit of walking back and forth and some stretching (she had not been taken from her cell for exercise since arriving). After this self-imposed fitness regime she washed in cold water, gave her teeth a quick brushing and attended to her hair with equal brevity. Since the interruption of her letter writing on the first day in her new prison, Steph had not attempted to continue. Her head had been too full of court proceedings. This morning however, with a little time before breakfast, she settled to do a bit more. She reread:

Hello John (and my little double troubles)

As I write this you are probably unaware that I have been moved to another prison. Hopefully by the time you are reading it you will have been told anyway.

That was as far as she had got on that first day. As she recommenced she realised that she still had not asked for the return address of her present place of incarceration. She assumed that John would have been told where she was and would be able to write to her anyway ... but she wanted to put the address on the letter ... and she felt rather stupid not knowing where she had been for the past few days ... and even more stupid for not having asked!

This prison is a bit different to the other one. I don't know if I am the only prisoner here but I haven't seen or heard any others. It is a very quiet place. I can't hear a sound at the moment, and probably won't hear anything until they bring my breakfast. The prison and the court are part of the same building so when I go to court it is just a matter of walking down the corridor. I was told when I was moved that it was necessary in order to be nearer the court ... but I didn't realise it would be this near.

Anyway, this is The Court of Truth. You should look it up on Truepedia. I wish that I had. It's an odd set up. Mark Welsh had told me a bit about it ... but it's more like a theatre than a court! And maybe for historical or religious reasons they seem to use archaic terms and language. I even find myself starting to sound like them when I answer sometimes! I really must stop that! Haha!

Anyway, I have been in the court a few times already and I am due back there today. I have no idea how much this is costing but there are loads of people involved and it seems a massive waste of money to me. One positive thing is that I have been allowed in this court with my dress on. Don't get me wrong, they are still trying to get me to take it off, but they are not barring me from the court room because of it. I am due in court again today at 10:30 ... and they do seem to be pretty good at time keeping here! Well, I expect that breakfast will arrive soon so I will sign off for now. Oh and by the way, my hair is long enough now to wear in a bun. I knew you would want to know that!

Steph folded the letter and put it in an envelope addressed to John. She would finish it after today's hearing and ask one of the warders for the return address. She put the envelope into her bag and took out her little notebook of "Stuff". She had taken paper from it for her letters but had not continued her diary. She looked at the few short bits she had written and found herself, almost involuntarily, making another entry.

To be honest John I don't care what all this is costing. I just want to hug you and Tim and May. This place is like some strange dream. Truepedia won't tell you what it's really like. I wish I wasn't here.

*

Breakfast was a fairly light affair for Steph. She could have had something cooked but preferred toast and coffee. A little while after breakfast she made a second trip to the toilet before the warders arrived to accompany her on the now familiar walk down the stone corridor to the court room. Steph stood in the dock, for what was now the fourth time. The scene was just as before.

"Good Morning Mrs Hugo, I hope that you have slept well," began Justice Couchan. "Yesterday We offered you the opportunity to elect one of our august number to act as counsel for you. On that occasion you declined the offer. Having, quite literally, slept on it have you changed your mind? Are you willing to identify one of our number, or have one identified for you, to assist you and give you counsel? We urge you most strongly to avail yourself of this offer ... for your own, ongoing benefit.... both spiritual and temporal." He paused and looked intently at Steph, before repeating slowly and pointedly, "...for your benefit Mrs Hugo ...*spiritual and temporal.*"

Steph did not know quite what to make of this. The court was silent. She had no *wish* to take any counsel from anyone. She had thought through her position and was being true to herself, just as she had been throughout. She had no *need* to take counsel. There was however foreboding in the silence and in the words just spoken ... and she remembered again, the moment after Mark Welsh had left her that last time, the one question that she had not asked.

"And if I do not accept your offer of counsel, what then?" asked Steph.

"If you do not accept our offer Mrs Hugo then We will proceed with matters on the basis of the facts and the things that you say, and have said, without the benefit of that counsel."

"And when you say 'proceed with matters' - what exactly do you mean? I have been brought here, to this court without explanation as to why. I have been asked questions without explanation as to their purpose. I have answered your questions ... without really knowing why you are asking them. Where is it all leading? Am I allowed to be told?" Steph surveyed the court. Her question was to each and every one present as much as to Justice Couchan. It was he who answered however.

"You have been brought here Mrs Hugo in order that we can establish the truth - and I am sure that We have explained that to you already."

"Yes, but the truth about what? And when you have found out the 'truth' ... whatever truth you are talking about ... what then?"

"Then, Mrs Hugo, We will proceed accordingly." Again, Justice Couchan held Steph with a steady gaze and with a gravity in his voice that made her anxious. She felt that both he and she were doing some kind of dance, skirting round the real issue - the real question.

"Well, have I been charged with something? Is there some 'truth' about a charge that you are trying to establish?

"Our questions so far have been leading us towards establishing whether there is a 'charge' as you put it. Having listened to your answers We now propose to inform you of the conclusion of Our deliberations." He paused and looked at Steph as if seeking her permission to continue.

"Well, at least that will explain what it is you think I have done wrong - if anything."

Justice Couchan made an open handed gesture and small nod of his head as if to say, "precisely - thank you". With that tacit permission from Steph he proceeded. "On the basis of the facts presented to Us, the questions asked and answers given We, the assembled members of The Court of Truth, believe the following indictments must be answered by Mrs Stephanie Hugo in order to finally establish the truth and therefore the action that must be taken in her case." He looked up. "Will the clerk please pass to Mrs Hugo the written indictments." A man in the court moved forward to the side of the dock. The young man who was, as usual, seated behind Steph in the dock, moved forward and took the document that was passed through a little hatch. He handed it to Steph and returned to his seat. This done, Justice Couchan continued.

"The court will adjourn for one hour to give you time to read through the document that you have just been handed, Mrs Hugo. When we reconvene I will again offer you the option of counsel before we proceed. Please return Mrs Hugo to her cell." With that, the young man and the warder stepped forward and Steph was returned to her cell.

She sat on the edge of her bed and looked at the piece of paper – "The Court of Truth, Justice Couchan Presiding: Indictments in the Case of Stephanie Hugo". Here, at last, was what it was this court considered she had done wrong. There were three indictments. She read and reread them several times. She had become used to legal phraseology, but as she had noted in her letter to John, this wording sounded archaic rather than legalistic. Nevertheless, the three indictments were clear enough and she spent the hour trying to formulate her response to each charge. Certainly there seemed to her to be assumptions in some of the wording that she would want to challenge.

*

John and the lady from the bank had worked out a route that they thought would minimise the chances of meeting other people, as they made their way to her house. The little party of four wound its way through alleys and side streets. Here and there they came across vandalised houses, sometimes with things burning in the garden, where items had been piled up and set on fire. Whenever they heard voices or saw people they stopped and hid. As well as being afraid of who they might encounter, all of them were silently afraid of what they might see. With all the destruction had people been hurt? Would there be dead people in the streets? As they continued their journey however they encountered no dead bodies, despite passing a number of buildings that had been attacked.

At one of the smashed houses there was a group similar to themselves - a man, woman and two girls picking through broken things and taking salvageable stuff back into the house. Tim had been the first to become aware of the voices from this little group and had grabbed his father's arm to silently bring the party to a halt in the alley where they were. They had crept forward until they could observe the four people while remaining hidden behind a wall. The man and the woman were both heavily tattooed and John could see the 'EM2' on each of them. Presumably this was a family. These were clearly victims and not perpetrators. Had they fled and returned or had they been present during the wrecking of their home? If they had been here throughout the destruction it would be useful to know what had taken place. Had they been physically attacked themselves? Molested? Injured? John and the lady from the bank knew that they would almost certainly encounter people sooner or later, so it was agreed that they should try speaking to this family now, and see what they could learn about the night's events that might help prepare them for any further encounters, and for what they might find when they got to their own houses.

It was decided that John would initially make his presence known, and only when he felt confident there was no danger, would he signal to the others to come out from behind the wall. Checking first to see that there were no other people about, John walked a little further down the alley to where the gate into the family's back garden hung crookedly by one hinge under an arch in the wall.

"Hello," he said standing in the aperture. The salvaging family stopped and looked up. None of them spoke. "Is this your house?" asked John.

"We're certainly not looters - if that's what you think," answered the man, bending again to pick up a wooden box.

"No, no. My house was attacked," said John by way of apology. That possible interpretation of his question had not occurred to him. "I just assumed that the same had happened to you."

The man stopped again. "You assumed right."

"May I come in?" asked John. The man smiled and then began laughing - almost hysterically, until his laughter turned to the edge of tears. He wiped a hand across his eyes and straightened himself.

"I'm sorry. Come in," he said, clearing his throat. The woman stepped forward.

"The kettle is still working. Would you like a cup of tea? I think there might be enough cups." She smiled.

"Well, I'm afraid there are more of us," said John, sensing that there was no danger from these people and signalling to the others to join him.

Tea was duly made, and with salvaged cups and two tin cans, the eight sat down and recounted their own stories of the previous night. As John had assumed, this was a family and this, their home. The man and woman were probably in their early to mid-forties and the girls were fifteen and ten years of age. The destruction had been carried out by no more than eight or ten men and women. The family had all been in bed when these people broke in.

"They seemed drunk, crazy," reported the woman. "I was terrified. I didn't know what was happening. They burst into our bedroom. We tried to fight them off. I was so afraid for the children. I wanted to get to them but there were too many of these thugs. They grabbed both me and my husband and shut us in the bathroom. I could hear them smashing things, shouting to one another to go to the next room, and things like that."

"We tried to get out. We were so afraid for the children," added the man, "but the door was one that you could lock from the outside ... old fashioned retro door with a key! We banged and shouted ... but had nothing to use to prise the lock or break the wood."

"I could hear mum and dad screaming and shouting above the noise," added the older girl, "and then I became very frightened. I could not imagine what was happening to them. Then the door of our bedroom flew open and in they came - into our room." She looked at her younger sister. "They pulled me out of bed. They stood me in front of a big cupboard in my room. It's heavy. They pushed it over. I think they were trying to kill me and they must have thought that they had, 'coz they left the room. They had smashed so much though, and the huge cupboard fell on an upside down table that held it at an angle long enough for me to wriggle out from underneath. I don't think I'll ever forget that though. My concern was also for my little sister." The younger girl hugged her sibling. "She had crawled under her blankets, and her bed was completely covered with broken glass, but she was all right. When the men had gone to do more damage in other houses we were able to release mum and dad."

"... and survey the wreck which had been our home," added the father.

John had no intention of questioning the girl's interpretation of the attempt to kill her. Turning over the cupboard on top of her had certainly seemed deliberate ... but he was relieved that there had been no beatings or use of weapons directed at the family members. The destructive violence had been unleashed on the family possessions, not the family.

"Did they make any threats or say why they were doing this?" enquired John.

"Not really ... did they?" answered the woman looking at her husband.

"No, not really," he said. "They all wore *PMV* insignia - some as arm bands, but a lot of them were wearing clothing - shorts and tops - and the tops had *PMV* insignia on them too."

"I told you, didn't I?" said the woman from the bank with a look of satisfaction towards John "...and I bet you and your wife had not joined the *PMV* had you?" she asked, almost rhetorically, looking at the father of the two girls.

"No, I pay my taxes and expect a police force and army to be maintained professionally to deal with unrest and crime ... not a bunch of volunteers ... volunteers who now seem to be vigilantes."

"I told you it was the *PMV*," said the bank lady to John.

"Oh yes, it's the *PMV*," confirmed the father. "I've been on the phone to a woman at work. Like me, she hadn't become a volunteer. Her house was attacked too. Same story - a bunch of people wearing *PMV* insignia smashing everything. She was scared witless."

"But she wasn't hurt?" enquired John.

"Not seriously," said the man, "though they pushed her about a bit - and hit her when she tried to stop them, but she was OK enough to talk to me on the phone. She sounded angry more than anything - though that might have been a cover-up for being frightened."

Once John and the lady from the bank had told their stories they thanked their hosts for the hospitality, and were about to set off on the remainder of their journey, when the woman said:

"I saw your 'EM2'. It's once in a blue moon that I see anyone else with one, and know what they must have gone through to achieve it. What were the chances ... and who would have thought two 'EM2' families would ... or even could, meet under circumstances like this? What sickness has caused this?"

John looked silently at the dejected little group. He didn't say anything in response. He didn't need to. The woman could see that John was as bewildered as she was. John simply repeated his thanks – and that of his 'family'- for the tea and they left.

The little band continued to be cautious, but after being ignored by a woman with a *PMV* armband who unexpectedly stepped out from a doorway as they passed, they became less fearful. The town was coming to life, and soon they had passed and been ignored by several people with *PMV* armbands. There were no tops or shorts evident. In many ways it appeared to be a normal day, and the people they encountered were going about their daily business. They seemed uninterested in this little party of four. The passers-by probably didn't notice the absence of armbands on the two adults - that is, not until they were at the top of the street where the lady from the bank lived.

As they turned into the street they met a group of three men walking towards them. At first, like everyone else they had encountered, the men didn't seem to pay them much attention but then, just after they had gone past, one said,

"Hey, hold up...!" and ran back to stand in front of the four saying, "You're him ... you're the bloke that's married to that red dress woman" and then, calling to his companions who were standing looking back, "...It's him, the bloke married to the bomber woman, it's him!" The two companions, not convinced, ambled back down the road.

"He's got no arm band ... neither has she," said one looking at John and the lady from the bank as they joined their companion. "Well, mate, what you got to say? You married to that red dress bomber, like he says?"

John was no match for these three if there was going to be trouble. "No," he said simply.

"Why aren't you wearing an arm band then?"

"Because I don't wish to ... or do you think everyone not wearing an arm band is married to, '*that red dress woman*'?" John emphasised the quote to highlight the stupidity of using the absence of an arm band as evidence that he was married to Steph, but realised this was lost on his accuser.

"Well, mate what you got to say?" asked one of the other two and then continued, "He's pretty good with faces," indicating his companion.

"No, I don't know what you are talking about," repeated John.

215

"It is you ... I saw you at the court. You were there for her trial and I was there for mine at the same time. I saw you," said the other again.

"I'm sorry, you're mistaken," said John a third time which was followed by the lady from the bank grabbing John's arm and rounding off the argument with,

"Too right you lot are mistaken ... unless my husband has been a bigamist all these years ... and if he has there will be some bombs flying ... from me!" The third assailant guffawed at this, though his companions didn't get the joke. "Come on John. Come on kids," said the woman beginning to walk the party away from the three while the chuckling one encouraged his comrades to leave the little group alone. John gave guilty, embarrassed and hushed thanks to his 'wife' once out of earshot of the three and they finally reached her house and ascended a couple of steps to the front door. It was intact and the house frontage looked undamaged. They glanced back up the street. The men still stood gawping after them. The bank lady put her key in the lock and they went inside.

*

"So, Mrs Hugo," began Justice Couchan, "have you had sufficient time to read the indictments that were handed to you?"

"Thank you Your Honour, I have read the indictments. I am assuming I have the right to challenge them?"

"Yes, indeed Mrs Hugo, you are absolutely correct, and We sincerely hope and pray that it will be possible to assist you in finding the way of truth that will mean that you are fully absolved of these indictments. In terms of that assistance We would, once again, encourage you to take counsel from one of Our number. Will you avail yourself of that offer Mrs Hugo? We earnestly urge you to do so."

Steph had already given this offer some thought. She had concluded that any advice would simply be advice to agree with whatever this court, just like previous courts, wanted. She felt confident that she was perfectly able to think and reason for herself.

"I am content with my own counsel, thank you."

"I will not conceal my disappointment or concern Mrs Hugo," sighed Justice Couchan with resignation, "- but the offer will remain open should you change your mind at any point in the proceedings. We will therefore consider each of the indictments in turn. We will read each one to you and then ask whether you accept the indictment as true or not true. If you accept it as 'true' then We will discuss that indictment no further. If you contend that it is 'not true' then it will be for you to challenge and explain to us the falsehood in the indictment. Is that clear?"

"Perfectly clear, Your Honour."

"Do you have any questions before We read the indictments?"

"No."

"In that case, We will start with the first indictment. You have your copy before you but I will read it aloud:

Indictment 1. Mrs Hugo denies Trueway and The Book of Truth electing instead to follow her own, individual conscience - her 'truth' - in guiding her behaviour, even when that comes into conflict with the former.

In evidence of this: Mrs Hugo accedes to and obeys her own counsel as dictated by her conscience which she also refers to as her 'truth'. She always obeys this and does not seek or accept counsel regarding her actions from significant others whomsoever they be - friends, family, work colleagues, police, judiciary or ecclesiastic ministers. In particular she does not accept the guidance of Trueway whatsoever when it is contrary to her own personal 'truth'. She believes firmly that the voice of her conscience is good, saying that, if it were evil she would quite well have known how to distinguish this since it would be advising harm to others.

Mrs Hugo defends her actions - even when deemed inappropriate or criminal by others in authority - on the basis of her conscience - her 'truth'. As to Trueway, she had deferred and refused to submit herself, her deeds, and her words to it (although many times required and admonished so to do) saying always that it is impossible to her to do contrary to what she had, in her Trial, affirmed to have done in accord with her conscience - her 'truth' and that for these things she will not refer to the decision or the judgment of others, including those of Trueway.

Here ends the First Indictment. I ask you, Mrs Hugo, Do you accept this indictment as 'true' or 'not true'?"

"Not true, Your Honour," said Steph firmly.

"Thank you, Mrs Hugo. You have said that you consider this indictment as 'not true'. Please tell Us what it is that you wish to challenge regarding this indictment. Take as long as you need Mrs Hugo. Remember We are all here for truth."

Steph looked at the indictment and her head began to swim a little - though she calmed herself with Justice Couchan's advice to take as long as she needed, and by telling herself that she was 'good' and needed just to be true to herself. She tried to remember what she had been thinking when she looked at it back in her cell.

"Well, I accept that I follow my truth ... but I don't see why that has to be in conflict with Trueway or The Book of Truth. I don't deny Trueway or The Book of Truth. And I don't recall there being much, if anything, said in my former appearances here in the court about not accepting counsel from friends, family and so on. That wasn't brought up was it?" Steph looked at Justice Couchan. She didn't feel she was doing very well in refuting this indictment.

"It is true, Mrs Hugo," conceded Justice Couchan, "that we have not covered everything here in the court. There is, however, ample documentation available to us to substantiate the claim that you ignore friends, family and work colleagues. However, that wording can, if you wish, be removed from the indictment - say the whole sentence from 'She' to 'ministers'. It serves only to illustrate the extent of your insistence in following your truth." Justice Couchan signalled to the clerk to remove the sentence, before returning his gaze to Steph. "The substantive point, Mrs Hugo, is that you place *your* 'truth' above that of Trueway as the ultimate arbiter in guiding your behaviour. By implication you regard yourself as infallible and Trueway as fallible."

"No, I would never say that I was infallible," retorted Steph indignantly.

"Then, let us put the truth of this indictment to the test Mrs Hugo," came Justice Couchan's swift rejoinder. "This court and these august Assessors speak with authoritative knowledge of The Book of Truth. This court is the ultimate voice of Trueway - of truth. Do you accept and agree to abide by its rulings and its requirements without question in terms of your behaviour?"

The trap was set - and whichever way she stepped she would be ensnared. Say 'No' and the indictment was proven. Say 'Yes' and she was agreeing to blind obedience. The words, 'without question' rang in Steph's head. To agree to this requirement would be to go against everything she felt she stood for. She had no choice. She would speak the truth.

"No."

"Be sure of your answer Mrs Hugo. To refuse to abide by the requirements of this court is to deny the authority, the unerring authority, of Trueway. Again, we offer you counsel that you might give further, advised consideration to your answer. Will you take our counsel?"

Steph remained silent. She could see now the way in which the remaining two indictments would follow a similar course to the first. Justice Couchan, his voice ever kindly, broke the silence.

"Then we must move on to the second indictment. You have your copy before you but I will read it aloud:

Indictment 2. Mrs Hugo has taken to wearing a red dress, refusing to remove and abandon it despite the advice of The Court of Truth that she should do so and failing to accept, that in light of this advice, persistence in wearing the dress is wrong.

In evidence of this: Mrs Hugo, in keeping with her 'truth', has taken to wearing a dress, which she has borne and still continues to bear, persisting in obeying her 'truth' in this matter, to the extent that she said she would rather die than give up this dress, adding that she will only abandon it if she concludes that it should be abandoned and not simply because a more powerful authority has demanded that she do so. She had even preferred not to have visits from her family, rather than remove the dress.

She has made it quite clear that if Trueway wished that she should do anything contrary to her conscience - that guidance that she did pretend to have received from an unerringly good, personal truth - she would not consent, whatsoever it might be. Thereupon she did not wish to refer to the decision of Trueway, nor to any one, whoever it be in the world, but to her own 'truth', the requirements of which she did always execute. This answer and all the others are not coming from a position based on a surface desire to be free to wear and do what she wants where and when she wants she said, but from a commitment to act in line with her truth although by the Judges and others of the Assessors, the ultimate determinant of truth, The Book of Truth had often been recalled to her, and it had often been shown to her that all faithful, Trueway Citizens are bound to obey The Court of Truth acting in line with the Holy Book of Truth and to submit to it their words and actions above all in matters of faith and in all which concerns sacred Doctrine and Ecclesiastical sanction.

Here ends the Second Indictment. I ask you, Mrs Hugo, Do you accept this indictment as 'true' or 'not true'?

"Not true," said Steph, though with resignation in her voice.

"Thank you, Mrs Hugo. You have said that you consider this indictment as 'not true'. Please tell Us what it is that you wish to challenge regarding this indictment. Take as long as you need Mrs Hugo. Remember We are all here for truth."

Steph's head no longer felt swimmy. She felt despondent. She knew now that no matter what argument she made this court would simply test this indictment with the requirement that she obey it and remove the dress. That would be the test of the court. There would be no questioning of the questioner. No questioning on the grounds of reason. Nevertheless, she would try.

"Yes, I agree that I wear a dress. I am here in full view. I also agree that I have refused to 'abandon' it, as you put it ... but only because nobody has provided adequate reason why I should. The indictment says that I have not removed it despite this court 'advising' me to ... but *why* is the court advising me to? Give me reasons that I can understand - reasons that make sense." She thought that summed up her thinking but on glancing back at the indictment added, "And I don't know why the indictment says, 'pretend' ... '*that guidance that she did <u>pretend</u> to have received from an unerringly good, personal truth* '. I do what I do in line with my conscience. Surely each person's conscience *is* good ... isn't it? So, as I see it there is no pretending. I don't *pretend* that my actions are guided by my conscience - they *are* - and I don't pretend that my conscience is good - it *is*."

Steph felt quite pleased with these points. Even if the court was going to put the indictment to the test in the way that it had before she felt she had, 'said her piece' and said it well.

"Very well put Mrs Hugo," said Justice Couchan. "You raise important questions, questions - in their general sense - that have been raised and pondered by many. Let us take your second point first - the use of the word 'pretend'. When penning the indictment consideration was given to using the word, 'believe'. Would you accept the wording if that change were made?"

Steph had not expected this. Certainly, 'believe' would remove any conscious intention on her part to deceive. She would say as much.

"Well, I think that saying 'believe' is better since 'pretend' makes it sound as though I am intentionally trying to deceive people - but I don't even know that 'believe' is right either. It still suggests that I am wrong and that following my conscience is bad in some way."

"And, Mrs Hugo, I think that is, in a nutshell, what this court - at the minimum - believes to be the case. In keeping with that minimum the clerk will change 'pretend' to 'believe' in the indictment. Why does this court consider that you are wrong in following this belief in your personal 'truth' rather than accepting the word of Trueway? This brings us to the first of your points - the demand that you make for reasons. Reasons have been proffered ... the wearing of your dress upsets people - 'alarm, harassment or distress' - to quote your previous trials. The wearing of your dress contravenes an order (the *Behaviour Restriction Order*) imposed by a duly authorised court. The wearing of your dress has caused you to be separated from your family - presumably causing them hurt as a consequence of that separation. These are all reasons, yet you do not accept these reasons. This court therefore has to ask whether the conscience that you follow - your 'truth' - is genuinely true, genuinely good ... or whether it is something that you *believe* to be good when it is not."

Justice Couchan paused and looked at Steph. She wasn't sure whether he expected her to make a response. He neither continued speaking nor invited her to speak. It seemed as though he was simply waiting for what he had said to settle like some dust of wisdom thrown in the air. She sensed it was futile to try and make the argument that the courts were wrong in interpreting complaints as genuine, 'alarm, harassment or distress' or that contravening the *BRO* wrongly presupposed that that order was valid in itself. She could argue that any hurt to her family, regrettable though it was, was a valid, limited hurt necessitated (and validated) by the need to fight for what was right - freedom - and she was about to launch into this when Justice Couchan, having given sufficient time to the dust, spoke again.

"So you see Mrs Hugo, we have stalemate. The courts - society even - say that they are right. You say that you are right. In this situation a final arbiter is required. That arbiter is Trueway. So, this brings us back to final consideration of this, the second indictment - your refusal to remove the red dress that you wear despite the advice of that infallible arbiter - Trueway. Here I will draw your attention to the final sentence of that indictment that all, *Trueway Citizens are bound to obey The Court of Truth acting in line with the holy Book of Truth and to submit to it their words and actions above all in matters of faith and in all which concerns sacred Doctrine and Ecclesiastical sanction.* If you are a Trueway Citizen Mrs Hugo then these words apply to you. If you choose not to obey this court then you choose not to obey Trueway and you effectively cast yourself out from the bosom of Trueway - a bosom where you are loved, protected and through which you can attain ultimate salvation. It is in your hands whether you excommunicate yourself from this. Again We offer you counsel at this point," Justice Couchan paused and looked gravely at Steph, "... and would urge that you avail yourself of it."

Steph felt herself trembling - a mixture of fear and anger - fear at the threat that lurked in the words and anger at the way in which, as had been the case previously, she was being given responsibility for what the court was doing. Refuse to take off your dress and you are choosing to absent yourself from the hearing, denying yourself the right to address the jury she was told - yet it was the court's decision - the judge's decision - not to allow her into the hearing. Here it was happening again - refuse to obey Trueway and you are excommunicating yourself from Trueway when the truth was that any decision of that nature was being made by the court, by Trueway. Steph would not take counsel from people who deceived themselves, deluded themselves with this failure to admit the truth to themselves.

Again she remained silent.

At this point Steph had expected that Justice Couchan would apply a similar test to the second indictment that he had applied to the first but, in face of her silence simply said,

"In that case we will progress to the third and final indictment. You have your copy before you but I will read it aloud:

Indictment 3. Mrs Hugo, through her letters and her actions in persisting to wear a red dress has incited and supported political unrest and a revolt against Trueway.

In evidence of this: The same woman did avow and acknowledge that she had corresponded with one Robert Cray, encouraging him to act in accordance with his personal truth - just as she was doing - in order to gain freedom and to do this without fear of consequences - political or personal - "since there is

222

nothing more important than freedom". She claimed that the only way to peace was through people being true to themselves united since, through acting united in those individual truths (as she was doing) change would be created more widely. Such a change - the destruction of Trueway - is being sought by Robert Cray and others working in line with their individual truths 'united' as advocated by Mrs Hugo. This is evidenced by Robert Cray's own words to Mrs Hugo that she had the support of him and others and by the symbol of the red dress that is always found in association with the bombings carried out by him and his colleagues.

Here ends the Third Indictment. I ask you, Mrs Hugo, Do you accept this indictment as 'true' or 'not true'?

"Not true," said Steph, though she realised as she said this that she had not actually listened to the indictment being read to her.

"Thank you, Mrs Hugo. You have said that you consider this indictment as 'not true'. Please tell Us what it is that you wish to challenge regarding this indictment. Again, take as long as you need Mrs Hugo and remember We are all here for truth," and then, after a pause, "... and for you."

Steph turned her eyes to the paper in front of her. She started to feverishly read until she got to the final words, "...him and his colleagues" only to realise that she didn't know what she had read. She couldn't remember. She had been reading but not taking it in. Her mind was spinning - jumping backwards and forwards between the first two indictments and the things that had been said. She started again to read. "Indictment 3. ...". She knew she hadn't had anything to do with stirring up unrest or revolt ... but what was she to say other than simply deny it? What argument could she make that was anything stronger, more persuasive, more valid than pantomime-like contradiction? Her silence seemed to go on and on. The silence in the court seemed to go on and on - waiting for her. She felt she was sinking, drowning in that silence. The room seemed to be getting physically darker as if she were sinking in water, drifting away from the light. The calm tone of Justice Couchan then rippled to her.

"You are silent Mrs Hugo. I urge you, I urge you sincerely, to take counsel. Will you?"

Steph looked out across the murky court room. The voice of Justice Couchan in her head, '*I* urge you'. She looked down at her hand holding the piece of paper with the indictments. '*I* urge you'. She felt suddenly tired, incapable of thought. '*I* urge you'. She needed to think. She needed *time* to think. All she had at the moment was a blank mind with his words, '*I* urge you' washing over it like ripples on the smooth sand of a beach.

"Yes." She heard herself say ... though it wasn't until she heard Justice Couchan speak again that she was sure she had voiced the word rather than simply thought it.

"I am glad Mrs Hugo. Is there any member of this court that you wish to elect to provide that counsel?"

Steph felt herself returning to the court as if from some other place. It was becoming lighter around her. She was beginning to breathe again, think again. She had said 'yes' to counsel. It would give her time, time to think.

She looked at the ranks of anonymous Assessors and at the Bench of three. She looked at The Justice Civil, silent, malevolent she felt and The Justice Martial pompous, bombastic and there, in the centre, Justice Couchan - an imposing, yet oddly kind figure.

"You, Your Honour, if I may," answered Steph. There was no hesitancy or uncertainty in her voice. She was back. She was thinking.

*

The unscathed exterior of the front of the bank lady's house made the interior chaos all the more shocking. The little group of four stood in a hallway that had once been modestly elegant, but was now completely wrecked. Pictures from the wall lay with broken frames and smashed glass on the floor. A vase lay in pieces at their feet, the red and yellow flowers that had been in it strewn about. Glass and broken crockery crunched under their boots as they went forward. A cracked mirror reflected their entry into the living room. There was very little left inside. Most of the furniture had been thrown out of the windows and now littered the garden, in the corner of which a bonfire still smouldered. They were startled by a robin that had found its way in and now flew out through a broken window. They went silently from room to room. Everywhere the devastation was the same. They came to a halt in the bathroom. The toilet was unbroken and the lady from the bank sat down on the closed lid. The two children perched on the side of the bath and John simply stood looking down at the poor woman feeling he should say or do something - but having no idea what. The situation was too overwhelming. Eventually, more to break the silence than anything, he said,

"Thank you again for what you did out there. That was quick thinking."

"That's OK - stupid louts."

"Do you think they were involved in this?"

"Who knows? I didn't recognise them ... but I didn't recognise any of the people that burst in either, so ... I don't know. I don't know." She sat, totally dejected.

"Do you have family - someone who can come and help with all this?" asked John.

She looked up. "Yes, there are people, assuming they don't have the same to contend with. I know a few of my friends were of a similar mind to me and had not joined up. If you go to the bank today Mr Hugo I am afraid I won't be there."

"You could come back to our house," suggested May kindly.

The lady smiled. "You are very kind. Thank you - but I will be fine and... well ... who knows what you will have to deal with yourselves?" At that moment there was a banging on the front door downstairs. They all froze.

"Can we get out the back?" John asked as they all started to make their way downstairs. The banging came again when they were half way down ... and then a voice called, "Kathy, Kathy ... are you OK? Kathy?" and more, urgent banging. With relief the lady from the bank flung open the door to reveal a very concerned gentleman in his sixties.

"Oh Colin, Colin, thank goodness ..." and with that she burst into tears.

John did not stay to enquire who Colin was - he was just relieved that someone had arrived who could help, and who would allow him to leave this good woman without feeling too much guilt. John didn't check to see if the three assailants from earlier were still down the street, but felt it best anyway to take Tim and May out through the back garden.

'Kathy', thought John as they left. *The lady from the bank was, 'Kathy'...*

*

The journey home was taken with caution - with alertness - but without an attempt to be completely unobserved. John felt they were likely

225

to blend in better if they behaved normally. This strategy appeared to work, though it seemed to John, that everyone was wearing *PMV* arm bands, and he felt sure that someone would suddenly pounce on him as the only adult out and about without one. As he and the children walked, he mentally rehearsed his response in the event that such a challenge occurred. He would explain how it had got torn off the night before, how he would not be so stupid as to be wandering around without it, if he was 'one of them', and how he would have it back on later in the day. As it was, he did not have to utilise this explanation. Although he felt that he stood out as if in a bright spotlight, nobody seemed to notice and he, Tim and May reached the turning into the close in which they lived without incident. At that point however the little party slowed, almost to a halt, with the shock of what they saw.

The first thing they noticed was not their own house, but Charlie's. A little hedge that he neatly trimmed was trampled. There was a pile of broken bits and pieces on his front lawn. On the path, where he would generally be sitting at this time of day, there was more broken stuff - including his radio. The windows had been shattered and it was possible to see further devastation in the gloom of the interior. There was some police tape over the gaping hole where his front door had been. There was no sign of Charlie himself.

They edged silently past Charlie's house and past unscathed buildings towards their own. They could see the police tape fluttering from the gate to their small front garden, and as they came closer, the now familiar pile of wreckage - only this time, it was the wreckage of their home, their lives. Bits of furniture that had, the day before simply been 'furniture', now became - for all three of them - intensely personal. It was 'their' furniture. Through its destruction, through the careless way it was tossed as rubbish in a heap, they themselves had been personally violated. They came to a halt, looking and feeling these feelings, no longer concerned about being seen or questioned. The sight of their home destroyed, and the ill intent towards them should have made them more afraid - but it didn't. It left them numb.

They stood on the street. The police tape - fragile as it was - formed a barrier that their good civil minds rebelled against crossing, even though the building beyond was their own home. Like Charlie's house the windows were completely gone as was the front door and they could see vaguely into the gloom inside. Without warning Tim ran forward screaming and tearing away the police tape. John was quickly after him concerned that there may be damage within that would be dangerous - dislodged furniture that might topple, broken flooring that he might fall through. Tim bounded into the dark of the house and John was about to follow when he was momentarily brought to a halt by a scream from Tim. As John was about to head into the gloom shouting "Tim" his son emerged, struggling in the arms of a huge man - a policeman judging by the insignia armband.

"Put him down," yelled John reaching for his son while May, who had now caught up, grabbed the policeman's arm, and was pulling it in an attempt to loosen the man's grip on her brother. She did not have to pull for long since the policeman released Tim quite willingly into John's grasp. John swung Tim round behind him and instinctively pulled May round behind with a scooping motion too.

"Why are you in my house?" demanded John. Before an answer was forthcoming there were voices behind John from the street.

"Told you it was him ... told you it was." John looked over his shoulder to see the three men that they had encountered close to Kathy's house. He looked back at the policeman.

"Mr Hugo, I am arresting you on suspicion of involvement in terrorist activity. You do..."

"You're doing what!" yelled John, all fear gone. The policeman continued with his regulation caution simultaneously reaching for John as two more officers emerged from the gloom of John's house. They moved swiftly and John was grabbed and held firmly by his arms. He struggled but it was no use. May and Tim did what they could, punching, kicking and grappling with the officers but then the three men from the street joined in and held the squirming children off.

"Let them go," yelled John in frustrated anger but it was no use. All three of them were firmly held. As John struggled he could hear the sound of a police siren growing louder and within seconds a police van pulled up.

John and the children were pushed into the street and towards the waiting vehicle.

"You were quick!" shouted the arresting officer to the policeman from the van who was now undoing the doors at the back.

"Yep – let's get them inside ... haven't you got cuffs?" came the response.

John looked at the speaker. The voice was familiar. To his astonishment it was the man he had met at the Causeway Cafe - Robert.

"What the hell ...," began John.

"Shut up you scum!!" screamed Robert bearing down on him ..." and get in the van. Get him in the van ... and the kids!" He ordered the group holding the struggling three. With the adrenalin of anger, fear and the need to protect his children, John managed to wrench an arm free. His fist lashed out at the officer holding his other arm and dazed him with a blow below his ear. John's second arm became free ... but it was too late. He didn't see the blow from Robert coming or even feel it. It was delivered with precision and John's world went black. After that he was unaware of being bundled into the van. He was unaware of Tim and May being bundled in as well, and secured in a cage before the doors were shut on the three of them. He was unaware of the calming words to his children from a woman in the back of the van, or of the way she cradled him as the vehicle pulled away and, as they picked up speed and began winding through streets, he was unaware of the sound of another police siren from another police van heading in the direction of his house.

*

The sound of keys and unlocking, and Justice Couchan entered. Steph had expected that she would be taken to some room with Justice Couchan for counsel. She had not expected that he would come to her. Here, in the confines of Steph's cell, he looked even bigger than in the court. In the court he was imposing. Here he seemed to fill the room. He was portly but tall as well - a bulk that seemed to swallow the air of the space. A warder came in with him carrying a folding chair. She placed the chair opposite Steph who was sitting on her bed and left the cell, closing and locking the door behind her. Steph was a little surprised to be left alone with such an important figure as Justice Couchan - especially since she seemed to be regarded as some kind of terrorist figure. He seemed to read her thoughts.

"Thank you for requesting counsel Mrs Hugo - and thank you also for asking that I provide that counsel. Do not be surprised that the warder did not stay. I asked specifically that we be left alone. I wanted you to be free to say what you think ... in fact for both of us to be able to talk freely. There are no sound or video monitors in here either. Whatever we say to each other is purely between the two of us." As he spoke he removed his yellow wig.

"Thank you," said Steph meekly.

"The court was asking you to consider Indictment 3 when you asked for counsel," began Justice Couchan. "What made you seek counsel at that point Mrs Hugo?"

Steph was relieved to be sitting in her cell rather than the court room. She remembered how things had gone dark in there, how she had stopped functioning, how she felt she needed time ... time to think ... time to work something out ... but that seemed the 'wrong' reason to be seeking counsel. She looked at Justice Couchan. What was he expecting her to say? She had to say something. She looked down. The paper with the indictments was still in her hand. She looked up again at Justice Couchan. He looked kindly. She had no sense of him being impatient with her continued silence. She looked again at the paper in her hand. She held it forward and quietly said,

"It's all lies - but I don't know what to say."

Justice Couchan remained silent, though he nodded thoughtfully and took the list of indictments from her. He looked at the indictments and then at Steph.

"You say they are lies - but are they? In court, full consideration was given to the first two indictments. It was clear that you follow your own truth, and sitting here now I can see that you are still wearing your red dress. It will not be for me alone to ultimately decide whether these first two indictments are determined as 'true', but I see little to suggest that they are not."

"But what does it matter if they are true? It doesn't harm anyone!" blurted Steph – almost in tears with frustration.

"It is not the purpose of the court to determine whether those indictments, of themselves, have harmed anyone. The court is simply there to establish whether those indictments are true. There is also the third indictment which the court has not yet considered ... and I can assure you Mrs Hugo that people are being hurt as a consequence of the unrest and the bombings that are taking place across the globe."

"But that has nothing to do with me," said Steph indignantly. "The words in my letters have been twisted - taken to mean what they don't. I have never incited or encouraged violence ... never. That's why I say it's all a lie."

"I believe you Mrs Hugo. I believe that you have never, *intentionally* sought to encourage unrest - at least not unrest that involved violence. The inescapable facts however, are that you have corresponded with Robert Cray and that you have encouraged individual freedom, and action, in line with personal conscience above the rule of Trueway. It is also inescapably true that you persist in wearing a red dress, and that violence is taking place throughout the World under the symbol of a red dress. Again, I must emphasise that it will be for the court to decide on all three of the indictments and not me alone, but the case for their truth appears quite compelling ... and any lack of intentionality on your part does not detract from that."

"But surely my *intentions* matter...don't they?"

Justice Couchan leaned forward and in an a hushed, almost conspiratorial, voice said, "They matter Mrs Hugo ... but they matter more to some and less to others depending on what is at stake." Justice Couchan sat back again before continuing. "I admire you, Mrs Hugo. You have integrity. You are being true to yourself but - and I don't think I over emphasise the situation - the rule of law, the authority of Trueway ... the very foundation and fabric of our society ... is under threat of destruction ... and I believe that you stand in a position where you must make a choice. That choice is to act in a way that will be seen to further that destruction or in a way that will be seen to help counter it."

"So what are you saying I must do?"

"There are three indictments. You must endeavour to show that each one is not 'true' or, at least, will not be true henceforth. For the first indictment you must agree to accept the decisions and guidance of Trueway above your own individual truth. As proof of your agreement you will remove your red dress, and in so doing counter the second indictment. The abandoning of your dress will also show to the World at large that you do not support and advocate the ant-Trueway activity that is taking place, so addressing - in part at least- the third indictment."

"To 'the World at large'?" queried Steph.

"Yes, your demonstration of the untruth of each indictment will be filmed and broadcast."

"So, in essence you are saying that I must sacrifice my own principles 'for the greater good' - or at least a greater good that the court has thrust upon me?"

At this, the Justice Couchan remained silent. What he thought and whether he agreed or disagreed, no longer mattered. He knew that Steph had understood what he had told her. Steph looked at him. She felt he still had something kindly about him. She held out her hand and took back the paper with the indictments.

"And if I refuse to do as you counsel? If I refuse to refute each of the indictments in the way you say? What then?"

"If you refuse Mrs Hugo, then it will be for the court to decide whether or not each of the indictments is 'true'. If the court finds that any are 'true' then..." He paused and looked long and hard at Steph. "Then it will be for the Justice Civil to determine appropriate sentence."

There was menace in that pause and Steph knew that this was the issue that she had been avoiding, but which was constantly at the back of her thoughts ... and had been since Mark Welsh had left her cell that last time in her former prison. It was with trepidation that she asked,

"And what is that sentence likely to be?"

"I cannot say what is 'likely'. It will be for the Justice Civil to determine sentence on the basis of guidance from the Book of Truth and in consultation with the Assessors as required. Her's will be a difficult job. There is no simple matching of a sentence to an indictment in the Book of Truth. Each situation is different. She will endeavour to make sentence proportionate to the *implications* of the indictments that are found to be 'true'. The more grave the implications are seen to be the more severe the sentence ... and I have to tell you Mrs Hugo that the implications may be evaluated by the Justice Civil as *very* grave." He paused, looking at Steph to emphasise this point before continuing.

"Consider the bigger picture, Mrs Hugo. There is unprecedented global unrest. Despite the identification of the *Individual Freedom Alliance* as being responsible, the so called, *Red Dress Bombings* continue. Because of this, some think that there must be other forces at work behind the *Individual Freedom Alliance*. There is fear and there is suspicion – and in the centre of all this, there is a woman who defiantly wears a red dress. Wittingly, or unwittingly you have become the symbol – the standard bearer, even - for all this unrest.

If you fail to abandon the dress and denounce the bombings then you will be seen to be condoning and supporting them – possibly even be in league with the unknown forces behind the *Individual Freedom Alliance*.

There is no guarantee that your abandonment of your dress and denouncement of the bombings will end the unrest, but your failure to do so would certainly be seen as likely to perpetuate the violence – and that has huge implications for Trueway. It is this which the Justice Civil will be considering in terms of sentence, should you ignore my council to do what is necessary to prove the indictments as 'not true'." Again Justice Couchan paused and held Steph in a silent gaze. She felt a mix of increasing anxiety and impatience, as he seemed to be avoiding the one thing that she wanted to know. She could stand this no more.

"Yes - but what sentences are open to her ... to the Justice Civil? Even if you can't tell me what is 'likely' ... what is *possible*?" Justice Couchan looked at Steph with resignation before eventually saying,

"Everything."

"What do you mean?" asked Steph.

"I mean everything. Everything from admonishment through imprisonment, to corporal punishment," again a pause, "… and even capital punishment."

Steph was stunned to silence as those words resounded in her head. Eventually she found her voice.

"Are you telling me that I could be executed for wearing a dress?"

"You wanted to know what was possible ... what options the Justice Civil had open to her." Justice Couchan sounded almost apologetic. "I have already said that I do not know what sentence is *likely* ... but I have tried to emphasise to you the gravity of your position. All I would point out, in terms of sentence, is that even in civil court your sentence was... appeals aside ... in reality, life imprisonment. I think it is therefore unlikely that the sentence of The Court of Truth, will be less than that if all the indictments are found 'true'."

Steph remained silent.

"I'm sorry, Mrs Hugo. It has not been my intention to frighten you or upset you. I have tried to be honest in the counsel that I have given. My counsel is simple. For everyone's sake, including your own and your family's, please take steps to disprove the indictments by agreeing to publicly obey the requirements of Trueway, remove the dress and denounce the unrest."

"May I have some time?" asked Steph.

"Of course. I will come back in a while." With that Justice Couchan stood, folded his chair, knocked on the cell door and was let out, leaving Steph alone. More alone than she had ever been.

*

It was half an hour later when Justice Couchan entered Steph's cell for the second time. That half hour had been simultaneously the shortest half hour of her life making her feel she had no time to think, and a half hour that had stretched away interminably like a long straight road to the horizon where it disappeared into nothingness, taking with it her life. She had however made her decision. When Justice Couchan re-entered her cell it seemed to Steph that she was somehow outside herself - hovering up on the ceiling looking down. There was Justice Couchan, a living mountain in her room sucking up all the air and there she was, small and naked sitting on the edge of her bed, and even smaller beside her, neatly folded, her red dress.

*

When John regained consciousness he was in bed under a crisp white sheet. The room around him was airy and calm with pale blue walls. He could hear birds singing outside through an open window. His head ached and he soon remembered the events that had taken place outside his house. He sat up looking round the room - where was he? Where were Tim and May? Caution subdued his instinct to shout their names in order to locate them. This place did not look like a prison, but he clearly remembered Robert and the imminent arrest of himself and his children. He remained still, straining to hear any sound that may give a clue to where he was or what was happening. At first he could hear nothing other than the bird song, but then voices and a little laughter. He slid out of bed and edged to the window to find himself looking out onto a very pleasant little lawn with flower beds, and to his astonishment and relief, Tim and May sitting in the middle of it playing with a puppy. Again, he resisted the temptation to call out. Was this real? His head throbbed. Was he hallucinating? He looked at his hands - touched the windowsill. All seemed real - but of course it would.

"Dad!"

John looked up to see his children running towards him with the puppy seemingly attempting to tangle itself in their feet.

"Dad, dad --- you're awake!" called Tim as he bounded onto the wooden veranda outside the window before bursting into the room through a door to John's left and flinging himself on his father.

"How do you feel dad?" asked May as she came into the room, the puppy squirming in her arms.

"I'm OK. A bit of a headache. Are you two OK? Do you know where we are?"

"We're fine," answered May putting the puppy down outside and closing the door. John looked at his children and saw nothing to contradict what May was saying.

"So, where are we? Do you know?"

"We're at the house we told you about, John," came a woman's voice from behind him.

John span round. He had not heard anyone enter the room. He instantly recognised the speaker. It was the woman he had met at the Causeway Cafe - Lisa.

"How is your head John?" she enquired, "I'm afraid that we had to give you a sedative as well as that rather heavy thump. I'm sorry, but we had to get you away from the police, and it seemed the only way. There's a jug of water by your bed." She pointed to the bedside cabinet where a glass jug stood, frosted from the ice cubes inside. "You should drink plenty. It will help. There are some pain killers on the cabinet too if you feel you need to take a couple. You've been unconscious almost twenty-four hours so I can get you some breakfast if you feel like eating."

John remained silent. He couldn't work out what was going on. His head throbbed. "I don't think I could eat ... not just yet."

"I'll leave you and the kids to have a chat. Show your dad the garden and stuff," said Lisa addressing the two young people. "I'll come back later, or if you want to see me and ask any questions ... or get some breakfast ... I'll be somewhere in the house so just wander and give me a yell. There's no restriction on where you go ... but please, until we have had a discussion and you understand the situation please, please don't try and leave. While you are here the three of you are safe." With that she left a puzzled John with his children.

*

234

Justice Couchan appeared genuinely relieved when he found that Steph had removed her dress, and when she confirmed to him that she would be obedient to Trueway. He explained that he would relay her decision to the court and that preparations would be made for the live video transmission of her public obedience to Trueway. This would take place the following day. A script would be prepared for her. When Justice Couchan left Steph he took her red dress with him.

Steph spent the remainder of the day and night alone, save for the times when food was brought to her. She felt a deep sadness and disappointment. She felt she had betrayed the dress - betrayed herself. She slept fitfully and did not feel refreshed. She left most of her breakfast and did not do her usual morning routine. Eventually, around 10:30 am two warders came to take her to where she was to do the video. They walked together down the corridor towards the court but, before reaching it turned aside through one of the doors, and Steph found herself in a room about the size of a school classroom. There was a welcoming smell of coffee and Steph realised how long it had been since she had smelled fresh coffee ... or indeed anything fresh.

The room was filled with all the paraphernalia of a broadcasting centre - though it looked temporary, with wires snaking across the floor and held in place with tape. The Justice Couchan was there, waiting for her, as was her red dress. It had been draped over the back of a chair - *not even placed on a hanger*, thought Steph.

The warders entered the room with Steph, closed the door and remained there flanking it. Justice Couchan - large and smiling - welcomed Steph and directed her to a chair - one of a group of comfortable armchairs around a low coffee table in the corner of the room. The seats were already covered with paper sitting cloths.

"Would you like coffee?" Enquired Justice Couchan as Steph sat down.

"No, thank you, I'm fine." He poured himself a cup and took up a chair opposite to Steph.

"Did you sleep well?"

"Not really," said Steph with a wan smile.

"You are doing the right thing, Mrs Hugo - really you are." He smiled reassuringly. "Let me explain what will happen. At the moment there are only the warders and myself here. I felt it was best to let you familiarise yourself with things before others arrived - the technical crew, and of course, The Justice Martial and Justice Civil." Steph listened. He was being kind but she felt indifferent. "This is the script that will be followed for the broadcast." Justice Couchan indicated a piece of paper on the coffee table and pushed it towards Steph. She obligingly picked it up and skimmed through it. It was not very long. "You will see," he continued, "that it takes the form of a dialogue - an interview - between you, myself, the Justice Martial and the Justice Civil. When the broadcast takes place this dialogue will come up on a screen in front of you so you won't need to look down at a piece of paper."

"An autocue," volunteered Steph.

"Yes, exactly," said Justice Couchan, "an autocue. As well as the autocue the things that you say will always be prompted by a question from one of us. There can be a rehearsal with the technical crew ... but I felt it might be helpful to you to go through it here, with me first to familiarise yourself in an unhurried way. Are you happy to do that? I have a copy for myself, if you are."

Steph wasn't 'happy' about any of what was happening, but if it was going to happen, then she could see no reason why she should not co-operate with Justice Couchan. They left the comfortable chairs and went to the centre of the room where he indicated a place for her to stand. There was a camera facing her and one immediately behind her looking over her shoulder. Justice Couchan took up a position next to the camera facing Steph.

"I will say the part of myself, the Justice Civil and the Justice Martial," he said. "I'm afraid that the autocues are not turned on yet so we will have to use paper copies - but at least you will have the opportunity to go through everything ... and you can always ask to do a rehearsal again using the autocues once my colleagues and the technical crew are here." Justice Couchan looked down at his copy of the scripted interview and then back at Steph. "So, there will be some preliminaries to set the scene. The camera will then go to me." Justice Couchan cleared his throat. "I'll start with my part now." He glanced at Steph and then back at the paper he held in his hand - then back at Steph again, "Oh! What am I doing? ... I almost forgot the essential thing. You must be wearing the dress at the start of the interview. Can you put it on please?"

Steph almost laughed at the irony of this senior judicial figure instructing her to put the dress on! She did as requested however. She was surprised at how little emotion she felt as the dress fell down over her body.

"Right then, I'll start," said Justice Couchan and began to read his part from the script in his hand. "'I am the Justice Ecclesiastic of The Court of Truth. Will the prisoner please state her name?'"

Steph read in a monotone, "'I am Stephanie Hugo'."

Justice Couchan: "'You have come before the court charged with three indictments. Why are you here today?'"

Steph: "'I am here to prove to you, and the World, that the indictments are false'."

Justice Couchan: "'Then we will consider the first indictment' ... oh I should say Mrs Hugo," said Justice Couchan momentarily abandoning the script, "That we have reversed the order of the indictments for the purpose of the broadcast. We felt that because of the civil unrest it was important to address that issue immediately. I'm sorry if that's a bit confusing ..." Steph managed a smile to acknowledge that she had heard what he had said but otherwise remained unanimated. She didn't care. "So getting back to the script, 'My colleague the Justice Martial will read the first indictment'." Justice Couchan moved slightly to his left to indicate he was becoming the Justice Martial before continuing. He then read the indictment accusing Steph of inciting unrest and revolt against Trueway. When he finished Steph looked down at the piece of paper and read her lines: "'I accept that my letters and actions may have contributed to unrest, but this was not my intention. I do not support such unrest and strongly condemn *it* and any revolt against Trueway. I denounce any bombings or violent action taken under the symbol of a red dress. I urge anyone involved in such acts of revolt to stop what they are doing'."

Justice Couchan smiled and then continued with the other two indictments. Steph dutifully, but impassively read her lines of response. Most significantly, and symbolically, she also complied when Justice Couchan, speaking the words of the Justice Civil, asked Steph to remove her dress.

Once all three indictments had been addressed Justice Couchan delivered the last lines from the script.

"'Thank you. The Court of Truth has heard your answers to the indictments and has found that you speak the truth'." Justice Couchan smiled and put down his piece of paper. "Thank you Mrs Hugo. I think that went well. After this point the broadcast doesn't require your direct involvement."

"So what happens?" asked Steph.

"Well," said Justice Couchan, with a tone that Steph read as bemusement, "the Justice Civil will pronounce sentence ... a sentence which I might now add will undoubtedly not be as severe as it might have been."

"But what will it be?" asked Steph, astonished that this, the most significant thing for her, appeared less than the central concern to Justice Couchan.

"I do not know," said Justice Couchan. "As I explained to you, the sentence is a matter for the Justice Civil."

Steph was silent with disbelief. She had done all this, yet still did not know the outcome for herself.

"Do you have any further questions, Mrs Hugo?" Steph remained silent. "In that case I will go and see if the technical crew, and the Justice Civil and Justice Martial are ready. Well, you may as well go and make yourself comfortable again," said Justice Couchan motioning in the direction of the easy chairs. "Help yourself to coffee. I won't be very long." He left and Steph went back to the easy chair. The warders watched her. She did not get herself a coffee. She did not want to do anything. She felt blank. As it was, she would hardly have had time to start drinking a cup of coffee before the door opened and Justice Couchan re-entered with a small group of people. The time between him leaving and returning was so short that Steph felt sure that all these people must have been in a nearby room simply waiting for him. It crossed Steph's mind that maybe the rehearsal had been as much a test of her co-operation as an opportunity for her to familiarise herself with the procedure.

She recognised the Justice Civil and the Justice Martial. The other people - mostly quite young - she assumed were the technical crew. They immediately busied themselves in preparing for the broadcast. Some took up positions on cameras, a couple went behind a consol, another couple went to seats behind a desk with an official 'Trueway' backdrop. Others adjusted lights and microphones. One young woman with a clip board spoke to Justice Couchan, the Justice Civil and the Justice Martial. She positioned them at a point close to where Justice Couchan had stood in the 'rehearsal'. She then approached Steph.

"We are ready for you now, Mrs Hugo. If you would come over?"

Steph did as requested, and went without guidance to the spot where she had stood only a few minutes earlier. She looked at the three justices standing opposite to her. Justice Couchan was in the centre flanked by the Justice Civil to his right and the Justice Martial to his left. Steph idly wondered why this process was being done standing and not sitting. She decided that it was probably to do with the taking off of her dress.

She looked at the camera operator who was about to film her. It was a girl - maybe twenty-five or twenty-six years of age. Steph wondered whether she knew anything of what she was filming or whether it was simply a job she had been hired to do. The girl, her slim figure and her hair style, reminded Steph of May. Steph felt a pang of guilt. She hadn't thought much about May ... or Tim or John. She wondered what they were doing, and for the first time, realised that they would see what was about to happen. It was as if she had been in a bubble of isolation. Why hadn't she thought until now, standing here, that her husband and children would see her in this interview? It didn't seem real. Was that it? Everything that was happening to her did not seem part of the world in which John, May and Tim existed. She had been, and still was, in a bubble.

"OK, can I have everyone's attention?" It was the girl with the clipboard. "The timing of this is flexible since we will cut into whatever is being broadcast on the regular schedules across media throughout the World so everyone can relax - there is no deadline for the start. Does anyone need the loo?" She looked round. A few head shakes. "Does Your Honour want a rehearsal?" The question was addressed to Justice Couchan.

"I am familiar with the text and procedure, thank you. Mrs Hugo," Justice Couchan looked directly at Steph, "do you want to rehearse?" Steph shook her head. She noticed the Justice Civil make a sideways glance at Justice Couchan. "Then let us proceed." Justice Couchan looked at the young woman with the clipboard who took this as her cue to begin the broadcast interview.

"OK people. We don't have cue lights in here so keep your eyes on me for cues. We will start with the announcement desk to do the schedule and media interrupt then, on my cue, His Honour, Justice Couchan will begin the interview. All three judges will just be head and shoulders in shot. Mrs Hugo will be full length. OK technical," she said turning to the two people behind the consol, "ready for the interrupt?"

"Ready," came the joint response from the two.

"Cameras?" she enquired looking around to a chorus of "OKs"

"Ready for broadcast?" she enquired looking to the two behind the desk with the backdrop.

"Ready," came the joint response.

She looked at Justice Couchan. "Are you ready, Your Honour? The script will be on the autocue. Is the autocue clear?"

"Yes, thank you," smiled Justice Couchan.

"Can you give me the first line please?" requested the clipboard girl.

"'I am the Justice Ecclesiastic of The Court of Truth'," read Justice Couchan.

"Excellent. Thank you. Mrs Hugo - can you give me your first line please?"

Steph looked at the autocue and obediently obliged, "'I am Stephanie Hugo'."

"Excellent, Mrs Hugo. Thank you. Can you please put on your dress?"

Steph did as requested. It was all so mechanical, so inconsequential - dress on, dress off - yet all this was taking place around that simple act.

"OK ... 5...4...3...2...1...," said the clipboard girl and her finger pointed at the technicians behind the console. Switches thrown by them and a 'thumbs up' to the clipboard girl who pointed at the two presenters behind the desk.

"Hello Citizens, we interrupt ..." began one of the two behind the desk and the broadcast had started.

*

While Steph was going through this process in prison, John was in a garden talking with their children trying to make sense of what had happened, and what was still happening. He had taken some of the tablets that Lisa had offered. His head still hurt a bit but he was beginning to feel much better. May explained how all three of them had been bundled into the van outside their house after John had been knocked to the ground. She and Tim had been terrified, but the men holding them were extremely strong and no matter how they struggled they could not free themselves.

Inside the van there had been a cage into which she and Tim had been locked before their unconscious father had been lifted into the van and laid on the floor. The woman, who they now knew to be Lisa, came into the van after John. She had shut the doors and the van had sped away.

They had seen Lisa give John an injection before cradling his head in her lap while the van rocked and swayed its way through the streets. At the same time she had repeatedly reassured Tim and May that neither they nor their father were in danger. She explained that she and the people she was with were not the police, and that the van was not heading to a police station or prison, but to a house where they would all be safe. When the van stopped and the doors were opened John had been taken out on a stretcher and they had been released from the cage. Tim said that he had thought about running but didn't want to leave May and his father ... and both the children agreed that once in the van, they had not witnessed anything violent. In fact Lisa had spoken kindly and appeared to be caring for their father. They had been allowed to accompany John to the room where he was left to recover. Lisa and others showed them to rooms of their own and offered them food and drink. They were allowed back to spend time at their father's bedside if they wished. Gradually their anxiety had subsided.

Had these people explained who they were or why they were doing what they were doing? John wanted to know, but all Tim and May could say was that they had been told by Lisa that she and the others were friends. The children had been given no fuller explanation. John was wary, but like his children, perceived no immediate threat. He wanted to go and find Lisa or Robert and obtain some answers, but since he and the children appeared to have freedom to wander, he felt the best strategy was to explore a little - see where the boundaries were to this property, and whether they really could leave if they wished. Tim and May had not explored far. They had been around parts of the house and the garden but had not wanted to venture far from their father. At John's suggestion they now headed down the garden away from the house. They crossed a well tended lawn and followed a little path between some shrubs and into a small clump of rhododendrons. On the other side they found a couple of greenhouses and a vegetable plot. A young man was watering a row of green shoots. He looked up as they approached.

"Morning," he smiled and then, indicating the shoots, "carrots. My name's Frank. How are you feeling Mr Hugo?"

"Better than I was."

"You look as if you are exploring," said Frank. "The end of the garden is just beyond the line of trees on the far side of the greenhouse. There's a gate onto the lane further round to your left. The lane leads down into the village. It's not a big place and there hasn't been much trouble there ... but I really wouldn't advise going down 'til you've had a chat with Yusef."

"Yusef?" questioned John.

"Yes, the person in charge of all this." He indicated the garden and pointed up towards the house.

"Oh, right. Mind if we go and take a look at 'the lane'?"

"Not much to see. Like I said - just follow the path down past the trees and then along to your left. The lane is generally not used much, but my advice would be to approach it with caution. The reason that there was little trouble in the village was because they are staunch *PMV*. You and the children have been in the media. You could be recognised. That wouldn't be good for you ... or for us ... but Yusef says that if you are going to trust us then we have to trust you."

"So, apart from Yusef and the people here in the house ... how many is that, by the way?"

"About half a dozen at the moment ... but it varies"

"So, apart from this half dozen, nobody knows we are here?"

"That's pretty much it ... but you really need to speak to Yusef to get the full picture."

"Why have the children and myself been in the media?"

"It sounds to me as though you really do need to speak to Yusef. If you want to see the lane ... and maybe prove to yourselves that you are free to go if you want ... then follow the route I have just told you, but after that I really think that you should go and find Yusef back at the house, and let him answer your questions."

"Thank you, I guess we will go and look at the lane – cautiously." John and the children then followed the path and found the lane. It was sunken with steps leading down from the gate where they stood and a bank with trees rose on the other side. The lane sloped gently downhill to their right. There were no vehicles or people to be seen. John opened the gate and took a few steps down to get a better view along the lane but they were on a curve and he could see no more than a few meters. Nevertheless it was clear that he and the children could go down to the lane and walk away if they wished.

"I should have asked him the name of the village, shouldn't I?" said John, more to himself than the children.

"Fordington," said May.

John looked at his daughter. "You know about the village?"

"Yes, Lisa told us - though we didn't know about the lane. She just said that we were near Fordington."

"Oh, right," said John recalling now that Robert had said that name when they had met in The Causeway Café. Village and lane established, the three started back towards the house.

*

Steph stood in her red dress, in her bubble, and listened to the clerk behind the desk apologising to the Citizens of the world for the interruption to whatever they were viewing and explaining what was about to happen. She paid no attention to the details of what was being said. She wondered whether John or her children were watching. She wondered whether some of her former work colleagues were about to see her. Were there casual acquaintances who would say - 'Oh, I recognise her, she used to come in the shop'. She wondered if Charlie was sitting listening to his radio. Then, a silent gesture to Justice Couchan from the clip board girl and it began.

"I am the Justice Ecclesiastic of The Court of Truth. Will the prisoner please state her name?"

All eyes turned to Steph - in the room and beyond. It seemed an age 'til she heard her voice echoing around within her bubble. "I am Stephanie Hugo ...hugo...hug...hu...h...". Then she heard Justice Couchan again. She wondered if it would have been better if they had not rehearsed it. It seemed such a pantomime going through this script, yet on cue, she again heard her own voice, "I am here to prove to you and the World that the indictments are false ... fals ... fal... fa ...". The voice of the Justice Martial then penetrated the bubble. It was harsher than Justice Couchan, more aggressive in tone.

"*...that you, Stephanie Hugo, through your letters and action in persisting to wear a red dress have incited and supported political unrest and a revolt against Trueway. What <u>will</u> you say to refute this indictment?*" The words were spoken with vehemence. There was a challenge in his emphasis on the word 'will' as if it might be changed to 'can' ... as if he was asking her what she could *possibly* say to refute the indictment since it was so obviously true. Steph looked out at him. She found his aggression pathetic. She remembered his pomposity in court. Nevertheless she would answer. Dutifully she read her lines, "I accept that my letter and actions may have contributed to unrest...," and so completed her response to the first indictment. There was less echo in the bubble now and the calm tone of Justice Couchan thanked her, and advised her that he would ask the Justice Civil to read the second indictment.

The voice of the Justice Civil was cold, and her eyes never left Steph as she spoke the indictment. It was clear that the Justice Civil knew the words and was not reading the autocue. The ice cold words cut into Steph, telling her that she should not wear her dress and that, "... persistence in wearing it...*is wrong*." The Justice Civil then asked her question. What was Steph going to do to refute this indictment?

Mechanically, Steph spoke her words:

"I am prepared to remove and abandon my dress, and so refute this indictment."

"Remove and abandon your dress!" Steph felt jolted. She had expected only the Justice Civil to speak these words but the Justice Martial spoke them as well. They spoke simultaneously - the pompous and the ice cold speaking as one. Steph froze. She looked from the Justice Civil to the Justice Martial and back to the Justice Civil. Steph felt the latter looked smug. She felt she was taking pleasure in her task - pleasure beyond simple fulfilment of duty, though Steph did not know *what* pleasure, or *why*, or from where in that woman's being it stemmed. Her pleasure was a secret one without evidence, concealed from any reasonable, let alone provable, accusation. Her male colleague, the Justice Martial, on the other hand, was clearly deriving some twisted gratification from the situation. He stood, arms folded, haughtily looking down on Steph with an obvious swelling of his member that he made no attempt to disguise. Here however, in this clinical cell, conducting this clinical duty, for this official procedure, Steph doubted that anyone would ever be in a position to question him, her or these events. They, the Justice Civil and the Justice Martial were, in fulfilling their duty, free. They were also hidden, shielded by the 'truth' of convention, of power, of expectation, of acceptance, of majority - of 'normal'.

Steph looked at Justice Couchan. In contrast to the other two his eyes looked pleading, though he stood perfectly still. Slowly she reached to the hem of her dress and pulled it up over her head. She folded it. She placed it on the table to her right as she had done in the rehearsal.

She looked back at Justice Couchan. She felt he looked relieved.

"Thank you," he said. It was part of the script, but he looked directly at Steph as he said it, and paused before he continued the words from the autocue. His voice was gentle as he spoke.

The third and final indictment reads: *That you, Stephanie Hugo deny Trueway and The Book of Truth electing instead to follow your own, individual conscience - your 'truth' - in guiding your behaviour even when that comes into conflict with the former.* What do you say to refute this indictment?

Steph felt small, deflated. Justice Couchan was being kind. He felt sorry for her. She looked at the autocue. She read aloud. "I fully accept the absolute, unerring infallibility of the Book of Truth and of Trueway. I will always obey and act in accordance with the requirements of Trueway. I will not follow the guidance of anything in conflict with this since such things will be false truths."

With a tone that Steph interpreted as relief, Justice Couchan spoke his lines. "Thank you. The Court of Truth has heard your answers to the indictments and has found that you speak the truth."

As with the piece of paper that Steph had used for rehearsal the autocue ended with these words but the girl with the clipboard did not do anything to bring the proceeding to a halt. Instead the Justice Civil began speaking.

"The Court of Truth has found that you have spoken the truth in relation to the three indictments and therefore the extent and limitations of the truth of each indictment is established. It is therefore my duty to state those extents and limitations and pass sentence accordingly.

The First Indictment: The court finds this indictment to be true but that there should be mitigation in sentencing due to your admittance of this and renunciation of it.

The Second Indictment: The court finds this indictment to have been true but that there should be mitigation in sentencing due to the fact that you have removed and abandoned your dress here today.

The Third Indictment: The court finds this indictment to have been true but that there should be mitigation in sentencing in light of your agreement to fully accept the absolute, unerring infallibility of the Book of Truth and of Trueway, and in agreeing that you will always obey and act in accordance with the requirements of Trueway and no longer follow the guidance of anything in conflict with this, since such things will be false truths.

That concludes the findings of The Court of Truth in relation to the indictments against you, Stephanie Hugo. It is now my duty to pass sentence. I do this not as an individual Justice but as the voice piece of the Book of Truth, the prescription of which I have considered on this matter in combination with the wise guidance of my esteemed colleagues here present and the exhortations of the combined wisdom of the Assessors of The Court of Truth. Having laid before these aforementioned the grievous nature of the indictments against you, but also the mitigating factors identified, the court sentences you to life imprisonment."

At first Steph did not hear the final words. In her bubble she had more or less switched off to the monotonous voice of the Justice Civil. It was the silence that returned her to full consciousness. It was then that she heard the words ringing in her ears - "...life imprisonment". She was being sentenced to life imprisonment. She had complied with everything advised by the Justice Couchan and yet she was being sentenced to life imprisonment nonetheless.

The bubble burst. With clarity she looked and saw. The three Justices - big, powerful, dictating, bullying, and herself - small, weak, alone, different. A criminal, a prisoner. But, even as a prisoner, even now she was free, free to be herself, free to follow her truth.

Silently, deliberately she lifted her dress, kissed it, put it on - and stood in crimson defiance, true to herself while rage boiled behind the eyes of the Justice Civil and the Justice Martial's impotence was plain to all.

Chapter 18: Meeting Marginals

When the broadcast from the prison terminated Yusef turned off the television and sighed.

"What now?" asked Lisa. There were only the two of them in his study.

"For her or us?"

"Both ... and John, and her children."

"*Que sera*," mused Yusef before sitting in thoughtful silence.

"Did they have to broadcast the sentencing?" asked Lisa quietly after a few moment. "I thought they just wanted the bits about the indictments ... get a message out, that they were making headway in defeating those behind the Red Dress Bombings."

"They're in chaos, Lisa - wrapped up in their nonsense and their incompetence. I suppose we may get further details of what went on in that room in the fullness of time. Whatever they intended, I don't think the script went like that. It's a good job we are nearly ready now. Where are John and the children? Have they made a run for it?"

"I don't know. I'll go and see if there's any sign of them. Do you want to see them if they are still here?"

"Yes, if they're still here. They will need a lot of help getting to grips with all this. They probably have no idea about what has been happening with Stephanie - and they certainly won't be aware of what we have just seen. If you can find them it will probably be best to bring them here. I know that we have told everyone to refer them back to me if they encounter them and they ask questions, but the sooner that happens the better. I wouldn't want them catching wind of a conversation or a news report. If they are hungry, and want to eat, then we can arrange for something to be brought here. Thanks Lisa."

Lisa met the group of three coming across the lawn towards the house.

"How are you feeling, John?" she enquired, as casually as possible, at their approach.

"I'm feeling much better now, thanks. The headache's pretty much gone. We went down and looked at the lane to Fordington. I've been through that village a couple of times over the years. I've often wondered who lived in some of these big houses. A man called Frank said that we should ask to speak to someone called Yusef."

"Sounds like you've been busy. You must be feeling better." Lisa was trying to keep the mood light, but knew that John and his children were about to find out things that were going to be hard to comprehend and accept. A selfish part of her even wished they had made a run for it - down the lane to Fordington. "Frank was right. You need to speak with Yusef if you have questions. In fact he asked me to come and find you. He's in the study. If you're hungry, he said that you could eat with him if you want." Lisa turned and the four of them walked the few yards to the house.

It was cool in the study. Yusef rose from a seat behind a desk where he had been reading. He walked forward, hand outstretched in greeting. "I'm sorry about the heavy handedness outside your house the other day, John - but we had to get you away ... and it had to be done convincingly."

"Hello Robert," said John shaking the proffered hand. "I am sure that there is an explanation for what you did, and for why my children and I have been brought here. We have been told that someone called Yusef will see us, and explain it all." John looking around the room.

"Come and sit down. There's a lot of explaining to do." He guided them to some easy chairs and all five sat down. He looked directly at John, "*I* am Yusef."

*

John didn't speak. His brain was racing. His brain had questions, but his brain also told him to leave the next move to this man who used two names. This man - Robert/Yusef - also held all the cards. John waited. He detected a hesitancy in this Robert/Yusef - a puzzling reluctance to begin.

"My name is Yusef Murphy. I'm a fifth generation Marginal. The name 'Robert' was one that I adopted in order to contact you, and to arrange the meeting we had at the Causeway Cafe."

John let that stark, and seemingly outlandish statement, sink in. John told himself not to be concerned with the veracity of what he had just heard, but simply to keep listening and questioning, in order to find out what this man claimed was happening, and why the Hugo family had been abducted. "So why did you write to my wife ... if indeed you did?" asked John.

"No," said Yusef, "I didn't write to your wife. A man called Robert Cray wrote to your wife. Do you remember, at the Causeway Cafe, the man with a hat and scarf?" John nodded. He also remembered seeing the same man knocked to the ground, on the night when so many were rounded up, and taken to the school. "That was Robert Cray. Robert had started writing to your wife for his own reasons as a textilist. He actually did invite her to stay with him, if she wished. I wanted to write to her directly myself, but as a Marginal there was no way I could do that. Robert was a well meaning, somewhat eccentric man, and I hoped that he would agree to write to your wife on my behalf, but unfortunately he refused. It was then that I contacted you, using his name, in the hope that I could correspond with her via yourself. That didn't happen either. The conversation we are now having, is in part at least, the conversation that I was hoping to have with you then. Sadly, we never got beyond our first meeting."

"I heard about the Marginals," piped up Tim all of a sudden. "They don't really exist anymore. They died out. Everyone knows that."

John didn't attempt to contradict or silence his son. Tim's assertion was as good a starting point as any, with which to begin to get more information, so he waited to see how this 'Yusef' would respond.

" 'Everyone' says that do they, Tim?" smiled Yusef, "well, you are looking at one now, so what do you think? Am I real?"

"You might be a real person, but that doesn't make you a Marginal," retorted Tim. John was pleased with his son's reasoning … and readiness to assert himself.

"Then I had better prove to you, that I am what I say, hadn't I?" Yusef looked at John. "Your son is right. I might be spinning you a tall tale, so I am happy to start with proving my claim, if you want me to. It won't take long, but I will need one of you to go with me to the front door - or if you prefer it, one of you could go with Lisa to the front door, since she is a Marginal too."

John felt suspicious. He didn't want to be separated from his children, even though he had witnessed no ill intent, and knew that they had been at the mercy of these people all the time he had been unconscious.

In the brief silence that accompanied John's indecision, May spoke. "I'll go with Lisa."

"Don't be anxious John," reassured Yusef. "Come over here. You can see exactly where they will go." He went to a door that led out of the study into a small adjoining room. Inside were monitors showing what appeared to be CCTV images of places around the property. Yusef pointed to one. "This is the corridor outside my study, leading down to the stairs." He pointed to another monitor, "Here are the stairs." He then pointed to a third monitor, "and here is the corridor to the front door. We can watch Lisa and May all the way. OK?" He looked at John.

"OK," agreed John, "but what happens when they get to the front door?"

"They walk out, and then walk in again one at a time, while we look at that front door monitor. It will make sense when it happens," assured Yusef looking at John's puzzled face.

"Come on," said May, boldly grabbing Lisa's hand. The latter smiled, and the two went back into the study. They soon appeared on the first monitor and John, Yusef and Tim watched their progress to the front door. As they went out together some unintelligible words and numbers flashed onto the screen of the front door monitor.

"There's a bio scanner in the front door?" queried John.

"Yes, there's a bio scanner." Yusef pushed a button below the screen and the encrypted bio-details disappeared. "Now they will come back in one at a time." The three waited a few seconds, and then Lisa appeared at the door. She paused and then entered the house. No figures appeared on the screen. She seemed to generate no data. She stood aside from the door. May appeared, paused and then entered. The screen came to life with encrypted bio-data. Yusef again pushed the button to clear the screen. "When Lisa and May get back I would be happy to go down while you watch me go in and out of the front door. The same thing will happen. I will generate no bio data."

He walked back into the study, and John and Tim followed. John considered whether there could be some trick involved, but he had not seen Yusef do anything to affect the screen. It genuinely seemed that Lisa did not generate any bio data when she passed through the scanner. They sat down, and in a few moments Lisa and May re-entered.

"Lisa explained to me what we were doing," said May to her father and Tim as she sat down. "Did you see my data?"

"Yes, … well, I saw a jumble of numbers on the screen that could have been generated by your biodata when you went through the door" confirmed John.

"…but nothing when Lisa went through?" queried May.

"Nothing that showed on the screen," said John, with scepticism still in his voice. "So Yusef, let's say that you and Lisa are genuinely Marginals.

What has it got to do with me and my children? Why have you brought us here? Why did you pretend to be the police, and come and arrest ... or should I say 'rescue' … or maybe even 'abduct' ... us?"

"You and your children were in considerable danger. I honestly don't know where you would have been taken, or what would have happened to you, had we not got to you when we did."

"But why?" asked John in puzzlement. "Even if what you are saying is true I still don't understand *why*. Why did you come and do this? What are we to you?"

"You're Stephanie Hugo's family, and she is a good woman. A good woman caught up in events ... like some of my ancestors ... good men and women caught up in events." Yusef surveyed the three of them. He paused. He didn't want to go on. He knew where it would lead. It was May that broke the silence. It was May that picked up on the unspoken, and the anxiety in her voice was undisguised.

"Where's mum? ...What's happened?" She looked to Yusef and to Lisa. "Where is she?" There was panic in her voice.

"Your mum's in prison May ... just as she has been for the past months," said Yusef reassuringly.

"But something's happened, something's different isn't it?" she said looking back and forth between Lisa and Yusef ... looking for which one was going to tell her the truth. "What is it ... tell us ... what's happened?"

"OK May ... it's OK," reassured Lisa - though her voice was not convincing, and she looked anxiously at Yusef.

"Your mother was moved to a different prison a little while ago," explained Yusef. He spoke calmly now, factually. "There was concern about the bombings that were taking place, and as you know, the bombings were becoming known as, 'The Red Dress Bombings'. The Trueway authorities thought that your mother may have something to do with the attacks because of her insistence on wearing her red dress. They found some of the correspondence between Robert Cray and your mother. The authorities already considered Robert Cray to be involved with the bombings, and so they felt the letters confirmed their suspicions."

"Even though both Robert Cray and your mother, almost certainly, have had nothing to do with any of the unrest," interjected Lisa.

"That's right," confirmed Yusef, "But in the end they forced your mother to denounce the bombings and take off her red dress. I think it was a weak attempt by the authorities to show that they were successfully tackling the bombings ... and maybe even an attempt to send a message to those actually responsible, that their cause was futile, and that they should stop."

"So when has all this been happening, and how do you know?" queried John.

"The prison move took place about a week ago. Your wife's denouncement of the bombings, only today."

"You seem to have a lot of knowledge about what is happening with my wife," said John, indignation as well as scepticism entering his voice. "Steph said nothing to me about a change of prison. How come you know all this?"

"There is so much to explain, John," said Yusef putting his hands on his head as if to suppress the volume of information endeavouring to escape all at once. "We have many people who provide us with information..."

"'*We*' and '*us*' being who?" interrupted John, possibly more aggressively than intended.

"Marginals, John. Marginals. There is a lot to explain."

"But what about mum?" interrupted Tim, frustrated at the way the most important thing in his mind, and that of his sister, was not being addressed. "Is mum all right?"

"At the moment your mother is alright Tim though she is still in prison I'm afraid. I don't know whether she will remain in her present one - which is in the capital by the way - or be returned to the local one, where she has been for most of the time. I am sure I'll get further information about your mum in the coming days - maybe even later today ... and when I do you will be the first to know, Tim." Yusef smiled. He turned to John. "Have I said enough to convince you that you, and your children, are not in any danger from me and the people here? If I have then I would like to suggest that we eat." He looked questioningly at the three. John nodded his agreement.

*

Eating done, Lisa suggested that she, Tim and May spend some time working in the kitchen garden. There was a lot that needed doing, and Frank was currently on his own. John felt comfortable with this, and the children seemed keen.

While Lisa went off with the two young people, Yusef took John on a tour of the house. It was quite a big place - a little like a small hotel or large guest house. They met a few people as they went round, but Yusef explained that several of the residents were out at work. John would have the opportunity to meet them later. Many of the people who lived in the house ate communally (though it was not a requirement) and John was introduced to the cook and shown the menu for the day. The cook was happy to accommodate requests from John and the children, if they were staying a while. As well as the house itself there was the garden. John and Yusef stopped by to see May and Tim, hard at work among the vegetables, before returning to Yusef's study.

"Tim and May seemed to be enjoying themselves," volunteered John, as Yusef and he sat down with freshly brewed coffee.

"Lisa will keep them busy in the garden for a while," smiled the latter, "... but I am sure, that if they get bored or tired, she will find something else. I needed to speak to you, John. I was honest with Tim when I told him that his mother was alright - but I did not explain everything. I felt that I needed to share it with you first." John felt a shiver. "I don't know why your wife began wearing her red dress in public, but her decision to do that at this time, placed her in a much more difficult - and dangerous - situation than she could have imagined. It also put you, Tim and May in danger, though she would probably have been ... and probably still is ... oblivious to this.

When you asked me how I knew so much about your wife I mentioned people who provide information. That was the truth but with regard to your wife's denouncing of the bombings, and abandoning her red dress, I did not require an informant. Her denouncement and abandoning was broadcast live to the World. Had the violence of the other night not driven you from your home, and had the authorities not attempted to arrest you, then you would have seen the news reports leading up to the broadcast ... and you would most probably have seen the broadcast itself. I have it recorded. You do not have to watch it. You may find it distressing ... but I think that you should see it, since your children will soon encounter it in the media, and I imagine that you will want to prepare them for that."

With some trepidation John agreed to watch the recording. Yusef played it through to the point prior to sentencing. John *did* find it distressing. Steph was a fiercely proud woman, and although he didn't understand, and guessed he would probably never fully understand, why his wife had been wearing the red dress, he knew that she was principled and that she wore it with integrity. To see her forced to abandon those principles and the dress in response to these strange indictments, and in so doing to implicitly admit to some responsibility for civil unrest in which she had played no part, left him heartbroken for her and trembling with hate at the injustice being done to her. The two men sat in silence for a moment.

"Thank you," said John. "I will have to think about how to explain all this to May and Tim."

Yusef took a deep intake of breath. "I'm afraid there's more, John. After the point that we have reached in the recording your wife was sentenced in relation to the indictments. The sentencing was also broadcast. Maybe the authorities thought that it would act as a deterrent, but for reasons I don't understand, the broadcast did not end immediately after the sentence had been passed." Yusef played the remainder of the recording. With dismay and disbelief, John heard the sentence of life imprisonment. He then witnessed his wife's act of defiance - an act of defiance that, in a single stroke, eradicated everything that she had previously said in regard to the three indictments.

John's silence was now longer than before. When he did speak the words came quietly, almost involuntarily from his lips. "What's going on? What's happening?"

Seeing the recording of Steph had somehow brought John to a stillness. He stared at his coffee cup. Since he had woken up everything in his head had been racing. Now, all of a sudden, came the stilling realisation that he had absolutely no idea what was happening. It was as if he were in some sort of nightmare or drug induced alternative reality. Did that broadcast of Steph really go out to the World? Maybe it was recorded by this man, Yusef. Maybe Steph was here somewhere in this house. Anything was possible in a world where nothing was making sense. John looked around. The house, the grounds, the lane. Was the village of Fordington really just down that lane? Was there anything he could be sure of? The night of things being smashed - that seemed real. That was before he was here, before he was dependent on this, 'Yusef'. The lady from the bank - Kathy - she seemed real. The family with whom they had drunk tea – they too seemed real ... and he could always talk to Tim and May about those people to be sure that they all had the same memory. John became aware that Yusef was silent. John looked up at his host.

"I heard your questions, John but you looked too far away for me to start to answer."

"I don't know what's real," said John without guile. He still didn't trust Yusef - maybe even less now than before, since John felt he could no longer trust himself and his grasp of reality - but he saw no sense in trying to disguise his confusion. "Why was my house attacked? Why did all that smashing go on? ... and Charlie, where's Charlie? He warned me; told me to get out. What's going on Yusef? What's going to happen to my wife? Have you got answers? Do you know?" John's voice was raised now in urgency.

"I can answer some of your questions, though I don't know who 'Charlie' is."

"He's my neighbour, a few doors down. He's blind. His house was attacked like mine. He rang me and warned me to get out, just before they came to smash everything."

"OK - I don't know anything about him but I can make enquiries. I'm afraid I can't tell you anything further at the moment regarding your wife. There are people who will find out and let me know, and then I can pass that on to you. I'm sorry I can't be more helpful." John didn't say anything. "Maybe it will be best if I start with the attacks that took place when your friend Charlie rang you. I am happy to let you sit with a TV or computer to get the latest if you wish. I have a few print newspapers too that you could sit and read. Needless to say different sources give slightly different explanations."

Televisions, computers, newspapers ... phones! They were all out there, all still available. The realisation rushed in on John of how cut off he had been since abandoning everything as he fled from his house in the middle of the night. Instead of sitting here confused why hadn't he asked to see a TV, a newspaper - anything to give him contact with the outside world?

"So, I can log in to a computer if I want ... email people? How about a phone? Can I phone someone?"

"Yes, John. You and your children are not prisoners here, but just as you were cautioned about leaving the grounds and going down the lane, so I think it is in your interests ... and that of your children ... to get a better grasp of what is happening before you decide whether you want to phone someone or send an e-mail or go back to your house."

"Well, maybe that is where you need to start - by telling me what *you* think is happening."

"I don't have all the answers, John. I can only tell you what I know."

"And what is that?" John looked challengingly at Yusef.

The latter met his gaze, and calmly said, "Trueway is dying."

*

Steph, once again in her red dress, sat on the edge of the bed in her cell. There had been angry words between the Justices and the technical staff after the broadcast had finished. Recrimination, blame and counter blame for the fact that the broadcast hadn't been terminated earlier - the Justice Civil blaming the girl with the clip board. The latter blaming the Justice Civil. Steph could hear it continuing as she was escorted down the corridor back to her cell. What she did not hear was the discussion between the three judges once they were alone.

"You said she was on board," was the accusation from the Justice Civil to Justice Couchan.

"I never said she was 'on board' as you put it. I said that she had agreed to follow the prescribed script ... and she did ... but you pushed, and kept the broadcast going for the sentencing. Why? Why do that? It was irresponsible - no, downright stupid."

"You said that you had told her that she would have a sentence of life imprisonment. Why shouldn't the broadcast have included the sentence? I thought she knew what was coming, and had accepted all of that."

"You know full well that I did not tell her she would have life imprisonment. I never told her what the sentence would be if she agreed to do what we asked. Hell knows the damage that you have now done!"

"Me? You're blaming me? How dare you! How dare..."

"Stop! stop!" interjected the Justice Martial. "What's done is done. The question is what do we do now?"

"In regard to *her* or the whole sorry mess?" fumed the Justice Civil.

"Let's start with Mrs Hugo," said the Justice Martial calmly. "I think we have some control, as well as duty, there. I am now much less certain about our influence regarding, 'the whole sorry mess' ... and I wouldn't advise that you allow anyone outside this room to hear you use terminology like that."

"Oh give me some credit!"

The three fell silent and momentarily stood looking at each other. The Justice Civil, her eyes ablaze, walked to a water dispenser in the corner of the room and poured herself a cup of cold water. The two men, for something to do as much as anything, went and sat down at a table. The Justice Civil joined them and put her cup down.

"Do either of you want water?" she asked. Heads were shaken and polite, 'no thanks' given. Peace and a professional attitude had been restored.

"So," began the Justice Martial. "Mrs Hugo has publicly defied Trueway and, as far as I can tell, the three indictments against her have, in that process, been proved 'true'. Is there anything contrary to that from a Civil or Ecclesiastical perspective?" His colleagues shook their heads. "Then, I look to you Justice Couchan, as Justice Primate, to advise on procedure."

"We return to the court to seek counsel - which will effectively mean ratification from the Assessors of the conclusion that you have just expressed. After that it will again be for the Justice Civil to determine sentence. Mrs Hugo would then be given one last opportunity to reconsider her stance regarding the three indictments before the sentence appropriate to her final position is implemented."

"I take it all this would be done within the court - no further broadcasting fiascos?" queried the Justice Martial.

Justice Couchan looked at the Justice Civil as he answered. "That is how I would see it."

"And carrying out of the sentence?" queried the Justice Civil. "Justice has to be *seen* to be done - especially, I would suggest, in light of the very public display of defiance from the silly ... from the Accused."

"I think that is something that would need to be considered in the fullness of time," suggested Justice Couchan cautiously.

"And under these circumstances what is the sentence likely to be?" queried the Justice Martial looking at the Justice Civil.

"Well, Justice Martial - 'under these circumstances' - I think there is only one sentence, and that is 'Eternal Reflection' - wouldn't you agree Justice *Ecclesiastic*?" The Justice Civil did not try to disguise her anger in emphasising the word 'Ecclesiastic'.

"The sentencing is a matter for the Civil Courts, and therefore is the responsibility of the Justice Civil within The Court of Truth," came Justice Couchan's calm response.

"Hypocrite!" blurted the Justice Civil with venom.

"Please let's not get ..." began the Justice Martial but was cut short by the Justice Civil.

"Shut up! You know," she said getting to her feet and pointing an accusing finger at Justice Couchan "... and you for that matter," looking at the Justice Martial, "that my hands are tied, and the ropes that bind them are essentially religious and military. You're hypocrites, both of you! Both the religious and military factions within the Assessors will demand harsh sentencing in accordance with the Book of Truth - in accordance with the stupid compromises that formed the foundation of Trueway all those years ago ... and which we have never, as a peaceful World society, had the courage to challenge. You both know that, and you both know that 'Eternal Reflection' is what the Book of Truth will lead me to, and which the Assessors and those they represent, will expect. So, don't sit there all smug saying it's up to me - saying it's my responsibility!"

"Then we must reconvene The Court of Truth," said the Justice Martial, ignoring the Justice Civil and rising to his feet. "I will do that ... and do it immediately. I leave you to speak to the awkward little trollop, Justice Couchan. Possibly you will be more successful in convincing her to co-operate this time ... though I doubt that the Assessors will accept any recantation - but that is not a matter for me." He left the room. The Justice Civil, already on her feet, followed him and Justice Couchan was left alone thinking of Steph.

*

A few weeks earlier, and John would have scoffed at anyone telling him that Trueway was dying. Even now his initial reaction was one of incredulity, but recent events had been so bizarre that this suggestion from Yusef didn't seem as absurd and implausible as it should have done. That however did not prevent a defensive and questioning response.

"Dying? Trueway? The entire World order? Do you expect me to believe that?"

"You asked me, John, and so I have told you. I can't force you to believe what I say."

"Well, what you have just said sounds pretty farfetched – but you are right, I did ask. So, now that you have given that very succinct response, maybe you should try and explain things a bit further – because what you have just said seems utterly implausible."

"Of course, but I can only tell you what I know. At the moment, as I have said, I can't tell you any more about what is happening with your wife, but I can give you a broader picture of what is taking place, and I think that should help you understand the situation in which she – and indeed yourself and your children - have become embroiled. Is that OK?" John nodded.

"In that case, can I start by asking you what you know about Marginals? Like Tim, you may believe they no longer exist, and you may not have been convinced by my demonstration with the door scanner – but what I am going to tell you involves Marginals, so it would help me to have some idea of your thinking."

"OK," nodded John. "You're right, I *am* still sceptical about you and Lisa, but I have no doubt that Marginals existed in the past, and I don't really see why there shouldn't still be some out there somewhere, though I don't remember the last time I heard anything about them in the media." As he spoke, he remembered his discussion with Charlie, who had thought that Marginals may have left the red dress cut-outs in the public gallery at Steph's trial. "I guess you could say I'm somewhat agnostic rather than atheist – if that makes sense?"

"It makes perfect sense, John. So, maintaining your agnostic stance, what are, or were, Marginals supposed to be? I'm pretty sure they will have been discussed in your history lessons at school –even if there's not much said about them in the media today."

"Well, my school history lessons were a while back, but as I recall, the Marginals were the remnants of the defeated, anti-Trueway terrorists who fled at the end of the Terror Wars. They settled in the margin just outside the Trueway borders – hence the name. They continued to launch attacks on Trueway for quite some time – but that has grown less over the years … much less."

Yusef nodded. "An excellent summary, and one that I feel sure would be recognised, and accepted by many Trueway Citizens. I certainly recognise it … but I don't think I can fully agree with it – but that is because *I* am a Marginal. My version of history is slightly different. But first, let's be clear about what we do agree on. Would you agree, that, prior to the Terror Wars, climate change, ecosystem degradation, corruption of the atmosphere and conflict based on nationalism or religion or philosophy of some kind, had set the planet on a course to self-destruction?" John nodded.

"And would you agree that a worldwide movement developed, aimed at preventing this self-destruction, through the creation of a unified world order which would become known as Trueway?"

"Yes, of course," confirmed John. "That was the fundamental basis of Trueway. Wars needed opposing sides. If the World was united ... then there was no opposing side. With no opposing side there would be no war."

"Exactly, John – and it was such a necessary goal, that there was a lot of motivation to consolidate Trueway, and for Trueway to be successful. Despite that however, the coming of Trueway would mean change – and many people find change frightening – threatening, even. For some people, Trueway may have been seen as a threat to their way of life, their heritage, their identity, their belief system ... all manner of things. And, where there is threat (real or imagined) there is resistance. For some, that resistance took the form of political argument or protest, but for others it took the form of an armed struggle. The people prepared to take up arms to prevent Trueway were in a minority so their only avenue was that of terrorism. Thus began the lengthy Terror Wars."

"Yes," interrupted John. "I don't think I have any argument with what you are saying – but how does all this relate to what's happening now?"

"Sorry, John, I'm not trying intentionally to be frustrating. It's just that I am about to tell you things that you are unaware of, and that you may find difficult to accept, so I wanted you to see that there is a good deal of history that we share and see as the same. Please bear with me just a little longer." John gestured for Yusef to continue.

"Thank you. My great, great Grandparents were born during The Terror Wars and lived in the period of transition to the early days of Trueway. Many of the things that you and I now take for granted as part of Trueway were still to be established. There was still no ban on wearing clothes for example. They were young people during the latter phase of the Terror Wars - pretty average people judging by the written records that

I have, and from the anecdotal information that has been passed down by word of mouth.

I guess it's with my great, great Grandparents that things might start to deviate from what you were taught ... or even from what a lot of students who studied history at university would have learned – but let me continue just a little longer with the history on which we agree.

The final military action of The Terror Wars aimed to rid the young Trueway, once and for all, of any internal terrorist threat. And, as far as Trueway was concerned, this final offensive was successful. The stable and peaceful Trueway in which you grew up is testament to that. That military action eliminated any armed groups opposed to Trueway. Many people in those groups were killed, and any that survived were driven to the geographically isolated, unmanaged areas of the globe where there was no eco-shield, no climate control, no domes with UV filters, no protection from cold or heat or storms. These areas are what I would call The Outlands. Yes, a part of that was just about habitable and could rightly be called "The Margin", but in some parts survival was virtually impossible. The people driven out to these places included my great, great Grandparents."

"So, are you telling me that your great, great Grandparents were armed terrorists – part of that, internal threat that was forced out by Trueway in its final - and successful - bid to create World peace?" interrupted John .

"They were certainly part of that original group of people that was forced out – but this is where our common understanding of history diverges. I am quite certain that my ancestors were not 'armed terrorists'. As I have already said, they seemed to be pretty average people. I have diaries that my great, great Grandmother wrote and I have seen similar diaries written by others that were forced out beyond the Trueway borders at that time. There is no doubt that some of these people had been involved in an armed struggle - and indeed small, but ineffective, incursions of Trueway continued for a period, as you have said.

The vast majority of people who were forced out however, were not violent or intent on the destruction of Trueway. They were people caught up in Trueway's process of ridding itself of any risk of failure. It was better, in the eyes of Trueway, to remove some innocent people, along with the dangerous ones, in the interest of the greater good. As a result, many very ordinary families were expelled – pushed out to The Margin and pursued even further into The Outlands. Many died there. My great, great Grandparents were among those completely ordinary people thrown out in this way. They survived ... but they would probably have had longer, happier and more fulfilled lives if they had not been ousted in this way."

"But," interrupted John again, "if your ancestors, and others like them, were not involved in anything 'subversive', then why would they have been identified for inclusion in this cleaning up process?"

Yusef fixed John with a steady gaze and spoke with measured gravity, "Your house and your neighbour's house were invaded and smashed. Were you, your children or your friend Charlie involved in anything anti-Trueway, John?" The latter remained silent. Satisfied that his point had been made, Yusef continued.

The Marginals were a disparate group. Trueway had given them that common name, but in reality they were pockets of people who differed greatly in background, culture, religion, geographic location and so on. For many - probably the majority - survival was the main, possibly the only, priority in those early years. As time passed however, links were made between groups. Co-operation and mutual trust grew, as they assisted each other in surviving. Gradually, as survival seemed more assured, planning and developing gained greater significance. Armed incursions into Trueway, all but ceased, as those involved in such activities were killed, died naturally or simply gave up. Very few weapons had found their way into The Margins anyway.

Infiltration however, did not stop. In the Margin people wore clothes through necessity, but undressed in Trueway, with the exception of biodata coding, there was little or nothing, to distinguish a Marginal from a Trueway Citizen. Over the years Marginals have infiltrated Trueway at all levels of society – but particularly at relatively senior levels. It is near impossible to mimic genuine osteodata in situations where advanced scanners are used – but for everyday movement, interactions and transactions, an implanted chip can make a Marginal indistinguishable from a Citizen."

"So," interjected John, thinking that he had spotted a flaw in Yusef's account, "how come your friend Lisa went through the door scanner without any biodata registering? And how come you asserted that you could do the same?" John felt that Yusef had just talked himself into a corner – but there was no hesitation in Yusef's matter of fact response.

"Because I don't have an implanted chip, John. I carry one of these." He took a small card out of the pouch round his waist. "I never wanted an implanted chip. This is something called a Bronofsky card. It is less advanced than an implant – but it's good enough for my purposes. It is the same for Lisa." And, with that matter-of-fact dismissal of John's questions he continued.

"So, as the Marginals gradually infiltrated Trueway, they looked for allies. Some of these were individuals, particularly those with power and influence, but some were groups - especially groups that were a bit *avant-garde* ... perfectly legal groups, but groups where a little secretiveness or 'odd' behaviour would be expected, and would not appear unusual to the authorities of Trueway. The Textilists proved perfect for this. Textilist groups existed all over the world. From Trueway's point of view they did not pose a threat. Indeed they were a bit of a safety valve. They allowed expression to people who might be a bit disgruntled with Trueway. Participants in textile groups might, at worst, be making a protest - but were more likely simply people who liked dressing up for their own personal reasons or secretive pleasures. Either way they were not a serious threat from Trueway's perspective. As such they provided a perfect cover for Marginal infiltration, global communication and organisation.

Patiently, over decades, from these textilist bases, the Marginals infiltrated most sectors and levels of Trueway society. With meticulous care they have identified, and made links with powerful Citizens within Trueway. They have formed a secret alliance – The Trueway/Marginal Alliance – or simply *The Alliance*. Although not everyone at a senior level of Trueway Society is a member of this covert group – many of the *most* senior are aware of it, recognise the necessity for it, and accept the legitimacy of the ultimate fulfilment of its goal – the return of Marginals to the centre of global society. That return would inevitably mean the demise or at least very significant adjustment of Trueway as it existed ... but there has never been any intention for that demise to be brought about by violence and the killing of Citizens.

Trueway believed that it had removed all possibility of challenge to its authority … but it hadn't. The memory of pain and injustice has survived. It has crossed the generations, and the descendants of injustice are now ready to realign Trueway so as to incorporate all Marginals, without the need for them to use such things as implanted chips or Bronofsky cards. That is why I say Trueway is dying, John."

"So, a revolution … is that what you are saying?"

"I would say 'realignment' – but semantics aside, I think you understand what I am talking about – and we are now on the brink of that seismic change."

*

Once again Justice Couchan stood in Steph's cell. This time she felt he looked smaller. Yes, his physical bulk was still there, but he no longer seemed to suck the air from the room. He seemed more a human than a mountain. She sat on the edge of her bed. She made no attempt to stand for him. He stood. He made no attempt to sit.

"The Court of Truth has conferred," he announced quite formally. "In light of your behaviour, especially recorded in the video transmission, the court has concluded that the indictments have all been proved 'true' and that there are no grounds for mitigation in relation to your sentence. I am here to offer you," his tone suddenly softened, "to implore you, to reconsider your position." He removed his wig. "It is not too late to recant and accept the clemency of the court."

Steph looked at him. She felt cold - physically within herself and emotionally towards this man that she had previously felt was genuinely supportive. "Clemency? Clemency is life in prison isn't it?" she said with vehemence.

"I cannot...," began Justice Couchan, but was cut short by Steph.

"You 'cannot say'? ... It's for the court ... or the Justice Civil ... or someone else. Don't patronise me. You knew, when your coaxed me into agreeing to that interview, that the outcome would be life in prison ... and you know now, exactly what the outcome will be for me whether I recant or whether I don't. Well, I don't want to spend the rest of my life rotting in a prison. Or are you going to tell me there would be options to appeal ... that it might not be forever ... dangle another hope that will get me to comply?" He remained silent. She looked at him, long and hard before concluding with a contemptuous, "I thought as much."

"Maybe you are right," he eventually said. "Maybe, although 'technically' the decision is not mine, maybe you are right, that I can

264

anticipate what the outcome will be for you. They say that 'where there is life there is hope' ... so appeals will, I am sure, be possible."

"So, if I don't recant and accept life in prison you are going to kill me."

"That is possi..."

"It wasn't a question," interrupted Steph, silencing him once again. "Well, kill me then - you and all your excuses."

Justice Couchan remained silent for some time before, "Please Mrs Hugo listen to me and consider."

"Consider what ... whether I want to live? ... whether I am afraid of dying? ... whether I can believe you? trust you? be convinced by you? I don't even know that agreeing to co-operate will result in life in prison do I? What's to say that I could do all that recanting – and denying of my truth only to be killed anyway?"

"It will not be an easy ...,"

"Not an easy death? ... Is that your tack now? Frighten me into accepting what you want?" Her eyes blazed as she looked at him. "Finish it! Kill me!"

After another short silence Justice Couchan said, "Are those your last words Mrs Hugo?" Steph remained silent. Justice Couchan knocked on the cell door. It was opened and he went to leave. He paused half in and half out. He looked back at Steph. "I'm sorry Mrs Hugo." Steph did not look up.

*

John had listened patiently to what Yusef had been telling him. What he had heard seemed no more than a revised version of history being told to him in order to justify what was currently happening ... a revolution to bring Trueway to an end in order to reintegrate Marginals. He had listened enough.

"So," said John rising abruptly to his feet in agitation, "You are a Marginal and it's the Marginals that are responsible for all the bombings that have been happening. This is the start of your revolution is it? Why have you dragged my wife into all this? Hey? She has nothing to do with your pathetic bombs ... but you seem to have stuck her right into the firing line with your prank paper dresses!" John was shouting now and his fists were clenched. Yusef remained impassive.

"No, John. The Marginals have not been doing the bombings - well not the main Marginal body or The Alliance. I don't know who is behind these 'Red Dress Bombings'." He spoke calmly. "The situation has become complex ... and sadly your family has become caught up in that complexity in just the same way that my great, great grandparents, and so many like them, were caught up in events that hurt them so unjustly."

John was angry, and Yusef's calmness and rambling explanation of what was happening, was fuelling his anger further with frustration.

"My wife is in prison. My wife is getting blamed for involvement with bombings, injuries and even deaths! I need some explanations, not mysterious references to things being 'complex'. I don't really care who is doing the bombings - you, Marginals, the man in the moon. I just want my wife taken out of this mess ... a mess she has nothing to do with. So, either tell me what you can do to help get her out or I'm going to leave here with my children and tell the authorities all about you and this place. I wonder how your version of history will go down with them. Maybe they will believe what you tell them about your revolution, and so realise that my wife has nothing to do with it – because she isn't a Marginal!"

"Alright John, alright," said Yusef, gesturing towards John with open palms as if to try and push him back to his seat without touching him. "I think it would be extremely dangerous for you and the children if you left here now ... and I think that the best thing that we can all do for your wife is to be patient and wait. Please hear me out. Let me sum up the situation."

The rational side of John, always strong, calmed him more than Yusef's outstretched hands. With the bombings, arrests and attacks on people like himself, Charlie and Kathy from the bank, Trueway was no longer a place he could trust and predict. He knew that that made him – and his children – very vulnerable. John sat down.

"Thank you, John. The Alliance of Marginals and senior members of Trueway has been working, through parliament, to create the necessary legislation for the democratically agreed reintegration of Marginals to society. Things have been prepared over generations ... and we were close to readiness ... *are* close to readiness ... but some people, some faction, has commenced these, so called 'Red Dress Bombings'. I do not know who these bombers are. It may be some over eager group within The Alliance itself. That would certainly explain why Trueway forces have had difficulty identifying and naming the perpetrators beyond the vague, *Individual Freedom Alliance* – which is almost certainly a Trueway fabrication designed to give the impression of progress being made when in fact it isn't. The arrests and the night of smashing are testament to how vague their real knowledge is. The bombings have, however, forced The Alliance to move to a rapid realignment rather than the originally planned progression through parliament. I can only hope that once the realignment is complete the 'Red Dress Bombings' will stop. The Alliance will be in control and I am sure will be better placed than Trueway to deal with any further unrest should the bombings continue.

"You seem to know a lot about all this," said John. "Assuming everything you say is true, you must be quite senior in the organisation? I'm surprised you have enough time to spend telling me all this."

"I am senior enough to be kept in the loop but my focus has been endeavouring to keep you and your family safe."

"Are we really that important? I don't see why - and does 'my family' include my wife? Do you have the responsibility for keeping her safe?"

"Obviously I cannot intervene directly to assist Mrs Hugo, but I have been liaising with others who are in a better position than me to do that, and as I have said, I will give you feedback as soon as I can. And 'yes', you are that important. The Marginals - the main Marginal body - has always been working towards what might be better considered a realignment of Trueway than a revolution. There was much that was good about Trueway ... much that *is* good - but it is complacent - complacent with the wrongs of its past, complacent with the regularity and comfort of its present. Change is necessary ... but we want change that does not repeat the wrongs of Trueway. We did not want, and do not want, violence and death – and our plans have been carefully made to avoid that. Your wife and her wish to be free to wear her dress has been usurped by some group - and given the timing - it is possible that The Alliance is implicated in some way. It is our duty therefore to do all we can to protect her and you from the harm that could come from that.

At the risk of repeating myself John, I cannot force you and your children to stay, but I think that you will be safer here than anywhere. I also think that I am likely to obtain news of your wife through The Alliance sooner than you or the media."

John was not convinced by this monologue but felt, on balance, that the best option for himself and his family was to remain at this house so simply left the room to find Tim and May with the parting words, "Then, I wait to have news of my wife."

*

It was probably no more than an hour after Justice Couchan left that the door of Steph's cell opened. It was her warders. She had to attend the court again. Steph complied and was soon standing in the dock looking at the three Justices and the tiers of Assessors. Justice Couchan spoke.

"Mrs Stephanie Hugo, three indictments have been brought against you and have been investigated by this, The Court of Truth. No effort has been spared in Our attempts to assist you in refuting these, most serious indictments and to help you regain your footing on the path of Trueway. Sadly, all Our efforts have been rejected by you. We, The Court of Truth, therefore find all three indictments shown to be true. As Justice Primate of The Court of Truth it is my duty - a sad duty that I fulfil with a heavy heart - to pass this finding to the justice Civil of The Court of Truth to determine sentence."

The justice Civil immediately spoke, reading from a paper in front of her.

"Mrs Stephanie Hugo, in light of the findings of this court and after consultation with the Book of Truth, my esteemed colleagues the Justices Martial and Ecclesiastic and the knowledgeable Assessors here present, it is my duty - a sad duty that I fulfil with heavy heart - to pass sentence in accordance with the prescriptions of The Book of Truth for the indictments against you that have been found to be true. The prescribed sentence, and the one that I now pass, is that of 'Eternal Reflection'. The sentence will be carried out tomorrow at noon. Take the prisoner down."

Steph was not given the opportunity to speak and made no protest when the warder stepped forward and took her arm. She did look at the three justices however and it was only the justice Martial that met her gaze with a look of satisfaction.

*

I don't have the return address to give you, wrote Steph as she attempted to finish her letter to John and the children. *This strange court has sentenced me to something called Eternal Reflection. I don't know what that is but in case I don't see you again I do love you.* After that she didn't know what to write. She put the letter back into the unsealed envelope. The night still stretched ahead of her. She told herself she would write more in the morning. She looked at her little note book of 'Stuff'. "I've got nothing to say to you," she said out loud, "except maybe that I'm scared." Then, for no apparent reason, the image of a little boy, his grandmother and a blue fluffy rabbit came into her head. Tears welled into her eyes and with shaking hands she picked up the book of 'Stuff' and through the blur of her tears wrote, "I'm Good".

At some point she drifted into sleep and was woken by the arrival of a breakfast that she did not eat. It was taken away and she was left alone. She re-read her unfinished letter to John and her children. She wrote no more before putting it back in the envelope. She didn't even sign it. The words 'I *do* love you' seemed fitting last words to them. *Last words*, she thought, *last words*. Anyone who can speak will say them. Last words. She looked at her book of 'Stuff'. The last words she had written in there were to the book; to herself. "I'm Good". Yes, those were fitting last words. Nothing more for the book of 'Stuff'. Anyone else? Anything else? Last words; last *word?*

'I'm good,' … but am I? Was he? Even bleeding from the knife he did not stop, would not stop, could not stop – the passion as red as his blood.

She took the pencil. The pale wood bed frame poked out from under the mattress and along its length she wrote,

Yusef. Did you hear her last words? – " You, Steph, Tell, Topsy, ~~Are~~ Our? Med". Now mine: I love May.

She put the pencil in her bag.

Chapter 19: The Room of Eternal Reflection and a Martyr on TV

John walked with May and Tim in the garden as the sun set. He had given them a synopsis of his discussion with Yusef earlier that day. The children liked the house and the people they had met, so had no objection when their father suggested they would continue to stay there for the time being. He did not tell them about the video that Yusef had shown him.

"Of course I have no idea how much of what Yusef said was true. The idea of a peaceful revolution... or should I say 'realignment'... if it is genuinely going to happen, doesn't sound like something that would be quick. This Yusef did seem to think his Marginal friends were ready for it... on the brink was the impression I got... but he didn't say how long he thought it would take... and I didn't ask.

"Let's just wait and get news of mum," suggested May.

*

So, this was it, the start of the last day, the start of the end. Steph had not been told what 'Eternal Reflection' meant, but she assumed it to be a euphemism for execution. She sat on the edge of the bed looking at her feet, observing the minute detail of the wrinkles on the knuckles of her toes. She felt numb and blank. Her toes formed a focus, pointless yet somehow calming.

A distant sound. Were they coming? Was this it? She waited. She strained but could hear nothing more. Her heart pumped harder and she felt a little sick. She looked at her toes again - pale, white, innocent - just toes. A sound again - definite this time, clanking, doors being opened, footsteps of feet with shoes, voices. Coming closer. She looked up. The voices grew silent but the footsteps continued and came to a halt outside her door. The little spy flap was slid open - "shhlink!" Eyes looked in at her then a key in the lock and the door opened. Steph sprang to her feet.

There were three female warders. Two stepped into her cell and flanked the door as the third came forward towards her.

"Good morning Stephanie, how are you?" she asked.

"OK."

"Step forward please and hold out your arms."

Steph did as requested and the warder placed handcuffs on her wrists. Steph's hands trembled and she clenched her fists to try and make the tremor stop. The warder bent down and fastened similar manacles to Steph's ankles. Without getting up the warder held out her hand and one of the others stepped forward and gave her a piece of chain about a meter long. She attached one end of this by a clip to a central loop in the short chain between Steph's ankles. She then stood up and attached the other end to a similar loop on the chain that joined the handcuffs. Again she silently held out her hand. The other warder stepped forward and handed her a further piece of chain, longer this time. One end of this was attached to the same loop between the handcuffs. Once attached the warder gathered up the rest of the chain.

"Bend your knees please, Stephanie."

Puzzled, Steph did as she was told.

"Not like that - do it so that your knees come apart."

Steph awkwardly turned her bent knees outward and the warder tossed the bundled chain between Steph's legs. It clattered to the floor behind her. The warder walked round and picked it up.

"Follow my colleagues please, Stephanie."

The two who had flanked the door now went out into the corridor and Steph shuffled forward as directed. The third warder followed on behind holding the chain. Steph glanced back at her bag still lying on the bed.

"There's a letter," she said.

"I'll see to it," came the peremptory response. "Please, follow my colleagues."

The two leaders waited side by side in the corridor. They had turned right - the opposite direction to that which Steph had previously taken to the court. They were large women and it was a narrow corridor so that Steph could not see much beyond them. She shuffled on until she was within a meter of them and then they started to slowly walk forward. Steph continued to follow and so it was that the four of them gradually advanced up the corridor – silent, apart from the chain and the warders' shoes.

The bizarre quartet made a number of turns in the corridor before coming to a flight of stone steps. The lead warders started down in unison - first step then stop, second step then stop. Steph reached the edge. She started to turn to the warder behind, but before she could speak or even question with her eyes, the command came,

"Jump!"

271

Steph froze. Was she really to descend the stairs in little jumps?

"Jump!" came the command again, this time accompanied by a shake of the chain.

Steph positioned herself on the edge of the top step. She felt she would go headlong if she just jumped forward. Instinctively she swivelled sideways and found that she could do it. Little, slightly sideways jumps, took her gradually down about fifteen steps. There she recommenced her ungainly journey. They went only a short distance before the chain between her legs was yanked back like reins being pulled to stop a horse. The two leaders continued a few steps more and Steph could see that they had come to a door on their left. They opened it and went in, standing either side as they had done when they entered her cell.

"Go on through please, Stephanie," came the instruction from behind.

Steph shuffled into a small room, followed by the third warder. The door was shut and her chains were removed.

"Take off your dress please."

Steph hesitated.

"We will take it off by force, if necessary."

Steph did as she was asked.

"Thank you," said the warder as Steph handed her the dress. "Now go and stand on the footplate over there and hold the two silver handles, please." The warder indicated a machine in the corner of the room. It looked a bit like a biodata body scanner. There were hand grips in the upright columns either side of the footplate where two outlines of feet showed her where to stand. Steph hesitated again. Was this it? Was she going to be electrocuted?

"Like this," said the warder moving forward and positioning herself between the columns.

"What is it?" asked Steph falteringly.

"A new type of scanner. It's part of the procedure. It won't take a moment – though it is a bit noisy."

The warder vacated the footplate and Steph fearfully took her place.

"Now hold the handles, and keep holding 'til I tell you it's finished," instructed the warder. Steph held the handles and waited. A low humming sound began. It grew louder and turned into something that sounded to Steph like metal rods being banged together before stopping abruptly.

"That's fine Stephanie. Thank you. If you could now come back to the door and put your dress back on?"

Steph did as she was asked and the chains were reattached. They left the room and recommenced their procession until, at the end of the corridor, the leading pair reached another door, went through and flanked the entrance.

Without bidding, Steph followed, and edged cautiously into a room with white walls. It was a much bigger space than the room they had just left - about the size of a school classroom.

"Keep going," came the instruction from behind. "Over to the right side, please."

The flanking warder to Steph's right pointed to a wall on which Steph could see metal rings, pulleys and hooks. Her head started to swim. The pointing warder impatiently gripped the top of Steph's arm and pulled her towards the wall. Steph made little scurrying steps, as best she could, and managed to avoid falling. The warder position Steph with her back to the wall. The warder who had been following Steph now came to stand by her side. She still had hold of the chain that dangled from the handcuffs and passed between Steph's legs. The warder reached up behind Steph and attached the chain to something on the wall. Steph felt the cool chain move up between her thighs until it became taught, pushing the dress into the cleft of her buttocks. The chain then suddenly jerked upwards pulling Steph's hands down and between her legs. The upward movement continued, forcing Steph to bend forward and go on tiptoe.

With Steph immobilised in this distressingly uncomfortable position, her three escorts left by the door through which they had all entered and closed it behind them. The room was silent except for Steph's breathing. She bent her head back, looking around her as best she could. In the centre of the room was something resembling a chair. It looked to be constructed of wood. It had a high back made of simple planks. The seat and legs resembled a box, similarly made of wooden boards. This chair had no arms. The rest of the room was bare. White tiles covered the walls. As well as the door to her left, through which she had entered, there was another door in the wall to her right. There were no windows.

She looked down. There were her little, white toes again. She still trembled and felt sick, but she focused on her toes, and gradually calmed a little. Steph remained like this, in the silence, for maybe ten minutes until, without warning, the door to her right opened and three people came in. These were not the warders who had brought her to this chamber. They didn't even appear to be warders as such. One was a huge, bulky figure draped from head to foot in black - a featureless shroud. The other two were young women – little more than girls – in their late teens or early twenties. They wore no clothes – not even shoes. All three came over to her. The large shrouded figure stood immediately in front of her and the two girls either side. She looked at her toes. One of the girls moved away, did something behind Steph and the chain loosen - but although her hands now fell forward Steph remained bent over, looking at her feet.

"Stand up straight please, Stephanie." It was the shrouded figure in front of her, yet the words were spoken in a whisper ... no voice.

Slowly, she straightened. She looked directly ahead at the figure's chest. The amorphous shroud concealed any clue to gender. The creature put its hand under her chin and lifted her head so that she looked briefly at the shrouded face before the menacing form turned and walked to the centre of the room. It stood between her and the wooden chair-like construction.

"Walk to me, please," came a whispered request, as a black gloved, left arm emerged from the drapes and beckoned.

Steph waddled forward, but was momentarily startled to a standstill, when the far end of the long chain attached to her wrists clattered to the floor behind her. Her movement had detached it from the wall. She started forward again dragging the chain with her. She was almost in contact with the outstretched hand before being told to stop. The two young women had moved alongside Steph to this point but now went off to stand one in front of each of the doors.

"Please go to my colleague over there, Stephanie," came the whisper. The gloved hand indicated the young woman to Steph's right. Steph turned, and began to do as she was told. A short swishing noise then broke the silence and a sharp sting shot through her buttocks. An involuntary "Ahh" escaped her lips.

"Faster," came the command - all the more sinister in this voiceless breath.

Steph moved her shackled feet as fast as she could, but again came the swish and the stinging pain across her bottom followed by the command to move faster. This happened a third time before she reached the girl who stopped her by holding out her hand and grasping Steph's shoulder. Steph stood shaking looking at the young woman, not knowing if the swish and sting would come again. The girl then took Steph's head in both hands. She leaned forward until they were almost nose to nose. The girl then moved her head back slightly before abruptly bringing it forward and spitting in Steph's face. She then dropped her hands to Steph's shoulders, and turned her round to face her colleague on the other side of the room.

The black shrouded figure stood half way between her and the other young woman. A black gloved right hand had now emerged from the shroud and in it Steph could see the lash that had been used to whip her.

"Now go to my other colleague please, as quickly as you can," came the whisper.

Steph started forward, the spittle running down her face. She went as fast as her small steps allowed. As she passed the shrouded form she tried to go even faster, but to no avail. Again she heard the swish and felt the sting three times before she was stopped by the girl's outstretched hand on her shoulder. Again her head was held, and again she was spat upon, before being turned around.

She was made to waddle back and forth like this until both girls had spat in her face three times and she was hardly able to see because of the spittle in her eyes. On each short journey the lash stung her three times as well - sometimes on her buttocks, sometimes her back, sometimes on the tops of her legs. The red dress had given her some protection from the blows – but not much. After the second girl had spat on Steph for the third time, and she was again stumbling back towards the other, the figure brought her to a halt.

The creature took her by the shoulders, turned her and leant in towards her. It came so close she could smell the sourness of the whispering breath through the concealing veil as it spoke. "I'm going to undo the cuffs and manacles, but you must not wipe your face. Do you understand?"

Steph nodded. "Do you understand?" it repeated with a more emphatic exhalation of breath.

"Yes, yes," whimpered Steph, almost inaudibly.

She had shut her eyes now in an attempt to squeeze out the spittle and the horror that was unfolding. She was aware of the restraints being removed from her feet and hands, followed by a noisy clanking as the chains were thrown to one side.

Again the whispered voice gave instruction. "Please turn round and face the other way, Stephanie."

She did as she was told, grateful, despite the pain in her skin, and her blindness, to be able to move her feet unrestricted. Hands took her arms on either side, and with incongruous gentleness, moved her backwards. She guessed the monstrous form must have silently moved away. The backs of her legs came in contact with something. She guessed it was the thing that looked like a chair.

"Sit down now please," said one of the girls.

The hands either side of her supported her reassuringly until her own hands, and then her bottom, met the wooden seat. It was cool through her dress but the soreness of her buttocks made sitting painful.

"Lean back."

Again the hands reassured her until her back met a cool surface, and she was sitting perfectly upright, her arms hanging limply either side. She was afraid to open her eyes and made no resistance as her arms were raised into a vertical position. Then something was deftly slipped over each hand and pulled tight round her wrists clamping her arms to the back of the seat. Her eyes shot open by reflex. Most of the spittle had now run down and she could see blurrily. Leather straps were round her wrists. They passed through wooden boards that formed part of the back of the chair. She tried to free her hands but they were held tight. With her hands fixed she was unable to move from her seat.

The two girls then looped a belt-like strap round her waist and passed it through slots in the back of the chair before pulling it tight to secure her torso to the upright. They then put straps round her ankles to attach her to boards that extended down from the front of her seat. She lifted her legs to try and prevent this but it was futile. Unable to stand she could do nothing but kick and struggle a little. The girls easily slipped big loops of leather around her thrashing legs one at a time, and while one girl held her leg the other pulled the loop tight round her ankle until it clamped her to the board. Finally straps were passed up through slits in the seat of the chair to secure each leg above the knee. Steph could do nothing to resist.

The back of the chair was hinged where it met the seat and was now lowered. From her knees to her finger tips she was now lying flat. All the time that she had been upright the shrouded figure had been behind her out of sight. Now, from her prone position, she could see it. The thing

276

stood there, an imperious apparition, observing proceedings. Movement drew her attention back to the two girls at her feet. The planks beneath Steph's leg were hinged behind her knees. The girls now raised these slats until they were level with the rest of the platform and secured them in this position. Steph was now lying horizontal on this surface of wooden boards with her body forming a straight line from the hands above her head, down her outstretched arms, through her scarlet clad body, to her toes.

The two young women now stood, side by side, almost to attention. In unison they gave a ceremonial bow to the shrouded spectre before leaving the room by the door to Steph's left. As they did so the door to her right opened and three new figures entered.

The three were covered from head to foot in shrouds like the figure behind her but their palls of concealment were white not black. Again, Steph could not tell whether the loose, billowing veils were hiding men or women. The figures were small with something delicate about them. They may even have been children. Each carried an object beneath a cloth. They advanced, ethereal like, until they stood, a line of white, mysterious acolytes, to one side of Steph.

One stepped forward, and removed the cloth from what it carried, to reveal a gold hoop about 20cm in diameter. The figure leaned across Steph who instinctively turned her head away. The figure made no remonstration but gently placed the hoop on Steph's head, like a crown, before returning to the line.

The second individual stepped forward and uncovered what it held - a ceramic pot. The figure went to Steph's right side. It dipped its fingers in the pot, and smeared something oily onto Steph's right foot and right hand before moving round to do the same to Steph's left foot and left hand. Steph felt she was being anointed. The small hand then smeared the oily tincture on Steph's thighs and up under her skirt to cover her belly before pouring the remainder on the dress itself. This attendant then returned to its place before the third white creature stepped forward.

When the cloth was removed Steph could see that this last one held a small knife. She recoiled at the sight of the blade, but could do nothing. Like its predecessor, the diminutive figure walked to Steph's right side. It gently lay the knife down on Steph's stomach, leaving it there while it continued walking to position itself below Steph's feet.

The faceless, white apparition waited motionless until the first of the three, the one which had entered carrying the hoop, came over and stood alongside. Simultaneously, they reached out. One gripped the board that passed beneath Steph's left leg and the other gripped the board that passed beneath her right leg. The two, white wraiths then appeared to glide away from each other. As they did so, the boards beneath Steph's legs parted and her legs opened like the blades of a pair of scissors. The process stopped when Steph's feet were about a meter apart. The white individuals then went, with ceremonial slowness, to where Steph's hands were secured and repeated the process with her arms. Steph was now, spread-eagle, with the knife still lying on her stomach.

The former hoop bearer returned to stand with the ointment bearer. The knife bearer moved to Steph's side, picked up the blade, and with an abrupt jerk of the arm held it menacingly aloft.

"No!" shrieked Steph – repeating the word hysterically as her body struggled for freedom and her head thrashed side to side in futile desperation.

The hoop was dislodged and fell into the gap above Steph's head. Any sound made by its fall lost in the echoing screams. Ignoring Steph's distress the knife bearer slowly took hold of the bodice of Steph's dress, pulled the fabric taught, and made a cut in it with the knife, before calmly returning to position with the other two.

Sobbing and shaking, Steph watched as the three bowed to the black figure before drifting away through the door by which they had entered.

As soon as they had gone, the monstrosity in black, that had overseen this strange ritual, stirred itself and with solemn deliberation began a circuit of Steph's prostrate form. It circled one and a half times like a vulture before stopping to stand between her feet. Steph was still trembling but her sobbing had stopped. She had no difficulty hearing the whispered words from the veiled mouth.

"Do you know who I am, Stephanie?" Steph, eyes wide in terror, gave a slight shake of her head. "I am *Sentence*." It moved forward and leaned over her, "I am the two in one and I am now completing my duty." Steph screwed up her eyes to try and block out this horror.

*

They sprang open again when she heard a sliding sound and was aware that she was moving. She could not see the creature called *Sentence*. She, and the whole device to which she was strapped, were in motion. She was gradually travelling head first, towards the wall behind her. Within moments she found herself entering a room. It was as if the wall had dissolved or been slid away. The room was well lit, though she couldn't tell from where the light was coming. As she entered she could see herself in the ceiling. It was a mirror. Glancing to her left and right she could see that the walls too were mirrors. When her feet had passed through the portal her conveyance came to a halt. The whole contraption then began to tilt, and slowly she found herself rising into a vertical position. Once upright she could look through the doorway into the room where she had been, the room where all the torment had taken place, the room of the white shrouded figures, the two girls, and of *Sentence*. There it now stood - a still, black, faceless spectre. Only gradually did Steph realise that it was turned away from her and that she was looking at the figure's back. There was movement and *Sentence* slowly turned round to reveal hands holding a large lighted candle.

The black apparition advanced towards Steph with ceremoniously measured pace, the flaming candle threateningly leading the way. This shrouded manifestation of malevolence did not come to a halt until it was within touching distance of Steph's suspended form. The contraption on which she hung had raised her so that the head of *Sentence* was at the level of her thighs. She looked down, but unable to bear the sight, looked up. The spectre was still there, along with her tortured self in the mirrored ceiling. She could not escape the torment.

She closed her eyes to shut it out. The spectre spoke:

"The anointing is complete. The flame awaits."

Steph's eyes shot open in alarm, and with horror she looked down at the candle flame.

"No! ... please, no!" Sentence seemed not to hear and continued speaking.

"The Court of Truth has read The Book of Truth with its eyes, yet has been blind to its meaning."

"No, no," repeated Steph as she made futile attempts to twist and struggling free of the straps holding her while the whispering voice monotonously continued.

"I, *Sentence*, will carry out my duty to both the blind and the seeing, for I am the two in one. I am the paradox and through the same action we will fulfil closure of our duty as demanded by Trueway while simultaneously opening the door to eternity here on Earth as required by The Book of Truth. For the first you must be punished."

With the word, 'punished' *Sentence* fell silent and the shrouded head tilted as if looking at Steph. This stilled Steph's frantic struggle.

"No, please, please, no," she begged in the brief silence before *Sentence* continued.

"For the second you must be lost."

Steph was no longer hearing the words as she quietly sobbed, "No, no, please, please," but Sentence completed the ritualistic monologue.

"For both, we thank you and ask your forgiveness."

Steph was still quietly whimpering, "Please ... please," when the flame of the candle was held to the hem of the dress. She screamed in pain and terror as the scorching flames consumed her dress, skin and tattoos to leave her hanging in raw agony. Steph, barely conscious, saw *Sentence* ceremoniously turn, and walk away. The black form then disappeared from view as a mirror backed door slid across the opening and she was confronted with the horrific reflection of her part incinerated self. She was in a box of mirrors, each side reflecting her and the opposite side - a box of eternal reflection.

*

Once again Couchan sat in Steph's cell – but now he was alone. She was no longer there. He didn't know why he had come. He had done his duty as a minister of Justice. He had done all in his power to help her. Ultimately the decision to refuse help had been hers. He knew he was trying to justify himself, to himself. She was not here. He sat on the edge of the bed where she had sat in her red dress – but neither she nor her red dress was there. In fact nothing of hers was there. Her boots and her bag were gone. He had asked the warders where they had been taken. The warders did not know. After taking her uneaten breakfast things away new warders, specifically assigned to carry out the sentence, had arrived to replace them. The regular warders assumed that these new warders must have dealt with her belongings. *Yes,* thought Couchan as he sat alone, *Dealt with her things just as they dealt with her – and despite my lofty status, my position as Justice Primate, I handed everything over, once my part was done – and now I don't even know where she, and everything that was here, have gone.* He could not justify himself, to himself.

He was about to stand and go, but as he put his hands down onto the bed frame, to help raise his weary bulk, he saw the writing. Its meaning eluded him, but he felt certain that it had been written by Steph. He took a pad and pen from his bag and copied it verbatim. Certain that he had it correct, he then scribbled through the words on the bed frame to make them illegible.

*

John sat with Tim and May looking out over the garden while they had their breakfast, when they noticed Yusef emerge from the house with a middle aged, portly gentleman that they had not seen before. He looked oriental. The two men walked with heads down. They were talking but were out of earshot. As they walked and talked they occasionally glanced at each other, but then they came to an abrupt halt. Yusef clutched his head as if hearing some incomprehensible news. The older man took Yusef by the arm and propelled him forcibly to continue walking. They disappeared behind the rhododendrons.

*

John found Yusef in his study later in the day.

"I saw you talking with a man in the garden earlier," said John. "A biggish man?" Yusef seemed distracted and did not look up. Neither did he make any attempt to answer so John was more direct. "Have you had any news yet about my wife?"

"I'm sorry John, not yet," came the response though Yusef still did not look up from the papers through which he was shuffling. He then pulled open a drawer in his desk and began rummaging there.

"When do you think you will hear? I did wonder whether that man - the one with you in the garden ... whether he might have had news. I hadn't seen him before."

Yusef at last looked up. "I'm sorry, John. As soon as I have any news I will tell you. What you probably also need to know is that it's all about to start, so I may be unavailable for a while ... or at least, not as readily available as I have been." He returned to sorting his papers.

"I assume that you mean this revolution/realignment of yours?" There was no response. Irritated at being ignored, John disparagingly added, "Saying that it's, 'about to start' makes it sound more like a play or a film than a world changing political event."

Yusef stopped what he was doing. He met John's gaze, but with a distant look in his eyes. "A surprisingly good analogy, John. I had never thought consciously of it that way ..." His voice trailed off. He dropped his gaze and nodded thoughtful, a melancholy smile on his lips. When he spoke, it seemed he was talking more to himself, than to John. "A play takes months of preparation and rehearsal, and then the show is over in an hour or two. What is now about to happen has been decades in the planning ... decades and decades and decades ... but, just like a play, I think it will be over very quickly when compared to all that planning time." He fell silent, simply staring distractedly at the papers on his desk before startling John with a sudden turn of his head and fixed him with a penetrating blue gaze. He spoke with an almost bitter tone, "Of course, that all depends on everyone playing their part - and there will always be someone who forgets their lines - won't there, John?"

The latter couldn't interpret the look or the tone. It was a look and a tone that seemed too intense for the question being asked. Before John had any time to respond the moment passed, and in a much more mundane voice, and with eyes back on his task, Yusef added, "Anyway John, someone usually improvises in such situations, and the play goes on, doesn't it? And when it's finished nobody remembers the minor slip, the minor error ... or the actor who made it." He tidied some papers into a wallet. John remained silent. "But, like I say, the play that is about to start will be over far more quickly than you might imagine. Right now, you will have to excuse me, for now ... my part beckons." With that Yusef took the wallet and made to leave, but stopped.

He turned to John. "You asked me why I was doing things for Steph and for you ... her family. I had heard about the way she was unjustly treated in court - denied a defence because she would not take off her dress. Etiquette above justice.

I saw the way the media, and as a consequence the public at large, ignored the important issues that she raised - the principles - often focussing on the inconsequential instead. I saw the way she was being usurped - by textilists for their cause, and more sinisterly by the 'Red Dress Bombers'. And, as I told you before, I saw the similarity with my great, great grandparents and others like them - collateral damage - in the development of Trueway.

Someone once said that we ignore the smallest infringement of justice by the system at our peril. Your wife held up a mirror to the courts. If they had listened then she would not have been in prison. She and her dress would not have become a symbol to be usurped. Because that didn't happen I now fear that 'the play' may have a different ending to what the author intended." With that Yusef left his study in the direction of the front door. John never saw him again.

*

At around 4:00am, on the morning following Yusef's departure, John was woken by activity in the house. He lay in the dark, listening. It wasn't the sound of panic, but there was a bustling, purposeful urgency to the scurrying feet and hushed voices. Every so often he was also aware of his window rattling and a sensation of the air in the room being squeezed. He was about to get up when his door opened a crack and a shaft of light cut across his bed.

"Sorry to wake you John," It was Lisa speaking in a whisper "… but it's started."

"What?" asked a still sleepy John.

"The realignment, John. The realignment has started. I thought you should know. I didn't want you or the children to be alarmed. We're all quite safe here. I looked in on May and Tim just now. They are fast asleep."

*

Yusef had been right about events moving quickly. The history books would say, that from start to finish, the overthrow of Trueway took only a week. When The Alliance, spearheaded by The Marginals, made their move the globally co-ordinated attacks were swift, limited, controlled … but totally effective.

From his discussion with Yusef, John knew about the Marginal use of textilist groups, of disaffected senior Trueway Citizens, of infiltration and of The Alliance but all that had not prepared him for the blitzkrieg of explosions and cyber attacks that began that morning.

If everyday Citizens had been alarmed by The Red Dress Bombings and puzzled by their purpose then they would have been mystified by what was happening now – but that mystification was not destined to last long. There had been no discernible purpose to The Red Dress Bombings. The attacks, during this Marginal-led week of change on the other hand, were devastatingly purposeful. In a world reliant on communication and information The Marginals, within a matter of days, had turned out the lights, turned off the internet, silenced telephones and halted transport in locations of their choosing. Thousands and thousands of explosions ... often small ... had severed cables, brought down bridges, blocked roads and toppled radio masts while processes reliant on information technology were halted by code.

Selective, global communication blackout and transportation gridlock was the result. Trueway ceased to function.

From where had the explosives come? How had they been secretly transported to their locations? How had so many Marginals infiltrated society? How had they co-ordinated themselves undetected? How had the computers been hacked? Answers (whether true or false) to these questions, would one day be provided, but when the overthrow of Trueway started it was bewildering. Outside of *The Alliance*, none had been prepared for this co-ordinated, pervasive and seemingly uncounterable strategy of crippling disruption or for the pre-prepared, diplomatic solutions then offered, and which were impossible to refuse.

In the years that followed that decisive week some argued the process had been bloodless. Some felt otherwise, and brooded with dark eyes. Yusef had told John that what was about to occur was a realignment of Trueway not a revolution, but nevertheless, the seismic events of that week became known as, *The Bloodless Revolution.*

John, in the company of his children, Lisa and a few other house members watched these things unfold. Owing to the intentionally selective nature of the communication disruption they were able to obtain information via the media. This was mainly internet based, and as the week progressed, almost exclusively from Marginal controlled broadcasts. John could indeed see why Yusef had picked up on his unwitting comment and likened what was about to happen to the staging of a play after years of preparation. Occasionally even the house experienced loss of signal and John thought of Yusef's enigmatic smile and reference to an actor forgetting the lines.

*

At the beginning of the following week the process of reconstruction, and indeed realignment, began. As Trueway died, NewWay was born. It was that quick.

The selective removal of communication and blocking of transport which had so rapidly brought about the demise of Trueway became the selective reinstatement of these things as NewWay emerged, phoenix-like from the ashes of its predecessor. Reassuringly familiar faces appeared in the media ... there really had been a bloodless *coup d'état* ... in fact no *coup* at all ... just a realignment. Here were the faces, the senior members of Trueway, to stand testament to that! But what of truth? What of all the finer detail of Trueway? What of the Book of Truth itself and the very unification of all matters civil, religious and military? There was nothing to fear. All that was good of Trueway would remain. For the vast majority of citizens there would be no discernible difference to their lives ... if that was what they wanted. NewWay was an enhancement, a progression, a development of Trueway not a destruction and diminution of it ... the natural growth that occurs with all organisms. Does a child stop being the same person just because it grows to adulthood? No, it has new freedoms and new responsibilities. So it would be with Trueway becoming NewWay ... fresh freedoms and fresh responsibilities.

The period of realignment would take more than a week, and clarification of those freedoms and responsibilities would be an ongoing process. However, within the familiar, vestigial frameworks of Trueway, there was an adequate structure for initial steps in that process to be taken without too much anxiety. Many of the same secular, and ecclesiastical figures with whom the Citizens of Trueway were familiar, were there to reassure and provide guidance. Alongside them and among them - as with the populace at large - were The Marginals. They had been the catalyst for change, the instigators of change and now the partners, the indistinguishable brothers and sisters in the development of NewWay. The old boundaries of Trueway may now be pushed further into the Margins and the people from the Margins taken within the umbrella of NewWay but there would no longer be any banished. All would now be as one.

*

Prior to the beginning of the phase of reconstruction and realignment, Lisa had advised that everyone in the house remain inside as much as possible. Now, with the violent phase of the realignment complete, the house members could relax and venture further afield. It was not long before Lisa was able to confirm that the police and military forces of Trueway had become the forces of NewWay and that the PMV had been disbanded. There was still uncertainty about the perpetrators of the 'Red Dress Bombings', but she was confident that if such random bombing recommenced, then NewWay intelligence would be better able to address the issue than Trueway had been. Given this information John now felt that it was time for him and the children to re-establish their life in the outside world – and Lisa agreed.

Of paramount importance to John was getting in touch with Steph. He had not told his children about the recording that Yusef had played to him - partly because it was upsetting, and partly because he was unsure of its veracity. Yusef had not been seen since John watched him leaving with a wallet full of papers. John had little confidence therefore that he was going to learn anything about his wife – or for that matter, about Charlie – from Yusef. Even Lisa could not establish where Yusef had gone. She felt that John's best starting point for getting in touch with Steph, was to contact the prison service.

"With the new administration you may even be able to arrange a visit," she said optimistically. "I know all the changes of NewWay aren't clear yet, but 'freedom' is a big issue for Marginals, and I am sure that Steph will be free to wear her red dress, and have visitors while wearing it. In fact, I would think her current sentence is likely to be quashed. Certainly, part of the longer term reconstruction and realignment process, will be the review of the sentences of current prisoners."

John listened and nodded thoughtfully but said nothing.

"The phones are working if you want to telephone the prison," volunteered Lisa. "I don't know whether your wife has been returned to the local prison or remains at the central prison in the Capital. It's probably best to start local. Yusef was the one who knew who to contact to find these things out. I wish I knew what has happened to him."

Thinking of Yusef rekindled John's feeling of distrust – and isolation. "No, I would prefer to go to the prison in person – see someone face to face. I think your idea of starting 'local' is a good one."

"Where will you and your children stay?"

"Good question," said John. "Last time I saw my house it was a mess. Do you think anything will have changed there since you and Yusef got us away that day?"

"I doubt it. You are welcome to remain here if you wish or swap a bit between here and your house while you get things back in order."

"Thank you," said John. "Any advice on how we get into town in the first place?"

"We can get you there," said Lisa with a smile.

*

John, Tim and May looked about them as they sped into town. They were being driven by Latia, one of the people from the house. John had asked that they be taken home first. As they travelled each of them was thinking that things looked much the same as they had always done - Tim probably with least surprise at that, and John with most. Initially they found themselves passing through countryside and there were relatively few people about, but as they came into the town they passed more people and the first, striking difference, became apparent - clothes. The vast majority of people were as naked as they had always been - as Latia, John and the children were now - but here and there could be seen splashes of coloured cloth. Some garments appeared to be genuine items of clothing – shirts, dresses, trousers, while others were clearly improvised.

"Where did the clothes come from?" mused John aloud.

"Probably Marginals ... or Textilists," said Latia. "Clothes were essential in parts of The Margin. I'm third generation infiltration and I don't have any. Never had any need for them."

John remembered his first meeting with Yusef at the Causeway Cafe when Yusef was calling himself 'Robert'. Although Yusef had clearly been feeding John a false story, John realised that there may have been some truth in there being textilist enthusiast groups that made their own clothes.

The car pulled into the close. There was Charlie's house - police tape still in evidence ... and there was their own house, much the same as when they had last seen it, with its broken door and smashed windows. They unloaded a couple of cases containing some essentials given them by Lisa and thanked Latia.

"Remember," she said, looking at the ravaged building outside which she had dropped them, "you are always welcome back at the house. There's a lot of work you're going to have to do here."

As the car pulled away the three of them waved, and then just stood looking at their house ... their home. At that moment their immediate neighbour - a woman with whom they had had very little dealing over the years beyond greetings and social pleasantries - came out of her front door. It was a second or two before she recognised them. She halted half way down her path, looking perplexed, uncertain.

"It wasn't me. It wasn't me, Mr Hugo," was all she said before she turned and scurried back inside.

Like the family that they had seen on the morning after the night of smashing, the Hugos would have to start the process of salvage and repair. For now they would just see what was left inside and whether any of it was functional. They would then go, as a family, to the prison. Depending on what they discovered there, they might then return to their house and see if they could make one or two rooms habitable, at least for the night. If that wasn't possible then they could see if a hotel was available. If all that failed, then they would have to take up Lisa's offer of a return to the house near Fordington. John had seen buses on the road and his car might have escaped damage since it had been in a garage a few streets away, so transport should not be a problem.

*

At the prison they reported to security, and John explained who they were. They were shown to a very pleasant visitors' room where they were told someone would attend to them shortly. Drinks and biscuits were available. It was about half an hour before a young man wearing a warder's armband came in.

"Mr Hugo?" he enquired politely.

"Yes," said John shaking a proffered hand.

"I'm afraid that your wife was transferred from here to the central prison some time ago. I've been in contact with the central prison, but they seem unable to help. They say that she is not, and never has been, in the main block, but that she was placed in the security wing reserved for The Court of Truth."

"Right," said John a little perplexed. "I knew that she had been moved to the central prison ... and thank you for telling me that she has not been returned here. Are you saying that she is still at the central prison?"

"I imagine so, sir - they just said that she was placed in the security wing."

"But they didn't say she had been moved again, somewhere else?"

"No, sir they just said what I have told you. I'm sorry sir. I can give you their number, if you would like to speak to them directly."

John took the telephone number of the central prison, though neither he, Tim or May had a phone. They had looked for phones, tablets and computers at their house but the place had been thoroughly looted of anything valuable. The three left the prison. They agreed that communication equipment was a priority so they headed into the centre of town.

So much seemed the same as it had always done. They popped into a shop and bought some cans of drink. As usual John made the purchase via his biodata. There was no query, so he assumed that the banks were functioning as normal, and that his account was unaffected by the recent events. He had hardly thought about work since the family's flight into the night. As soon as he had a mobile device he would check to see if his salary was still being paid in, and establish exactly what was happening with his job.

They arrived at the electrical goods store from which John had bought his last device. It seemed much the same as the last time he was there, and John's customer account was still active. Tim and May knew exactly what they wanted and were keen to get back into 'real life'. They had had no communication with their friends all of the time they had been away. They had had no communication with anyone. A different reality had existed at the house near Fordington ... but now, back in town seeing everything 'as normal', brought home to them the realisation that all this ... the town, the shops, the people, their friends ... had been here all along, still going about things as usual. They knew that things had happened. They knew that things had not gone on exactly 'as usual' ... and expected that when they were again with their friends, they would talk about how events had unfolded in the 'real world', while they had been ensconced within the house. Nevertheless, everything around them was so familiar - so much 'the same' - that superficially at least, it seemed that if one could pluck out the last few weeks from the passage of time, and pull together the loose ends of past and future, one wouldn't notice the difference. They were wrong.

As John busied himself with the transaction, and as Tim and May wandered round the shop in excited anticipation of their new phones, 'the difference' rushed shockingly into their lives. A photograph of their mother appeared on every screen in the store that happened to be broadcasting the news at that moment. It was an image that had been taken from the broadcast that she had been forced to make - the broadcast that May and Tim had never seen, and about which John had never told them. It showed Steph in her red dress. There was no audio. All the screens were silent so that differing broadcasts in the store did not create a jangling cacophony. May and Tim fell silent also. What did this mean? Why was their mother on the screens? They stood frozen to the spot until a second later the word, "Dad!" was blurted urgently from their lips as one voice.

*

As with all broadcasts, the image of Steph was soon replaced by something else and then something else after that. For John, Tim and May there was no knowing whether these later images related to Steph or not. The man in the shop, surprised by the sudden shout, and recognising the name of Hugo went to speak, but then seemed to check himself. He waited awkwardly to see what John would do. John, shocked though he was by the site of his wife on the television, regained his composure quickly. He presumed that, at the very minimum, the man in the shop had seen the original broadcast, and John didn't want anything said to Tim and May until he had had the opportunity to speak to them about that.

"Let's get these," John indicated the phones, "then *we* can sort out what all that was about." He looked pointedly at the store assistant. Whether because of John's look, or simple store etiquette, the shop assistant restricted himself to matters of business. That completed, John and the children left the shop with John carrying the mobiles.

Chapter 20: And the Chamber was Empty

The three made their way, on foot, to the wreck that was their house. They were all in a state of puzzlement and anxiety about the silent broadcast, but as they walked, John had the added dread of having to tell Tim and May about the broadcast he had been shown by Yusef. He now regretted not having grasped that nettle sooner. Amidst the wreckage of their home, he gave his belated explanation.

John assumed the broadcast would be available on line, and told his children that if they wanted to view it, he would make no attempt to prevent them. To his relief both said that they did not want to see it – at least not at this point in time. John had always been very open and honest with his children, and now he could see no way of shielding them from whatever would emerge when he investigated what they had seen on the televisions in the shop. John suggested that he would do the relevant internet searches and then tell them what he had discovered. He knew that he could not prevent them from doing research of their own, but again they said that they were content with him finding things out, and telling them. All they wanted to know was that their mother was alright.

John found a recording of what they had seen and also several other articles covering the same material. The audio, which they had not been able to hear in the shop, said:

"*Police are investigating the disappearance of Mrs Stephanie Hugo. Mrs Hugo, who made the now famous gesture for freedom when she defied The Court of Truth by donning her red dress while on live media broadcast, was imprisoned in the security wing of Central Prison. She had been on trial at The Court of Truth on indictments relating to her alleged denial of Trueway and involvement in the Red Dress Bombings. Justice Couchan, who was the lead justice in a panel of three at Mrs Hugo's trial said:*

'On several occasions, both within the courtroom, and in private meetings with Mrs Hugo, I endeavoured to guide her, and gain her agreement to take the appropriate steps to prove false the indictments against her. This she refused to do as can be seen from the record. As a consequence The Court of Truth was left with no choice, in fact had a duty, to find the indictments proven as 'true'. The court, per se having fulfilled its duty then handed the question of sentence and implementation of sentence to the Justice Civil. The sentence that she

announced to the court and to Mrs Hugo was that of Eternal Reflection. I heard this sentence given by the Justice Civil. I also heard her command the warder to, 'take the prisoner down' - the customary order for a prisoner to be removed from the court to the cells. Mrs Hugo was then taken from the court. That was the last time that I saw her'.

When asked to give details of Eternal Reflection, Justice Couchan made reference to The Book of Truth where it is described simply as, 'suspension within a mirrored room where the view in any direction reflects back to infinity'. He confirmed that a room for this - the only one of its kind - exists within the security wing of Central Prison. He also confirmed that when senior members of NewWay opened this chamber it was empty.

When asked, in a number of interviews, whether the sentence had been implemented, Justice Couchan humbly confessed that he did not know. He repeatedly said that sentencing was the responsibility of the Justice Civil, and advised that all enquiries on that matter be directed to her.

The Justice Civil, when asked whether the sentence had been implemented, said that she assumed that it had but that her duty ended at the point of determining and pronouncing sentence in accordance with the appropriate guidance. It was not her duty to implement the sentence, oversee implementation of the sentence or indeed to witness implementation of the sentence. There were specialists within the prison system for that.

Our enquiries have not yet identified who these 'specialists' are, but a spokesperson for NewWay said that the police are now investigating matters, and their investigations will be focusing on events following the point when it was ordered that Mrs Hugo be 'taken down'. At the present time the whereabouts of this heroic woman are not known."

All of the other articles that John read said much the same thing. Some of the articles however had photographs of the Justice Civil and of Justice Couchan as well as the one of Steph. John printed off one of the short articles with the photographs. He explained to Tim and May what he had discovered about the broadcast they had seen in the shop and then handed them the article with the photographs. They both looked in silence at the piece of paper. John said nothing. Were they looking at the picture of their mother? Were they realising that this may be the final image they would have of her? He doubted that they were reading anything of the article having already been told its content. It was May that looked up and met her father's gaze. She pointed to the picture of Justice Couchan and said, "That was the man in the garden with Yusef." She had confirmed what John had thought when he had first seen the photograph. The portly gentleman that they had seen take Yusef by the arm that morning was Justice Couchan - the man who had been presiding over Steph's trial in The Court of Truth.

*

A year after John and the children had learned of Steph's disappearance her whereabouts remained unknown - to them and to the world at large. The police investigation had uncovered some information about what had happened after Steph left The Court of Truth that last time, but it was limited. Three prison warders, interviewed independently of each other, confirmed that Steph had been taken from her cell the following day. She had first been taken to a room where she was scanned by something like a bio-scanner that made a noise. They didn't know the purpose of this device. It wasn't something they had seen before. They had then taken her to what proved to be the antechamber of the mirrored enclosure of Eternal Reflection. They confirmed that Steph had been wearing her red dress, that her hands and feet had been manacled and that they had left her secured by a chain to one of the walls. They had not seen a mirrored room and knew nothing about such a room. They knew nothing of what had happened after they left Steph. When asked how they had received their instructions two said that they had been directed by the third - their senior officer, and she said that her instructions had been received from 'the court' via email. She assumed that the e-mail had been written by the clerk of the court, but on whose instruction she did not know. Despite extensive investigation the writer of the email could not be identified.

The only information about what may have happened to Stephanie Hugo from that point onward came from a witness who voluntarily identified herself to the police. This was a young homeless woman. She said that she had been approached on the street by a lady offering her a one-off job. She didn't know who the lady was, and didn't think she would recognise her again. All she could remember of her appearance was that she was of average build, had no distinctive tattoos and was 'oldish'. She might have been oriental or white but definitely wasn't black. The lady had told her the job was a bit like an acting job in which she and another girl would have to spit at someone. The young woman said that she thought it an odd sort of job but wasn't going to refuse what sounded like easy money.

She was taken somewhere by glide car. She wasn't sure where, but the other girl was there just like the lady had said. She was introduced to the girl - but didn't pay attention to her name. The two of them watched a film - a kind of cartoon film - showing them what they were to do. They then had a brief rehearsal. After that they were then taken to a room where there was a man ... at least she thought it was a man ... dressed from head to foot in black. She never saw his face and whenever this figure spoke it was always in a voiceless whisper. The man in black took them into another room where there was a woman chained to the wall wearing a red dress. The other girl and she then acted out their parts. This involved unchaining the lady in the red dress and spitting in her face when the man in black told them to. They had then strapped the woman in the dress to a 'kind of chair'. After that they had both left the room and picked up cash payments that had been left in envelopes for them.

A private auto-glide then returned her to a place close to where she had been recruited. She assumed that the other girl was taken back to somewhere in similar fashion. She had not seen the girl or the lady again. She had come forward to give her evidence after seeing pictures of Steph and hearing about her in the news. She didn't recognise Steph for certain but thought it must be the same person because of the red dress.

Some people believed this testimony. Others thought it too farfetched…while others thought that it might be true … but was simply unreliable. Would the truth ever be known?

Epilogue

Almost two years on from John's discussion with his children in their vandalized home, the family had moved to a new district and were living in a new house. Nothing more substantive had been learned about what had ultimately happened to Steph than was known when they had sat amidst the wreckage. In years to come nothing conclusive would emerge, though theory and speculation would abound. Eventually one of the theories would resolve itself in the collective mind of the people to become the truth of what had happened to Stephanie Hugo. Irrespective of the nature of that eventual truth however Stephanie Hugo, for many people, took on the mantle of hero and martyr almost as soon as NewWay came into being. The red dress and the room of Eternal Reflection became symbols of this hero - this martyr. It became common place to see people wearing a brooch in the form of a red dress or a pendant of a reflective glass cube that became known as an 'eternal reflection' or sometimes just a 'reflection' or an 'eternal'.

Also, two years on from Steph's sentencing by The Court of Truth the Justice Civil had been removed from office. No criminal charges had been brought against her, but it was argued that even if she had no direct part in the disappearance of Steph, her lack of knowledge of what happened after sentencing showed her to be grossly incompetent and unfit for her post. In practice this removal from office was interpreted to reflect a belief (unprovable) that the Justice Civil was indeed responsible for the disappearance of Stephanie Hugo. Following her dismissal the Justice Civil made a speech that later came to be referred to as 'the domino' speech.

"I have no regrets. I carried out my duties according to the law. Had I not done so I would have been criticised as a maverick - making my own rules - but because I followed the law and the result is not to some peoples' liking I am accused of not having done enough. I did my duty according to my remit. I have a clear conscience. In the absence of knowledge about the true events, those charged with discovering the true events must find someone to blame. Stand up a line of dominoes so that they knock each other over when the first one is pushed, and as the last one falls blame the domino that hit it - but don't look further up the line to who pushed the penultimate domino ... or the one before that ... or the one before that ... and certainly don't ask about the hand that pushed the first one or stood the dominoes in a line in the first place."

At the end of those two years there was no news of Charlie. His house remained empty. It had been boarded up. There never would be news of Charlie. He was one of the 'Lost' for whom there was no record of death and no mention in the history books beyond his contribution to one of the statistics illustrative of the wrongs of Trueway.

*

Two years on from The Bloodless Revolution things were very calm throughout NewWay – surprisingly calm some might say – but, as the leaders of NewWay repeatedly pointed out, there had not been a 'revolution', only a 'realignment'. Whichever label was used however the events of that week had not been part of the democratic process of Trueway. NewWay therefore had to be given political legitimacy. This was not difficult. The Trueway/Marginal Alliance had a significant majority of liberal minded politicians in the Continental Council. Legislation recognising and legitimising NewWay had been drafted well before the week of The Bloodless Revolution and it was a simple matter to put this before parliament and have it passed into law. Traditionalist and conservative politicians may have been frustrated and angered by this – but NewWay was utilising the existing political framework of Trueway. All the politicians in the various tiers of government remained in office (unless they chose to resign) and all of these politicians had been elected in accordance with the constitution of Trueway. They were the legitimate representatives of the people. Structurally nothing had changed other than the name of 'Trueway' being replaced by 'NewWay'. Yes, it was true that changes were taking place under NewWay that had not – and arguably *would* not have taken place under Trueway ... but these changes were being enacted by the same parliament – the same people elected under Trueway and therefore with the same legitimacy.

Another very significant factor contributing to the stability of NewWay was the complete cessation of Red Dress Bombings. Some argued that the bombings had been done by Marginals and not the IFA – or that the IFA was composed of Marginals. Others argued that there had never been an IFA. Others argued that the IFA had ceased bombing because they had achieved what they wanted. Some people claimed that the bombings had stopped because the Marginals, that had now been welcomed back, knew of secret arms stashes and routes into and out of what had been Trueway, and so were able to intercept and put a halt to the activities of the IFA. The generally accepted 'explanation' was, that irrespective of the detail, the need for IFA bombings… or any bombings… ceased under NewWay. The media and the vast majority of the populace lost interest in the different theories, and nobody satisfactorily explained the little red paper dresses. All that mattered was there were no more bombings.

The first two years of NewWay therefore saw little political disquiet. The lives of the majority of NewWay citizens were unchanged in most significant respects. They felt happy and settled. There were occasional reports in the media about this politician or that group of people complaining about clothes or some other aspect of change but there was certainly no appetite for a counter revolution among the people at large – at least not yet. "There will always be moaners and complainers," people would say dismissively because they felt it had nothing to do with them … and they felt that it never would.

*

Since Steph and her disappearance were very much a news topic in the early days of NewWay, John had unavoidably come into the public eye as well. Thankfully the children had been shielded from a lot of the media attention and as new, unrelated things hit the headlines any interest in John and his children rapidly faded. John left his job, and after a period without work took up a new post. He thought about using a false identity – even changing the family name officially but it proved unnecessary, so rapidly was yesterday's news forgotten.

The media made little attempt to pursue John and the children. Their absence was compatible with the growing cult of Stephanie Hugo which did not sit comfortably with the mundanery and potential contradictions of a genuine suburban family rather than a stylised one. There were facts about Steph … facts that could be established through very fresh records … but any records were tainted. They had been produced under Trueway and new truths emerged rapidly creating currently palatable legend in an astonishingly short period of time.

Initially, John devoted all his time and energy to trying to find Steph or at least trying to establish what had happened to her. It consumed him, but with each lead pursued by the police and authorities failing to establish anything, he gradually had to accept that he may never find her or establish the truth behind her disappearance. He never stopped hoping, but after the changes of house and job his focus shifted. For John, now more than ever, what mattered to him were the children. Tim and May carried their mother within them. That was what mattered, and if they had children, then something of Steph would be passed on to them, and through them, to the next generation. In the end, children were all that mattered. Children were the record of the past and the opportunity of the future – their own and the World's.

*

As Tim approached fourteen years of age John watched him with pride. John felt that he was already showing the signs of turning into a fine young man. His school reports were positive in every way. He worked hard academically and was progressing well. He was a successful sportsman. He had many friends - some of them appearing to John to be very good friends, boys and girls who seemed to be reliable and supportive of each other. John thought his son was a good looking lad too. He could see Steph in him. Very importantly to John, Tim's behaviour was excellent. There had been no repetition of the difficulties that had forced a move of school a few years earlier, though with the move of house Tim had again had to change school as had his sister.

John marvelled at the resilience of both children. They had been through so much, and even if the media did not pursue them, there was no escaping the reminders of their mother's disappearance. Headlines would periodically appear when a new witness was thought to have been identified or a new theory was postulated. Then there were the red dress brooches and sparkling 'eternal reflection' pendants that were increasingly seen in jewellers' shops, in advertisements and on the people walking down the street every day.

John found these pendants difficult to cope with and detested them for the remainder of his life. They formed a relentless reminder of his wife. On the one hand that was painful because of the love he had had for her and the memories that were invoked. On the other hand it stirred feelings of guilt. Could he have done more to protect her – persuade her to stop what she was doing and get out of prison as Charlie had urged? Could he have pursued the authorities more doggedly to establish what had happened to her? And then there was the worst guilt, the fear that the answer – or at least, part of the answer - to these questions was that his love for her had faded. He told himself that if this was the case, then his wife was to blame – or at least, in part to blame – because of her determination to give greater weight to the principle of being free to wear the dress then to the principle of being with her family. How can one go on loving a person that has abandoned you for a dress, and forced a separation that could so easily, in his mind, have been avoided?

John struggled with these emotions, often pushing them from his thoughts by filling his mind with other things –Tim, May and work – but there were always the sparkling trinkets and emblems to remind him, and sometimes, alone at night, he cried. He never discussed these feelings with his children, and although the three of them talked about Steph, the frequency of such discussions reduced with time. He allowed that to happen – and was glad that it did. He regarded it as part of the healing process. He never asked May or Tim about their reactions to the glittering 'eternal reflections', feeling it best to, 'let sleeping dogs lie'.

Initially May had found these emblems upsetting. They made her imagine terrible things about what happened to her mother. It took many years before she could remain completely calm inside while talking to anyone who was wearing one – though eventually she would come to wear one herself.

For Tim however, they quickly became invisible. Maybe he habituated to them because they were so decorative and almost ubiquitous - trinkets that he could easily dissociate from the warm lady who had cuddled him, told him bedtime stories, kissed him better when he grazed a knee, told him off when he had not done as he should; the warm lady who had borne him and who had loved him.

Did she love me? the question was one he had asked himself - whether directly in words or in muddled, questioning feelings. He had asked it as he tried to reconcile that warm lady with the one who had deserted him for a red dress. That was very much how he saw it - or felt it - his mother had deserted him ... and had done so for a dress. In contrast, Tim looked at his father - the person who had stood by him. He hadn't always seen John like this, and indeed there were times now (and would be times in the future), when he rejected him as weak. Why did his father always seem so meek and accepting ... surely he could have done more to protect his wife ... rescue her even? Why so indecisive ... like the time he hovered outside the house in the morning following the night of smashing? Why so gullible... like the time he believed that Tim had really done those bad things at school because he wanted to go to prison in order to be with his mother? Then, at other times, Tim would wonder who would have cared for him when his mother was in prison, or what would have happened if John had not believed him - believed *in* him - and stood by him, when his school turned against him for his wrongdoing.

Tim occasionally thought of those 'wrongdoings'. He wondered why it was that his school had been so uncompromising. He knew that his father had argued that the school should be forgiving, because that was what The Book of Truth said, and Tim wondered why his school had, nonetheless, not forgiven him. He had heard teachers say that people should be forgiving. How many times had he seen and heard teachers tell children after a squabble to say sorry to each other, and forgive each other? Heard them quote The Book of Truth even. So why hadn't they forgiven him? Sometimes he thought that it must be because what he did was so bad. Sometimes he thought that it must be because *he* was bad. Sometimes he thought it was because the school, teachers, the world was stupid. Most of the time though, he mused for a moment and then became engaged in something else, and thought no more about it until the next time the question popped into his head. Then, when he was by himself in the countryside, a series of events began that would change that.

*

Tim spent a good deal of time with his friends, but nevertheless enjoyed his own company, and was often at his most happy when wandering along by the river, or sitting under a tree with nobody else around. He liked the solitude and enjoyed listening to the sounds - sounds that were often missed when there was chatter. There were the gloopy gurglings of the river, mysterious rustlings in the hedge, the breeze in the branches, the whispering of leaves, the rasp of a distant crow or the repetitive call of a wood pigeon perched on a post.

One evening after school, when sitting still under his favourite tree down by the river listening and watching in this way, he had seen a little brown bird. It darted from left to right in front of him and disappeared behind long grass. It was about as big as a robin - but wasn't a robin. He didn't know what it was. He knew it wasn't a sparrow. He would have puzzled no more about it had it not reappeared like a little brown dart going in the other direction. Even then he would not have given it much thought, but when it appeared for a third time a little later he became more curious, and more certain that if he stayed still where he was he would see it again. Sure enough, it wasn't long before he was proved right.

Tim sat and watched this performance until he felt he should be going home. He wondered what the bird was, but despite his enjoyment of being in the countryside and with nature, he wasn't all that interested in birds, and to him it was just little and brown. Still, he was pleased that he had seen it ... and rather pleased with himself for realising, and correctly predicting, that he would see it again and again if he just waited.

"Try looking it up," suggested his father when Tim told him of his ornithological encounter.

"Bit diff dad ... it was a little brown bird! Lots of them ... though I know it wasn't a sparrow or a robin."

"Robins are red - so it obviously wasn't that if it was brown," said John

"Robins aren't red they're brown with red chests," retaliated Tim

"Same difference," came John's repost.

Tim smiled. He knew his dad was teasing him. He enjoyed silly conversations like this - but John's silliness was a bit more purposeful on this occasion and he continued, "So, if you can tell a robin from a sparrow because of the colour of its chest then there must be something about this bird you saw that tells you it's not a sparrow - right?"

Tim could see the logic of where his father was leading him and jumped ahead. "Well, I know it wasn't a sparrow ... but I don't know how I know. I just know."

"In that case it was a sparrow!" said John with mock triumph.

"It wasn't!"

"Was"

"Wasn't! Wasn't! Wasn't! .... to infinity Wasn'tsis" laughed Tim, intentionally using the childish phrase, that he and his father had used, in such mock combats when he was younger.

"Well, in that case it probably wasn't," agreed John with a smile, "but if you see it again look carefully at it. Listen too ... it may have a song. Try and see what it is that makes it 'not-sparrow'. Oh ... and a tip before you do that ... have a closer look at sparrows first!"

Tim did as his father suggested and looked at sparrows. There were loads of them about. The house where Tim, May and John lived had a small garden and sparrows regularly flitted in and out of that. They appeared outside the window at school, on fences in the park, tweeting in masses in bushes along the side of the road. When he started to look at them Tim was surprised that they were all not exactly alike, but by looking carefully, he was able to see the common features. Then, with the help of an online ornithology guide and a book, he started to establish the features that might help him identify his mystery bird.

Tim didn't have the opportunity to go back down to his spot under the tree for a couple days, and when eventually he had the time, he hoped that the bird would still be around ... especially since he was now an authority on sparrows. He settled down under his tree. He waited for about an hour. There was quite a bit of bird activity. A couple of blackbirds, a blue tit (or maybe a great tit), some ducks flying in to a water ski landing on the river and some pigeons but not a little brown bird darting back and forth. He got fed up and went home.

He told his father this disappointing news.

"How long did you wait?"

"Ages .. about an hour I think."

John mused. An hour sitting still as a thirteen year old waiting for something that might not happen was pretty good he thought. "Mmm -- pity, especially given how you had checked them sparrows out! Maybe you should go again at about the same time you saw it. Maybe it's a creature of habit," suggested John encouragingly.

"OK," said Tim cheerily. "It was after school. Today's Saturday, let's hope his habits don't include resting at weekends!" Later that day Tim went back to his tree. He sat still, not really believing that the bird would appear - but it did. Just as before, it darted back and forth repeatedly with a gap of a few minutes between each passage. It stopped on a couple of occasions, and Tim was able to see that its beak was more pointed than those of the sparrows he had been watching. And there was no black throat, like on some. For Tim, it might still be just 'a little brown bird' ... but at least he felt that he could now win the 'not-a-sparrow' argument with his father. To go the next step and identify it would be the, 'icing on the cake'.

With the help of his phone, and the features he had noted Tim narrowed down his 'little brown bird' to, sedge warbler, dunnock, corn bunting or meadow pipit. Since the little bird always disappeared behind the grass to one side of where Tim was sitting Tim wondered whether there might be a nest there. He moved his position in an effort to see where the bird went the next time it flew past. To his delight it came to the ground and disappeared into the grass. A short while later it reappeared and took off and then a little while after that returned to the same spot in the grass.

Tim waited for the bird to take off again. As soon as that had happened he kept looking at the spot from where it had emerged, and set off in the direction of his gaze, not even glancing away to see where he was placing his feet. He went very slowly as he got close. The grass into which he had seen the bird disappear was in effect a curtain behind which there was a nest. It was on the ground, and to Tim's astonishment, was occupied by a little brown bird. There were two little brown birds! Of course there were two ... why was he so stupid? A mother bird and a father bird … one sitting on the eggs and one fetching food. He stood stock still. The little bird must have seen him but it didn't move. Very slowly Tim walked backwards until the angle was such that the bird disappeared from his sight behind the grass curtain. He turned slowly and crept away.

With elation he told May and his father about his discovery. John reacted with excitement, and wasn't putting this on simply to appear encouraging to his son. May was probably equally excited, but reacted with pleased restraint in order to maintain her cool in front of her younger brother.

"Did you get a shot ... or a clip?" asked May. Tim hadn't even thought about taking a photograph. He'd been too concerned about the possibility of disturbing the nesting couple. The idea was appealing though, and he knew he could do it if he was careful. He had a stand for his phone - or better still he could use a real video camera, link it to his phone and then watch the nest without going near once he had set it up! Or maybe he could use his phone on a stand and link it up to May's tablet? The ideas spilled out of him.

The options were discussed with John, and watching the nest became a family project. With a real video camera of John's it was possible to zoom in on the nest from a safe distance once a platform had been set up in a nearby tree. The camera then linked to a tablet enabled one of them - most usually Tim - to sit comfortably at an even greater distance and watch the nest. When enough watching had been done the camera could be released from the platform with no risk of disturbing the birds and taken home. The whole process could then be repeated as and when the family wanted.

Although not down at the nest every day, Tim made regular visits after school. He wasn't there for the moment when the eggs actually hatched, but he soon found the parent birds scurrying back and forth to feed four little demanding mouths. After a couple of days he began to tire of what was pretty much the same routine, and on the third day of feeding, decided after about twenty minutes, that he had had enough and would pack up and go home. In fact, rather guiltily, he felt that he didn't want to see the process through to when the chicks fledged ... despite the help that his father had given him in setting up the platform and providing the camera at his request. *Well, maybe I will come back just to see if I can catch sight of one of them fledging,* he thought. He knew when the chicks had hatched so there must be guidance on when fledging was likely to take place.

With that guilt-soothing thought he decided he would pack up for the day, and was just about to turn off the tablet, when something brown moved at the edge of the nest. It wasn't either of the parent birds. They were nowhere to be seen. There were just the four chicks. The brown thing moved again and then the pointed face of a stoat appeared over the edge of the nest. Tim didn't know it was a stoat, only that it was a brown furry animal. Swiftly the brown head lunged into the nest and grabbed a chick. Tim sat transfixed looking at the screen. The furry creature disappeared from view with the chick. Moments later it appeared again to grab another chick. Tim looked up and across at the grass 'curtain'. This was happening just over there hidden from view behind the grass. When he looked back at the screen there were two chicks and no furry creature but moments later it was there again taking a third chick. Horrified Tim stood up. The tablet fell to the ground. He was rooted to the spot. He wanted to rush across but his head told him that it was too late already. He looked around. There were large stones - flint. He grabbed one and ran towards the grass curtain but slowed as he approached. The nest was empty. The brown furry creature was nowhere to be seen. One of the chicks was there beside the nest. It appeared to be dead. The other three were gone. Tim guessed that he had scared the animal off before it could take the last one away to wherever it was taking them. He hurled the stone as far as he could with all his might and screamed.

He went sobbing to the camera and took it down from the platform. He didn't want to see the parent birds when they came back. Those birds had worked so hard flying back and forth to feed those chicks. They were good parents - and hard work and goodness should be rewarded ... not punished like this. He sat on the ground with the camera and the tablet and he cried. He cried and cried. He cried more than he had cried for his mother. Then he could cry no more. Then he just sat. Then he hated himself for sitting, not moving not doing something when he first saw the creature on screen. Why hadn't he picked the stone up then, moved quicker? Killed the ugly, murdering thief! Why? Why was he so useless? He looked out across the grass. Where had the creature gone? Was it still there eating the baby birds? If he went searching, could he find it and kill it? No, it was probably hiding and eating somewhere or maybe feeding the chicks to its own young down a hole. Then it hit him in a flash. It could be exactly that. The furry creature could be feeding its young. If he had killed the furry creature those young would starve. He looked at the camera in his lap. What if he had been watching the furry creature's babies down their hole, and a boy had killed the furry creature with a stone, so that it never came back?

It was at that moment, sitting there in confusion with tear-stained cheeks, that Tim became reconciled to 'acceptance'. He wasn't consciously aware of this, but it happened, and the lack of forgiveness of his school inexplicably popped into his mind. Just as inexplicably, after this encounter with the stoat he never again puzzled over the attitude of his former school.

*

On her sixteenth birthday May went to the deactivation centre. Following the demise of Trueway, the practice of automatic biodata encoding at birth had been ceased. People could volunteer to have their newborn children encoded and a lot of parents continued the practice. They could see benefits to having biodata and few disadvantages. NewWay however emphasised individual freedom, and so made it possible for people who had been automatically encoded at birth, to have their osteodata deleted by a process similar to that of wiping a computer disc. Parents could elect to have their children's biodata eliminated in this way and anyone over the age of sixteen had the right to decide for themselves to have it deactivated. John had not opted to have his removed, and had not pursued removal of his children's biodata. May's birthday present to herself therefore, was to go to the centre and have it done.

The deactivation centre was as clinical as a hospital, and the person that called May into the interview room was even referred to as a nurse. With a keen sense of irony May knew that she had passed through a biodata scanner as she entered the building, and that the nurse already had all the data about May that was required. May would not need to fill out any forms or produce ID.

"You are obviously keen!" said the nurse looking at May's date of birth, "and shouldn't you actually be in school at this time?"

"We operate flexi-time attendance. This is a remote study period so I guess I should be doing school work ... but I can catch it up later."

The nurse smiled. "Well you're here now and this won't take long. If you will just undress please and remove any jewellery? You can put your clothes and bag on this chair. Any jewellery can go in this tray. When you've done that, I would like you to stand over here with your feet in the foot marks on the floor." The nurse indicated a spot under an arch that looked very much like a biodata body scanner.

May had taken to wearing clothes very early in the post-Trueway period. She had not expected to have to undress for deactivation and resented the request to do so – not least because it would reveal the little white scars on her arms and some of the fresher red lines on her legs; tiny cuts that she had made herself and that only she and one or two close friends knew about.

She understood why she might have to remove jewellery, but couldn't understand why she had to be completely naked for deactivation - a process which she understood to be essentially electromagnetic. As well as a dress she was wearing a pair of panties and sandals. When the nurse was looking the other way May pulled the dress over her head and slipped off the sandals but kept the panties on. She stepped forward towards the foot marks shielding her legs with her hands.

"The panties as well please," said the nurse glancing round.

"Why?" demanded May belligerently.

"It's just procedure - we have to be sure there is nothing that will interfere with the process - buckles, pins ... that sort of thing."

"There's no metal in panties!" said May indignantly.

"I'm sorry, it's simply procedure ... anyway some people have piercings and body jewellery and the like."

"I'm sixteen. Body jewellery isn't allowed 'til eighteen years of age!" May had no intention of having body jewellery either as it happened - or tattoos. She had rejected that idea long ago, seeing them as 'old fashioned'– though she did like to colour her hair.

"I'm sorry, if you aren't willing to remove your panties then I can't proceed with the deactivation," said the nurse deliberately avoiding eye contact with May and starting to move away from the foot marks as if to go to the door.

"Alright!" said May angrily pulling off her panties and throwing them down on top of her dress before putting one foot up on the chair and pulling open her labia. "See? ... No metal, no jewellery ... happy?"

The nurse, having glanced what May was doing ignored this apparent show of petulance, and without looking, said, "If you would just like to come over here now and stand where I showed you." May did as requested as the nurse walked over to a glass fronted booth.

"And if you could just hold the handles either side of you," came the voice of the nurse over a tannoy from within the booth. May looked down. There were hand grips within the upright columns of the arch. "That's it. Thank you. If you will just remain like that. There will be a bit of noise, but just stay as you are 'til I say that the process is over. Ready? 3, 2, 1."

A low hum started. This grew to a crescendo that sounded to May like someone banging two saucepans together before stopping abruptly.

The nurse emerged from the booth. "That's it; all done. You can get dressed now if you want."

May hurriedly put on her clothes. It had probably not mattered a great deal if the nurse had seen the scars but May still felt irritated, and simply wanted to get away from the deactivation centre. The process had all been so quick however that she felt she needed to be sure that the deactivation had worked.

"So, that's it? I'm deactivated?"

"Yes, it's all done."

"Aren't you going to check? Pass me through a bio-scanner? Make sure?"

"I've done hundreds. Believe me. You are deactivated. If you will just come with me to the front desk your deactivation certificate will have been printed already, as will your ID card. You will need to keep both of those safe. They can be replaced, but it can be a lengthy process because of the need to verify who you are. With the ID card you can readily begin the process of obtaining travel documents and the like ... if you haven't already started that process while you had biodata." The nurse looked at May with a smile - but it was a smile that said, "And I bet you haven't done anything like that!"

May collected her certificate and card. She glanced down at them with no real intention of reading them before putting them in her bag, but was glad she made this cursory inspection.

"You've given me the wrong one," she said confidently to the man behind the desk.

"Sorry, miss," he smiled. "You're the only person we've had in this morning as you can see. I've only run off the one set."

"Yes, but this is for someone called Lepton. I'm May Hugo."

"Like I said, miss, that is your certificate and your ID card. They have been derived direct from your osteodata prior to deactivation, and you are the only person who has been in this morning so the only data that I have processed."

"This is stupid," said May with great irritation. "Get me the person in charge. I might only be sixteen, but I know who I am!"

Hearing raised voices, the nurse came through.

"Is there a problem?"

"I've been given someone else's certificate and ID card. It's a good job I looked. I nearly walked out with them."

The nurse looked at the man behind the desk.

"I've told her that she has been the only person in today, and that this is straight from her osteodata."

"He's right," said the nurse. "There is no mistake."

"Of course there is a mistake – I'm May Hugo and this says, 'May Lepton'." She held up the certificate in front of the nurse's face. "How hard can it be to see that there is a mistake?"

"Yes, miss it says, 'May Lepton' because your osteodata says, 'May Lepton'. Now, I know nothing about you or your family but I *do* know about the scanners and I *do* know about osteodata. If the scanner says,

'May Lepton' then your osteodata says, 'May Lepton'. If there has been a mistake then it is a mistake that was made when you were initially encoded."

"Show me the biodata read out from the scanner," demanded May, not really listening to what the nurse was saying.

"It's not usual policy – but I don't see why not. Show her the data please Chris."

'Chris' tapped the keyboard and swivelled the screen so that May could see it. A lot was just numbers and incomprehensible code though she could read the name, 'May Lepton' and see the date and place of birth which corresponded with her own.

"Most of this is gobbledygook!" remonstrated May.

"Well, we are a deactivation centre miss. You wouldn't want us having a screen that disclosed how much you had in the bank and other private information. All we need to know for reference is what you see there. Everything else is encrypted and all the private stuff needed from your osteodata for your secure ID is now encoded on the card."

"This is clearly somebody else's scan. Do me again," commanded May looking at the nurse with fire in her eyes.

The nurse made no move, but stood impassively waiting the split second needed to see the moment of dawning in May's eyes before saying, "I did not pass the legislation that allowed sixteen year olds to deactivate. I just do the procedure that my position requires and permits. I suggest that you go and discuss this with your parents or guardians – but I can assure you that your osteodata identifies you as May Lepton."

May realised that she was going to get no further by arguing with these two.

"I'll do that and be back," she announced as she span round and left. Her blood was boiling with the image of the self-satisfied curl on the lips of the nurse throbbing in her head.

Once alone however she calmed. She began to think more clearly and to ask questions of herself. She needed to go somewhere and think. It was a hot day so she went into a shop and picked up a bottle of water. She went through the checkout just as she had done thousands of times before but this time it was different. This time an assistant stepped forward.

"Excuse me miss - you must pay for that."

May had no money or electrical payment device. Evidently the ID card that was now in her bag did not act in the same way as her biodata. She could no longer pay for things automatically. She put the bottle of water down.

"Sorry, I don't want it."

May left the shop. She now knew she had been deactivated.

*

The incident in the shop had not only confirmed to May that she was deactivated but it also brought home to her how different things would now be. She had thought about some of the ramifications of not having biodata, such as needing to pay for things manually, but had done little in practice to prepare herself for this. She had not discussed deactivation with her father in any serious way but once, when it had come up in general conversation, he had advised both her and Tim against it for practical and common sense reasons. Now, thinking about the ID card in her bag bearing the name Lepton, she wondered whether there might have been other reasons motivating his advice.

Before going for deactivation she knew that she would dread going back home and telling her father what she had done. She knew he would be angry and would ask why ... and she knew that she would not have an adequate answer. She had, however, pushed these thoughts and fears to the back of her mind. It would be a difficult encounter but one, with time, which she felt would resolve itself. But now, she was being told that she was someone different to who she thought she was. What Pandora's Box would she be opening now, if she went home and told him she had deactivated?

Maybe that box would have to be opened. Even if she said nothing today, she knew he would eventually find out. He would see that her allowance was not diminishing, that no purchases were being credited to her. The time would certainly come when he would ask her to 'pop to the shop' for something and she would have to admit she had no means to pay. There would be forms to fill in as well. She had some school exams coming up and these required verification of identity which was usually done via her biodata. The family would probably go on holiday in a month or two as well, and without biodata she would need travel documents of some sort. What if she fell ill? The doctor would not be able to use her biodata to help diagnose the problem and help stimulate her own bodily resources to combat the disease. She had known all this before going to be deactivated but it was all part of what she had put to the back of her mind … something to be dealt with when it *needed* to be dealt with. The urge to deactivate had been strong – so strong – and now it was done – but if she had given scant regard to the obvious consequences of living a life without biodata she had, at least, been aware that there were consequences. She had not been prepared for deactivation to raise the question of her very identity. She needed to sit and think. There must be times when her biodata had confirmed that she was May Hugo. There must!

May had lied to the nurse about flexi-time attendance at school, but she had no intention of going into school now or of going home. She had to think things through. She wandered into a small park and sat on a bench. She knew that she was still May Hugo – but she felt that she was someone different. She could feel the scratches on her legs. They were not especially deep but they were sore. She had been making these little cuts on herself periodically for quite a while. She hadn't done them for a bit but things at school hadn't been going too well – unlike Tim who had been getting straight 'A' grades. She didn't begrudge Tim his success – or did she?

Looking back it seemed their father was always more pleased when Tim did well, and more concerned when he didn't. She hadn't been aware of it when she was younger – well not consciously – but gradually she came to feel that no matter how hard she tried, her efforts were never appreciated or recognised, as much as those of her brother. Whether real or imagined, she perceived more and more injustice as she got older. On the night of the smashing their father had grabbed Tim's hand to help him escape, while she had scurried along behind. But then again, her brother was younger, smaller. Did she tell herself that at the time? He needed to be helped – but she was older, more able to fend for herself? Is that the explanation that she had given herself for doing the extra housework and cooking in her mother's absence? At least her mother had abandoned them all, and not just her. Then again, maybe even her mother was motivated most strongly to get away from *her*. Maybe she, May was fundamentally the problem - fundamentally bad in some way.

She didn't want to be 'bad' – though she felt that if all her best efforts were never good enough, then she might just as well be. She had seen Tim get their father's attention when he started stealing from friends at school, so maybe that was the tack she could have taken – but she feared that it would not have worked, and if it didn't work, then that would only have confirmed that she was not as good as her brother, as *needed* as her brother - as *loved* as her brother. The cutting was better. It let stuff out with the blood. Was that natural for women – flushing out failure with blood? A failed egg, a failed baby flushed out each month in blood?

She opened her bag and looked in at the certificate and the ID card attached to it. She closed the bag and looked around her. It was then that she became aware of a man sitting on a bench a little way off. There were other people around but they seemed to be paying her no attention while he seemed to be watching her. She opened her bag again and looked inside for something to do before closing it and casually glancing across at him. She felt sure he looked away when she glanced over. May thought he might be in his thirties ... but she was poor at estimating age. All adults looked 'old' ... though this man was not as old as her father. He was clothed - a light blue shirt and cream trousers. He looked back across at her, and this time it was May's turn to look away.

She had noticed people looking at her recently. May didn't recall being watched like this in the period of Trueway. Was that because she was younger then and less aware of what people were doing? Maybe it had something to do with everyone being naked. There was no variety of clothing to look at, and no wondering what was beneath the clothes. Maybe it was because of DAMP Law. She hadn't known about such things as she grew up but there was much talk and rejoicing when it was repealed – and she and her teenage friends were the first in many decades to experience adolescence without DAMP. Then again, maybe it was because she simply hadn't noticed. What was this man on the bench thinking? She couldn't see into his mind. She couldn't even see through his clothes. She got up and walked casually out of the park.

She walked back the way she had come. She crossed the road and looked back as she did so. The man had left the park as well. Was he following her? He seemed to be. She started to feel a little apprehensive. Without thinking she went into the shop that she had been into before. It was cool and she went over to the fridge where she had got the water before. She took a bottle. She glanced back. The man had come into the shop as well. He was looking at the shelves close to the door. May put the bottle back in the fridge. She felt stupid at having come into the shop a second time, knowing she would again have to leave empty handed. Without looking at the man she went through the checkout and out of the shop.

"You've been deactivated." The voice came from behind her. The man had followed her out. May turned. He was definitely talking to her. There was nobody else. He was smiling.

Her heart was pounding but she wasn't sure if it was apprehension or excitement. She had been deactivated less than half an hour, and already her world was different. "What's it to you?" she asked. "Is that why you watched me go through the till - to see how I would pay? Well, I didn't pay so how can you know?"

"You didn't pay because you didn't buy anything."

"I didn't have enough."

"I could give you some."

"Why would you do that?"

The man shrugged and then smiled saying, "You seem nice. Are you?"

May had never been asked if she was nice. "Not for me to say. Seems an odd question. Has anyone ever asked you if you're nice?"

"Not that I can recall," he chuckled before continuing, "Do you want that bottle of water? It *is* a hot day." May shrugged. "Well, I'll go into the shop and buy it for you. If you are still here when I come out then I'll know that I was right. I'll know you're a nice girl." He looked at her steadily, then went into the shop. She watched him saunter up the isle towards the fridge where the water was kept, but lost sight of him. May's heart was racing. She started to walk away but stopped. She looked back through the glass. She couldn't see him, but she could see the checkout. She waited. Why wasn't he at the checkout yet? Was he giving her time to leave? She started to walk away once more, but something compelled her to go back and look again at the checkout. Still he wasn't there. She would go. Maybe that was what he wanted. She turned to leave, but as she did so, she saw him coming down the aisle towards the tills. He didn't look out but simply went to the counter and handed a bottle of water to the assistant before then handing her something else. What was it - coins? A card? May wasn't sure. Did this mean that he was deactivated too?

"You're still here then." He smiled as he handed May the cool bottle.

"Thank you."

313

"I know somewhere we can go," he said, before adding, "... if you still want a bit of money that is?"

May stood, trying to think. She opened the bottle of water to stall and give herself time ... but no thoughts came. She took a sip from the bottle.

"I should have got two ... it is a warm day." May handed him the bottle. "Thank you. See? I said you were nice. It's only a short walk to the place." He held the bottle out to her as he began to walk down the street. May found herself walking too as she took the bottle from him. She continued walking - following the man.

After ten minutes he turned into a narrow alley between buildings. He paused for May to catch up. She stood at the end of the alley. She watched him. He faced one of the walls and took some keys from his pocket. He appeared to open a door - though May could not see it clearly - and then disappeared from view. May stood, her heart pounding and her hands shaking. Cautiously she went down the alley until she came to a door. It was open. Inside it was dark and cool. She was looking down a corridor. She could not see the man. She pushed the door until it was right back against the wall. She took a deep breath and went inside. She slowly edged down the corridor.

"Close the door behind you," came the man's voice from ahead of her, "and you must tell me your name." May looked back at the street.

"OK," she tried to say but all that came out was a shaking, "O" from her dry throat. She opened the bottle of water, dropping the cap from her fumbling fingers as she did so. It clattered on the tiles. She gulped a mouthful and pushed the door. It closed with a click. She bent down and picked up the screw cap from the bottle. When she looked up he was standing ahead of her in the corridor.

"In here," he said indicating a room and disappeared inside. May went and stood on the threshold. The furnishing was sparse - a table, a couple of chairs, a cupboard, a basin and a bed. "Come in," he invited. May stepped in, and without being asked, turned and closed the door.

When May stepped out into the alley again she had money to buy her own water, and a good deal more besides. She was glad she had never told the man her name. She was sore and she felt a little sick but she also felt changed. She felt she had made a transition.

*

With no intention of going into school late or of going home early May wandered where her feet took her. She knew that she should be thinking things through further - working out what to tell her father about having been deactivated. That would entail admitting that she had skipped school. She knew she should be thinking about these things but she couldn't focus. Her mind wandered along with her feet. She was sixteen years old and she had just had sex with a man whose name she did not know and who did not know her name. He had never asked how old she was. If he had done would she have told him the truth or would she have said eighteen - the age of consent? She wasn't sure ... but he didn't ask. It struck her then how arbitrary it was, that at sixteen she could not consent to sex but could consent to be deactivated.

A glint of something bright in the sunshine flashed across her face. A woman walking towards her had an 'eternal reflection' on a chain around her neck. The woman walked past without looking at May. Even had she looked, she would almost certainly not have recognised her as the daughter of Stephanie Hugo, the woman whose life (and possibly death) she symbolised on the chain round her neck. At first May had thought a lot about her mother and what had, or had not happened to her. Was she dead? Was she alive somewhere? Now, as May walked along, it was the absurdity of it all that was uppermost in her mind. Under Trueway her mother had been a criminal. She had been imprisoned, tried and sentenced. Under NewWay she was revered - a martyr. It all seemed so arbitrary.

Having walked for about an hour May realised that the houses had become sparse and she had passed out of the main built up area of the town. She still hadn't managed to focus her thoughts and so she continued walking. As it got later she thought about turning back and going home. The chances were that her father would not realise that she had not been at school. There were a couple of birthday presents there too that she had left unopened - as a treat for herself when she got in, she had told him.

May stopped and turned to go home. As she did so she saw a sparrow. It sat chirping on a wall. She took a sip of water from the bottle. The sparrow hopped along. It brushed against a flower and disturbed a moth. Almost too quick to see, the sparrow caught the moth in its beak and flew off. *The sparrow's rules are not arbitrary*, she thought. *It only has one - survive*. May thought about the money she had in her bag. May loved her father and her brother. She had loved her mother too. May turned again and started walking. She did not go home.

THE END

About the Author

Asthouart* is a pseudonym. I created 'Asthouart' in the year 2000 so that I could have an on-line presence for my creative hobbies that was separate from my actual personal and professional life. Asthouart has mainly been responsible for drawings, paintings, sculptures, photographs and the occasional poem. At the moment, Asthouart is still alive, and can be seen wandering around in Canterbury, England – especially in the early hours of the morning down by the River Stour. He has been known to venture further afield and secretively leave pictures in random places for passers-by to find and take. A practice he calls #artabandoned. The following two books are currently (May 2022) in manuscript:

> *The Red Dress* (A prequel to *The Unnatural Woman*)
> *The Eternals* (A sequel to *The Unnatural Woman*)

*Asthouart is a combination of three words: as-thou-art.
It is based on the wording from an inscription in St Eadburgha's Church, Broadway, England that reads: 'As Thow Art, So Was I. As I Am, So Shalt Thow Be.' In other words, *I used to be alive just like you, and one day you are going to be dead, just like me.* When I created the name Asthouart I did it from my memory of the inscription. It wasn't until many years later that I discovered the spelling discrepancy of 'thou' and 'thow' … and by then, it was a bit too late to change it.

Printed in Great Britain
by Amazon

13141028R00185